For Victoria, my better angel

In the past, war was fought on battlefields.
In the present, it is fought online.
In the future, it will be fought in people's minds.

—ISOBEL LOWE

OMEGA RULES

BY ERIC VAN LUSTBADER

THE EVAN RYDER SERIES

The Nemesis Manifesto
The Kobalt Dossier
Omega Rules

THE SHADOW WARRIOR SERIES

The Ninja
The Miko
White Ninja
The Kaisho
Floating City
Second Skin
The Death and Life of
Nicholas Linnear (ebook)
The Oligarch's Daughter (ebook)

THE TESTAMENT SERIES

The Testament
The Fallen
Four Dominions
The Sum of All Shadows

THE SUNSET WARRIOR CYCLE

The Sunset Warrior
Shallows of Night
Dai-San
Beneath an Opal Moon
Dragons on the Sea of Night

THE JASON BOURNE NOVELS

The Bourne Legacy
The Bourne Betrayal
The Bourne Sanction
The Bourne Deception
The Bourne Objective

The Bourne Dominion
The Bourne Imperative
The Bourne Retribution
The Bourne Ascendancy
The Bourne Enigma
The Bourne Initiative

THE JACK MCCLURE NOVELS

First Daughter
Last Snow
Blood Trust
Father Night
Beloved Enemy

THE PEARL SAGA

The Ring of Five Dragons
The Veil of a Thousand Tears
Mistress of the Pearl

THE CHINA MAROC SERIES

Jian
Shan

OTHERS

Sirens
Black Heart
Zero
French Kiss
Angel Eyes
Batman: The Last Angel
Black Blade
Dark Homecoming
Pale Saint
Art Kills
Any Minute Now

ERIC VAN LUSTBADER

OMEGA RULES

HEAD
ZEUS

An Aries Book

First published in the UK in 2022 by Head of Zeus Ltd,
part of Bloomsbury Publishing Plc

9 7 5 3 1 2 4 6 8

A catalogue record for this book is available from
the British Library.

ISBN (HB): 9781803282084
ISBN (XTPB): 9781803282091
ISBN (E): 9781803282060

Printed and bound in Great Britain by
CPI Group (UK) Ltd, Croydon CR0 4YY

Head of Zeus Ltd
First Floor East
5–8 Hardwick Street
London EC1R 4RG

WWW.HEADOFZEUS.COM

OMEGA RULES

PROLOGUE

VIENNA, AUSTRIA

Armistad was in the cemetery when the hammer came down. He'd been expecting it, sooner or later, but still . . . It happened very quickly, which, now that it had begun, was a blessing, as his assignment was at an end. During this last week in Vienna, he'd come here at the same time each weekday. In field agent terms it was sloppiness, at least to an outsider. To him, it was an invitation, and in Armistad's line of work, the opposition never passed up an invitation. They might have held second thoughts except, having anticipated his Vienna endgame, he'd spent increasing time with Sofia, a definite vulnerability for a field agent. During the previous weeks he'd packed on a few extra pounds just to complete the picture of boredom and incipient indolence.

Now his meticulous preparations were about to bear fruit; he'd drawn out the opposition at last.

He'd been drifting through the narrow leaf-strewn path between the iron grave markers of drowning victims and those denied a Christian burial. Forgotten in life, hidden in death. Despite being so near the Danube, the Friedhof der Namenlosen cemetery was difficult to find along Alberner Hafenzufahrtsstrasse, squeezed as it was between the Alberner canal and a looming building materials storehouse with its signature triple yellow silos, visible through the miserable stand of willowy tree trunks. The grass at the entrance was unmowed, patchy as a mangy dog's flanks.

He liked to come here at dusk when the shadows were long and the air melancholy with the ghostly voices of the unremarked dead. Not that Armistad believed in ghosts or any such paranormal claptrap. Still, he had to admit the silence within this cemetery was different from all others he'd visited, completely undisturbed by the noises of the city. Despite the intimate proximity of the industrial complex, it was almost palpable, lying against his skin like a drift of leaves.

Armistad loved cemeteries, loved their silence, their proximity to eternity. Within their grounds he could think perfectly clearly, could parse the events of the day, set them into the framework of the past week, consider his progress, the advances along with the missed opportunities.

During this time, he found the voices of the dead helpful, wise as they were, outside time and the fretfulness of human existence. They gave him perspective, the ability to turn off the constant torrent of minutia he was trained to glean from his environment. Wedded to Parachute, a massive corporation even by the standards of the gig economy, he was on the surface indistinguishable from a field agent in the employ of any clandestine government agency.

But the truth was Parachute was an animal of an altogether different nature and working for it was a blessing for someone like Armistad, who could not abide bureaucracy and the fools who made it their life's work. Parachute was richer, more powerful, and far more influential than any government on earth. Its internal patterns, rules, and code of ethics were set by Marsden Tribe, the company's founder, himself an eccentric. He had over a million avid Twitter followers; often his tweets moved the equities markets.

It was through his eccentricities that he created the revolutionary breakthroughs in quantum computing that formed the foundation of the present company. Before Tribe, quantum computers needed to be cryogenic, using qubits requiring a temperature of around -460 degrees Fahrenheit to operate, a lethal environment for humans. Somehow Tribe got his quantum computers to work at 30 degrees Fahrenheit, moving an infinite number of qubits one hundred times faster than all those lagging him in the field. This was the first in a long line of proprietary break-throughs. In other words, Tribe had ensured for Parachute a wide and unassailable business moat. Subscriptions to its online software suites were in ultra-high demand by the largest, deep-pocketed corporations across the globe; Tribe refused to sign a single nation-state client. He had also resisted the calls to take Parachute public—the infusion of money this would bring meant nothing to him; total control meant everything. The thought of Marsden Tribe reporting to a board was ludicrous.

Armistad was himself a nonconformist who Ben Butler, his control at Parachute, appreciated and deployed to maximum effect. Truth to tell, he wasn't that happy with Butler being his control. Butler was a cripple and, in his opinion, a depressive; Armistad didn't like being reminded of one of the worst outcomes of a career in the field. Death he could handle, but being a cripple, nuh uh.

These thoughts ran through his mind in a fraction of a second as he watched a slim man make his way along one of the aisles parallel to the one Armistad himself was on. He was dressed for the chilly December weather in an overcoat, a charcoal wool suit, pale-blue shirt, and paisley silk tie. He had a prominent nose, slicked-back hair, and carried a clutch of fresh white lilies wrapped in green paper in one hand. The man never so much as glanced at him, which was a tell in itself. No field agent worth his salt would check out his target directly.

Armistad felt his muscles tense in response to the perceived threat. He stopped to observe a grave marker with a poorly formed wrought-iron Christ, painted silver, here and there encrusted with rust like cankers on old flesh. Now he was a step or two behind the suit, who continued on as if he were perfectly unaware of Armistad's presence.

The only other figure in Armistad's field of vision was Karl, the slender caretaker, earbuds connected to an ancient iPod, wheeling his cart filled with brooms, rakes, and an assortment of clippers. A fixture at this time of day. He did not look Armistad's way, but paused for a moment to shake out a cigarette and light it, a prearranged signal to Armistad, then pushed his cart on. He stopped to adjust one of the old wrought-iron lamps that lined the aisles, cocking his head reflectively to make sure the angle of the head was correct. Nodding to himself, he moved on again, taking out a wide-headed broom as he did so.

Meanwhile the suit had stopped in front of a grave marked by a Christ on the cross and, just below, a lantern with thick red glass panes. A breeze gusted, rattling the last of the leaves, turned yellow and rust. Birds flitted from branch to branch, last searches before moving on to their hidden nests for the night.

Karl had crossed to the path Armistad was on, head down, concentrating on clearing the cracked concrete of dead leaves. The suit, staring at the image of the crucifixion, had not moved. Unconsciously, Armistad fingered the hollow amulet hung from a thin silver chain around his neck.

Now the suit was turning away from the grave marker. Karl lifted his head, the bristles of his broom sweeping up a surf of leaves. Armistad's right hand moved even as the suit dropped the lilies, revealing the pistol, silencer already attached. It came up aimed at Armistad's chest. But Armistad's throwing knife was already a blur, burying itself to the hilt, connecting the suit's tie to his pierced heart. His arms flung outward, forming a cross like the grave markers as he stumbled, fell to his knees.

Armistad advanced through the field of graves. Behind him, Karl stood as still as all the Christs in the cemetery, gazing at the unfolding scene, cigarette ash mingling with the leaves at his feet.

The suit's mouth was opening and closing like a hooked fish. His lips and eyes were bloody. Now he was drooling. Coming up to him, Armistad kicked him on the point of his chin and, with a sharp crack of his knees, he collapsed backward.

Karl turned away, heading back down the path, still listening only to his music. Armistad bent over the corpse, checked all pockets for any form of identification, but all he found was five thousand in euros. Nothing to identify who his would-be murderer was. But then he hadn't expected to find anything, not on a well-trained field agent.

And yet, on the other hand, perhaps something was overlooked. Using the heel of his shoe, he pried off one of the suit's thick-soled brogues. Maneuvering the brogue into the light with the toe of his own shoe, he peered closely at the bottom, saw imprinted there: **WESTFALIKA**, **Москва**.

Russian, he thought. *Now that's interesting.*

Switching his attention, he pulled out the knife, stepped smartly back to avoid the sudden gush of blood. He wiped the blade on the satin lining of the suit's coat. As a last order of business he sent a brief encoded text update to his control via his cell phone. He was about to turn away when he changed his mind. Stooping again, he scooped up the bouquet of lilies. It would make the perfect present for Sofia.

■   ■   ■

And, indeed, he was correct. Sofia delivered a lingering kiss when he handed her the lilies. She held them to her breast, her eyes alight. She loved lilies. Loved the color white. It was only after she had put them in a cheap plastic vase with water, set the vase on the coffee table in the living room, that he noticed the tiny drop of crimson marring one petal, gleaming in the lamplight. Sofia hadn't seen it as yet, and Armistad was determined that she wouldn't. Crossing the room, he brushed the blood off the lily with the pad of his finger.

The lamplight threw a golden aura around Sofia. She was wearing a dark-red chenille robe, her pale feet padding silently across the floor of his apartment, a two bedroom in a modern high-rise on Hertha-Firnberg-Strasse, just south of Vienna's center. It had the benefit of overlooking a small garden below the terrace outside the bedroom where he and Sofia slept, fought, made love. The apartment was bright, clean, furnished in Danish modern—simple lines, neutral fabrics—which suited him. He wasn't comfortable living in fussy, old-world quarters, where dampness, mold, and the memories of past wars were sure to be lurking.

Sofia's somatotype was right in his wheelhouse: a full-figured woman with the long legs of a model, blond hair blunt-cut to just above her shoulders, full lips and a sharp chin, wide-apart eyes, night dark. She was whip-smart, as well. She worked for Simon & Trebbilowe, lawyers to many in the gig economy, so Parachute was a name known to her. She even did business with a couple of Parachute people—he had checked—though not of course anyone in the secret directorate overseen by Isobel Lowe, where Armistad worked. She was familiar only with Parachute's multifaceted public face.

As Sofia had decided to take a shower, he stripped off his outer garments, went to the sideboard, poured himself three fingers of whiskey. Drink in hand, he stepped into the bedroom just as the bathroom door closed. The shower began to run, and he sat on the side of the bed, savoring the whiskey as it burned its way down to his stomach.

Sofia's voice drifted through the door. "Want to join me in here?"

He did, but he had some work to do while she was behind the closed door. "Give me a couple of minutes," he called out.

"Don't miss your chance to soap me all over," she said. "And I mean *all* over."

Smiling, he took out his throwing knife, cleaned and lovingly oiled it.

He'd met Sofia in Bar Onyx on Stephensplatz, ironically near St. Stephen's Cathedral. He favored the place; it was quite posh. Glittering like a handful of jewels, it roosted on a high floor in a corner building; it boasted floor-to-ceiling windows, affording patrons spectacular views of the city.

She had been sitting at a lounging area with a group of women more or less of her age, late twenties, early thirties. At some point, he had to pass by in order to refresh his drink—he liked seeing his drinks made, not trusting waiters to hand them to him, an old habit that had served him well. On his way back, he discovered her eyeing him and he smiled. She smiled back. He was going to invite her over to his sitting area when she rose and walked away into another area of the bar. He assumed she was using the ladies', but moments later he saw her appear on a narrow terrace, forearms leaning on the hand-worked cast-iron balustrade. As he continued watching her, she pushed both shoes off. She stood there barefoot, seemingly tense, uncertain. Then she peered down at the busy square below. Her pale hair was blowing across her cheeks and he could see that her bare skin was pebbled from the cold.

At once he rose and, following the path she had taken through the crowded bar, found the inconspicuous doorway out to the terrace. She turned her head, her dark eyes on him as he approached.

"You're not thinking of jumping, are you?" he said when he was near enough to grab hold of her if her answer was yes.

She laughed deep in her throat. "What gave you that idea?"

He gave her bare feet a significant look.

"Oh, no." She briefly put fingertips to her lips. "I'm just a barefoot girl at heart. I belong bicycling down a country road on my way to buy milk, bread, and butter."

"What are you doing in the city then?"

"Making money," she replied. "What else?" The smile on her lips went straight to his heart.

He invited her back to his sitting area. At first, she declined, but at his gentle urging she agreed, and that was it. She came back here with him that night and more or less had never left.

Soon enough, the eager blade looked just as it had before he'd used it at the cemetery, gleaming in the circle of light thrown off by the bedside lamp. The suit had not been his first kill, nor would it be his last. He rolled more whiskey around his mouth, swallowed, while briefly gripping the amulet around his neck. It was made of titanium, lightweight and durable.

He held out his right hand, saw there wasn't a trace of a tremor. He had been unnerved by his first kill, which had come upon him all at once. He did what he had been trained to do without conscious thought. Muscle memory. But afterward, the nightmares had started. They kept up until his second kill. It was as if the two canceled each other out, and from then on he was golden, working his way across Europe as needed. You would not think a gig economy corporation would need people like him—and certainly the thought would never occur to anyone on the outside looking in—but nowadays espionage was not the sole province of governments. Governments could no longer be trusted except with incompetence. And since Parachute, like most gig companies, lived on the bleeding edge of constant breakthrough innovation, it required heavy protection from hackers and corporate spies. These days if you wanted something done you needed to do it yourself. That was Isobel's philosophy and he happened to know it came straight from the top, from Marsden Tribe, Parachute's once-in-a-generation genius.

"Love," Sofia called, "are you coming? It's lonely in here."

He laughed, put away the knife, and rose, shucking off the rest of his clothes. He was padding toward the bathroom when the slider to the terrace exploded inward. Instantly, he grabbed the necklace, buried it in his fist. Seconds later the figure was on him. A knee slammed into his testicles and with a groan he doubled over. Head pressed into the carpet, the muzzle of a pistol pressed against his temple, Armistad prepared himself for death.

"Where is it?" the male voice grated.

"Where's what?" Armistad figured he had nothing to lose by lying.

The muzzle pressed harder. "We know you have it. Tell me where it is."

"I have no idea what—" He broke off as the barrel of the pistol whipped against his cheek, opening skin and the flesh beneath. He felt the wet heat of his own blood, the warmth of it in his mouth.

"Enough bullshit." The figure had bent low, the harsh stink of stale cigarettes and garlic sausage enveloped him.

"I guess you'll just have to kill me," Armistad said.

"As you wish."

The muzzle pressed against his chest, beneath which his heart beat like a triphammer. Armistad closed his eyes and tried to catch the lingering musk of Sofia. Not a bad scent to be his last.

The percussion rocked him. A weight came down, smothering him. He had read that the brain lived on precious seconds after the body died. Was this what it was like, being smothered? Was death on the other side?

Then, at once, the weight was lifted off him and he saw Sofia, a small but deadly Kahr Arms ACP .380 in one hand, rolling the body of the intruder off him and onto the carpet. She was wearing her carmine chenille robe.

She knelt down. "Are you okay, love?" She examined his bloody cheek. "We should get you to a hospital."

"No hospital." With her help he sat up. His mind was still trying to process what was happening. It wasn't every day you were on the point of death one minute and safe the next. Even for him this was a first.

"A clinic then."

"No." He said it firmly so she'd know he'd closed the subject.

"Okay." She eyed him as he got to his feet. "But what the hell is going on?" She pointed at the corpse. "Who is that?"

"No clue." Armistad sat on the end of the bed. His nerves were still twanging uncomfortably, but at least his thoughts were beginning to clear. He watched her while she went back into the bathroom, returned with a washcloth soaked in cold water. She pressed it to his face. Her eyes were cloudy with anxiety and worry.

"Why did he attack you?"

Armistad shook his head, and she sighed.

"Okay, let's at least get you into the shower so you can clean up. Then we can figure out this puzzle."

"Out," he said, rising. "We need to get out of here. Now."

She gestured. "Not with you looking like that."

She took him into the bathroom where the shower was still running. He stepped in, the hot water sluicing over him, easing his knotted muscles. Luxuriating in the lassitude coming over him, he gestured for her to join him.

It was only when she smiled at him that he wondered what she was doing with a weapon while she was supposedly taking a shower, but by then it was too late.

"Oh, fuck," he said, fisting his amulet tightly.

"Ah, no. Not tonight, love."

She shot him twice between the eyes with the ACP .380.

As he slumped to the wet tiles, she pried open his fingers, releasing his death-grip on the amulet.

"Ah, so there you are, love," she whispered as she ripped the titanium oval from its slender silver chain.

PART ONE

PARACHUTE

1

WASHINGTON, DC

It had been raining for three days when Ben Butler tried to kill himself. Evan Ryder let loose a string of expletives as she raced through the blessedly light early morning traffic. Part of her mind was in shock. Ben—her Ben, her patron, her control, her partner in the field. Her rock. She could not wrap her mind around this new reality.

She had received the call from Isobel at just after 5 A.M. and, like receiving news about a death in the family, could not believe what Isobel was telling her. It was a mistake; it must be. Ben would never attempt to take his own life. Her eyes filled with tears as she hurriedly dressed and slammed out the door of her apartment. And here she was not fifteen minutes later almost at her destination, after having hit 100 mph, slewing and, once, fishtailing around corners, and shooting through every red light in her path. Trying to keep her emotions in check, she slowed to a more moderate speed as the downpour sluiced against the windshield. The wipers, even at max speed, couldn't get rid of the rain fast enough. Her thoughts were in turmoil and it was all she could do to keep herself together.

As she turned onto California Street NW, the Italianate villa became plainly visible. Though Isobel Lowe enjoyed a high-ranking position in Parachute, she worked out of her home in DC, this three-story cream stone and butterscotch stucco villa near the corner of California Street NW and Massachusetts Avenue, near Rock Creek Park, rather than in Seattle, where the Parachute main campus sprawled across countless acres. With good reason, almost no one knew of her existence or of the directorate she ran. Outside of her own meticulously vetted people, only Marsden Tribe and a pair of his trusted assistants were aware of her and her team, and even those two knew only that she was in charge of corporate security. Which was true, but merely one small facet of her overarching remit.

Parking on the street, Evan raced through the gray downpour, up the steps to the villa's side door. The key she used fit into the conventional Yale doorknob lock, but just inside was an inner door locked in an altogether different manner—it used an algorithm derived from each individual's biorhythm. This ultra-secure mechanism, developed by Tribe himself, might have seemed a tad over the top for Parachute, a Platform as a Service company, a pioneer in quantum cloud computing and cross-application services, but it was right on the money for Isobel Lowe's directorate.

Evan and Ben had been recruited by Isobel over five months ago while Ben was still recovering from the bullet wound that had shattered his hip. Back then, his prognosis wasn't bad—the surgeons had assured them that he'd be able to walk, albeit with the assistance of a walker and then a cane.

But it was not to be. A month ago, when Ben still couldn't even stand, further tests revealed that the hip bone had shattered with such force that several slivers had acted like internal shrapnel. So deep were some of them that it was deemed too dangerous to get them out. For the rest of Ben's life he would be confined to a wheelchair.

That's when the real difficulties began.

Evan was through the inner door, flying into the kitchen, where Akiva, ex-Mossad and one of Isobel's security people, stood waiting for her. He was a deceptively slender man with a thick black beard and blue eyes. He led her up the narrow back stairs that once served as the kitchen staff's access to Isobel's quarters.

On the second floor, she found Isobel in one of her half-dozen studies. This one was ringed by flat-panel TVs, each tuned to a different news net.

"How is he?" Evan said as Isobel turned away from the screens.

"The doctor's in with him," Isobel said in her soft but commanding voice. A former Mossad operative herself who knew Ben since long before Evan ever met him, Isobel was as willowy as she was toned, with devilishly wide-apart tawny eyes and an enigmatic smile.

Evan's mind whirled in this room filled with so many voices: CNN, Fox, MSNBC, CNBC, BBC, RT—the Russian News net, Al Jazeera, Sky News, Firstar 24/7, Newsmax, One American News, and TNSC-Titan News and Streaming Corp, the ultra-conservative network owned by Samuel Wainwright Wells, multi-billionaire, media mogul, and most importantly for Isobel, major magnet for right-wing fringe groups, believers in conspiracy theories, the more outlandish the better. The Earth is flat. Democrats are socialists, Democrats are fascists, Democrats are under the sway of the Deep State, controlled by Jews, the Moon walk was a Hollywood fake (Jews again), 9/11 was perpetrated by the American Deep State as an excuse to invade Iraq, Democrats engage in Satanic rituals attempting to melt all the guns owned by the faithful, in human trafficking of young girls, babies, cannibalism, alien lizard-men. You name it, they had a conspiracy for it. And, for the love of God and Wells, don't you dare try to confuse them with facts. Facts did not exist; neither did science. Jewish inventions all. "I'd rather live in Russia than under Democrats" was one of their rallying cries.

Isobel saw the distressed look on Evan's face and with the push of a button on her console muted the sound on all the feeds, though her staff downstairs continued to scrutinize their own screens, even slowing them down to ID facial tells, inadvertent mannerisms, and the like. Blessed silence emptied the room, allowing Evan to breathe again.

"What happened?" Evan was too anxious to sit down.

"He slashed his wrists."

Evan's heart contracted and she felt tears trembling in the corners of her eyes. Angrily, she wiped them away with the back of her hand. "He hasn't been able to come to terms with losing the use of his legs."

Isobel regarded her sadly. "If this response is any indication, he never will."

When Evan pointed out that it'd only been a month since he'd gotten the worst-case news, Isobel said, "I've known Benjamin longer than you have. He's not cut out to be a cripple."

"Can I see him?"

"As soon as Dr. Sheren gives his okay." Part of Isobel's attention was on the Titan 24-News Hour. The Breaking News banners scrolling across the bottom of the screen detailed the chaotic scenes of an Omega rally outside the Texas state capital.

"How they adore Omega," Isobel said.

"Worship it, really," Evan added. "The outlets owned by Wells are allowing this shit full rein."

"It's even worse on 27chan. No one knows who controls that internet posting board."

"My money's on Wells."

"Proof?"

Evan shook her head. "Bits and pieces. Wells is a media mogul. He knows how to manipulate the media."

"So do several other multi-billionaires," Isobel pointed out. "Plus, these days you hardly have to be a billionaire to manipulate the media."

Of course Evan knew that, but she had a specific reason why she suspected Wells—his wife, Lucinda; she just wasn't ready to share her suspicion because Lucinda happened to be one of her sisters. "Yes, but I've discovered that Wells is a student of propaganda history. He knows the word from its origin in 1718, when a committee of cardinals in charge of foreign missions of the Catholic Church had its name changed to the *Congregatio de Propaganda Fide*, the Congregation for the Propagation of the Faith.

"More to our point, he is specifically fixated on the Big Lie, a clever technique employed to great effect by Joseph Goebbels. Adolf Hitler wrote about it in his autobiography, *Mein Kampf*."

Isobel nodded. "An infamous political strategy so simple it's virtually infallible: make the lie big, outrageous even, keep saying it, and eventually the people will believe it."

"It's been used by dictators and presidents here and abroad every decade since," Evan said. "Ben and I identified the string of Big Lies Omega was disseminating. That's why we made Omega our top priority. We've been putting out its fires for over two years. But until we take care of that disease at home, our work will continue to be undermined."

"I hope your intuition serves you well because—" Isobel's cell beeped, interrupting them, and she gestured. "Right, then. Doc says he's ready for visitors." She led Evan out of the study.

They stepped down the hallway. "He was unresponsive when I found him," she went on, "but when Sheren kicked me out he was conscious and seemed in minimal distress."

"Thank God Zoe doesn't have to see this," Evan said.

"No. And she's happy in Germany with your family. Your niece and nephew are her dearest friends, and your newfound parents sound like extraordinary people. Ben had good reason for sending her to stay with them, and it wasn't just so he could recover without worrying about caring for her. He knew he was on a psychological precipice. We have to help him down, Evan."

Evan nodded. Looking in, she saw the back of Ben's head. He was in a chair next to the bed, Dr. Sheren bending over him, checking the bandages on his wrists. Two bags hung from a rolling metal frame—one filled with blood, the other with a saline solution, hydrating him while he received the infusion.

Evan's eyes began to sting. She was on the verge of tears, struggled to hold them back. She needed to be strong, positive when she stepped into the room. But it wasn't going to be easy. She and Ben had a complicated history. When they worked for the federal government he was her partner in the field before becoming her control. Years ago near the end of a long and difficult mission the desperate exigencies of their situation, their nearness to death, drew a curtain over Ben's marriage and, acting on their mutual attraction, they spent the night twined together. Afterward, as if by divine punishment, both Ben's wife and Evan's sister Bobbi had been murdered, quite possibly as blowback for the success of their mission. Guilt was an altogether too passive term for what they continued to suffer.

The two women stood on the threshold, unaware that Bobbi's death had been staged by her FSB handlers, that she had been tasked with terminating Ben's wife, which she did, deftly and neatly a week before she was exfiltrated out of DC, out of the country, and into the arms of her new bosses in Moscow. As far as the world at large knew, Bobbi was dead.

Isobel handed Evan a folded slip of paper. "The update on your first mission."

Evan frowned as she took the paper. "Why didn't you give Ben the update yourself?"

"It's Operations. Your responsibility." She sighed. All at once she seemed exhausted. "It should come from you."

Evan felt something in her stomach clench. "Bad news?"

Isobel made no reply. Opening the note, Evan read the terse report.

Evan closed her eyes for a moment. "What a monumental shit show."

As she looked up, Isobel said, "I'm still trying to sort the details." She cleared her throat. "It's time you saw him."

Evan nodded, turned away. Taking slow, deep breaths, she centered herself and entered the bedroom. The doctor glanced up as she approached, but Ben didn't turn his head or move at all. He sat still as a rock face, staring out the window through the rain-streaked glass.

"Ben," she said as she came up beside him.

"Ah," he replied, in a voice thin and sere as a winter reed. He did not, however, turn his head to look at her. "You came."

Sheren nodded to her. Before he left the room, he said softly, "I've given him a mild anti-psychotic." In reaction to her shocked expression, he explained. "It's just a precaution, to keep his mind settled, nothing more." For a moment, she heard him murmuring to Isobel, before they moved down the hall out of earshot.

"Of course I came." She struggled to keep her tone from faltering, seeing the bandages on his wrists close up. "Why wouldn't I?" She jerked her gaze away, concentrating on his face.

"I wasn't sure she would call you."

Evan frowned. "Why wouldn't Isobel call me?"

"Maybe she gets too much pleasure out of taking care of me."

Evan wiped away a tear, placed a hand on his shoulder. "Maybe right at this moment you need taking care of."

"You know Israelis." Lost inside himself, he seemed not to have heard her. "All nails and thorns on the outside, inside a molten chocolate cake."

She gave in, knelt down beside him. "Ben, this isn't you."

"It is now."

"No," she said, "it isn't."

Now, at last, he turned his head to look at her. His eyes were bleak, angry. "Oh, Evan . . ."

She placed a forefinger gently on the inside of his bandaged wrist. Ignoring his wince, she said, "Right here is proof you're the same Ben as you've always been."

He shook his head mutely.

"If you'd really wanted to kill yourself you wouldn't have slit your wrists crosswise. You would have made the cut lengthwise, along the vein. That way you would've bled out before anyone could get to you."

"Odd," he said, turning back to stare out the window, "I feel like I've bitten down on a bar of copper. I can't get the taste out of my mouth."

It took Evan a moment to realize he was talking about the taste of his own blood. "Look, I get it. You thought you'd be able to walk—"

"That's what the surgeons promised. Over and over." His voice was bitter, rageful. "Now they've done a one-eighty. So what the hell does that mean? It means they fucked up when they went in. They should've—"

"No, Ben. The damage was already done. The nerve connections were severed at the moment you were shot."

"They say."

"They worked hard on rebuilding your hip. Five hours—I was there, at the clinic. The German doctors did an amazing job. The permanent damage was hidden from them. But in any case there was nothing they could've done. Isobel's own surgeon made that perfectly clear."

Ben shook his head. "Even the Coke Isobel brought me tastes of copper."

Time to change tactics. The soft sell both she and Isobel had been peddling not only wasn't working but as she saw now was enabling him to sink lower into self-pity.

"Listen, you," she said, her voice suddenly sharp-edged as a razor, "stop being so goddamned selfish."

"Badgering now? I thought . . . But now I've had enough. Leave me alone."

Abruptly, she stood up, went to the open doorway, but when Isobel made to come in she shook her head, put a finger across her lips, and slowly closed the door. Taking out her mobile, she pressed a speed dial, listened as the connection was made.

"Hey, cookie. How are you? . . . You in school with Wendy and Mikey? . . . Lunchtime, yeah . . . Ha, learning German, are you? . . . Russian, as well! Too good . . . we'll have a conversation soon enough, right? . . . I miss you, too, cookie . . ." She turned her head to look at Ben.

He was staring at her in anger. He shook his head vehemently, his intent clear as a bell. Evan raised her eyebrows, held the phone out toward him. He just shook his head again and looked away.

Evan acquiesced to Ben's refusal and turned from him, walked over to the window. "No cookie, I'm not with him right now . . . Of course I will. And I'll talk to you again in a few days." As she cut the connection, she bit her lip and thought, *Damn it, Ben, come back from wherever you are.*

Silence fell between them. When she couldn't take it anymore she came to stand by his chair. The rain had lessened but the sky was still low and roiling. She put the lightest of hands on his shoulder.

"How I hate winter," he said, leaning almost imperceptibly into her touch. "The trees look burnt, they look like skeletons. It seems life has shrunk away, leaving an empty hole, nothing but the cold and the dark coming down earlier and earlier."

"Until January twenty-second when the new administration takes over. I'll bet we could get our old jobs back." She'd said this lightheartedly, with a smile in her voice because neither of them would ever work for the federal clandestine services again. She chuckled, but he gave no response. She went around, stood between him and the black outlines of the trees.

"Ben, listen to me, if you kill yourself I'll never forgive you; Isobel will never forgive you—you know how unforgiving Israelis are."

As she hoped, this brought the ghost of a smile to his face.

She took a breath before she brought home the ultimate consequence.

"Worst of all, Zoe will never forgive you." There was no longer even a trace of humor in her voice.

He turned to her and his gaze held none of his previous anger; it was full of pain and longing, and then a sudden animation, a spark of life that hadn't been there a second before. She picked his cell phone off the small table by his chair and put it into his hand. "Call her, Ben. Don't be afraid. She needs to hear from you. It's important she knows you're okay."

His gaze fell to the phone in his hand. Something galvanized inside him then, and he switched on the phone, hit his daughter's speed dial number.

■   ■   ■

"Dad!"

Ben closed his eyes, allowed her excited voice to flow over him as she asked how he was.

"I'm fine. I want to know all about what you're up to."

"Dad . . ." He knew that tone of voice. Zoe could be like a dog with a bone.

"No really. Coming along really well." But even he could hear the wooden tone in his voice. And of course Zoe, who could read him like an open book, picked up on it right away.

"Okay, Dad. What's up? You haven't called in a bunch of days. Are you really okay? You can tell me the truth. You know you can. Don't keep stuff from me—I always know when you do that and, you know what, I start to think the worst."

A memory surfaced of his father, always away on business, whether it was with real clients or not. His mother's eyes red, dark half-moons beneath them.

"Dad?"

Zoe's plaintive voice returned him to the present, and he knew he didn't want to do to her what his father had done to him. He did not want to shut her out.

"Right, well, the truth is I haven't been tip-top lately. The doctors have no idea whether I'll be able to walk again." He forestalled her response. "Before you go on, honey, I don't want you to come back yet. It's important to me that you live your best life right now. I know you love it there with Aunt Evan's parents and Wendy and Mikey. In any case, I'm still at Isobel's place. She and her staff are taking great care of me."

"Have any of them ordered a physical therapist?"

"You mean a physical trainer."

"No, Dad. I mean a physical *therapist*."

"Doesn't matter what you call them. Well, if the doctors are right—"

"They don't know everything, Dad! Don't listen to them," Zoe said heatedly. "I've been talking to Dr. Stan." That was what she called Dr. Reveshvili, Evan's birth father. "He worked on you in the beginning, remember? He thinks a physical therapist is just what the doctor ordered, lol."

Ben had met Konstantin Reveshvili and his wife, Rebecca, the previous spring, when Evan discovered who they were. They ran a high-end psychiatric clinic in the countryside near Cologne, Germany. It was there that Evan and Ben had gone to recover at the end of their mission rooting out the Omega stronghold in Romania. It was there that Ben had had his hip surgery, began his recovery. But not only for that did the Reveshvilis loom large in Ben's world. They were the birth parents of Evan and her late sister, Bobbi, but also of the twins Ana and Lucinda. He had shot Ana to death last year; Lucinda was married to Samuel Wainwright Wells.

"And there is a difference, Dad—a big one. Dr. Stan says a physical therapist knows much more, can call on a lot of what he called 'modalities' to help you."

Both the Reveshvilis were incredibly smart, innovative physicians. Konstantin had been reluctant to release Ben into another doctor's care, insisting that his recovery was just beginning. Ben had great respect for him, but had wanted to get back home. But now if it was his opinion that Ben should be in the care of a physical therapist maybe he should hire one.

As if reading his mind, Zoe said, "Dad, he even has the info on the person you want to see in DC. Her name is An Binh. Dr. Stan says she's awesome. I'll text you her contact info, okay?"

"Okay," Ben said.

"Dad, please promise me you'll hire her."

"I will. Scout's honor," Ben said, truthfully. He realized that he had not just unconditional love, but also great respect for his daughter. She wasn't even nine years old yet, but she was a fully formed person, with a sometimes frightening maturity forged from the early loss of her mother, her father's unconventional life, and the mysteries of her own innate nature. He heard her breath in his ear and he felt better than he had in a long time. The boundless energy, the surety of youth—of Zoe, in particular—had injected him with much needed vitality.

He looked out the window, saw a bird alight on a bare black branch, heard its call even through the glass. "Now tell me all about your adventures in the German countryside," he said to his beloved daughter.

2

NUREMBERG, GERMANY

Having deplaned from her flight from Vienna and passed easily through immigration, Sofia made her way through Albrecht Durer Airport, a place she knew well. However, she was no longer Sofia Moretti. Her hair was now a deep, lustrous burnt sienna, her eyes the color of sea glass now that she'd ditched her contact lenses. There was in fact a Sofia Moretti who worked at the company she told Armistad about, and which she had no doubt he'd called to check. But the real Sofia Moretti was still in Vienna, never having met Armistad or knowing a thing about him.

She had entered Germany under the name Katie Harden, a favorite identity of hers. Katie worked for an international cosmetics company domiciled in Zurich, Switzerland. She liked airports, the ultimate no-man's-land, neither here nor there, the gray place where people were either spaced-out in limbo or hurrying through on their way from one location to another. Here she was invisible. Here she could think what she wanted, do what she wanted without consequences. Here, between death and rebirth, identities dropping away, she could gaze into the emptiness at her core with neither anger nor humiliation.

She stepped into the Mövenpick restaurant, was shown to a table she had pre-booked under the name Harden and immediately ordered a Doppelbock beer. Instead of burying herself in her mobile phone, she kept her bright, quick gaze on the people around her, those entering the restaurant as well as the ones passing by. As was her wont, she cataloged them by both style and wealth—or lack thereof.

For women it was always handbags and shoes. The stylish, the wealthy—even old money—were fanatic about the quality of their shoes and the stylishness of their handbags. They could be wearing overcoats that had seen better days, outmoded skirts or pants, but the shoes and handbags were always top-notch and en mode. Men were a completely different story—the wealthy or business big boys wore suits of impeccable lines, fabric, and tailoring. There were those with rumpled clothes and hair, but the thing that set them apart was their faces—always well-groomed, healthy-looking skin. And manicured nails.

It was the little things that gave people away, she thought as she sipped her bitter beer, like nails. When she was Sofia she had no-nonsense square-cut nails without polish. Now she sported long acrylics painted brilliant crimson. She wore an expensive man-tailored suit and high-heeled pumps, an auburn wig. No one with whom she had come in contact in Vienna, not even Armistad, would recognize her now.

Armistad. It was a shame she had to kill him; she had rather liked the guy. For a field agent he had a number of features she found enjoyable—first and foremost he was an excellent lover. She'd miss that. Not that she felt even an iota of remorse. She was unable to feel either remorse or regret. Conscience she had none. She lived in the moment, as if standing in the rain she felt only one drop at a time. Anyway, one of these days she'd find a better lover.

The waitress had set down laminated menus, but she had hardly glanced at the one facing her, satisfied with her beer and her thoughts.

Konrad Mischler arrived precisely eight minutes after she entered the restaurant. The man was nothing if not precise. He wore an exquisitely tailored cashmere jacket and wool slacks, striped shirt, a tie emblazed with medieval rampant lions. His hairless face was freshly scrubbed. Slightly shiny, as if it had been waxed. Mischler was older than her by several decades, his thick hair silver-gray along the sides, reminding her of a skunk's pelt.

"Herr Mischler," she said, "what have you brought me today? A loaf of your finest bread, or a clutch of croissants perhaps."

Mischler produced the hint of a smile. This was a joke between them. Mischler was a Swiss German. Mischler was the occupational name for bakers, though he himself was a vice president of a large and prestigious Zurich bank.

While they ordered lunch, she wondered how Herr Mischler would react if he knew he was talking to Kata Romanovna Hemakova, acting director of Zaslon, the Russian FSB's most secretive action directorate. But, of course, she wasn't Kata, either, having assumed that identity after she had killed the real Kata. Before that, after she had been exfiltrated out of Washington, DC, she had been code-named Kobalt. And before that? Originally she had been Bobbi Ryder, an identity she rarely recalled, aside from when the name of her sister, Evan, was brought up by her FSB superiors. Then she married and became Bobbi Fisher, a superficial sham of an identity even greater than that of her childhood. But then why should she remember her past? At the time of her exfiltration her Russian handlers made sure Bobbi Ryder Fisher, orphaned twice— once by the death of her adoptive parents and again by the demise of her Russian birth parents—was officially pronounced dead. Buried now, a stranger she had never met in her grave. In the odd times she was obliged to remember her younger self it was as if she were viewing someone else, a character in a film she watched in a dark Moscow theater. She was so buried in identities that they were all partially that character up on the movie screen and at the same time contained nothing of her at all.

Herr Mischler was a cutout, someone otherwise unaffiliated with the FSB, whose sole job was transport—small objects only, he had made that stipulation quite clear when he was recruited some years ago. Like most cutouts he was used sparingly and, in his case, for only the most discreet transfers. As far as Herr Mischler was concerned, she was just another cutout, or possibly one of the many worker bees buzzing through the vast FSB hive.

Their food came and they spent a pleasant forty minutes chatting amiably about this and that as if they were old friends catching up with each other's lives. There was absolutely no hint from either of them that this meeting was anything but what it appeared to be. This masquerade was, of course, Kata's life. As for Herr Mischler he was old-school Swiss, seemingly trained from birth to maintain a congenial expression through any and all difficulties, should one arise, even though with Herr Mischler one never did. He made sure of that.

Over coffee and a shared dessert she passed him a small box, gaily gift-wrapped, with a small pink bow. "For your daughter." Herr Mischler did indeed have a daughter, as well as two sons, but the box held the titanium holder she'd ripped from Armistad's clenched fist. In it was a SDXC micro memory card.

"My goodness." The box disappeared in the blink of an eye. "How kind you are to think of her."

She smiled. "I know she'll love it."

Herr Mischler nodded. "A gift from you, so there is no doubt."

Their business concluded, the check was called for. Being a consummate gentleman Herr Mischler paid the bill with all the finesse befitting his station in life.

After he left, the plates were cleared and Kata asked for a double espresso, which was duly brought. Taking her first sip all thought of Herr

Mischler evaporated from her mind. It was as if he had never existed. Now she awaited the second part of her rendezvous, the nature of which was far less determinable than her meeting with the Swiss banker.

Much as she hated to admit it, Lyudmila Alexeyevna Shokova was the only person on earth with the ability to intimidate her. She didn't fear her, exactly—fear was another emotion unknown to her ever since she was a teenager. But undoubtedly there was something—something she could not explain . . .

. . . And here she was, tall, slender, stately, with her unnerving ice-blue eyes. Her blond hair was hidden by a stylish white Sherpa newsboy hat. Her long overcoat was open, revealing a lustrous sand-colored silk shirt and a pale-orange chiffon slit maxiskirt, and high boots the color of dried blood. Those eyes never left Kata's as she entered the restaurant, ignored the hostess, and strode directly to Kata's table and sat down opposite her. She asked for ice water only.

When they were alone, Lyudmila said, "You fucked up."

Kata wanted desperately to lick her lips but held herself in check. Nevertheless she could feel every beat of her galloping heart. "What, no hello, how's it going?"

"I know how it went." While others might have leaned forward, using their bodies to intimidate, Lyudmila sat unnervingly still. "You killed Armistad."

"I had no choice."

"Of course you had a choice." Lyudmila's gaze did not stray from Kata's face. The ice-blue eyes did not blink. *How does she do that?* Kata wondered. "There's always a choice."

"Not this time." She handed over the copy she had made of the SDXC memory card.

Lyudmila didn't even glance at it. "You could have charmed it off him, but you didn't trust yourself."

"I didn't know where it was until—"

"No, no. The trouble with you, Kata, is you're bloodthirsty." Lyudmila had not so much as touched her glass of ice water. "The trouble with you is you're too much in love with the act of killing another human being. You're in thrall to the thousand-mile stare on your victim's face when the bullet or the knife goes through him. I bet you wonder what it is they see." Lyudmila's hands wrapped around her water glass. "You're like a heroin addict. Killing is your high. Nothing else compares." Now at last she took a sip of water. When she set the glass down, she said in a measured tone, "Correct me if I'm wrong. Please."

Customers moved in and out of the restaurant, eyes glazed from hours of travel, breathing recycled air, and sitting without respite. Kata automatically scanned the faces of all the newcomers, searching for anomalies that would alert her to trouble.

She said nothing. She knew if she put up any more excuses Lyudmila would humiliate her in far worse ways than she already had, and, honestly, she'd deserve it; the truth was she did enjoy killing—it filled the gaping hole inside her if only for the few seconds the victim inhabited the gray world between life and death. Besides, she needed Lyudmila, who was, at this moment, her most potent source of power and protection from the very organization she had been working for since long before she was exfiltrated from the United States.

"Listen to me, Kata." Lyudmila modulated her voice lower. It was softer now, all the spines and edges gone. Now it was as if they were having a fireside chat. "You are my eyes and ears inside the FSB, particularly the special action directorates of which you are a part. I set you up there. I gave you life at the FSB when powerful forces were arrayed against you. I opened the way for you to validate yourself with your erstwhile enemies." She meant Darko Kusnetsov, director of the FSB, and his close ally, Slava Baev, director of SVR, the chief action group, and Kata's immediate boss.

Lyudmila's penetrating gaze dropped finally and it was all Kata could do not to gasp in relief. She felt released from iron bonds.

Lyudmila swept the micro memory card off the table and into a reader she had pulled from her overcoat. "You gave the Swiss banker the original?" Her eyes moved back and forth over the lines that appeared.

"Of course. Wrapped as if a present for his daughter." Kata found her voice at last, though it seemed a bit creaky with the scare Lyudmila had put into her. "All pink paper and bows."

Lyudmila's head snapped up. "What the hell? This is gibberish."

Kata had seen the lines of code when she'd copied them from the original. "It's a cipher," she said. "It has to be."

"Not like anything I've ever seen. Looks more like chicken scratching than a cipher." Lyudmila sighed. "If we don't even know what it is, I don't know how we can break it. In which case, the Vienna affair will have been even more of a clusterfuck." She tucked the reader back into her voluminous overcoat. "Do you know what's going to happen now? Happen because of your bloodlust? Your masters are going to send an agent out to Vienna."

"What? What for?"

"To make sure you haven't left anything that could be traced back to them."

"But I haven't. I was perfectly—"

"In this instance, no one is going to take your word for it, even those who love you the most." She meant Baev and Kusnetsov, of course. "Protocol is unwavering on this point. Moscow Rules. A clean-up agent or agents must be dispatched to the scene of the murder you committed." She pursed her lips, a sure sign of her displeasure. "Someone you won't know, someone you hope to God you never meet. An agent from Department 73—the clean-up crew who in this case will deal with the Austrian federal police. These people are specially trained in a remote facility so secret even I haven't been able to discover where it is. And not for lack of trying, I assure you. The name of the facility is *Devyatyy Krug*."

"Ninth Circle," Kata said. "As in Dante's Hell."

"Correct." Lyudmila nodded. "These individuals are very, very nasty pieces of work. *Devyatyy Krug* has taken their souls. They're called *ovoshchechistki*."

"Peelers." Kata frowned. "I don't like the sound of that."

"Nor should you," Lyudmila replied drily. "The *ovoshchechistka* will be coming not just for Armistad; there's another body in that apartment—an FSB hitman."

"That was an outsourced team, the one at the apartment and the other one at the cemetery," Kata protested. "Ex-cons. Professional murderers plying their trade for money rather than favors as they did when they were serving out their sentences. No connection to the FSB."

Lyudmila shook her head. "Doesn't matter. You say you're in the clear; they see a leaky boat."

"Then I should head back there."

"That's precisely what you *won't* do." Iron in her voice now, and Kata subsided. "I don't want you anywhere near that place. You were right to get out of Vienna, out of Austria as quickly as you did. One good decision anyway." She lifted a finger. "You need to learn the difference between a sledgehammer and a silken cord."

"This again?" Kata felt the urge to turn away but the other woman's ice-blue gaze held her prisoner.

"You killed Armistad, one of your sister's field agents. Evan surely will be drawn to Vienna so you cannot be there. She thinks you're dead, as does everyone else, and it is to your benefit—"

"And yours," Kata interjected.

Lyudmila shot her a piercing look. "Naturally. I only do things that will benefit me. Isn't that what we humans do? We were born selfish—that, my dear Kata, is the actual Original Sin. The idea of amassing knowledge being sinful is the precinct of autocrats and religious hierarchs."

She pursed her lips. "In any event, the fiction of your death allows you immense freedom in our world of shadows. You will not do anything to jeopardize that advantage."

She shook her head. "No, you'll go straight back to Moscow and I'll tell you why. My latest intel informs me that when it comes to Omega there's an ideological split forming within the FSB."

"What part of the FSB?"

Lyudmila bared her teeth. In what might have been a smile or something else altogether. "That's what you've got to smell out. You're good at smelling out the rot; better than good, Kata." Her teeth were exceedingly long and very white. "No more distractions. Please do not forget that you're management now—don't let your murderous instincts distract you from your purpose: moving up the echelons of the FSB. To take the next step you must ferret out the wheat from the chaff inside the FSB. I need to know what these factions have in mind regarding Omega before I make my next move. Am I clear?"

Without waiting for an answer, Lyudmila called the waitress over, ordered double espressos for both of them. She sat quite still, staring at a space behind Kata or nothing at all. Thinking. Their order came. While Kata sipped hers, Lyudmila downed her espresso in one large gulp, as the Italians do.

Kata, still angry and humiliated by how Lyudmila could manipulate her, snapped, "Here's an idea. Why don't you contact my sister. Evan always did have a way with ciphers. I used to make fun of her. 'Of what possible use is studying the history of ciphers?'"

"And what was her reply?"

"A smile, Lyudmila. She smiled like a crocodile."

Lyudmila shook her head, her eyes narrowed. "Sometimes I don't understand your humor at all."

"Maybe that's 'cause I grew up in America."

Lyudmila ignored the comment. "Book yourself on the next flight to Moscow and, as I said, get to work on your Omega mystery. Keep your head down and your ear to the walls. The FSB, like all Russian institutions, is monolithic. The fact that there is a split within it portends something ominous. I need to find out what."

Kata grimaced. "My expertise is in the field. I—"

"My dear, as I have already pointed out your proficiency at killing is hardly your only outstanding attribute," Lyudmila interrupted, clearly not interested in Kata's compulsive hunger. "You've had your brief vacation, and I trust you've sated yourself. Time to get your head back in the game. Your ability to charm your higher-ups is invaluable. Baev, yes, he's fairly easily manipulated by someone as clever as you, but Kusnetsov is a hard man—extremely hard. It takes a singular talent to win him over. And yet win him over you did. As director of the entire FSB he must forever remain in your crosshairs. He is aware of much more than he lets on—more even than you imagine. Like a woodpecker on a tree trunk you must find the vulnerable pith beneath the holes you have made in his armor." Then she laughed, not harshly but not softly either. "Just make sure you don't kill him."

3

Evan was in the kitchen of Isobel Lowe's villa. Perched on a high stool, one of four set along one side of the green granite-topped center island, she was picking at a plate of eggs and bacon the cook had made for her, staring at the report of Armistad's murder. It was good to be a billionaire, she was thinking, to take her mind off the terrible failure she and Ben had absorbed, when Isobel entered. She asked the cook for a plate of fried eggs and labneh with harissa, and a glass of pomegranate juice.

"How is he?" Evan asked.

"Better. Much better. He's sleeping now. Dr. Sheren gave him a sedative before he left." The juice was served from a ceramic jug. Isobel took a sip, placed the glass down on the granite with great precision. "I don't know what you said to him, but . . ."

"It wasn't me," Evan replied. "Well, not only me. It was Zoe."

"Ah." Isobel nodded. "I never think of children. Just like me."

There was a silence for a time. Then the cook set Isobel's breakfast down in front of her. She had added a small saucer piled with warm pita cut in triangles.

Isobel slid the point of a triangle into the soft cheese, took a bite. "He needs a human anchor."

"He has Zoe."

Isobel waved a hand dismissively. "Besides Zoe, I mean. An adult."

Evan looked down at her eggs and bacon, which she had barely touched and which had grown cold. "I doubt that's possible now," she said softly. "After Lila's murder and the guilt . . . he felt . . ." Her voice faltered.

"It's all right." Isobel's voice was soft as velvet. "I know what happened between the two of you."

"It was a mistake."

"Now why would you say that?"

Evan lifted her gaze to find Isobel looking at her frankly, without judgment. "You know why."

The other woman shook her head. "It was a matter of need, of necessity, actually. The tension of the mission had hit a boiling point. It required release in order for you to continue. I see no guilt in that."

Evan made no immediate reply. She had never thought of her one night of sex with Ben in such a pragmatic light. Perhaps only someone outside the situation could see it that way.

"Thank you," she said softly. "But it will never happen again."

"Of course it won't. He won't allow it."

Evan observed reflections in the egg yolks. "Did . . ." She paused, steeling herself to ask a question that had been nagging at her ever since Ben had taken her here last October when she was hurt.

"You want to know if Ben and I ever had an affair."

Evan looked up. "Yes."

Isobel shook her head. "No."

"Do you love him?"

"What a question! Of course I love him, but not in the way you mean." Isobel smiled. "My sexual interests reside in another sphere."

"Ah." When Isobel cocked her head, giving her an unguarded look, Evan went on. "I just, well, now I feel a bit foolish for suspecting you two might be amorously involved."

Isobel laughed softly and, half-turning on her stool, said, "Eliane, Evan's breakfast is shivering. Please make her another."

"Don't bother," Evan said. "I'm not hungry."

"Appetite or not, you'll eat," Isobel ordered. "You need to keep up your strength." She tossed her head. "The last thing I need is one of my agents passing out in the middle of Vienna."

Evan sighed. "Okay, then. But I'll have what you're having. That labneh looks good enough to eat."

Isobel laughed, pushed her plate and saucer over. "Then by all means have some with the pita."

Evan reached for the pita and following Isobel's lead dipped a corner into the labneh, took a bite. It was delicious.

"How did he take the news of Armistad's death?" Isobel asked.

"About as expected." She took another bite, chewed reflectively. "You reached out to An Binh?"

"The PT woman?" Isobel nodded. "She came fully vetted by your father, but we did our own deep dive. She'll start work tomorrow morning." She looked at Evan with concern in her eyes. "You really think this is a good idea?"

Evan shrugged. "My father recommended her. Besides, what's the downside?"

Isobel hesitated a moment before saying, "It could get Ben's hopes up."

"And that would be wrong why?"

Isobel said nothing, looked away. Well, Evan thought, she had been pessimistic about Ben's recovery right from the get-go. She'd seen too many battle casualties as a young woman in the Israeli army.

Evan had just dipped another bit of pita into the labneh when her mobile buzzed. She turned away, her heart beating faster. The pattern of the vibration alerted her to the fact that the material coming in was from the sandboxed section of her phone, meaning the area completely cut off from the rest of her phone's data, securely compartmentalized inside its own hacker-proof space.

Only one person possessed the credentials to contact her in the sandbox: Lyudmila Shokova. Now a friend of a unique stripe, Lyudmila had been an apparatchik for the FSB and, after, the Politburo itself. But she had climbed too far, too fast, and her male colleagues purged her from the government on bogus charges. A price was put on her head, but through her vast network of contacts she was smuggled out of Russia, going to ground. She was always three or four steps ahead of her pursuers, all the while further building out her own clandestine network, the ultimate purpose of which remained unclear to everyone but Lyudmila herself. In any event, one of her objectives was undermining the current Russian regime, which she had come to despise.

This time, however, there was no personal message from Lyudmila, per se, just 55KBs of a text document. Evan opened it and began to read. As she did, she scrolled faster and faster, her jaw nearly dropping open.

"Good God!"

Isobel leaned forward. "What is it? What d'you have there?"

Evan turned the phone so Isobel could see, but Isobel just shook her head. "It looks like a child's scribbling—no letters, numbers, even in other languages."

"Look—there at the bottom. Intel from your agent."

Isobel frowned, used her finger to scroll back and forth. "This is a whole bunch of nothing."

"Maybe it's been enciphered. My source—"

"Your Russian source, yes?" Isobel looked up. "But I can't make heads or tails out of it."

"You suspect it's Russian *dezinformatsiya*?"

"I'm considering the source. I'm thinking this is a joke."

"When it comes to work, my source doesn't have a sense of humor."

"Evan, the Russians killed Armistad. Why would a Russian share this with you?" Isobel said, ignoring her.

"I'm Russian," Evan countered.

"You're as Russian as I am Israeli, Evan. I love Israel, I love its people, by and large. My disagreement is with its current government. I think you can say the same for Russia, yes?"

"Not quite yet," Evan said. "The time I've spent inside Russia has been filled with tension, fear, and a sense of extreme urgency. But I take your point."

"We're Americans."

"For better or for worse."

Isobel gave a bitter laugh. "Yes, we've been through the shitter lately, haven't we."

"To say the least."

"Bottom line, the text she sent you is suspect. First and foremost, if Armistad was killed for this how in the hell did she get her hands on it?"

"The last signal we got from him four days ago was that he had ID'd a Russian thug shadowing him."

"The Russians. Always the Russians," Isobel said meaningfully.

"You don't know her."

"My point exactly." The look Isobel gave her was as hard and dark as obsidian.

"Then you'll just have to trust me. She's a friend. A friend—trust—doesn't come easily in this business; I hardly have to remind you of that. She's on our side. Everything she's ever said to me, every piece of intel she's provided me has been true."

"So you trust her."

"With my life."

"Why?"

"She's protected me more than once. She's laid her life on the line for me."

"Really?"

"Yes. Really," Evan said with emphasis.

"This Russian woman must be extraordinary indeed."

"I'm not immune to your tone of voice."

"Evan, how the hell did she get the file we were after?"

Evan took a breath, let it out. "My best guess is she took it off the Russian who murdered Armistad."

"So she was in Vienna."

"Probably not. Knowing her she had an operative on site, possibly tailing the Russians—because from what we understand there were two, not one."

"That was Armistad's mistake."

Evan made no response; there was nothing to say.

Isobel stared down at the remnants of her breakfast, which had also now grown cold. "So." But still she hesitated, then sighed. "How do we handle a putative cipher that is composed of neither letters nor numbers?"

Evan had been taking a closer look at the cipher. "Good Lord," she said now.

"What?" Isobel's eyes narrowed. "What is it?"

"I think the cipher is written in Akkadian." Akkadian was an extinct East Semitic language used by the Babylonians and Assyrians during the Bronze Age. "I recognize the cuneiform style but I can't read it."

"Give it here." Isobel reached her hand out and Evan gave her the phone. "Akkadian is the first Semitic language, a precursor to Aramaic. Along with other extinct Middle Eastern languages, I studied it at university." She shook her head. "But this doesn't look right."

For a time nothing was said between them. While Isobel was concentrated on the mysteries of the cipher, Evan's old breakfast was whisked away, replaced by her new one, hot from the stove. Judging that Isobel's translating was going to take some time, she took up her fork and another triangle of pita and began to eat. She had no desire to be castigated again for not keeping up her strength. Besides, Isobel was right, as Ben had told her she was about most things.

She was halfway through her eggs and labneh when, with a bolt of insight, she abandoned her food, rose from the stool. She crossed the room to a line of drawers, scrabbled through each one until she found what she wanted. The item flashed like lightning as she brought it back.

"Isobel, give me the phone, I have an idea."

Evan held the cell in one hand and the small mirror she had found in the other, so that phone and mirror were facing each other.

"Look," she said. "The cipher is written in mirror image."

"But you still can't read it, can you?"

Evan shook her head.

Isobel shrugged. "So maybe this isn't Akkadian after all. Maybe it's nothing."

Evan considered. "You could be right, but why? Why go to the trouble to send nothing to the American Omega cadre? People died over this." She shook her head. "No, I still think it's more than just nonsense." She looked at the cuneiform, was again sure it was Akkadian, so why couldn't she read it? She looked up at Isobel. "What if the Akkadian is not only mirrored, but also enciphered."

Isobel huffed out an exhalation.

Evan gave her a *Let's be calm* look. "One step at a time. Input the mirror image into the quantum computer, then run every bit of code-breaking software Parachute has in its arsenal and see what comes up."

"Hm." Isobel tapped her forefinger against her lower lip. "First we'll have to download the Akkadian alphabet, syntax, and the like. Then my coders will write a program so the computer recognizes Akkadian cuneiform."

"A piece of cake," Evan said.

Isobel gave her a wry smile. "It'll take a bit of time. Obviously, Akkadian isn't in the database and converting language into code will be a challenge." She shook her head. "This is quite the mystery." She transferred the full file to the isolated Parachute server, then handed Evan back her cell. "Don't worry, this gets top priority."

She stood. "Meanwhile one of our planes is waiting to take you to Vienna. I've started the ball rolling repatriating Armistad's body but I want you to vet the body first, then retrace Armistad's whereabouts in the hours and days immediately before he was shot to death. Find out where and who this message came from."

4

Pasha Rodionovich Shutkov entered Vienna as a civil engineer for a well-known German firm. His credentials were complete, authentic, and unimpeachable; the Moscow *stsenaristy—scriptwriters—*were particularly good, very detail oriented, one could say almost anal in their thoroughness.

The title "civil engineer" tickled Shutkov's funny bone, deeply buried as it was. For, in fact, as a first rank *ovoshchechistka—*a *peeler—*he was in a sense very much a civil engineer, cleaning up the mess the SVR shadows left behind in the real world. The SVR, a division within FSB, carried out its foreign work—often wet work, meaning blood was spilled.

He took a taxi to the museum quarter and from there walked to Mariahilfer Strasse, the main shopping street. Crowds filled the pedestrian-only area, people buying all manner of electronics, household goods, clothing, and the like. His mother's family had once owned a café near here, but that was a long time ago and though he made it a point to stop into Rickoffer's Café when he was in town, it was nowadays run by people he didn't know and had never met. The café still had the best apple strudel *mit schlag* in Vienna, though. The thick hand-whipped cream was his great-grandfather's recipe, he'd been delighted to discover, its secret being a tipple of apple brandy in every generous portion. Just the thought of the decadent dessert made his mouth water.

However, at the moment he had important business to conduct. He opened the door to Fifth Avenue, a high-end clothing boutique between a fashionable shoe store and a shop with a gaudy front window hawking the latest mobile phones and smart watches and wearables.

The place had the air of an atelier. Walls were painted a rich cream, the ceiling high above a pale blue, as if illuminated by a skylight. Chestnut shelves filled with shirts, pants, and sweaters lined the side walls interspersed with racks of jackets and suits. A customer was admiring a new suit in one of the floor-length mirrors, while a young woman knelt to pin up the cuffs.

As always, Brigid, the proprietor, a handsome, very proper Viennese woman in her early fifties, emerged from behind the counter filled with socks, ties, and a smattering of expensive watches, to greet him. She had a round face, and a figure to match. Impeccably dressed, coiffed, and polished, she smiled, kissed him on both cheeks, then, as was her way, she took one of his thick, hard hands briefly between hers.

"Such a pleasant surprise when you appear," she said. Earnest, controlled, not effusive: Austrian through and through.

They chatted for a moment or two before she said, "And how is your *schatzi* Alyosha?"

"Alyosha Ivanovna is just fine," Shutkov said. "She asks to be remembered to you," he lied.

"She should come with you the next time you visit," Brigid sighed. "I would show her all around Vienna while you work. The real Vienna. We'd have such fun."

"That's very kind of you." Alyosha would never visit Brigid, would never in fact set foot outside of Moscow. She wasn't Shutkov's sweetheart, she was his lover, one of those young Russian women who was made to be taken and used over and over until the years rendered them useless.

Shutkov was fond of Brigid; he often took her to dinner when he was in town. She was smart, funny—in short, good company. She was the one person he did not enjoy lying to.

She gestured, leading him over to a neat stack of sweaters. "You came at a fortuitous time. I have just now laid in a new store of cashmeres. I have them all in your size."

Five-A, as it was known among locals, was stocked with the most exquisite men's cashmere sweaters in a veritable rainbow of colors. As he always did, Shutkov bought three and, as she always did, Brigid had all his purchases at Alyosha's apartment that evening.

"And as always," Brigid said, "I'll pick out something special for your *schatzi*." She tapped her forefinger against her lower lip while her gaze lifted toward the second floor, which housed the women's clothing. "Perhaps a dress this time, eh?"

"Perfect," he said, as Brigid gathered up his purchases. "Maybe something in yellow."

"It will be my pleasure." She nodded. "And now, darling, Noemi is anxiously awaiting your arrival."

He gave a smirk at Brigid's very Austrian joke; Noemi didn't know the meaning of either anxiety or anticipation. He had never met anyone who so utterly lived in the moment. He reluctantly admitted to himself that he envied her perfect sangfroid.

He passed through a packed storeroom with a niche to the left where a seamstress worked beneath a brilliant gooseneck light. She paid him no mind as he opened another door, stepped through into Noemi's workshop. This space was far larger than might be imagined from the shop itself, reaching back some one thousand square feet. Noemi was in the middle of making coffee when Shutkov entered. The sharp tang tried to override the smells of hot metal, electronics. Ranks of laptops and servers surrounded her on two sides, beyond which was arrayed a bewildering variety of equipment whose purpose was opaque to him.

Noemi was a stringer for the FSB, though not strictly speaking a part of it. By design she had no knowledge of the workings of the organization or of its byzantine politics. Besides which, she, like Brigid, most assuredly didn't want to know. A disaffected Moroccan of Spanish descent, Noemi was all about her expertise in forgery. She liked money, too, no doubt, but her joy was in creating docs that were indistinguishable from legitimate ones.

Slender, virtually hipless, with a face as long as if it had been dreamed up by El Greco, and spidery fingers so deft she could put a surgeon to shame, Noemi was a master of her trade. What she had for him was a complete bag of tricks to transform him from a civil engineer to a chief inspector in INTERPOL, a surprising and unwanted legend for him.

Shutkov frowned when he scanned the docs Noemi had made for him. He glanced up to see she was already waiting for his response. "My orders were to receive a legend attached to Parachute, Armistad's company."

Noemi bared tiny ivory teeth. "Should have, wanted to, couldn't, so there you are, Chief Inspector Rene Bouchard of INTERPOL."

Shutkov made a face. "Explain, please."

Noemi sighed. He hated when she did that, implying she was speaking to an idiot.

"Do you know anything about quantum computing?" she asked.

"Of course," he said, stone-faced.

"But like practically everyone else on earth you don't understand it." She waited in vain for his refutation. Her eyes sparked as if powered by electricity. "Parachute is first mover in the quantum computing space. Its revolutionary solution to computing at unimaginable speed is, of course, proprietary. Their quantum network is impregnable, even against the newest quantum cyber-attacks of ransomware, worms, Trojans, you name it. Every Forbes 500 company licenses one or more of Parachute's quantum suites including their cyber-security solution. I can't match that; no one can, at the moment, though certain nation-states, including your own, are trying their best to catch up. On top of that, Parachute has deployed the RevBits cyber-security suite as its first line of defense. I can't even touch the RevBits without setting off alarms, let alone hack it. Worse, the company will trace that probe right back to me no matter how I try to cover my tracks."

"Blah, blah, blah." He made a face. "I'll find someone who can."

Noemi burst out laughing. "Who are you kidding? I'm the best, better than the Chinese, the Iranians, the North Koreans, your own Fuzzy Bear."

"Fancy Bear."

She smirked; she knew very well the correct name. "Who cares? I'm better." She made a gesture. "So go ahead, Chief Inspector. Waste your time. Take your best shot at hacking Parachute."

When he said nothing, she poured herself some coffee, drank it straight off, black as night. She did not offer him any.

When she was finished, she said, "Now I have to give you a brush cut."

He sat on a stool, ready but unhappy to have his thick locks shorn. She thrust a hand mirror at him and he looked at his reflection: the yellow-gray eyes of a wolf, wide brow above eyebrows like gull wings. High cheekbones and a narrow chin gave his face a diamond shape.

"Like what you see?" Noemi asked as she took the scissors to his hair.

Pasha merely grunted.

"Well, I can scarcely blame you." Noemi snipped. "You have the lips of a high-priced whore."

■ ■ ■

The following morning Chief Inspector Rene Bouchard presented himself at the front door of the building housing the late Armistad's apartment. The federal cop at the entrance checked his creds, told him the apartment number, then waved him inside.

He was obliged to repeat the process in order to gain entrance to the apartment itself. Once he did so, he introduced himself to Brigadier Ku Geistler, a tall, distinguished assistant inspector in the federal police with a ramrod-straight bearing, salt-and-pepper hair, and a face like a hatchet.

The brigadier did not greet him warmly, even after glancing at his ID. His eyes were like granite chips as they looked Shutkov up and down. "What is INTERPOL's interest in this double killing? The American is a businessman; representatives from his company will be arriving later today to see to the repatriation of the body."

"And the other man?"

Geistler huffed, making it clear that whatever patience he possessed was at an end. "As for the other man, he has yet to be identified." His attention was briefly detoured to a subordinate who handed him a paper to sign. That done, he turned back to Shutkov. "So I ask you again, what are you doing here?"

"This other man aligns with a profile of an international embezzler we've been after for almost a year."

Geistler put his fists on his hips. "Is that so?"

"Well, I won't know until I see him in the flesh, as it were."

The brigadier's eyes grew icier if that was possible. "He's in the morgue. Right beside the American."

Shutkov assumed the subtle posture of a supplicant. He had determined nothing else would work with this Austrian prick.

"And nothing else will do?"

Of course nothing else will do, you imbecile, Shutkov thought. "I'm afraid not, Brigadier." Now he hoped that it would be Geistler who would accompany him to the morgue.

Geistler took a look around the living room, his heavy gaze alighting on one after another of his men. He snapped his fingers. "Hausmann," he said. A young man with ginger hair and a ridiculous narrow mustache turned from what he was doing, his expression questioning and obsequious in equal measure. "Take this INTERPOL personage to see our victims. It seems he needs a guide through our delightful house of the dead."

■   ■   ■

In a morgue you do not expect to be served coffee. On the other hand you do expect the morgue to be drab, utilitarian, and when it comes to interior design a bit derelict. As for Vienna's morgue, it was as spotless as a Swiss hotel. The walls featured what appeared to be a fresh coat of white enamel, interspersed with stainless-steel doors, spotless and polished as an officer's jackboots.

Like Virgil, Hausmann turned out to be an excellent guide through the land of the dead. He required no directions to the cold room, a vast dazzlingly white space dominated by a row of stainless-steel tables upon which autopsies were performed. The corpses were stored in refrigerated slots that took up the entire wall to their left.

Shutkov had contrived that they arrive during the lunch hour, when the house of the dead was deathly still. Not even the squeak of transfer trolleys or murmur of voices came to them when they crossed the threshold.

A lone, white-coated attendant stood waiting for them, hands crossed in front of him like a funeral director. The features of his face were unremarkable, his expression lugubrious. His pallor, however, was extreme, like a mole rat, a creature whose skin was visible only by moonlight. His ID tag marked him as one Hans Pfister. He and Hausmann seemed to have met before. He gave the cop a deferential nod. "The American?" he inquired, taking a step toward the refrigerated wall.

"The man who was with him," Hausmann said.

Nodding, Pfister stepped to a drawer on the second level, pulled on the handle, and the draw slid noiselessly out. "Ready?"

"Go on," Hausmann said, while Shutkov shrugged.

And there he was. Shutkov cursed silently but vigorously. Well, this mission had certainly gone sideways and fast. There was no way he could leave this corpse here because, even though he hadn't yet been autopsied, sooner or later he'd be identified through dental work, if not fingerprints, and he'd be marked out as a Russian. Bad for everyone involved, especially his bosses. They would of course deny all knowledge of him or of Russian interference on foreign soil. But then INTERPOL would in fact become involved, and then, inevitably the Americans, sending repercussions throughout the clandestine networks. The Americans especially did not take kindly to their people being murdered by hostile entities. They might not be as severely vindictive as the Israelis but not by much. Plugging these bloody leaks was the raison d'être of the *ovoshchechistki*. As a peeler it was Shutkov's responsibility to get matters under control. "*Ne ostavlyat' sledov—Leave no trace.*" That was the peeler's motto.

This shit show had gone from urgent to extreme. Extreme measures would have to be undertaken. Shutkov knew this, did not for an instant shy away from what was expected of him.

He would not have been able to look at himself in the mirror if he quailed now.

"There was another body," Shutkov said now. The two men looked at him, uncomprehending.

Pfister spread his hands. "I beg your pardon, but this man and the American Herr Armistad were the only ones—"

"Not in the same room," Shutkov snapped, and had to rein in his impatience. The quicker this was over and he got out of here the better. "A man was brought in the same day as these two. Another unidentified male."

Pfister nodded. "Well, yes, but how did you—"

"Let me see him . . . Please." He had to work hard to get the last word out. *These fucking Austrians and their hypocritical civility*, he thought. *Civility is for civilians.*

Pfister stepped to his right and slid out a drawer three columns over. He said, "Here you go," and pulled down the shroud to reveal the head and upper chest. Shutkov was at least pleased to see that this one hadn't yet been autopsied either. Business must be good at this dead end of the city.

The other one, Shutkov thought. *I was right. Those idiots, sending criminals to do a professional's job. When will they learn?* Without taking his eyes off the waxen face, he said, "Where was this one found, if not in the same room with the other two?"

Pfister took up a board with a sheaf of papers clipped to it. He paged through, then cleared his throat. "Friedhof der Namenlosen cemetery, sir."

At which, Shutkov's head snapped up. "He was found in a *cemetery?*"

"That is what it says here." Pfister tapped the paper he'd been reading from. "Yes, sir."

This was an unexpected twist, and Shutkov spent all of ten seconds pondering it. Then he turned on Hausmann and, stabbing out with the ends of his stiffened fingers, broke the cricoid cartilage in the cop's throat. Hausmann's hands flew up, but it was too late, his air supply was cut off. He gasped, suffocating. As the cop collapsed Shutkov was already rushing at the shocked Pfister, twisting him around so that he faced away, then with a vicious twist broke his neck.

Quickly now, he stripped off his clothes, set them on top of the first Russian who Pfister had pulled out. Then he climbed into Pfister's outfit, making sure the ID tag was only half-visible. Then he carried first Hausmann and then the lighter Pfister over to the far end of the wall of drawers. He found an empty drawer in the last row at the bottom, slid one corpse atop the other, made sure the drawer slid back with no problem, closed it up.

Returning to the open drawer in which the first Russian lay, he produced from the secret pockets of his shed clothing four packets of thermite wrapped in aluminum foil, shiny side out. He laid one at the head and at the foot of both corpses. Each of the four packets had a short magnesium fuse sticking out of it. Now the tricky part. The fuses, by design, burned fast. He needed to ignite them and get as far away as possible before the super-hot blasts incinerated the dead Russians, making them unidentifiable.

No problem. He had practiced this maneuver over and over again before he set out on this assignment. It was an alternative of last resort that as it transpired he was forced to use. One lit, two. Next corpse. One lit. He heard a noise at the door—a voice raised, querying. Calling out to Pfister. Three fuses were lit; he was committed. The door began to open, Pfister's name hanging in the air like an executioner's axe.

Shutkov lit the fourth fuse, sprinted for the half-open door, ran straight into one of Pfister's assistants, slamming him off his feet. He bounced off the opposite wall of the corridor, his eyes losing focus.

Shutkov didn't wait to see whether he was conscious or unconscious. He made tracks out the way he had come. Three orderlies stood just outside the building, smoking, drinking coffee, and chatting. They barely had time to register Shutkov flying past them when the blasts shook the building, sending a vicious shockwave down the length of the central corridor and out into the afternoon's uncertain sunlight.

5

MOSCOW

All across its icy surface Moscow seemed to have changed while Kata had been in Vienna. So close to Christmas, a festive winter mood gripped the city. Wrapped in its winter twilight even now in the early afternoon, Red Square's transformation into the site of the annual December festival, with rides for the children and temporary shops selling all manner of gear for the adults, was all but complete. On the river side of the grounds long strings of ruby lights in the shape of a glittering Christmas tree ornament had been hung, illuminating the faces of delighted children.

Far from there, in the grim building where she worked, apparatchiks strode to and fro, armed with stacks of intel, interoffice memos, reminders of the day's appointments. It all seemed the normal frantic hustle and bustle, but the veneer holding things in place seemed to have worn dangerously thin during her absence. Underneath she could sense the ever-present jealousy, fear, and throttled rage nearer the surface, like the fug in a tavern. Not that any of the drones who passed her seemed aware that anything was different. Their minds were totally focused on the here and now, the punishments to be meted out were they to fail in their quotidian tasks.

She rode the elevator up, strode down the corridors until she arrived at the office of the head of the SVR. Comrade Director General Baev was sitting behind his massive desk on the far side of the office. All penitents seeking an audience were required to navigate the expanse of red carpet. It was deliberately thick, to make it less easy to walk across.

"Baev," she said when she was perhaps ten feet away.

For a moment he said nothing. The only sound was the scratching of the nib of his pen across the paper on which he was writing. At length, his pen paused above the paper as if he was unsure how to continue. "The minister wants to see you," he said without looking up. He meant Darko Vladimirovich, otherwise known as Minister Kusnetsov, head of the FSB.

Kata stood with her back very straight, hands clasped at the small of her back. "Have you any idea of the meaning behind the summons?"

"You're dismissed, Kata Romanovna."

Baev continued scribbling on the paper before him.

■　　■　　■

Kusnetsov's suite of offices was three floors up. Rather than waiting for the elevator, Kata took the stairs, two at a time, feeling the stretch in her quads and hamstrings. The exercise felt good.

The minister's immediate domain was in the western section of the seventh floor as far back as the corridor went. Unlike the bare hallways on the floors below, this one was decorated with a number of black-and-white photos of Russian soldiers raising their flag in victory in foreign lands. She recognized Iraq, Afghanistan, Syria, the main seaport in Ukraine.

She knocked on the heavy wooden door, opened it without hearing a voice beckoning her inside. Across the room rose two high desks not unlike judges' bancs on either side of the door leading to the minister's sanctum. Meant to intimidate visitors and underlings alike, they nevertheless had no effect on Kata. The creatures behind either desk were as changeable as chimera: a warm smile one minute, the next an icy gaze that could cut the unwary in two.

"The minister is expecting you," said the one on the left without seeming to move her face at all. The one on the right was busy sharpening a pencil that didn't need sharpening, which told Kata all she needed to know. She girded her loins as she stepped through the wide doorway, closed the door behind her, went past the high desks into Kusnetsov's office proper.

It was a large office with a high remote ceiling. Three windows on the right-hand wall. The left wall sported a pair of blow-up photos of the hunting expeditions he'd been on with the Sovereign. There was a lot of blood and not a little gore. In one photo the Sovereign, knife in one hand, was crouching over the corpse of a massive stag, mugging for the camera. Kusnetsov, shotgun in the crook of one arm, was idly smoking, seemingly looking at something out of the camera's range. A locked cabinet ran along the wall below the photos, where, it was rumored, the secrets of over one hundred thousand Federation citizens, living and dead, slept until roused to use by the minister.

He was standing by the window farthest along the right-hand wall, looking out. His fringe of salt-and-pepper hair gave those who didn't know him the false impression that he was mild-mannered, even monkish. Nothing could be further from the truth. He was always in attack mode, like his beloved tiger sharks, with which he swam weekly after hours at Moscow's aquarium. "The city is in a festive mood," he said, gesturing at the lights strung up on lampposts. Then he turned toward her, his eyes glittering black and predatory in the reflected light from outside. He wore a dark-blue suit, white shirt, maroon tie. Stylish it wasn't, but then FSB officers were hardly known for their style. A blood-red enamel star was affixed to his left lapel. "I, however, am not."

"When are you ever in a festive mood?"

One corner of the minister's mouth quirked up. He often found both her quickness and her boldness refreshing, she had quickly discovered. The tricky part was judging his mercurial moods. He tapped out a cigarette, lit it with the scarred lighter he had taken off an American agent he had killed back when he was a field agent. "The last time was an evening at the aquarium not so long ago when you shoved your predecessor into the shark tank." He took a deep drag of the cigarette, let a lazy cloud of blue smoke wreath his head. "Afterward we had quite a memorable dinner." He stubbed out his cigarette in a massive malachite ashtray. "Too bad Slava was with us." He was referring to Baev, her immediate boss. "He can be such a bore."

Kata was pondering this comment when his face darkened. "Kata, have a seat." When she complied, he went on. "Hear me. I am extremely unhappy with the Vienna affair. At this moment the mess you left is being sanitized, by Department 73, no less."

"You may not know this, Minister, but there were two other of our own field agents—maybe even from Department 73, I don't know—in Vienna. They caused this mess. I could have been killed while I was with the target."

"Your bad luck. The Vienna affair was not in your remit. You could have assigned it to any number of your female field staff."

"My office was getting stuffy."

"Mm." He went behind his desk, sat down. Leaning forward, he unlocked a drawer on the right side. Out of it he took a Janz EM revolver, expensive, exacting, terrifying, and placed it on the desk. On its grip was embossed the same Russian star sigil he had pinned to his lapel.

Kata did not know what to make of this. She sat very still, wondering if he could hear the thunderous beat of her heart. With some effort she went into prana, breathing slowly and deeply, approaching a meditative state to keep herself from jumping out of her skin.

Kusnetsov stood up, came around the end of his desk, taking up the Janz almost as an afterthought, though she knew full well the gesture was just theatrics. Or was it? The atmosphere had changed. Kata could feel the icy wind sweeping down from the Siberian steppe, invading the room, encircling her at Kusnetsov's command.

Hefting the pistol he walked slowly around the chair she was sitting on until he stood in back of her, close enough for her to hear the rustle of his suit as he moved. "Listen to me now, Kata. I allow you a degree of independence because of your extraordinary capabilities."

All at once, she felt the chill muzzle of the Janz against the back of her head. "But never forget that you are on a leash. It may be longer than others'." The muzzle pressed inward until it ground against her skull, so hard she was obliged to bend her head forward as if bowing in obeisance to her lord and master. "Doesn't mean I can't and won't bring you to heel at a moment's notice."

She felt his arm move. "Are you listening to me, Kata?"

Before she had a chance to reply he pulled the trigger on the Janz. The dry click sounded like the jaws of a tiger snapping closed. Then a wave of relief swept through her.

Kusnetsov sighed, pulled the trigger again. And again, the dry click on an empty chamber. "Are you imagining that I am foolish enough to put an empty Janz against your head?"

She coughed and at last found her voice. "Taking on the Vienna remit was rash."

"As usual when it comes to criticism you have missed the point." He pulled the trigger on an empty chamber for a third time.

"Often with you words have no effect. Or, worse, have the opposite effect." He clicked his tongue against the roof of his mouth; it almost sounded like the action of the fourth empty chamber. "Actions are what penetrate that thick skull of yours."

He released her from the iron prison of the Janz's muzzle, returning to her field of vision to pull up a chair across from her. He had pocketed the pistol. He crossed one leg over the other, as if they were two friends having a heart-to-heart. *Well*, she thought, *we are having a heart-to-heart, but we certainly aren't friends.*

Prana. The deep, meditative breathing had saved her from humiliating herself by hurling.

"The point is you get off on stalking along the edge." Kusnetsov lit another cigarette. "Perhaps it was a mistake to make you acting head of Zaslon." He took a deep drag, lifted his head, directed smoke at the high ceiling. "Perhaps you would like it better back in the field taking orders from someone you can surely outthink and outsmart, hm?" He regarded the glowing end of his cigarette. "Someone who knows how to take orders as well as give them." His gaze slapped her like a physical blow. "What d'you think?"

He had treed her, boxed her in like a fox in the hunt. She was tough, and that toughness ran far deeper than he might understand. Shrugging off the impact of his actions, she said, "Are you giving me a choice?"

The minister appeared to consider this for a moment. "You know, I should. I really should." He pursed his lips. "But no. This is no choice for you to make; it is mine." He puffed away for a moment or two, his eyes unfocused, lost in thought. Then, quite abruptly, his gaze pinned her in place. "I'm not going to reassign you. You have too much yet to bring to Zaslon. But—" He raised a forefinger. "It seems to me that all you require is more . . . shall we say stimulation . . . to keep you satisfied." Like an old building tumbling to make way for the new, his cigarette shed ash onto the floor. "In that regard I am taking you to a party tonight—a private party, where you'll get to meet a number of fascinating individuals who, I have no doubt, you will both charm and amuse."

She blinked. "That's it?"

He put out the cigarette butt with his fingers. "What d'you want, flowers?"

6

VIENNA

"What d'you mean, turn around?" Evan said. "I just got here. I just stowed the flight bag with all my money and papers in an airport locker." And then with a clutch to her heart. "It's not Ben? He's all right, isn't he?"

"Ben's fine." Isobel's voice in her ear had that tinny, echoey quality that could only come from multiple layers of cyber-security constantly switching location.

Evan was frazzled from the flight, lack of sleep, inedible food. And then at the terminal discovering the heavy presence of both federal police and soldiers.

"He's had his wig-out," Isobel went on. "He talked to Zoe again. In fact, I have a strong sense that he'll be operational within the week."

Relief and stubbornness vied for control of Evan's mind. She picked her way through the thicket of passengers seeking entrance to the departures terminal and stepped outside. A chilly wind circled her like a dust devil and she wrapped her coat tighter around her. "Then I'm not coming back to DC."

"Yes, you are," Isobel said. "The atmosphere in Vienna just turned toxic."

Evan turned her head in both directions to look once more at the lines of cops and police. Something big had happened between the time she boarded the plane in DC and debarked here in Vienna. "Toxic how?"

"Moscow sent an *ovoshchechistka*."

"A peeler? I've never run into one."

"Consider yourself fortunate. These individuals are as hellish as it gets. They've been trained since birth—no fear, no remorse, no conscience whatsoever."

"Killing machines, in other words."

"Correct. And Moscow sent not just any peeler," Isobel said. "They sent Pasha Rodionovich Shutkov."

"Never heard of him." Evan maneuvered her way through the crowd towards a taxi queue.

"I wish I hadn't either." Isobel took a breath. "In fact, I fervently wish he didn't exist."

"That bad?"

"Worse. He just set fire to the Vienna city morgue. The Russian who Armistad signaled you about and another one who must have come on the scene afterward are now completely unidentifiable."

No wonder the police presence at the airport. "And Armistad himself?"

"Roasted then melted inside his stainless-steel drawer."

"Mother. That must've been some fire."

"Thermite, is what I'm being told."

Evan gave a low whistle. She'd used thermite in Romania last May; she knew firsthand how hot a flame it produced.

"Now you see why you need to exit Vienna ASAP."

"In fact, I don't."

"Oh, hell, Evan. Do I have to spell it out for you? I don't want you within fifty miles of that morgue."

"I have no intention of going anywhere near it. My destination is somewhere else entirely." She'd reached the curb, relieved to see there were plenty of taxis available. "Besides, security is now a major issue at the *flughafen*. Departures is crawling with law enforcement personnel. They're interrogating every passenger leaving."

"Shit."

"And I'm right in the middle."

"Congratulations," Isobel said archly. "If I'm not mistaken that's right where you're happiest."

Evan chuckled. "Ben talks too much."

"Ben tells me next to nothing, actually. I learn from direct observation, not hearsay."

This response gave Evan pause. She'd had mixed feelings about Isobel from the moment she first met her. She still didn't know her much at all. Instead, she put her faith in Ben, in their long relationship. In Isobel's innate integrity. But, when you came right down to it, who really knew anyone? Especially in the espionage game where every individual was like a set of nesting Russian dolls, an apt analogy, she thought with a wry smile.

"Okay, well, I know to stay away from any form of law enforcement and I'll try to make my stay here as short as possible."

"Stick to that plan, Evan."

"As far as possible. But you know no plan survives an encounter with the enemy."

"That's not a truism," Isobel retorted. "It's an excuse."

"Send me a photo of this Pasha Rodionovich Shutkov."

"If I could find one I would. I've been scouring but no luck. Stay in touch."

Evan pocketed her phone and slid into the backseat of a waiting cab. She gave the driver an address on Alberner Hafenzufahrtsstrasse. As the taxi entered the endless flow of airport traffic she remained tense and alert, but as soon as they were clear of the airport, she sat back and watched the city traffic passing in a blur.

The car stopped on the narrow street, trees, barren now, on either side. Behind them, three yellow silos rose into the chilly air. Leaning forward, Evan paid the driver and got out. Immediately, the grind and roar of nearby heavy industry filled the air. What an awful place for a cemetery, hidden away in the armpit of the city, but, she supposed, apt for those who remained forgotten.

As she stood on the street, carefully scanning what she could see beyond the entrance to the Cemetery of the Nameless, her cell rang. Isobel, calling her again.

"Evan, I really do need you back here for several reasons," Isobel said in her ear. Evan, at this point, was only half-listening. Her mind was on finding Karl, the caretaker Armistad had identified in his last signal before his death.

"Evan, are you to listening to me?"

"Right. What is it?"

"I want to get this straight. This file Armistad intercepted and which you got via your mystery Russian, was purportedly on its way to Omega here in the States, correct?"

"That was our intel."

"And Armistad, one of our agents-in-place in Western Europe, establishes himself in Vienna."

"Right."

"Because he learned that this e-file was going to be routed through that city."

"Exactly."

"Armistad sets up an rdv with his contact, who claims he has intercepted the message."

Evan kept her mouth shut because she knew where this was going.

"But before Armistad can pass on the Omega e-file he's shot to death by a Russian field agent, who, unaccountably, is after the same prize, takes it from him, and subsequently, lo and behold, you get it from your source."

Evan closed her eyes for a moment. "Haven't we been through this already, Isobel?"

Isobel sighed, but said nothing more, giving Evan permission to change the subject.

"What about the cipher?" Evan asked as she stepped through the entrance into the cemetery. Up ahead was a low cylindrical building built of stone, stuccoed and painted a dirty ocher. It might have been the mausoleum or the business office but whatever it was it was locked up tight and appeared to have been for some time.

"My coders are just finishing inputting the Akkadian. Apparently, the language has been a bitch to translate. It isn't like Latin or ancient Greek or even Sumerian. They'll keep at it, don't worry." Isobel took a breath. "In the meantime, stay safe." She disconnected.

The sky was low, the early afternoon light pallid as a corpse's face. A gust of wind rattled the stiff branches of the trees, like skeletal fingers, sending a shiver down her spine. She passed along the side of the cylindrical structure and was immediately surrounded by a legion of metal Christs on crosses, marking almost every grave in sight.

She passed slowly down the center aisle. Her eyes narrowed as she tried to look at the cemetery as Armistad had. What had happened here after he'd killed the Russian? What had happened to him on the day he was shot to death? The only one who could know was Karl. She had to find him.

Dead leaves crunched under her footsteps as she passed along one aisle after another, one stark grave marker after another, old, rusted, crumbling, askew. She thought there was nothing sadder than a cemetery without flowers—even wilted and dead.

Days were short here, and the afternoon was already dying, crowded out by shadows, elongated and dark as a forest stream. No one else was in sight. Periodically, she paused, nostrils flaring, scenting and listening, but nothing untoward presented itself. Abruptly, the wind changed direction, bringing with it the canal, and perhaps even the river Danube beyond, full of rank mud and gasoline. She imagined rainbow slicks on the surface of the water.

Apart from the low cylindrical building and a small shed filled with tools, there was no other structure in the cemetery. Disappointed to have found nothing, she texted Lyudmila through her cell's sandbox for a photo of Pasha Shutkov, then made her way back toward the entrance. She paused when she saw a small door at the rear of the round building accessed by three shallow steps. She climbed them and tried the door. It stuck a bit, but then opened. Inside, it was dim, the only light coming in through oriel windows near the top of the walls, which unlike the exterior here formed a five-sided space. Pulling out a small LED flashlight, she turned it on, stuck it between her teeth in order to keep both hands free as she moved the beam over shadowed corners.

Playing the beam of light around she could see that she had been wrong. This was no mausoleum or archive office. But of course why would there be an archive of the forgotten and now hidden? What the space had once been she couldn't tell, but now it served as someone's home—most likely Karl. There was a sandstone desk, a couple of well-worn but clean armchairs, a sofa in desperate need of recovering, but looking comfortable enough. A military-made bed stood against one wall. Nearby was an electric heating ring and, farther along the wall, a sink and a refrigerator that looked like a relic of World War II. Shelves along the wall on the opposite side were filled with books, mainly well-read novels, but also a number of thick volumes on the philosophy and strategy of war by the famed Carl von Clausewitz, a major-general in the Prussian cavalry, including his own *On War*. She thought that interesting: Clausewitz, not Sun Tzu. Weren't the Prussian's theories on war outmoded? What did that say about Karl's mindset? She suspected it meant something but didn't yet have enough information to intuit precisely what. In the middle of the room hulked a CRT TV, a blank-eyed dinosaur, in which she saw her distorted reflection.

Sending her flashlight's beam upward, she could make out a network of security cameras that had been bolted on the walls high up near the ceiling, looking like spiders at the center of their webs. Tiny red LEDs indicated the system was functioning. Evan looked for their source—a computer console, a screen with readouts—but could find none. Karl had hidden the guts of the system well.

Completing a circle of the interior made clear that no one was currently in residence. Everything was neat and tidy. Nothing seemed to be disturbed. She checked her cell—no answer from Lyudmila, and Isobel's warning stuck in her mind like a burr. The red-eyed spiders blinked at her implacably, recording invisible messages. She left all the lights off.

There were three doors along the wall opposite the door to the exterior. One led to a small but neatly appointed bathroom with a stall shower. The door next to it revealed a clothes closet. The third opened onto a gritty concrete stairway leading down into what she assumed to be a conventional basement but turned out to be something quite a bit more. For one thing the stairs went down much farther than they ought. For another, once she had descended to the concrete floor, what she saw was not a traditional open space, but a long tunnel whose end was far enough away that her light could not reach it. Crypts? No; as she walked along, she saw no signs of interment. In fact, the walls were the same as the floor and flat ceiling: reinforced concrete. Gradually, it became clear that these must have been built during World War II. They were thick, utterly immobile, without a crack to be seen. The atmosphere was icy, still as death, except for the slither and slap of echoes, made by the river.

The tunnel sloped steeply farther down, as if once put to a purpose she could not fathom, but then after a time leveled off. It was so deep she suspected it was going under the river, a secret way to gain the far shore, but it was only a dead end. Dimly perceived, a wall rose up in front of her constructed of what looked like plates of dull metal, studded with enormous bolts. Maybe the construction company had run out of money or had changed its mind. In any event, there was nothing for her here. No sign of Karl or that Karl had ever been down here.

All at once the tunnel filled with the shriek of metal against metal, a door she could not see. She turned and stepped forward, trying to peer through the gloom, when a stupendous roar caused her to start. *Not a tunnel*, she thought in those last seconds. *A sluiceway.* She lifted the beam of light just in time to see a boiling torrent of river water flinging itself headlong at her.

7

Bobbi as Kata returned to the townhome she had acquired, along with everything else the original Kata owned, after she had killed her. It was a quarter to seven. The party Kusnetsov had ordered her to attend with him was scheduled for nine. She might have had plenty of time to get ready had she any idea what to wear. In this department, she was clueless. The minister had been concentrated on meting out her punishment, and, she suspected, had deliberately neglected to tell her what kind of party it was, who exactly would be in attendance, or what the dress code was. In the matter of these essential details she was running blind.

Crouching near the base of her front door, she saw that the hair she had left across the edge was still intact. Unlocking the door, she stepped in, turning on the lights as she did so. Everything looked exactly as she'd left it when she'd departed for Vienna. And yet, something made her pause, nostrils flaring. She moved silently through the foyer and at the edge of the living room stopped still. Her head swiveling from side to side, her sense of wrongness elevated. A scent had invaded the house, so subtle most people would have missed it. Kata was not most people. The odor was so ephemeral she lost it several times before it registered. The smell of masculine sweat, not of a hardworking laborer, but that of a suit jacket that hadn't been dry-cleaned in ages.

She drew a knife from the sheath inside her boot, one of the weapons she had taken from her office after absorbing the minister's shellacking. Backing out the way she had come, she opened the front door and stepped out onto her front step. Gripping the knife's hilt between her teeth, she shone her cell phone's flashlight down to the area where she had seen the hair she had pulled from her brush. And there it was, still half-stuck to the jamb. Plucking it up, she examined it under the light. It was dark-brown or black, difficult to tell. But what was clear was it wasn't one of her blond hairs. Someone had taken hers and replaced it with one of their own when they left her house seemingly undisturbed.

Back inside, she went through each room carefully, knifepoint first. Shadows preceded her, then fell behind as she passed one light after another. Not a thing was out of place in the foyer closet, the living room, the den, the kitchen, the hall bathroom. Upstairs, it was the same. She went through the second bedroom that served as her de facto office. In fact, via her homemade security devices, she ascertained that her laptop had not been accessed, had not even been turned on.

So what the hell was going on, she wondered as she crossed the lintel into the master bedroom. At which point, she let out a gasp. There on her comforter were three boxes, each tied with a blood-red ribbon. Two were larger, low rectangles; the third was clearly a shoebox.

She first checked her bathroom and closets, saw that nothing was disturbed, then she stepped to the bed and, using her knife, cut the ribbons—their color either merry or ominous, she had no idea which. They reminded her of the enamel star affixed to the lapel of the minister's suit jacket. As it turned out, for good reason.

When she opened the smaller of the two rectangular boxes, her muscles relaxed. Pulling back the pink tissue paper, she discovered a black Alexander McQueen V-neck woolen grain-de-poudre dress. She knew precisely what it was because she had been eyeing it in a store window in Vienna. Lifting it out, she checked the size, which was correct. She held it against her, looking at herself in the full-length mirror affixed to the door of one of her closets. Something fell to the floor: a thick square envelope. She picked it up, opened it. Inside was a notecard with *Nosit' kol'tso* written in Kusnetsov's own hand. *Wear the ring.*

He meant, of course, the ring set with a large square-cut emerald, its facets sharp as a razor blade. Though it cost a king's ransom it could hardly be classified as jewelry. It had belonged to the Kata whose identity she had assumed. The original Kata was an assassin; the emerald was her weapon of choice, slicing it across her victims' vulnerable throats as they sat, all unsuspecting, sipping drinks and dreaming of bedding her.

Now she had to wonder what Kusnetsov had in mind for her at the party with this command.

Shrugging, she tossed the card aside, retrieved the ring from beneath a false bottom in the lower drawer of her bedside table and slipped it on. The emerald glittered like the eye of a serpent. She went back to the dress. Packed neatly beside the McQueen was a black YSL Kate evening bag in grain-de-poudre embossed leather. An ensemble fit for a tsarina. How on earth Kusnetsov had pulled this off she had no idea. Her delight lasted all of thirty seconds; she was too canny for that. Turning now to the largest of the three boxes, she found a sweeping coat of black cashmere with collar and cuffs of arctic fox fur. Last came the shoebox, in which were nestled a pair of Christian Louboutin spike-heel pumps that started out black at the tips, gradually turning a deep ruby at the heels.

This was going to be one hell of a bash if Kusnetsov was going all out on her, she thought, as she undressed. In the bathroom, she turned on the shower, stood for a moment looking at her face in the mirror, as wisps of steam curled around her cheeks, and thought about the oldest inducement in the world: the stick and the carrot. He had given her one mother of a carrot after the intimidation he had subjected her to. Not that it was going to matter to her; he had stepped over a line—her red line, which was as thin as a razor's edge. Lyudmila was right about her in every way, shape, and form.

Fuck him, she thought, eyes blazing. *Fuck him and the broomstick he flew in on.*

Ninety minutes later, she was showered, made-up, primped, dressed, and ready to go. She was just about to call a ride when her cell phone buzzed. The minister had sent a car for her. It and its driver were waiting outside.

Of course.

Time, she thought, *to step into the kitchen and start cooking a goose.*

■ ■ ■

Something awaited her on the backseat, a small rectangular box with the name of a high-end jeweler embossed on the lid. Kata almost never wore jewelry, not even in her well-off married life as Bobbi Fisher, finding even simple diamond stud earrings vulgar and contemptible, the more expensive the more vulgar and contemptible. She had never been one to draw attention to herself, preferring the shadows, like a baby bat.

Settling back in her seat behind the driver as the car rolled through neighborhood after neighborhood, Kata opened the box to find a necklace unlike any she had ever seen. Running her fingertips over it, she laughed softly. Strung on a platinum chain were emeralds alternating with polished shark's teeth. She knew Kusnetsov had had this made specially for her. She understood that the minister intuited she would balk at wearing a necklace, no matter how expensive, so he had it made of two elements that would appeal to her. Ever since she shoved her old boss into the aquarium shark tank where Kusnetsov swam with the tiger sharks, cementing her position near him in the FSB, the shark had become a symbol connecting them in a curious way through death.

And yet, she knew this connection to be false, that Kusnetsov was using it to manipulate her. She hated what he had done to her earlier today. Though he had revealed himself to be a sadist she was no masochist—this was no match made in Russian heaven. But she had her orders from Lyudmila. She was committed to being a double, Lyudmila's mole inside the FSB, an incredibly valuable one at that. The unique position she was in, she understood, was her power—power over Kusnetsov and over Lyudmila. Both needed her, each in their own way, and that, finally, brought a smile to her face.

She draped the string of emeralds and shark teeth around her neck, manipulated the lobster claw clasp. The glittering arc lay along her skin, midway between the hollow of her throat and the top of her cleavage. It radiated its own power, an admixture of wealth and danger, doubly so when she drew the emerald on her finger close to it. Which was precisely what Kusnetsov wanted.

The car slowed, then rolled to a stop. The driver got out, went around the front of the car, and opened the rear passenger door. Minister Kusnetsov slid into the seat beside her. He turned, grinned slyly as his eyes picked out the necklace in the dim light of the plush interior.

"Good evening, Kata." His voice was odd, no more than a purr. "I see you're ready."

For what? she asked herself.

But by then the car was already knifing through the thickening traffic on the road.

8

Mud and grit filled her nostrils. Something hard and heavy had slammed into the side of her head so violently she must have blanked out for a moment. She was now deep under the swirling water. She wanted to clear her nose of debris but until she could grab a lungful of air that was impossible. She had breath-trained herself; she could survive without air for almost four minutes, which was more or less the equivalent of an expert free diver, but she was being whirled around so quickly she lost her equilibrium, and with it any sense of direction. She no longer knew which way was up, which way was down. Add to that the fact that she couldn't see a thing in the churning mud and detritus-filled water, and she was completely lost.

Striking out with both arms, she sought to find a wall or even the floor to push against, but it seemed there was nothing but the violence of the river, for which she was unprepared and, without solid guideposts, unable to survive.

Gradually, she felt the pressure building in her lungs, the fire that preceded a desperate need for oxygen. But relief was not to come. She would remain here in this dark, watery limbo, eyes staring, mouth open in a silent scream as the water rushed down her throat and into her lungs.

Her bones turned brittle as twigs, her muscles gelatinous, while her blood thickened, slowed, her heart beating against her rib cage ever more frantically like a trapped animal.

Finis.

But then again perhaps not.

She ceased to tumble. A slow but immensely powerful tide began to drag her in a single direction. Her arms lifted, her heels met the solidity of concrete. Her arms flared out. She felt a pressure in her armpits. Dimly aware that she was in the grip of something. A force more powerful than the boiling, frothing, filthy river water. The pressure on her lessened, water streamed off her in thick, cloudy tentacles. Her autonomous nervous system recognized the change for what it was before her mind, still gripped by vertigo, did. Involuntarily her mouth opened and she sucked in air. Gasped. Choked. Head turned sideways, she vomited water.

Hard against her back, the concrete slope down which she had walked, all unwitting, into the sudden violent flood. Pulled farther up, out of the churning depths, she lay, the entirety of her concentrated on breathing in, out, in, out. In, out.

Returned to life.

Her eyes fluttered open. She blinked a number of times to clear them of grit, looked up at the face hovering over her, deep lines etched into the sunken cheeks and forehead.

Karl, the cemetery's caretaker and Armistad's contact. Her savior.

But as her vision cleared she saw the expression of horror on the face, the bloodless, waxen skin. It was only then that Karl's severed head was dropped onto her chest. The dead eyes, already beginning to film over, stared at her as if she were a demon from hell. The mouth was half-open, the blackened lips pulled back in a snarl. His tongue was a clump of dead flesh, curled up at the tip like the head of a viper.

"Here we go," a voice said in St. Petersburg–inflected Russian. And she was hauled up, slammed against the sweating wall of concrete. Braced to a sitting position. A fetid stink infested the sluiceway. She sniffed. It was also coming from her sodden clothes.

"Get up," he said. And then, more sharply, "Get up!"

When she didn't comply, he bent down. "Do you know who I am, American *shpion*?"

She looked up at him blankly.

"Do you?"

"Whoever you are"—she cleared her throat—"makes no difference to me."

He slammed a fist into her jaw.

"Now do you know?"

She looked up, grinning at him through her bloody teeth. "Ah, yes. Now I recognize you. *Gryaznaya pizda*."

With a growl at her abominable curse, he reached down. When he grabbed her by the collar of her jacket, she lashed out, both hands slamming against his ears. He reared back, his hands coming off her to cup his ears. Now was her chance. She lifted herself onto her feet, made to go after him, but her legs collapsed and she tumbled onto the floor in a heap. She tried again but could not even draw herself up to her previous position, back against the wall. A wave of vertigo overtook her and she groaned, head hanging down onto her chest. There was a peculiar sound, ragged yet rhythmic, a handsaw trying to get through sheet metal. It was a moment more before she realized the sound was coming from her chest. Her mouth had a metallic taste, her throat felt as if she had inhaled fistfuls of sand.

Oh God, she thought wildly. *Oh God*.

Pain ripped through her as her antagonist pulled her head up by her hair. He stared into her eyes. This close she saw the gold flecks in eyes the color of storm clouds, swollen with rain. *So Cassius*, she thought woozily, *with that lean and hungry look.*

He shook her until her teeth rattled.

Get me on my feet, you bastard, she thought, trying to shake the cobwebs while closing her mind off from the pain wracking her body and head. *Right this moment I can't do it myself.*

As if reading her mind he lifted her to her feet.

"Come on, you fucking bitch." He spat at her feet. "Let's see what you soft Americans are really made of."

And then she kneed him in the groin. It wasn't as powerful a strike as she wanted, but it was all she could muster and it got the job done. As he bent over, she leapt on him, and they both crashed down onto the wet concrete. She rolled him over and over, knowing she had only seconds before he recovered sufficiently to finish her off.

She caused them to pick up momentum as they went down the incline, faster and faster, until they hit the water. The water slowed her down and she had to exert more and more effort to keep them rolling. The deeper they went the greater the tug of the water. She felt him grappling for her, reaching out, his hands taut, fingers arced into the semblance of claws. But now, even injured as she was, she had the advantage. She had been here before, she understood the seething murk, could pick him out while he was as good as blind, blinking the detritus out of his eyes as fast as he could. Too fast to make her out clearly. To him she was a shifting shape, moving too fast for even his quick reflexes to home in on.

All at once, she felt his thumb contact her neck, blindly searching for her collarbone. Found it, and he kept it there as they whirled into the deepest water, applied appalling pressure so that her lips drew back from her tightly clenched teeth. He would have her if she didn't retaliate with savage violence. Leaning in, she chomped down on the meat of his shoulder, tearing through clothing and skin, into muscle and sinew. Like a predator with its prey she shook her head back and forth, ripping the mouthful of his flesh down to the bone.

He opened his mouth wide, his scream immediately annihilated by the turbulent water. He choked on a shard of wood, and she climbed atop him, mashed his face down as far as it would go. Let him see how it felt to drown.

His limbs flared out, their flapping becoming weaker and weaker, until at length they merely lifted and fell with the churn. She let go then. It was harder than she imagined, her own death grip more difficult to relax.

Lungs bursting, she pedaled backward, oriented now, dragging herself up the concrete slope before collapsing in exhaustion. She lay like that, water lapping at her ankles. For the moment she could go no farther. Instead she concentrated on breathing, slowly calming her heart rate, ridding herself of the excess of adrenaline, while she stared blankly up at the featurelessness of the sluiceway's ceiling. She willed herself not to think, to empty her mind of everything unrelated to regaining her strength. Time passed, she had no idea how much. At some point she was able to rise up onto her elbows. She remained in that position, staring at the black oily water, until she became aware of a pain in her hip. Blindly she reached down, pulled a cell phone from beneath her. Her heart raced, thinking it was hers, but, no, it was his—Pasha Shutkov—for her antagonist could be no one else. Her phone was lost in the arm of the river he'd let into the sluiceway.

She stared at the polluted mass of water that remained inside the tunnel. Protected from the turbulence of the river, it lapped gently against the sides of the sluiceway. Nothing disturbed the surface. Shutkov would not emerge now or ever.

■ ■ ■

If it wasn't for the immense pain she was in she would have fallen asleep in Karl's shower. As it was she was obliged to hold onto the spout in order to keep herself vertical. Crawling back up out of the tunnel had taxed her body to its limits. The journey had been slow and torturous, the worst of it having to drag herself like a centipede up the steep staircase a step at a time.

Now, standing in the spray of warm water, she mindlessly trod her filthy clothes under her feet, as if she were a farmer's wife beating the grapes into what would become wine. Once, her grip slackened, slipped off the spout. She fell to her knees, her forehead pressed against the tiles as the water fell upon her bent back. The brackish stink of the river coming off her clothes brought her back and, painfully, she climbed back onto her feet, eyes closed, dizzied as she had been when the water first closed over her.

Toweling off, she tended to her wounds as best she could with antibiotic ointments, salves, and bandages she found in the bathroom cabinet, wincing all the while. Nothing she could do about the bruises already starting to darken and swell. At least, after feeling herself all over, she discovered no broken bones. In the galley kitchen she drank two large glasses of water, careful not to swallow too fast. Her raging thirst slaked, she crawled into Karl's bed, pulled the covers up to her chin, and with a deep sigh, was swallowed by a deep and dreamless sleep.

Only to awake with a gasp, her heart pounding against her ribs. A shadow loomed over her, a shape slowly revealing itself. A figure stinking of the slime of the river, bending over her, dripping moisture onto her. His eyes were as yellow and lambent in the semi-darkness as a wolf's.

Shutkov!

"Pasha . . ." His name, uttered, fell like dust from her mouth.

She tried to rise up, but his hands were on her, pushing her back down onto the bed, a pressure on her chest, a feral leer on his face, her ribs about to crack.

"You won't get rid of me so easily, American *shpion*."

She could smell his sour male stench beneath the flux of the river coating him. Drops fell on her face, warm as a fever. She tried to move, but he had her pinned.

With the crack of a dry branch under the onslaught of a snowstorm, a rib broke. Then, *crack! crack! crack!* over and over as her chest caved in, crushing her heart . . .

. . . Gasping, she sat up in the strange bed, in the strange room, cold and hot at the same time. Sweat rolled down her cheeks, dripped off her nose, drenched her hair, armpits, and thighs. She took breath after breath, looking around wildly. No sign of Pasha Shutkov or anyone else for that matter.

A nightmare, then.

In truth, she was all alone in the dark.

9

MOSCOW SUBURBS

The dacha was lit. It glimmered through fir trees illuminated from the lamps around the periphery, black at their tips. The driveway, a long serpent of newly laid asphalt, foretold of a great deal of property to which the dacha was attached. It had taken nearly ninety minutes to get here, the last thirty along a two-lane lined with trees and, latterly, a narrow, forested road. Even this far outside of Moscow, land was in short supply, so this property spoke of enormous wealth and standing within the Federation.

Kusnetsov's car slowed, rolling to a stop, but though the driver got out and came around to the rear door on the minister's side, he did not open it. Neither of the car's occupants had said a word during the drive, but now the minister turned to address Kata. The light from outside gave the interior an emerald sheen. Filtered through the tinted bulletproof glass, it seemed to gather at Kata's chest, the emeralds there blazing as if with a life of their own.

Kusnetsov glanced pointedly at her ring before rapping on his window. Kata seemed to feel her blood congealing into ice. So she had been correct to suspect he meant to use her abilities here at the party. All the rest of the hellaciously expensive finery he'd curated and provided was just window dressing, concealing her true purpose beneath the sheen of designer fashions.

The driver opened the minister's door, then went around and opened Kata's door. The night chill was bracing, and she was glad for the heavy coat and the thick fur she now pushed up to her chin. The minister stood behind the car, beckoning. Apparently they weren't going inside just yet. The back of her neck began to tingle and she was instantly on her guard. She felt her heartbeat thumping against her rib cage. What did he have in mind?

He gestured. "Walk with me, Kata," he said as soon as she was beside him. He pointed to a spot ahead of them. "There's a short track through the woods. We'll take that."

The moon became occluded by thickening clouds. The wind changed direction and she could smell snow in the dry air. He lit a cigarette, handed it to her. When she declined, he shrugged, took a deep draw on it himself.

They left the lights behind as they turned onto the path. It was narrow, hemmed in on both sides by tall pines and firs. The ground was softened by a mat of fallen needles. He did not switch on a flashlight; he seemed to know the way in the inky depths. But he did not lead her far before he halted, turned to her. He wore a thick charcoal curly lambskin coat over what she considered to be a hideous umber-colored suit. The ever-present enamel star was pinned to his lapel.

"First," the minister said in a soft cloud of exhaled breath, "this is not a state function." His face was shadowed, lit only by the glowing end of his cigarette, which barely even highlighted his prominent features. She wondered then if he had deliberately stage managed this entire interlude. "Second, the gathering does not exist. Not officially. Not anywhere."

"So," Kata responded, "not a party then."

"That all depends." With the end of his cigarette close to his mouth Kusnetsov showed his teeth, a kind of horrible smile. "On what you will bring to it."

"You can be so clever when you put your mind to it." This far from the center of Moscow, miles from Lubyanka Square, she felt she could take verbal liberties. But who was she kidding? She had not forgiven him for subjecting her to Russian roulette in a clumsy attempt to frighten her into submission. Very Russian, and precisely the wrong way to focus her attention. In another time, another reality, she might very well have taken his life sometime tonight in recompense. Now, she judged, would be a better time than most. She imagined running the razor-sharp edge of her emerald across his throat, jumping back so the gout of blood wouldn't mar her expensive outfit. Actually, she'd quickly come to love the feel of the luxurious fabrics against her body. But her life belonged to Lyudmila. She had pledged herself to the rogue FSB officer and erstwhile Politburo member, who was now dedicating herself to bringing the deeply corrupt Federation hierarchy to its knees from the inside out. "So what am I to expect?" she went on.

"Inside this dacha are ten people. The men are of high rank and great importance. The women—well, you know how it is here. The women are decorations."

Meaning, Kata thought, the men are rapists and the women are penned like sheep.

Kusnetsov took another hit of the cigarette, let the smoke drift out of his nostrils, as if he were a dragon slowly awakening to a new age. "I will introduce you to the men. I will not mention their names. This is deliberate. This is to set you apart."

Meaning, she thought, to warn them that she was his and his alone.

"Is that clear?"

"Perfectly. Is that all?" she said archly. He was talking to her as if she were a field novice, but there was a deeper rage roiling inside her.

Kusnetsov continued to ignore her ripostes. "These men are all important, each in his own way."

"Clear."

"You will be the only female of rank in the room."

Was he trying to make up for his bestial behavior this afternoon? Was this—and all the expensive clothes he'd had bought for her—his roundabout way of saying he was sorry? She could scarcely credit it.

"Tonight is your, how shall I put it, your official coming-out party."

"I won't embarrass you."

He laughed that strange laugh of his, which had about it, whether he knew it or not, the stench of condescension.

"You had better not. Your trial period has ended early. You're now the permanent head of Zaslon."

Now she knew for certain that he had meticulously scripted this entire scenario beforehand. "I'm gratified." Her voice was neutral, strictly controlled. No matter what he did now, what favors he granted her, what praise he might bestow, she would never forget what he had done to her. What the fuck did he think he was doing? Hazing her, like horror night at the frat house?

They began retracing their steps back toward the light and the dacha. Snow was falling now and she was having trouble negotiating the soft ground in her Louboutin pumps. Kusnetsov was behind her and she tread lightly and carefully, determined not to stumble in his presence.

As they walked, Kata thought of her meeting with Lyudmila in the Nuremberg airport. Her new status advanced her another step forward in Lyudmila's plan—a piece moving across the board of Lyudmila's design. She didn't understand it yet. Possibly she wasn't meant to. Each to her own silo, that was what Lyudmila would say—what she did say the last time Kata had asked her.

"Kata?" They had broken out of the forest. In the open, the snow was already sticking. Soon it would begin to pile up. "Is that all you have to say?"

She gathered her wits into the present. "Being grateful isn't enough?"

"Of course it is," he said with false lightness. Clearly she hadn't given him the answer he was expecting.

She nodded. "Shall we go in?" She moved toward the front door, which was flanked by two FSB agents, their suits shiny with wear. Also, they smelled. But now the minister held her back.

"One more thing. About your intervention in Vienna. So far our people have gotten nowhere trying to decode the file destined for Omega you took off the American agent."

Her eyes grew hard as chips of stone. "I put my life on the line getting it. They'd better try harder." But she was pleased. She hoped Lyudmila was having better luck.

Kusnetsov surprised her by saying, "That is not the issue."

She looked at him, eyebrows raised.

His voice darkened with his expression. "Shutkov is gone."

"What d'you mean, 'gone'?"

"He's failed to check in—twice. He's dead, Kata."

"Shutkov? There must be another explanation."

"The fallback protocol is dead silent, as well."

"Well, then."

"Yes."

"I'll go myself."

His eyes narrowed. "Your permanent position precludes any such forays. Your remit is to stay home." He took a breath. "Besides, your sister is currently in Vienna."

Kata's heart turned over. "Did Evan terminate Shutkov?"

"What do you think?"

Of course she did, Kata thought.

The minister took a step closer, his mouth practically at her ear, his voice nearly a whisper. "We went to a great deal of trouble to provide proof of your death when we exfiltrated you out of America. It's one of your great strengths. You are forbidden to cross her path."

He stepped back, but kept his voice low. "Given Shutkov's departure from this vale of tears it must be assumed that he was betrayed." His countenance darkened even further. "What d'you think?"

"Knowing my sister it's altogether possible that she found out he was in Vienna through any one of her contacts."

"And why haven't we hunted down her contacts and rolled them up?"

"That's not in my remit," she said mildly, the better to throw his words back at him.

He grunted. "When it comes to Ryder nobody seems capable of surviving a face-off with her."

"Then you haven't come up with the right adversary." She was making it clear that she wasn't part of the "we" he was speaking of. "That person would need to check off a hell of a lot of boxes to qualify. I mean, she even shut Shutkov down and he was the elite of Department 73."

"What a thorn in my side she has turned out to be."

"The Sovereign can't be pleased."

He gave her a murderous look just before he went up the steps, showed his credentials to the guard even though his face was known here, and preceded her through the door into the overheated interior of the mysterious dacha and its even more mysterious occupants.

10

"Nothing?"

Ben shook his head. "She's turned off her GPS, which means she's deep into Moscow Rules."

"A good thing, then."

Isobel Lowe, wrapped in a long woolen sweater, stepped between a pair of pear trees and entered the small cloister in the back garden. It was screened from the street by nine-foot-high hedges, thick as brambles, shaded from the summer sun by a honey locust. But now, in the dead of winter with the sun low in the sky even at 1 P.M., shadows ruled all day long, until night seeped slowly in, dissolving them in a deeper black.

Ben was sitting in his motorized wheelchair, staring at his cell phone. "What's so fascinating?"

He shook his head. "Scanning 27chan."

"Allegedly the Omega posting board."

"It's akin to Reddit," he acknowledged. "These extremists incessantly posting here are obsessed with the Deep State. According to them, the Deep State is so entrenched in the federal government it continues irrespective of who the president is, which party is in power."

Isobel rolled her eyes. "The Deep State. Christ on a crutch."

"According to 27chan it's built on the backs of Jews and the libs—as they call the lefty Democrats. All of whom are Satanists." He lifted a finger. "Here, listen to this. 'The Deep State has set up a worldwide network of human trafficking in babies and young children. These poor things are sold and traded like NFTs, sacrificed in rituals to summon and appease the devil, buried alive in the foundations of new corporation headquarters in order to ensure enduring prosperity for their businesses, and, God help us all, roasted and eaten in elaborate dinners straight out of those of Henry VIII.'"

Isobel snorted. "Why do you read that shit, Ben? These people are stark raving crazy."

"I agree." Ben looked up from his cell to fix her in his steady gaze. "But their insanity is dangerous. Exceedingly dangerous. That's why Evan and I have been pursuing them for the past two and a half years." Ben could not get the bitterness out of his voice. "We lost a lot of people along the way. The latest being Armistad."

He glanced at her as she sat down on a wooden bench beside him. She had had the house renovated with ramps inside and out to accommodate him. As for getting down from his second-floor bedroom, he insisted on doing that himself by gripping the banister and bumping down on his bottom. It had hurt but he didn't care. He'd be goddamned if he was going to give in to being an invalid. Following his most recent talk with his daughter, Zoe, he'd burned his self-pity on the pyre of determination. He recognized that Evan had been right to force him to talk with Zoe immediately after his attempt at suicide. Zoe calmed him, centered him, focused him on the future. Her future. Speaking with his daughter at that dark moment had taken him out of himself, and he was grateful for that. More grateful than he could ever express to Evan for making it happen, for saving his life—again. Evan lived in a special place inside him, one he kept locked away, often even from himself. The truth was he was too cowardly to examine that place too closely lest his feelings spill out, inundating him. He could not allow himself the luxury of loving her. He'd loved his wife and because of the world he lived in she was dead, murdered by his enemies inside Russia.

Seeing his troubled expression, Isobel took his cell phone out of his hands, set it aside face-down beside her on the bench. "They've gotten under your skin, haven't they, Ben?"

"Omega?"

She searched his eyes. "They've become more than a professional target. This is personal."

"For Evan even more than for me," Ben replied, acknowledging the truth of what Isobel had said. "Two of her sisters."

"You shot one to death last year."

"She was choking Evan."

"That must've been difficult for both of you."

"To tell you the truth I don't know what it was." Ben took a breath. "Neither of us had ever met Ana before that night. Even worse, Evan was pretending to be her dead sister Bobbi, who Ana was expecting. She died without Evan telling her who she really was."

Isobel's gaze was level. He knew that look. He knew her so well. She was trying to get at something—something inside him he didn't want to look at.

"Ben, do you really think it would have made a difference had Ana known?"

He shrugged. "Not to me. But as for Evan you'd have to ask her."

"She'd never tell me."

The ghost of a grin passed across his face. "That's true enough."

"The two of you hold so much back," she said softly. "Especially from each other."

"Our history is complicated."

"So is ours," she reminded him. "But we talk, don't we?"

He nodded. After a time he said, "It's different with her."

"I know it is." Isobel waited a beat. "Possibly better than you do yourself."

He looked down at his hands, fingers laced in his lap. "It was never so hard for us, was it?"

"No. But I had a relatively uncomplicated upbringing. You can't say the same for her."

He nodded sadly. "Two sets of parents, two other sisters she never knew existed until seven months ago, when she also discovers and meets her birth parents for the first time. Now two of her sisters are dead, and I killed one."

She handed him a plate he hadn't noticed before. On it was a tuna salad sandwich on rye with a sour pickle on the side. "You need to eat."

He looked down at it with no little skepticism. "And you think this will help me how?"

"No one thinks constructively on an empty stomach." She took half the sandwich, bit into it, chewed, watching him until he began to eat his half.

He swallowed a mouthful. "Good," he said, grunting in pleasure. "You are right, as always. But I think you need to take the Omega threat more seriously."

"Nothing could be further from the truth, Ben. Believe me. I take it seriously. I understand this started two years ago with Nemesis. Samuel Wainwright Wells along with the ultra-right-wing party in Germany. Wells was funding Nemesis. Now it's Omega and once again he's right at the heart of the same evangelical conservative cabal."

Ben nodded. "Omega is Nemesis under a different name, it's in fact the overarching organization that Nemesis was a part of. These people are far from done."

"Agreed. But right now this is about you, not them. Ben, I'm just look-ing out for you. You and Evan were targeted by what appeared to be Samuel Wells or one of his American Omega cohort. Now you've been seriously hurt."

He reached over and picked up his cell phone, waved it like a flag. "And I'm saying I don't matter. The Omega insanity infesting 27chan has spilled over onto Twitter and Facebook and what with the gathering storm of shootings, more and more violent demonstrations, it's getting to look like Armageddon out there. Compared to that threat my health is nothing."

Her eyes were aflame. "Not to me."

"Look, Izzy. It's not that I don't . . ." He carefully put the plate with the remains of his half-eaten sandwich on the bench where his phone had been. "Omega wants to tear apart the fabric of this country. They want to set American against American, enflaming a second Civil War. Because in their hearts they never stopped fighting the first one. Their desire is the destruction of the rule of law that's been respected and followed since the Founding Fathers signed the Declaration, announcing our in-dependence from England and King George III. They're after nothing less than a white Christian nation."

He looked down at his cell briefly, then back up at Isobel. "The post-ings all over the internet are getting more and more hate-filled, vitriolic, more threatening, and most scarily more unified. What might once have been small groups of loose cannons are coming together. And I think Omega's the orchestrator. It's in the process of building an army out of what once were disparate militias."

She wiped her fingers and lips with a paper napkin. "Okay, okay. I hear you loud and clear."

"No, you don't. You're far too pragmatic. These people, they're over-whelmed, alienated and disillusioned. That's nothing new, of course, but while those people historically turned inward, often destroying them-selves with alcohol or drugs, these people have come under the influence of an altogether different drug: the religion of Omega. Omega has de-luded them into building a fantasy world where they have all the power, where no one who is traditionally in government can say or do anything to dissuade them. As sure as we're sitting here they're coming, Isobel. And God help us if we're unprepared for the assault."

PART TWO

THE
RESOLUTE
DESK

11

FAIRFAX COUNTY, VIRGINIA

The 12,000-square-foot mansion, white as sun-bleached bones, sprawled over the nexus of the 16.5-acre estate. This beautiful pile of stones had as many rooms as January has days, and a staff to service all of them. However, this staff was unlike all others. The complement of six men and six women had been painstakingly vetted using the resources of the DC Metro Police. They were also trusted members of Omega, sworn and initiated into the organization.

In the private parlor of the mansion built at the exact center of this vast and incalculably wealthy estate stood Lucinda Wells, third and only living wife of Samuel Wainwright Wells, media and energy mogul and one of the three richest men in the western hemisphere.

Lucinda exited the parlor, moving as if gliding on ice. She was given to wearing ankle-length dresses made specially for her by particular high-end couturiers. In return for her being seen in public wearing them, the grateful couturiers gifted her with their product free of charge.

But it wasn't only in public Lucinda wore these fashions; she wore them all the time, home or away. She did this, she told herself, as a manifestation of the power she held. Also, though she might be loath to admit it, as a reminder of how far she had come from her unhappy beginnings in Russia and then, after running away, in Slovenia where, as Luzida Horvat she began to remake herself, where she began to climb the mountain of the material world.

Lucinda went silently through rooms bedecked in dark wood wainscoting, gilt cornices, ormolu clocks, crystal chandeliers, silk sofas that no one sat on, buttery leather chairs with not a hint of a depression from anyone's hindquarters. She found these spaces, a bastard product of her husband and his first wife, at best in bad taste, at worst oppressive. Most ominous were the paintings of bloody moments in history—stag hunts, battles at sea and on land—and the hulking bronze sculptures and baroque marble busts. Enormous portraits of the Wellses, separate but equal, hung on either side of a mammoth fireplace that could have sheltered six people. There was nothing anywhere in the mansion to indicate that there had been an interim wife several years before Lucinda; that marriage had been brief and meaningless.

Lucinda could not abide the amount of money spent on showpieces. Money was not for buying the most expensive of everything. During her young adulthood in Slovenia there was hardly enough money to live. Spending as much of it as possible on useless luxuries was unthinkable. Initially outraged she in due course conceded defeat. She had once considered the mansion's interior a battlefield but weeks of suggesting they sell everything only antagonized her husband. It occurred to her that maintaining the interior was Sam Wells's ham-fisted way of keeping the memory of his first wife alive. Now it was as if she walked through a desert; she saw sand dunes only, stretching into the distance. This was not a difficult feat. She had more important matters on her mind, most unknown to her husband.

Through the first-floor rooms, hallways, back passages she went, until she arrived at a wall in which was set the etched bronze door of an elevator. Stepping in she rode it down two levels, exited beneath the cellar proper into and then through the wine cave.

Once past that, a set of double doors led into the Oval Office of the White House. This astonishing replica was authentic in almost every detail. The repurposed space, however, was the size of a university lecture hall, vastly larger than the original Oval Office. At the far end was a raised stage, at the back of which, to one side, hung the American flag, a gold eagle at the top of its pole. On the other side was a second flag: pure white, with a gold O in its center bisecting a black cross. At the apex of this pole were a pair of sculpted ravens facing each other.

Between the two flags rose an eighteen-foot cross constructed of enormous hand-hewn hardwood beams, blackened by fire. Bisecting the vertical beam was a golden O.

Lucinda bypassed those doors, instead turned left down a long narrow corridor where a smaller door led to a short flight of stairs. At the top, she pushed through a velvet curtain the color of oxblood and positioned herself in a wing of the raised stage. She peeked out. Across from her in the other wing was her husband. Their eyes did not meet.

Presently, there were twenty-six people in the enormous room, all of them standing. Mostly men, but some women, as well—senators, congressmen, Pentagon generals, chiefs of police. All were grim-faced, standing at attention, facing the cross. One more congressman hurried in, took his place beside the others. Now the complement of twenty-seven was complete. The double doors were closed. A thick slice of silence descended, like the blade of a guillotine.

The lights lowered, as they do in a theater. The meeting was about to begin.

A spotlight illuminated Samuel Wainwright Wells as he stepped to the center of the stage to thunderous applause. He was closely shaven, his pink cheeks glistening, his blue eyes piercing, shining like stars in the nighttime firmament. His were the eyes of a young man, the seventy-nine years of his life having dimmed the color not one iota.

Wells lifted his right arm, pointing behind and slightly to the right of him, and a second spotlight illuminated an ornate wooden desk that stood before the enormous wooden cross.

"Behold, a miracle!" His voice rang out, strong and solid as a roof-beam. His words unfurled like a magic carpet, lifting his audience up and away from the mundane world. The words were living things, flash of fire, roll of ocean deeps, chill of snowcapped mountaintops. They danced in the air, swollen with meaning, holy, irrefutable.

"The original Resolute desk in the president's Oval Office was constructed from the timbers of the HMS *Resolute*, a nineteenth-century ship in the British Royal Navy. It was gifted to President Rutherford Hayes by Queen Victoria in 1880." He nodded sagely. "That, my dear compatriots, is friendship.

"The Resolute desk you see before you is made from the lovingly salvaged planks of the First Presbyterian Church in Clarendon, Arkansas, which was destroyed in the Civil War when the entire town was torched by the invading Union Army. Unlike the HMS *Resolute*, the house of God where these timbers are from was boarded, breached, and burned by the enemy. Our enemy. As then, so now. Nothing changes. Except we are here now. Each day we grow in power, creating a network of dedicated followers—their eyes filled with our vision, their ears echoing with my voice. Their hearts are determined. They will do as they are told. They want what we want: to make America white again, to take back from the immigrants, the fomenters, the wicked, the violators of our Constitution that which is rightfully ours. Our land, our schools, our businesses. No longer will our houses of worship be breached, boarded, and burned.

No longer will God be banned from our lives. He must infiltrate every aspect of our lives. We are the standard-bearers who light His way, who make His voice known throughout this once great land of ours."

His voice rolled out through the room like thunder through the Rockies, like bronze church bells ringing in the holy days. It sent shivers through the assembled. Their eyes were locked on him as if he had just descended from heaven. Voice like a whip, voice like a velvet noose, Wells wove a spell around them.

His smile was like the sun breaking through rough storm clouds. "Good afternoon, my dear comrades in arms. It is a privilege to speak with you, to see you all here. I know how very patiently you have been waiting for this moment. I know how meticulous your preparations have been, how extensive, how clandestine. It is important to me and to Lucinda that you know all your hard work—and particularly your unwavering devotion—is recognized, valued, prized.

"You—all of you standing before me today—represent mankind's better angels. The work you have done, that you continue to do, that you *will* do in the coming weeks and months of chaos, will bear God's precious fruit."

The distance between Wells and his audience appeared to shrink until it seemed that he was among them, his words rushing through them like a tide, buoying them up, raising the new world from the ashes of the old.

"Recall our work is not salvation, my loving compatriots. We, who know the depths of His secrets, we who hear His voice through me, we are already saved. Our work, my dear friends, is salvage. As the righteous forebears salvaged the beams and trusses of the holy Clarendon church, as they saved what they could from the invaders, as they erected a new, more glorious church on the foundations of the old, we, the righteous of today and of tomorrow, must salvage this country. We must save it from itself. It is our sworn duty because it is God's will.

"To do that we must return to the beginning, to purity. We must do what our brave and righteous forefathers failed to do. We have waited since our defeat in the Civil War for this moment when our strength is at its peak. The Supreme One has spoken to me. He tells us that we must put down the unholy, atheistic insurrection fomented by immigrants who bring drugs with them, who traffic in girls, by the dark of skin, pedophiles, and homosexuals who have polluted this country. They who wish to take from you your America. They who have defiled it, turned it into a zoo without cages. We must put them down like the rabid dogs they are. We must at every turn limit their ability to vote. This country can ill-afford an incursion of dark-skinned people in public office, making decisions for us, taking away our essential freedoms."

His audience was rapturous with righteous terror, for he spoke to them of the demons all around them, the eternal damnation that awaited them if they did not give themselves over to him, to Omega, wholly.

"Deluded are the ones who preach that religion is transactional. You give your faith to a priest or a minister and as a reward your soul is saved." He raised his arms. "We say no. No, no, no! Because what you're asked to give is your *blind* faith—a belief that God will take care of you. It's dangerous because nowhere in that transaction is there any mention of truth."

Wells seemed to swell in the spotlight, to grow to superhuman proportions. "We know better. We do not walk through life deluded by one lie after the other. The trust has been revealed to us, my friends. It gives us the righteous strength to reject the commonly received truths. The real truth—the truth we witness here—lies hidden behind the falsehoods that the demons like George Soros, Hillary Clinton, Barack Obama gleefully feed the liberals, the godless gays and transgenders, the people of color, all of whom are taking away your God-given privilege as white people meant to rule America. Our forefathers fought and died to make America for us—and only us. They annihilated everyone in their path—as we must do."

He took a step toward them. His body was trembling with the terrible power within him. "We all know that America was nothing before our forebears came with civilization. America had no culture, no roads, no factories, no industry. That's *all* us. *We* built America and now they want to take it away from us? God provided for us. We made America great. Us." He pointed a long forefinger into the darkness of the room. "Not them. Us."

Monstrous applause that boomed like thunder through the Appalachians, shaking the entire room.

"For I am the demiurge," he cried, after the accolade subsided. "The chosen one to bring the Light of the Supreme One. I, who will lead you out of the darkness, the lies, the trickery, the temptations offered by those who decry the great and holy work—criminals, drug dealers, gang leaders, all of whom have one goal: to prey on you, to take your jobs, with the help of the UN to take your weapons, so you are help-less before this ungodly mongrel horde. They kill babies before they are born. They lie with each other—man to man, woman to woman—in shameless debauchery. Mark my words, unless they are stopped they—all of them—will suck this once great nation dry so there's nothing left for us.

"All this wickedness must end! Satan's evil multitudes must be wiped from the face of America, from *your* home, from *your* rightful land! Now! It is the Supreme One's will. I hear His voice inside me. He has guided me every step of the way. You know the Truth of this, good comrades in arms. Here we stand, the resolute legion that blocks the pit to hell and we say, as He says, 'No more! No more!'"

Everyone shouting in unison with Wells, "No more!"

Silence then, and the darkness of the cave from which man emerged to find God. When the lights came up, Samuel Wainwright Wells was gone, the cross with the symbol of Omega was shining like a beacon in the twilight. And in front of it, in front of the holy Resolute desk, stood Lucinda Wells, spotlighted, back as straight as any soldier at parade rest, ravishing, alluring. Resolute.

She waited for the right moment, spread her arms wide, mimicking the cross behind her. "Gentlemen and ladies, you have heard the words of my husband, our demiurge, our anointed one. You have witnessed the youth in his eyes, the blush of his cheeks, above all the thunder of his voice. Is he seventy-five years or fifty-five years old? Who can say, even you who have just seen him. Even I, who am his constant companion, his friend and confidante. Even I cannot say." Her eyes flashed and it was as if the allure she possessed was projected out into the room, af-fecting equally the men and women standing before her. Hers was an allure totally unlike that of her husband's but no less powerful for that. Possibly it was stronger still in the seductive silken darkness it conjured, for there were never-ending rumors on 27chan and other like-minded internet newsboards that Lucinda Wells was indeed the embodiment of Omega's Holy Spirit, which, since the dawn of Gnosticism, contained not a grain of the male essence. "What I can say is that his vigor remains undiminished. The Holy Spirit is within him, the Holy Spirit inhabits every cell in his body. He does not age as you or I age. He is a wonder, a living miracle."

But what the entranced assembled heard was: "I am a wonder, the Holy Spirit incarnate."

Her hands swooped and dove as if she were a mesmerist. "And now . . ."

Lucinda took a step to the side as a screen lowered in front of the symbol of Omega. A projection glowed in its center. The famous Titan logo: the stylized letters TNSC within the gold O bisecting the black cross they all knew stood for Omega. But as they watched, another logo swirled, slowly forming into the letters TFSN encased in a five-pointed star.

"Today, my friends, we are announcing that Titan has bought Firstar 24/7, the worldwide satellite network. Within the week, Titan-Firstar 24/7 will be broadening the reach of Samuel Wainwright Wells's vision, philosophy, political and business viewpoints, broadcasting them through Firstar's satellite network to every country in the world with television, internet, and cable connections.

"We will be the first and only conservative broadcaster disseminating the gospel worldwide!"

Heads turning. Smiles sprouting like flowers in spring. Thunderous applause. Whooping and hollering as if they were a bunch of good ol' boys.

"In addition, the totally redesigned Titan-Firstar 24/7 app will be available on all platforms—Apple, Android, and the like—as well as all operating systems."

More applause, fists in the air now. Oh, what a fine time they were having!

She donned a mask that covered the lower half of her face. The attendees did likewise. The masks were white, emblazoned with the gold O and black cross logo. Only then did she begin the prayer, the one they used daily here, the one her audience was expecting, the one they venerated as they venerated Samuel Wainwright Wells.

"I acknowledge one great invisible God/unrevealable, unmarked, ageless, and unproclaimable/the unknown Father, the Aeon of the aeons/who brought forth in the silence with his Providence: the Father, the Mother, the Son/and the nine demiurges/each in their time revered by the righteous, scorned, branded liar and false god/by the others who cannot comprehend meaning/in the gospel of contradictions. They do not know the Secrets/consecrated, exalted by He/who is the unknowable God.

"I embrace the Light of the one church/which revealed to me the demiurge/ Interior, Invisible, Secret, and Universal/the foundation of the Light of the great unknowable God."

She put her hands together, bowed her head, and every witness bowed her or his head with her. They were hers; she knew it, they knew it. The Supreme One might speak through Samuel Wainwright Wells, but he spurred them to action through Lucinda Wells.

"Gathered here today we have the prime movers in Omega. In all, twenty-seven of you, though you represent the will and voices of 250,000—a quarter of a million American patriots. You, their representatives, the twenty-seven strong and true. Not an informant among you; the FBI be damned, you are vetted hourly, your communications sent out in micro-bursts the government can never find even if its NSA flunkies knew where to look."

A brief spate of laughter, but no one looked at one another. She was the sole object of their attention. They had been indoctrinated and trained well. They were believers in Omega to their very bones. White supremacists all.

"Twenty-seven is a godly number," she continued, "a prime number in Omega lore. Two and seven equal nine. There are nine judges identified by the Supreme One. Nine demiurges down through the centuries who serve as conduits through which the Supreme One's will is made known to us, his acolytes. For he can never be seen, not by us anyway. But the demiurges—they can see him, they can speak to him, they are chosen to carry out his will.

"In our long history, there have been eight demiurges. Samuel Wainwright Wells is the ninth. The ninth, my friends, meaning he is the last and most powerful, destined since birth to carry us forward into the promised land.

"So ready yourselves for December twenty-first, for the assault on the fourteen blue states we have targeted. Ready your constituents, inform your trusted allies, summon your militias, extend our rallies. Keep their teeth on edge, their knives sharpened, their firearms locked and loaded for the Longest Night."

She flung her arms wide again, head thrown back, assuming the ecstatic posture of the best televangelists. "Four days," she called. "Four days until the first phase to our path to the promised land is cleared of obstacles. Four days until blood is shed, four days until destruction is rained down upon our sworn enemies, four days until every blue state that harbors the wicked, the agnostic, the apostate is set on fire! They will burn, I promise you that! Our enemies will burn! Four days until the insurrection that gives us back the America we know and love!"

The meeting was over, but the final phase of Omega's rise had just begun.

12

MOSCOW SUBURBS

Kata and Kusnetsov were met in the foyer by male servants who took their coats, brushing the snow off them before hanging them up. Her mind was working in overdrive. At last she understood the complexity of the clever web within which the minister had enmeshed her, and despite her antipathy for Kusnetsov she had to admire his ingenuity. He had deliberately humiliated her—he wanted to build up her enmity for him!—and then he had showered her with rewards, elevated her, taken her to what he termed a coming-out party at which she would be the only powerful female. Swinging back to humiliation again, he had let her know that her intervention in Vienna had not only been foolish but costly, as it had necessitated the notoriously thorny Department 73 sending Shutkov, their best *ovoshchechistka*, who had been killed for his efforts. It was clear to her now that Department 73, and possibly others, blamed her for his death. She suspected that Kusnetsov promoting her was a way of keeping her in Moscow, away from the field. The irony was that Lyudmila would be pleased; Kata's restless, bloodthirsty heart would not be. In one blow the minister had put her in her place and reminded her that he was protecting her from those in power who might now have a grudge against her.

She realized her cheeks were numb, as if they had been injected with Botox. She wondered if she would be able to speak, to not embarrass herself and, by extension, Kusnetsov, who right now held her life in his hands. Since her return to Moscow she had felt herself balanced on a knife edge, but now the edge seemed particularly sharp, the fall from it instantly lethal.

She turned away from her expensive coat, from her contemplation of how cleverly she had been outplayed. She stepped forward into the aural surf generated by the party already in progress. What had she expected this gathering to be? Either one of those famous bacchanals high-level *nomenklatura* were notorious for: men with fat faces gleaming with sweat pawing a bunch of subservient women. Or a staid affair filled with grim-faced men, smoking cigars, drinking iced vodka, gathered in weedy clumps, whispering of money and power, while the women, shunted off to one side, stared at each other, bored to tears. What she found was an altogether different scene than either she had imagined. Six men—high-level *nomenklatura*—and four women, surely their mistresses—for wives were home with the children where they belonged—were ranged around a square baize-topped table. On it were a pair of boards the color of lapis lazuli. Each long, narrow board consisted of thirty squares, each referred to as a house. Three rows of houses, ten in each row. With a shock that brought her to a halt, Kata recognized a game almost as old as time—the ancient Egyptian game of Senet. The object of the game was to move through the squares, the thirty houses representing life and its many obstacles. You won by removing all your pieces off the board at the thirtieth house, and thus you passed into the afterlife, which the ancient Egyptian venerated with their entire souls.

But the real shock was that Senet was being played only by the four women—two players to a board. Standing behind them, the men continuously bet on their favorite for each game, the odds swinging back and forth with each move of the players.

She caught up with Kusnetsov, who led her in a circle, introducing her to the six men, one by one. No names, let alone rank or title, were mentioned, but Kata intuited that they were being presented to her in ascending order of their importance. She knew none of their faces, although she thought the heavyset man with a beard seemed familiar. Perhaps she had seen him at FSB headquarters. They were all within a certain age range, these men—she estimated in their fifth decade, neither young nor old. Seasoned, yes. That was the word she would use to describe all of them. There was a strange energy to the room, as if the men were engaged in a greater purpose. There was a throttled fervor in their eyes.

Watching them as a group through the golden glow of the candlelit room was starting to weird her out. Even the regular circulation of servers with trays laden with Champagne, caviar-topped blini, smoked salmon on triangles of toast did nothing to assuage her sense that she'd fallen down a particularly bizarre rabbit hole.

The minister leaned into her, breaking into her thoughts, and asked her softly if she played Senet. She responded without looking at him. "You already know I do. I was taught it by Lyudmila Shokova after I landed in Moscow for my original debriefing. While I was sequestered in a Moscow safe house, subjected to Lyudmila's expert interrogation masquerading as an intake eval, she suggested we play Senet. When I told her I didn't know how, she offered to teach me."

"How lovely of her," Kusnetsov said through his teeth.

"Afterward, she claimed it was the best way to get to know me, to sense my motivation for defecting."

At the mention of Lyudmila he had stiffened, which was her purpose. She knew he was discomfited when her name came up, so she went on. "I could see that she was an excellent player—masterful, I would say, once I learned the game completely."

"Since you swallowed her style, could one say that you yourself are a masterful player?"

A corner of her lips quirked up. Instead of answering, she said, "You haven't yet introduced me to the four players. But then as you pointed out women are not so important here."

"Or anywhere in the Federation, for that matter," he added, a clumsy but telling blow, like the flat of his hand across her cheek. Her hatred flared inside her, igniting from the glowing coals she would never bank until she pressed a weapon to his throat and watched death arrive behind his eyes. "Apart from you, I mean."

Too little, too late. And anyway she knew he didn't mean it. Another trinket tossed her way that, when it came time to cash it in, would have no value. But now her gaze removed itself from the men to regard the four women. At once, she realized they were no mistresses or paid escorts. They possessed neither the carefully controlled movements of a mistress in public nor the hard neon flash of an escort with her calculating meter running.

The quartet was slim, blond, beautiful, as if cut from the same cloth by one divine tailor. But their beauty was marred by the perfection of their features; they didn't look entirely real, as if the skin on their faces had no pores. Apart from the one clad in yellow, there was a certain waxen quality to them, something bloodless. Kata wondered if they were stoned. Despite being nameless to her there was an easy way to tell them apart. They wore outfits of different colors: red, blue, green, yellow, like the four winds, the four elements, the four gates of an ancient fortress.

"So there's no fun anywhere to be had in my coming-out party?"

"Fun?" The corners of Kusnetsov's mouth turned down as if the word was like a squirt of castor oil. "Just concentrate on the play." His teeth shone brightly in the candlelight. "You're up next and I'm betting on you. Massively."

She snorted softly. "What is this, a remake of *Casino Royale*?"

"Nobody watching a Bond film would know what Senet was." He was dead serious. "The game is hardly cinematic. It's played too quickly, like the way the Chinese play mah-jongg."

"You mean the correct way."

"The only way," he acknowledged.

And, indeed, he had a point. The players were tossing their black-white paddles, moving their pieces at breakneck speed. To the novice or the uninitiated the board of thirty squares would seem all too easy to navigate. Nothing could be further from the truth. As in life, traps were waiting for the unwary player, along with setbacks, and sudden attacks by your opponent. And while setting up roadblocks was possible, they were difficult to complete before being wiped out. There was strategy to Senet, and the skill of the player was essential for winning, but in large part victory depended on luck. In Senet, as in other games of chance, you had luck or you didn't. There was no explaining that phenomenon but it existed all the same. In Senet Lyudmila had luck, and so did her pupil, Kata.

One game ended, as the player in blue had just swept her last man off the board into the afterlife. There was applause from some of the men, grumbling from others as money—a great deal of it—changed hands, from losers to winners.

As the woman in the yellow cocktail dress pushed her chair back Kata could see something in her eyes, a peculiar flash like anger—a genuine emotion in any event, and this intrigued Kata for it set her further apart from the other three. For an instant, their gazes engaged. Her eyes were like pale topaz gems, her face thin yet with prominent cheekbones. She had a wide forehead, rosebud lips, and small ears that Kata inexplicably found endearing. Then the moment vanished in the noise and smoke and the woman in yellow left the room. Kata thought the moment could mean something or nothing at all. Maybe simply her imagination at play, a drowning woman grasping for the last spar from a sinking ship. But in that instant she realized this was the last place on earth she wanted to be. A moment later, the heavyset bearded man slipped away from the crowd as well. A planned assignation? With this crowd and in this atmosphere, why not?

Oblivious to anything but his objective for the evening, the minister gestured. "Your turn." His hand gripped her shoulder briefly as he lowered his voice so only she could hear. "Do not fail."

She sat in the vacated chair, across from the blonde wearing a blue cocktail dress that left one burnished shoulder bare. As she did so, the second game came to a halt, annulled by a signal invisible to her.

Blue gave Kata a cursory once-over, then never looked at her during the entire game. She was good, aggressive, but impulsive as well, which served as her downfall. As the game progressed it appeared to the casual viewer that Kata had fallen behind. She had left men on squares 14, 15, and 26, while Blue moved her men relentlessly forward toward 30, the final square from which she could move her men off the board and into the afterlife. But then Blue's lead man landed on 27—a trap, necessitating her moving the man back to the first free square before 15. From there, Kata picked him off. Then, and only then, did she move her men forward. From then on, Kata attacked her opponent's men, sending them far backward where her own men were lying in wait.

The game was over in eight hectic minutes. In truth, Kata could have won in half the time but there were two other opponents to take on and she didn't want to get ahead of herself. But halfway through the game with Blue she got bored, formed a three-man blockade and ran the board into the afterlife.

Next came Green. Like Blue before her she gave Kata no more than a cursory glance, her gaze steadfastly on the board. She had learned from Blue's mistakes, avoiding Kata's early traps, but in doing so she gave herself away. Within three moves Kata had her pegged as impatient and greedy, wanting to own the board all at once. Kata preyed on this weakness and the game took a scarce five minutes.

The ending caused something of a hubbub in the crowd, the men, and Green and Blue pushing closer as the woman in red sat down opposite Kata and the board was reset. Her opponent's outfit was a crimson shantung sheath skirt and a sequined top so low-cut fully half her breasts were visible.

Unlike the previous opponents she fixed Kata with a rock-steady gaze. There was the hint of a smile on her wide lips that could have been interpreted as either caustic or ironic. Neither of those were good, Kata thought. But they were helpful. Gathering insight into an opponent was an integral part of a winning strategy. That neither of the previous women would look at her foretold their innate weakness.

No such weakness presented itself with Red. She was quick, decisive, and relentless. By midgame she and Kata were almost at a standstill, neither one holding the edge over the other. Twice Kata had tried to build a blockade with her men and each time Red intervened and broke them up. Attacks on either side set the men back to the first row of squares. With the passing of each moment Kata gained knowledge of her opponent's strategy and mindset. Unfortunately, this time the knowledge only served to prove over and over again that her chances of winning this game were diminishing, as if they were on a highway and Red's car was accelerating away at such a pace she'd never be able to catch up because she was already going flat out.

Gradually, as Red's men broke through and, one by one, slipped off square 30 into the afterlife Kata's confidence began to crack. She saw this as a sign, an omen, an inevitability in her life—an obstacle she could not overcome.

This is my fate, she thought bitterly, *to lose at the most inopportune moment.* When everything she had worked for since aligning herself with Lyudmila was in jeopardy. If she lost she would lose the minister's respect. She would be finished inside the FSB and of no use either to Lyudmila or to herself. She'd be consigned to a life as a minor functionary, ground down to a nub by the cruel and uncaring Russian machine.

As the game slipped further and further through her fingers, she thought, *This moment was foretold from the moment I was born. Evan knew how to deal with our adoptive parents; I didn't.* In that moment she understood the anger seething under the surface of her life. *Old or new,* she thought, *what does it matter? I still have nothing.*

And now, facing defeat at Senet in this mysterious dacha in the pine forest north of Moscow, she was gripped by a wild rage—the primal rage of the tiger who had been shot and does not know whether at the next indrawn breath she will live or die, only that the virulence of the pain was mixed with her fury until it was impossible to separate one from the other.

And that was when she saw the opening, the mistake her opponent had made. Her turn. A throw of the paddles was in her favor, and she made her move, the first of a half-dozen down a path toward Red's defeat. The method of her victory. All her men off the board, all of them safe and secure in the afterlife.

◼   ◼   ◼

Kusnetsov was grinning broadly, but she brushed by him with only a cursory nod and pushed through the crowd of men who wanted to meet her, talk to her, take her hand, kiss both her cheeks, press themselves against her, copping a feel under the guise of wanting to get to know her.

She asked one of the female servers to point out the restroom and was directed down a hall that branched off to the left. Black-and-white photos, indistinct with age or mist, hung along the walls between frosted glass sconces that threw triangles of pale light across the deep dove-gray carpet. She had not seen the woman in yellow since she had disappeared on the far side of the clutch of Senet gamblers.

The toilet was in the rear of the first floor. It was occupied, so Kata swung around, went up the staircase to the second floor, where there were two rooms—a bedroom and a study. Between them was a connecting bathroom, which also had a door to and from the hallway. She went in, emptied her bladder, then stared at herself in the mirror, not fully comprehending the face she saw there. Not for the first time she wondered whether she had ever had her own identity. So many years spent crouched in Evan's shadow hadn't allowed her the time to develop any emotion but anger, any desire but to run away from a life she so despised. She thought about her parents—her birth parents, not the couple who had adopted the two Russian girls. What had they been like? Would they have treated her any differently? But why should they have? They gave their daughters away to strangers, like good little Russians agents. But they were dead and buried. Lyudmila had taken her to their graves. She had stood at their feet, thought fleetingly of what her life might have been like if . . . If, if, if . . . She remembered the discomfort, as if someone were standing on her feet, the awkwardness of saying goodbye to people she never knew but who had known her intimately. Had it been raining that morning? Drizzling maybe? Or was that just how it had seemed to her? Certainly, the moment had been deeply creepy. Like now. This place was creepy, its residents, though temporary, or maybe because they were temporary, creepier still. There was no telling what they would do here, even now what was transpiring downstairs. She felt somehow safer up here in the quiet. The clothes she was wearing, the clothes Kusnetsov had bought her made her feel vulnerable, as if she were stripped bare, naked in front of the creeps downstairs. This was not how she should be feeling, not how she imagined this night going. She could hear Lyudmila's voice in her head, admonishing her, and she felt ashamed, diminished, weak.

She was about to steal into the study to look for evidence of who owned this dacha and why it had been chosen for this secretive high-level party when she heard the sounds. She turned toward the closed door to the bedroom. As she stepped toward it, she heard the noises more clearly—an altercation, or a scuffle of some sort?

When she heard the sharp crack of skin against skin, she turned the doorknob, silently inched the door open. She caught a glimpse of yellow, the dress thrust up over the girl's head. She was up against the far wall while the heavyset bearded man prepared himself to enter her.

He turned his head and Kata caught sight of his face in profile, his expression, his slitted eyes—it was just a flash, but as with many things in life it illuminated a darkness deeper than any midnight. She was thrust roughly back to Copenhagen.

■   ■   ■

She had been on a trip to Sumatra that Evan had planned for them, but she needed to get to Copenhagen, a city Evan had no interest in, to secretly meet with her FSB contact, an agent named Leda. Kata had been Bobbi Ryder then, Evan's little sister, and had easily guilted Evan into a stop in Copenhagen. Once there, she had manufactured a fight—not so difficult either, even a bit enjoyable in its way—to make sure they'd split for the day. But she'd only spent an hour or so with Leda before her contact handed Kata off to a man—her superior, Kata had surmised. She got into his black Citroën at the west gate of Assistens Cemetery and they drove off. His name was Sergei but she hardly paid attention. Why would he tell her his real name? She was sure Leda hadn't. All these people used operational names in the field, she already knew that much. In fact, that was one of the things that excited her the most: to get lost in a false identity, to be submerged in lie after lie like a set of Russian nesting dolls, so no one could see the real her.

She was surprised when Sergei pulled up to a hotel. He was thinner then, had not yet grown a beard. Silently they got out. Silently they entered the hotel lobby, took the elevator up. *Now my real schooling starts*, she thought. He waved her into his room, which was decorated in Danish Modern, which was to say completely anodyne to her taste. You could fall asleep in this room without even trying. It was dim, the drapes still covering the windows. Two lamps on either side of the bed were lit. The room smelled of tobacco and towels burnt in an industrial dryer.

He drew a fistful of tiny airplane-size vodka bottles out of the mini fridge, emptied them into a pair of glasses. She was only seventeen, she hadn't tasted much alcohol; Evan had forbidden it. She rolled it around the glass. It seemed oily. Sergei upended his glass, swallowed the vodka in one. Since this was obviously the Russian way she did the same. The last thing she remembered was the fire rolling down her throat.

The next thing she knew she was up against the wall. Her leggings were down around her ankles, her underpants a tight band around her knees, hobbling her. Her nostrils flared at the rank animal smell of him. He took her like a beast in the forest, slamming himself against her bare buttocks. Again and again, while he made grunting noises like a pig at a trough and lights exploded behind her eyes. Pain. She blacked out. When she came to he was still working on her. One arm snaked around her shoulder, his hand grasping her throat, cutting off her windpipe each time he thrust into her. More pain. Another blackout.

When she came to the final time he was sitting on a chair whose legs looked like the stripped bones of a deer. He was fully clothed, legs languidly crossed at the knee. He was smoking a cigarette, exuding an air of complete satisfaction. With hooded eyes he was staring at her as if waiting for her to awaken from a nap.

The moment she opened her eyes, he said, "You'll do."

■　■　■

She had lost track of time, of where the two people in the room were. She blinked, saw a blur and was greeted by a nose full of fist. Blood splashed hot, tasting of iron, as she reeled back against the edge of the door. Her right ankle buckled, the stiletto heel snapped off her pump, and she staggered. She saw the woman in yellow half-sitting, half-lying, her face as pale as the colors of the postmodern rug beneath her. Blood at the corner of her mouth, sliding down one nostril, a bruise blooming on her cheek. She had wrapped her dress around her thighs, arms tight around the hem as if that would keep her safe from his predations. But it was already too late for that.

Sergei's rough hand grabbed Kata by her necklace, which was too much—just too much, and with the edge of her hand she deep-bruised the nerve cluster on the side of her attacker's neck. For a moment he went stock-still. Time enough for her to drag the edge of her hard-cut emerald ring vertically down his chest, slicing through his clothes, the skin beneath. Blood spread, staining his pure white shirt. He was a big man, as she had noted downstairs, but now close up she was exposed to his power, his bull chest matted with black hair. The muscles of his arms like steel cables, and somehow he got on top of her. Teeth gritted, close-set eyes alight, he bore down on her chest with one knee, while imprisoning her hand with the emerald ring.

He slapped her with his free hand as he must have done with the woman in yellow. It was like being slammed with a concrete block. Kata saw stars, was close to blacking out, and once again the hotel room in Copenhagen rushed back at her—the Danish Modern furniture, the closed curtains, the smell of him, the bestial grunting. The pain. The flashes of remembrance like looking at a traffic light gone wild: red, yellow, green, all of them at once, none at all. Naked and vulnerable and along with it a terrifying creeping paralysis. This is a dream, she had told herself, all the distance she could get from the violence of the rape. The sense of being invaded. The pressure inside her. The grunts. The pain, the pain, my God, the pain . . .

She felt the broken-off heel against the fingers of her ringless hand. A black rage came rushing out of her memories like a ravenous wolf released from its cage. Sergei had his other knee on her forearm, but she did not care. Her rage lent her the strength of three men, more than enough to grab the heel around its thicker end and jab it into the meat of his thigh with such force it punctured his trousers and skin, embedding itself in the dense muscle.

"Bobbi, you prick," she spat.

His lips pulled back in a rictus of agony as she ground the heel deeper into him.

"Bobbi Ryder, remember me?"

His teeth clacked together, then began to chatter as he lost control of his facial muscles. He was so heavy and her position so compromised that she could only get him part way off her, but not enough to squirm out from beneath him. Then, unexpectedly, helping hands arrived from the woman in yellow. She hauled as Kata pushed until she was free. Sergei lay on his side, inert. He'd passed out.

Scrambling up, Kata took a moment to catch her breath before she thanked the woman.

"Alyosha," the woman in yellow said. And after Kata introduced herself, added, "Well, I think we have each other to thank, don't you?"

"How badly are you hurt?" Kata asked. "Are you all right?"

Alyosha gestured. "The sonofabitch did his best to destroy both our outfits."

They sat side by side, backs against the bed, and laughed. What else was there to do? Kata allowed the black rage to slowly slide out of her, covering Sergei like a shroud. She had no intention of telling Alyosha about her previous encounter with him. That horror was locked away again, tight and secure. The very idea of sharing it with anyone turned her stomach inside out.

"Did you win?" Apparently, the silence had gone on too long for Alyosha. "I bet you play Senet like a wizard."

"I did. It wasn't so difficult."

"It is for me." Alyosha laughed, but she was trembling, the shock just starting to hit her. "To tell you the truth no one around here plays well, including me."

Leaning over, Kata wiped blood from the corner of Alyosha's mouth.

"*Blyad.*" *Fuck.* Alyosha rose, went unsteadily to the night table, picked up the metal ice bucket with a bottle of vodka sticking out of it, along with the two glasses next to it, came back and sat down, placing her bounty on the floor between them.

"A lot is good," she said, holding up the frosted bottle by its neck. "More is better."

Kata took a convulsive gulp, winced as the fiery liquid rolled into her. "Your hand always this heavy?"

"Exigent times call for exigent measures." Alyosha drank and then they remembered to clink glasses.

"*Zdorov'ye,*" Kata said. *Health.* When she saw the drops of blood in the clear liquor, she put her glass down, rose, crossed into the bathroom, returned with two wet face cloths. With one she wiped the blood from Alyosha's face, then wrapped a fistful of ice in the cloth, pressed it gently against the bruise on the side of Alyosha's neck.

"Hold it there," she said, then made an ice pack for herself and, wincing, pressed it against her nose, where she had been hit.

Alyosha nodded, then gestured with her head. "You in any pain?"

"Nothing a bottle of vodka won't cure."

They laughed together as Alyosha refilled their glasses, this time almost to the brim.

"This ought to get the party started," Kata said. Then she glanced over at the unconscious man. "I know this prick from a long time ago. Sergei he said his name was, but I knew that wasn't his real name. Do you know him?"

"Borya Igorevich Arsenyev." She wiped her mouth again with the back of her hand. "He made money on the early games. Then he followed me up here."

Evan turned back to Alyosha. "Friend of yours?"

At this, Alyosha burst out laughing. "That's a good one. But, no, no, I have no male friends. Even my two brothers I hate. But in the FSB—" She shook her head. "My God, never."

At this point, Borya groaned and stirred slightly. Alyosha got to her feet, stepped over to him, and kicked him smartly in the side of the head. He subsided once again into silence.

"Good one," Kata said, as Alyosha returned to where she was sitting.

"He had it coming," Alyosha said, as she sat back down. "And then some."

"As long as neither of us takes out the heel of my shoe he won't bleed to death." Kata guzzled some more vodka, which had started to stoke a nice little fire in her belly.

She glanced across to Borya. "What does this little prick do when he's not battering women?"

"He's in charge of Department 73."

"Home of the *ovoshchechistki*," Kata said. "The peelers."

Alyosha's eyes opened wide. "You know about them?"

It was Kata's turn to laugh. "I'm the head of Zaslon."

Alyosha's eyes grew wider still. "You? A woman?"

"I'm very persuasive," Kata said with another laugh. "No, it's not what you think."

"Then you must have something on Minister Kusnetsov."

"You would think." Kata shook her head. "But no. I'm just exceptionally good at my job."

"I'm in FSB SIGINT. I'm good at what I do, too. Since when does that count for anything?" Alyosha shook her head. "The FSB is just like the internet, they both hate women."

Kata couldn't argue with that.

Alyosha went on. "So Zaslon exists. Really."

Kata nodded. "Really." She made a face. "The last peeler Department 73 sent out was terminated. My new remit is to—" But at the look on Alyosha's face she broke off. "Alyosha, what is it?" She pulled the other woman closer to her. "Did Borya do more than—?"

Alyosha shook her head. Tears and blood mingled on her lips and chin. "The man I love is a peeler. The best one 73 has." She looked down at the front of her dress. "He sent me this dress from Vienna just today."

Kata's heart dropped, seemed to stop beating for a moment.

Alyosha ran her hands over the dress, through the dried blood. "I was going to wear it the first night he was home."

"Is his name Shutkov?"

Alyosha's head snapped up, and she gasped. "Oh, God, Pasha. Oh, God. No."

Kata stared into those sea-glass eyes, now clouded with tears. "Pasha Shutkov was your lover?"

Alyosha collapsed in Kata's arms, sobbing inconsolably. Kata was at a loss. A sense of tragedy—the death of parents she never knew, a despised sister the very thought of whom still churned the pit of her stomach and, above all, a loss of self, combined to make her uniquely unsuitable to feel empathy on any level. And yet this woman, more or less the same age as herself, harbored the same deep-seated anger that was eating away at Kata from the inside. Kinship on a level she had never hitherto experienced worked as a metaphorical lever to open something inside her, something that caused her to put her arms around Alyosha, press the other woman close, inhale her scent, taste the saltiness of her tears on her own lips. Then she felt Alyosha's arms snake around her waist in response, and a tingle slid down her spine along with a warmth that had nothing to do with the vodka she had consumed. The truth was she had never held someone, never been held with the love a mother should feel for her child. The two of them rocked together, gaining something inexplicable from each other.

Even with her cheek against Alyosha's hair, even while being held, Kata's mind refused to slip into neutral. But she judiciously waited until she judged Alyosha had recovered sufficiently. "Downstairs, when you got up from the table you gave me a look." She thought Alyosha would deny it, but she didn't.

"Why?" she asked.

"I saw the anger behind your eyes."

Kata was taken aback. "Anger?" Was she that transparent tonight or was Alyosha's insight so astute?

"It smolders like a poorly banked fire."

Kata shook her head. "You're mistaken."

"It smolders still."

"I think—"

"It's like looking in a mirror."

A tense silence enveloped them during which Kata forgot everything outside this room, outside the pale topaz-blue of Alyosha's intense gaze.

It was Alyosha who cut through the thickening silence. "Listen, Kata, it doesn't matter why we are angry only that the anger lies deep inside us, sometimes in a place even we cannot reach."

Something loosened inside Kata. "And then we feel out of control."

"Yes."

"We know there is nothing to be done."

"Yes."

Kata's eyes clouded over. She felt enclosed in a darkness that welled up from inside her. "I think that's why I kill, Alyosha, why I'm so good at it. Why I love it so much."

Alyosha appeared unsurprised. "It makes sense, doesn't it? For that moment you are in control. No matter how brief, that moment brings release."

"Yes." Kata reached out, took Alyosha's hand in hers. "You are the first person—"

"And you." Alyosha nodded.

"Is that how you . . . ?"

"By killing?" Alyosha shook her head. "I don't have it in me. My release is solitude. Utter and complete isolation."

"How do you find a place like that?"

A rueful smile passed across Alyosha's face. "Only in the deep desolation of the place Borya works." Her mouth quirked. "Ironic, isn't it? I find peace within sight of where the *ovoshchechistki* train."

"Is that how you met Pasha?"

Alyosha nodded, touched her forehead to Kata's shoulder for a moment before pulling away. Her eyes again swam in tears. Reaching out Kata wiped them away with her finger. "Borya found us once, in the pine forest. He had grown suspicious and followed Pasha."

"What happened?"

"He told me tonight. Tonight when he would mete out my punishment for as long as I could remain conscious." She shuddered. "He said he was a master of that kind of thing."

Kata cupped Alyosha's chin, said gently, "But he won't harm you now. He never will. No one will harm you. I won't let them, understand?"

Alyosha nodded, then ducked her head, pushing her forehead into Kata's shoulder, as a younger sister might. *But what*, Kata asked herself harshly, *would I know about that?*

"Alyosha." Kata moved the other woman so she could look into those gem-like eyes. "Can you tell me where you go to be alone?"

"It's a secret," Alyosha whispered. Their faces were close.

"So is Zaslon."

"Yes." The glimmer of a smile crossed Alyosha's lips. "You trusted me."

"I will tell no one," Kata said. "I swear on the lives of my parents."

"*Devyatyy Krug* is in the middle of the largest forest in the Tarasovo district," Alyosha said. "Like most everything in Russia it's ironic. The area hosts a number of eco-hotels, along with quarries and mining sites." She grunted. "Imagine: Muscovite families sunning themselves beside pristine pools while not ten kilometers away workers are dying of any number of lung diseases." Finishing off her vodka, she continued, "Anyway, Tarasovo is thickly forested—many, many hectares of evergreens. In the center of one of them is the Ninth Circle, the heavily secured compound where the *ovoshchechistki* are schooled and, sometimes, buried."

"The ones who don't make it through the training."

"That's right."

"So they're not sent home."

Alyosha made a face. "Not even in a coffin; too many secrets there. They are disappeared six feet under."

Kata glanced over at the big man lying on his side. "Under Borya's orders, I imagine." When Alyosha nodded, she added, "So he was the one to send Pasha to Vienna."

"Oh, no, not at all. Pasha was Minister Kusnetsov's choice." She made an animal sound deep in her throat. "If it had been up to Borya, Pasha wouldn't have gone anywhere until he agreed to get the tattoo."

Kata knew tattooing was a major sign of strength and toughness among Russian men, curiously taking their cue from incarcerated criminals. "What tattoo?" she asked.

"The same one that's on Borya's chest." Alyosha pointed. "You can just make out a piece of it, where you slit open his shirt."

On hands and knees Kata made her way to the sprawled figure. She saw part of a horizontal crosspiece tattoo and figured it might be a cross. Peeling back the torn shirt she saw the tattoo was indeed a cross, but the overall design was one she'd never seen before.

"It's obscene, isn't it?" Alyosha was by her side. "Something about . . ." She shook her head. "Anyway, Pasha refused to get it, even when Borya pressured him. He told me he'd started investigating the tattoo and what it meant, a very dangerous thing to do in his small department."

Kata could see what she meant. Just below the crosspiece was what appeared to be an oval or the letter O integrated near the bottom. Kata stared at it as if mesmerized. The longer she stared at the peculiar tattoo the more she seemed to get lost in it.

"Looks like an English 'O,'" Alyosha said. "Doesn't it?"

Something clicked inside Kata with the force of the jaws of a crocodile snapping shut, and she thought: *Omega. This is the Omega sigil!*

It was at that moment Kusnetsov made his presence known. "There you are. I've been looking—" It was only when his gaze fell upon Borya lying insensate on the floor with the heel broken off Kata's shoe buried in his thigh that his face shut like a vault. *"'Tchyo za ga'lima?"* *What the fuck?* "This is the last straw, Kata." Advancing like a storm into the room. "You have crossed the line. Nothing will save you now."

13

Evan awoke with the name Clausewitz foremost in her thoughts, like a neon sign, blinking in code, but as she sat up with an animal cry of pain, it flew from her mind. She sat on the edge of Karl's bed, curled over, head in her hands, sweaty and chilled, amid the whirlpool sheets, still damp with her sweat. Her teeth chattered, a chill running through her. She felt hollowed out, wracked by flashbacks of being held under the water, desperate to get away, her antagonist coming after her, lunging, fighting, lambent eyes like lamps in the swirled dimness of the water, teeth bared as if he meant to spit in her face. The raw hatred.

And then she felt the wrongness. *What kind of life am I living?* she asked herself. *Through what twisted lens am I seeing the world around me, devoid of laughter and love, filled only with loneliness and death.* But at the same time she knew there were no answers to these questions, at least not now, and not in the foreseeable future. Only as death spread its spidery hands through her would the answers be made clear.

One last shiver to clear out the jams, to pull herself back into herself.

She was thirsty and famished, but first things first. After switching on all the lamps, she padded into the bathroom, saw the wet morass of her clothes on the floor of the shower, and knew they were unsalvageable. Short of burning them, nothing would get the stink of the river's inflorescence out of them.

Throwing them into a corner of the room, she turned on the shower taps, and when the water was almost scalding she stepped in, lathered up, and let the heat seep through her aching muscles as the hot water cascaded over bruises the color of overripe eggplant. She still winced as water splashed over the wound in the side of her head, but the pain was dull now, feeling like yesterday's trash. She toweled off, wrapped herself in another towel, returned to the main room and raided Karl's closet. Dressed in an inconspicuous outfit of dark-brown trousers, striped shirt, socks, and a pair of his work boots. Karl must have been a small man; the boots weren't a bad fit, especially when she added a second pair of his thick socks made of rough wool.

She fixed herself some food while she drank a glass of cold water. She turned on the TV, watched as Sky News reran an egregious bit from TNSC, the Wells-backed TV network. She managed to get through half of the fawning interview with a group of wildling protesters at a rally in Washington, DC, one of many across the country, who, to a person, insisted that Democrats were pedophile Satanists, "sworn enemies of white Christian society." They all wore masks covering the lower half of their faces, white with a black cross bisected by a gold O. The interview ended abruptly when a melee broke out on the fringes of the crowd between the protesters and Capitol Police and quickly encompassed the whole. That was bad enough, but then the scene cut to the Titan studios where a senator from Wisconsin said, "God bless those courageous people for standing fast against socialist forces trying to take away their rights as individuals. They're fighting for solid American principles. They only want what is due them as white God-fearing citizens of this once-great nation that is being torn apart by the socialist, atheistic left."

A loss of appetite caused Evan to turn to CNN International. She came in on the middle of a story about the latest mass shooting at a black church in Georgia—thirteen dead, scores wounded, and the church set ablaze. Another tragic statistic in a year when the number of mass shootings had already tripled from those of previous years. Three-minute footage of firefighters, police, flashing lights, emergency rescue vehicles, and stricken faces held behind police lines as the church burned was repeated over and over while talking heads speculated ad nauseum on the possible motives, the identities of the perpetrators, the hand-wringing at the use once again of illegal assault weapons.

She switched to another streaming network only to discover that the Washington Project, the most prominent action organization to come out against Wells and his constituency, was inundated with scandal. The CEO of the project had just stepped down following accusations by two female aides of inappropriate behavior of a sexual nature. In addition, the secretary stood accused of cooking the project's books, diverting millions in donations to a personal offshore account.

In other words, newsworthy elements of both the right and left were dirty as sin—liars, crooks, schemers, and amoral pricks, thought Evan disconsolately.

She was about to turn off the TV but switched back to CNN first to find the current news item interrupted by the flash of a breaking news bulletin. According to the newsreader, "Highly placed informed sources tell us that Titan News and Streaming Corporation are readying a major announcement that will reportedly change the landscape of television news." More Samuel Wainwright Wells, more Lucinda Wells. Her blood ran cold at the certainty of confronting her last remaining sister on opposite sides of the moral universe. She recalled all too vividly Isobel's concern that when push came to shove she might not be able to put her remit before family. She had been firm in her answer, of course she had, but for the past seven months part of her had wondered what would have happened if Ben hadn't killed Ana. That her sister was insane and homicidal was beyond question. *But isn't it natural for me to want to help her?* she had asked herself over and over. *Isn't that what anyone would do for her sister?*

And so, she wondered what would happen when the confrontation with Lucinda came.

To get her mind off her remaining sister, she switched to YouTube, listened to part of Marsden Tribe's TED Talk. It was audio only; Tribe had forbidden video at the talk. She found his voice soothing and what he said uplifting: "We have embarked on an age of exploration previously unknown in the history of humankind. This exploration is threefold: outer space, unlocking the secrets of gene therapy, and reaching into the deepest levels of the human mind. Our lives are now accelerated to a degree unimaginable even five years ago. Data surrounds us. We live in a data-driven world. We must learn to embrace it, rather than fear it. For most of us that is not an easy transition. It is much like meditation. Concentrate, learn, persevere with intention and patience, and once you do, a whole new universe of knowledge opens to you. The danger for all of us is serenity. Serenity breeds mediocrity. Serenity kills innovation. But how to handle the petabytes of data streaming constantly? The answer is quantum computing, being able to process a terabyte of data in a nanosecond."

Still exhausted, she slipped again into a brief sleep, slumped on Karl's sofa. She dreamed of holding Karl's head in the cupped palm of her hand, much like Hamlet held the skull of Yorick. Death, Hamlet realized, was the great leveler. In death both he, the prince of Denmark, and Yorick, his childhood court jester, would be the same. But in her dream, Karl—or rather Karl's head—spoke to her. What he told her was of the greatest import but when she awoke with a start she could not remember a word he had said. She rose, prowled restlessly around the room, but try as she might to hold onto the dream, it had slipped away.

And then she stopped dead in her tracks. She was facing the bookcase with the Clausewitz histories of warfare and only now did her mind register what her eyes had seen the first time. There were two copies of the same volume. Now why would a cemetery caretaker who was also an espionage cutout have two copies of the same book? Clausewitz was quite boring—and often wrong—read even once.

She took the volumes from the shelf, sat back down on the sofa, and opened the two copies side by side. At first glance, they seemed identical, but then, leafing through the one on the left she saw several pages were torn out—four, to be exact. Turning to the other copy she found the first missing page intact and began to study it but could find nothing that would make the page special. The same was true of the other three.

Returning to the mutilated book, she paged through again, but nothing anomalous stood out. She was about to close it in disgust when she caught a glimpse of something on the end paper in back. Opening the book up fully, she saw four sets of numbers, all of unequal length.

Heart beating faster, and ignoring the resulting throbbing in her head, she opened the intact book to the first page Karl had ripped out of the other. She ran her fingertip along the lines of text, keeping in mind the first set of numbers. There she found what she was looking for. Once you knew to look for a cipher, it was easy enough to decode. Karl had used a simple substitute letter system, working backward, so, for instance the letter A was Z, B was Y, and so forth. It took her twenty minutes to find the letters on the lines the cipher revealed. At the end of which time she had a name and an address on Handelskai Street, near the river in the tony Leopoldstadt district.

She sat back on the sofa, closed her eyes. Her head was spinning and she could feel whatever she had eaten lying in her stomach like a fistful of stones. With a start, she remembered she had come out of the water with the Russian's cell phone—to her he was and always would be "the Russian"; she could not bear to think or speak his name—but couldn't remember what she'd done with it. She got to her feet and looked around, found it lying on the floor by Karl's bed. It felt icy in her hand, as if she had just taken it out of the freezer. When the screen came to life, she was momentarily stunned to see how much time had passed—it was nearly 11 PM. Quickly, she scrolled though his address book. Nothing. Ditto text messages. Everything had been erased before confronting the enemy. He had done what he should have done, leaving her with nothing.

She knew all the required numbers by heart. She started to punch in Isobel's private cell number, then midway through stopped and deleted it. The last thing she wanted to do was to tell Isobel and Ben what had happened. They'd assuredly order her home instantly. She wasn't prepared to do that. Not by a long shot. She was on her way to the address on Handelskai Street contained in Karl's cipher. She'd pick up a burner phone from an electronics store and text Isobel, but not before she'd finished what lay in store for her.

She resisted an urge to drop the phone, grind it under her heel until it cracked like a rifle shot and flew apart. *Finis*. Really *finis* this time. But then she had a better idea.

■ ■ ■

She wrapped herself in a tweed overcoat that smelled of tobacco and, she assumed, Karl, and, with an almost overwhelming feeling of relief, she left the cylindrical building. Back out on the street, she called for a taxi to pick her up at the cemetery's entrance. When they arrived at the far end of Handelskai Street, she handed the driver the Russian's phone, which he happily accepted in lieu of euro as payment.

She stepped out of the taxi and the smell of the river hit her like a slap in the face. She choked and she felt her gorge rise alarmingly.

Breathe, she told herself. *Breathe*.

Hurrying beneath the shelter of the new building's front door, she ran her eyes down the bell ledger until she arrived at Camina Wagner, the name spelled out in the last spurt of numbers in Karl's cipher. She pressed the bell and waited. Perhaps Fraulein Wagner wasn't home. Perhaps she wouldn't let a stranger in. Perhaps she wasn't a Fraulein at all but a Frau and her shaggy, smelly husband would answer the buzzer and the front door.

She stared up at the lightless sky, crowded with restless clouds, the color of charcoal, gravid with rain or wet snow. Whoever was in Camina Wagner's apartment buzzed her in. No intercom palaver, no questions asked. *Interesting*, she thought. *And curious*.

On the far side of the marble lobby she ascended in the small elevator to the top floor and, after having a cursory look around, stepped to her right, down to the end of the corridor, which she judged to be on the river side. Thinking of the river sent a tiny tremor through her, at which she felt thoroughly aggrieved.

The door at the end opened while she was still a few paces away. As she came abreast of the doorway a diminutive Thai woman in traditional garb smiled at her, somehow making the expression noncommittal.

"May we help you?"

"I'm looking for Camina Wagner," Evan said.

The Thai woman's dark eyes regarded the visitor without revealing a thing. If she was surprised to find on her doorstep a woman with a bandage on the side of her head and bruises around her neck she kept it to herself. "Everyone who comes calling wants her," she said in clipped British-accented English.

"Tell her—" Evan was about to say, tell her Karl sent me, but her well-honed instinct intervened. "Tell her I've been sent by Clausewitz."

The Thai woman blinked, as if coming out of a reverie. "Clausewitz." She said it slowly, as if tasting it like a piece of ripe fruit.

"That's right," Evan said. "It's urgent."

"I'm sure it is." The Thai woman stepped back, her slippers soundless on the polished wooden floor. "Enter. You are expected."

How could I be expected? Evan asked herself.

"My name is Belle."

"Evan."

The Thai woman nodded, gesturing. "Please, this way. Once you are settled I will bring refreshments."

Evan followed Belle through the entryway into a spacious room, inexplicably devoid of furniture, with large French doors to their right that led out onto a wide terrace overlooking the river. The doors could be thrown open in summer. Now they were locked up tight against the gathering chill.

They passed through the room into a lushly carpeted hallway hung with Shunga, erotic Japanese woodblock prints, between closed doors on either side. Evan paused in front of a print depicting a woman, in the throes of ecstasy, wrapped in the arms of an octopus.

Belle turned, came back to stand beside her. "This Shunga is most famous. You like?"

"I'm just wondering whether this woman is experiencing eight orgasms at once."

Belle's laugh was as soft as a petal falling from a rose. "That is the point of the design, no? Maybe you want to stay an hour or so after your meeting with Camina. Yes? I can arrange it, no problem. That hour will be good for you. Very relaxing. Here you will find relief, guaranteed."

And then the penny dropped. Evan understood why there was no furniture in the front room. Clients were encouraged to linger only with their chosen woman behind these closed doors. It appeared that Camina Wagner was, among other things, the madam of a discreet, high-class brothel.

Double doors at the end of the hallway led into a large office that, judging by the comfortable-looking furniture arranged to create a cozy conversation nook, clearly also served as Camina's study and relaxation area.

When Belle ushered Evan in, Camina rose from behind a functional glass-and-steel desk, dominated by a laptop plugged into a large plasma monitor. It could have belonged to the CEO of any business in the world. But this wasn't any business in the world—it was one specific business that needed to remain in the shadows.

All this went through Evan's mind as she watched Camina Wagner approach her. She was slight, dark-skinned, of perhaps Turkish extraction, though it was difficult to tell. Evan judged her to be in her late thirties. She was a handsome woman with a powerful face and a stride that spoke of her solid decision-making.

"Peace be upon you, sister," Camina said in the traditional Muslim greeting.

"And upon you, peace," Evan replied.

Evan introduced herself. As Camina took her hand Evan felt a tingle of energy so subtle most others would not have picked it up. She looked into the other woman's eyes, saw the flash of understanding. In that moment, Evan decided this woman was worthy of her trust, and her shoulders relaxed. She thought of Belle saying, *Here you will find relief.* She realized that she would like that, very much. She felt spent, physically and emotionally. Her encounter with the Russian had delivered a body blow more devastating than she had at first realized. This, however, only made her more determined to keep going until she found answers to the question of who wrote the electronic file that Armistad had died for, and why.

"You look like you've just been spat out of a cement mixer," Camina said in a no-nonsense style. Evan found this refreshing, being used to the often-necessary circumlocutions of her trade.

Evan gave Camina as much of a smile as she was able to summon up. "You should have seen the Russian." She still couldn't bring herself to say his name.

A sad smile spread across Camina's face. "I have seen him . . . well, before you got hold of him, and believe me I didn't like what I saw." Her voice was deep—a contralto, rather than a soprano. It was colored by a hint of barely hidden sorrow and had about it a certain reedy quality that made it seem as if several people were speaking at once.

"Sit." It was an order, but not a difficult one to obey.

Evan dropped gratefully into a deep upholstered chair, watched Camina cross to a tabouret set against one wall. She went through several drawers until she found what she was looking for. Returning with a syringe, she pulled off the sterile plastic covering. "Now sit back and rest your head against the upholstery."

Evan eyed the syringe with suspicion. "What the hell's in that?"

"You can't go around with the wound in the side of your head, now can you," Camina said rhetorically. "What I have in here will heal it sufficiently within six hours so it won't get infected."

Evan looked at her skeptically. "What, are you a doctor, also?"

"I'm far more knowledgeable than a doctor." Camina smiled. "Now please do as I say."

Reluctantly, Evan complied, face tilted up to the ceiling. Camina was careful and precise. Evan barely felt the injections even though they were into the sensitive flesh just above and below her eyes. At once, she felt a coolness steal through her, followed by a burst of heat like an engine's ignition before the coolness returned.

"What's in the injection?" she asked.

"A cocktail of my own design." Camina dropped the used syringe in a hazardous waste receptacle. "Green tea extract, birch polypore, *fomes fomentarius*"—she cocked an eye—"shall I go on?" Since no answer was either expected or required she called for Belle.

While they waited, she picked up a remote that had been lying on the table and pressed a red button. A painting hanging above the tabouret rose up revealing a flat screen monitor. Another button pushed and a familiar interior filled the screen. Karl's apartment within the Cemetery of the Forgotten. No wonder Evan couldn't find the guts of the CCTV · monitors placed around Karl's living quarters. They were here in Camina's office.

"There is your Moscow-sent *ovoshchechistka*." A moving shadow came into a bar of light from one of the oriels. "Pasha Rodionovich Shutkov." The scene switched. "He's looking for something," Camina said, continuing the narration. "Of course he is. He's a peeler, sent from the bowels of

FSB hell to clean up anything that can lead back to the Russians." The scene switched to yet another angle. "But he doesn't find anything. He's not as clever as you are."

Evan, heart in her mouth, made no reply to the compliment. She knew what was coming. And there it was: the Russian coming up behind Karl as he emerged from the bathroom. A short vicious struggle ensued, which ended abruptly, shockingly with the Russian slicing through Karl's windpipe with a long thick-bladed hunting knife, cutting through flesh, viscera, and nerves, down to the bone, and, once Karl hit the floor, hacking through the bone itself to sever the head.

Camina clicked the remote and the screen blanked, the painting slid noiselessly down, and everything was as it had been in the room, as long as you were immune to the repercussion of the atrocity that had been committed on Karl's body hanging in the air like the stink from the river that refused to leave Evan's nostrils.

Camina took a seat across from her. Belle entered with a tray on which rested a porcelain tea service, along with small plates of Middle Eastern sweets, so perhaps Evan's assessment of Camina's background was correct. Belle poured them both tea—a bracing mint varietal—then silently withdrew.

"So." Camina sipped her tea, looked at Evan over the rim of her delicate cup. "So, given that's the last we see of Shutkov . . . now that you've seen the before, care to share the after?"

Evan considered, couldn't think of any reason to lie. "I drowned the Russian in the river water he let into the sluiceway below Karl's quarters."

Camina set her cup down without taking her eyes off her visitor. "He didn't go easily."

"Not easily, no."

"Ah, well, you'll be all the stronger for that struggle." Camina picked up one of the small plates, offering the small pieces of halvah. "Try one." When Evan gave her a dark look, she nodded. "I know. But they are special, flown in directly from my confectioner in Istanbul. Even just one will lift your spirits." She smiled. "I promise."

Evan gave it the side-eye. "Any *fomes fomentarius*?"

Camina's laugh was like velvet, and she shook her head.

Evan let the triangle melt in her mouth. Everything Camina said about it was true, and she understood why halvah was so good. After all, it was the Arabic word for sweetness.

Evan, deciding to adopt her host's directness, said, "I don't know what happened to Karl's body. I didn't find it in his quarters. I didn't even find any blood."

Camina wiped her fingertips on a cocktail napkin. "What would you have done with the body?"

"I would have buried it in the cemetery," Evan said without thinking.

Camina nodded. "That is where my people will find Karl, I have no doubt. We'll give him a proper burial." She paused a moment. "It's more than you can do for your own agent."

She meant Armistad, incinerated in the city morgue by the Russian peeler. She acknowledged the comment with a curt nod.

Camina said, "Now, how may I help you?"

"Omega," Evan said simply. "Karl passed on a—"

"A purported top-secret internal document. Yes, I know."

Evan said, "So, is there anything you can tell me about Omega?"

Camina rose, crossed to the windows. A wet snow streaked the glass, turning the city to melting wax. Unbidden, Evan gained her feet and stepped across the room. Standing next to Camina she offered her a square of flaky baklava. Camina laughed, took it, popped it in her mouth.

She looked into Evan's eyes. "What I can tell you is this . . . Omega's members see themselves reflected in their leader; they *want* to believe. The leader knows this and preys on this fatal weakness. It sets Omega apart from all the other sects. Omega makes its devotees special; it reaffirms to them over and over that only they know the world's true meaning: whatever their leader says is the truth that they must follow. They are inoculated against facts. When their leader's words are repudiated by multiple sources outside their inner circle they become even more certain of their path. In fact, the more the leader's 'truth' is denied by the Other, the firmer their belief in its godliness."

Evan stood stock-still for some time, her gaze moving from Camina's face to the bleary darkened windowpane, which showed her only a distortion of her reflection and the room behind her. She was beginning to understand and this sent a chill deep into her bones. What she had been battling for two years was an altogether different beast than she had imagined. It went deeper into the darkness, was more entrenched, more rooted in the deepest soil of the United States.

"I see by your expression that you have correctly absorbed the true danger of what you are facing." She placed a hand on Evan's shoulder. "I have one more thing to tell you but first why don't we find you a proper set of clothes that fit and don't smell of Karl."

She took Evan into another room, with a mirrored wall that turned out to be an enormous closet. Sliding open the door, she gestured. "Please. Choose anything that strikes your fancy."

"Oh, I couldn't," Evan exclaimed, eyeing the rich abundance of dresses, skirts, trousers, and jackets.

"You can," Camina said, "and you will."

Running her hand over the fine materials, she protested, "But I don't have enough on me to pay you. All my money is stowed at the airport."

"This is not an issue," Camina assured her. "Please." She gestured again. "It is my pleasure."

As Evan went through the vast inventory, Camina continued her narrative. "I have told you all I know about Omega, but there is another who may consent to give you more immediately useful information. I cannot guarantee it. But it is the only way for you to go, for he knows the origins of this festering disease. And believe me when I tell you that without knowing how and why Omega began you will never defeat it."

She went to her desk as Evan tried on an outfit, ripped off a slip of paper, wrote two lines in a neat hand, then scribbled a note on another. She gave them to Evan—the name and address of the contact and a note to deliver to him. Evan read them twice, memorized the name and address, which was in Nuremberg, handed that slip back to Camina.

"Have you ever been to Nuremberg?" Camina asked.

Evan shook her head.

"Plenty of ghosts inhabit those streets at night, just not the children's storybook kind." Camina's countenance was altogether serious. "It's no joke, but you'll probably find out for yourself. The past is particularly strong there, close to the surface, spread across the city; it was never truly laid to rest."

Evan had chosen a pair of black jeans, a dark gray collarless shirt, and a knit sweater, over which she drew on a waist-length jacket of black leather lined with shearling. She kept Karl's boots, but changed into a pair of Camina's woolen socks, softer than either of the ones she had been wearing.

Camina, approving, accompanied Evan across the office. At the double doors, she halted, standing close enough for Evan to smell her scent—a heady combination of amber and attar.

Evan said, "I know I'm in grave danger. Moscow must know by now that their *ovoshchechistka*, their peeler, is dead. Now they'll send another because they know the job is not yet finished. The peeler will be coming after me."

"Mm, I'm not so sure of that. My contacts tell me that Department 73 is in imminent danger of a top-down purge."

"Who might your contact be?"

Camina gave her the side-eye, which in her case was altogether chilling. "You don't expect me to tell you."

Evan shrugged. "Not really. That would violate security protocols."

"I will tell you that my contact is unimpeachable."

That was precisely what she had told Ben when he'd asked her who her Russian contact was.

"Pasha Shutkov's death has shaken morale inside the department," Camina continued. "For the moment, Moscow is reluctant to wager another death of one of its own on foreign soil." Camina shook her head. "So, no, you have nothing to fear from another peeler, at least in the immediate future." A slow smile spread across her face. "Lyudmila wanted you to know that."

Evan's heart thudded in her chest. "Who?"

Camina shot her a sardonic look. "Come now."

Evan felt relief flood through her. "Ah, you're part of Lyudmila's network."

"As are you."

For her own equilibrium of mind, Evan had kept her thoughts away from that thinly veiled truth. Because now she was, in effect, a double agent. Just as Bobbi had been in the years before her murder. She and Bobbi, one and the same. For a brief moment her blood ran cold and internally she shook herself like a dog coming out of the rain. Something lodged deep inside her heart seemed to have sprung a leak, obliging her to turn away from Camina, wipe her eyes before they were overrun.

"Are you all right?" Camina's hand on her shoulder, gently like a mother soothing her frightened child.

Evan nodded, but for the moment not trusting herself to speak.

"Perhaps this is not the best idea." Camina's tone had changed. It was deeper, more authoritative. "You've been through a lot already. You're running on empty. Time now to rest."

"I can't do that; I can't stop now, not when I'm close to finding out who sent the cipher that got one of my own killed."

"You won't do him, or anyone, any good if you collapse. Nuremberg is a dangerous place—especially for you."

Evan forced herself to gaze into her host's eyes. The leak in her heart had vanished; she'd made sure of that. *I'm perfectly fine now*, she told herself. But she knew she wasn't; she knew Camina was right. Exhaustion was hovering in the corners of her vision.

Camina smiled, raised an arm. "Come now. I have a spare room where you can spend the night." Her smile widened into a grin. "And I assure you that Belle will make you the best meal in the city."

Evan at last acquiesced. "Thank you, Camina."

"It's my pleasure, *habibti*." She led Evan back through the warren of formal sitting rooms, down a wood-paneled hall and through a set of wooden doors, into what appeared to be her own private quarters. She set Evan up in a small but comfortably furnished bedroom with a canopied bed and a window overlooking the water. A door on the far wall led to a bathroom clad in Moroccan tiles, making her feel as if she were in a riad in Marrakech.

"Please, make yourself at home." Camina gestured. "There's water in the pitcher and anything else you might want just pick up the phone and tell Belle. All right?"

"Again, thank you."

"A long hot shower, a good night's sleep and you'll be yourself again."

It wasn't quite like that. Evan flinched as the spray of hot water hit her battered body, but soon enough as she soaped up she was able to relax into it. Drying herself, she stumbled to the bed, groaning in ecstasy as she sank into the mattress. The underside of the canopy was embroidered in beautiful Arabic script: O Allah, I seek refuge in You from this journey's hardships, and from the wicked sights in store.

■　■　■

When she woke it was early evening; she'd slept nearly an entire day. Camina was waiting for her. They ate a delicious meal served by Belle. And then it was time to go.

On Evan's way out, Camina handed her a cell phone. "A burner, totally clean. It is perfectly secure; unhackable."

Evan took the phone, nodded gratefully. She was reminded that following Isobel's summons home she had been flying naked—no control, no backup. But what was the point of calling DC? Evan couldn't go home, not now, not until she found out everything she could about the origins of Omega, and about the e-file meant for its American wing.

"I simply wanted to offer you a choice," Camina said as Evan put the phone away. "I wanted you to know that you *have* a choice." She cocked her head. "Has anyone told you that? Ever?"

A rueful smile from Evan. "I don't believe so, but I'm grateful that you have."

Leaning forward Camina kissed her on the cheek. "If you were my sister, *habibti*, what fun we would have!"

A delighted laugh escaped Evan. It would be difficult leaving this extraordinary woman.

Camina's expression grew serious. "Now listen to me, Evan. Certain people have a knack for tracking a marked individual down and finding them even when that individual is certain they are invisible."

"Meaning me," Evan said. "I'm the marked individual."

"I'm afraid you are, and as I have told you Nuremberg for you is extremely perilous territory."

"I handled Pasha Shutkov, didn't I?"

"You did, and that was quite a feat." Camina stepped closer, lowered her voice. "But as well-trained as Shutkov was, you will now be dealing with another level of adversary."

"Tell me," Evan said in the same hushed tone.

"In Germany—in Berlin and in Nuremberg particularly—there are small groups of mercenaries. Not many, but they're extremely active. They'll take money from anyone—literally everyone."

Camina's hand on her arm, a gentle squeeze. "Have a care, Evan. You are clearly important to Lyudmila, which means you're important to me."

Evan felt a pool of warmth in the pit of her stomach. With an actual pang of pain she realized how much she missed Lyudmila.

"One other thing." Camina held out a slim black plastic wand five or six inches in length.

"Thank you," Evan said, "but I don't use eyeliner."

"And it is my hope you will never need to use this." She pressed the eyeliner case into Evan's hand, leaned in, whispered a word or two in Evan's ear. Evan put the case away with the cell phone.

Camina smiled as she kissed Evan on both cheeks in the European manner and held her close for a moment. They broke apart, as if reluctantly.

"Peace be upon you, sister," Evan said softly.

Camina smiled. "And upon you, peace."

14

After the revival, as she privately called it, after addressing the troops before their final battle, after leading them in a prayer which meant less than nothing to her, but which she delivered in stirring fashion, Lucinda Wells took herself into the back kitchen. Here she would not be disturbed by butlers, footmen, the cook, or the servers, all of whom knew better than to set foot into one of her sanctuaries. She busied herself in the pleasing ritual of making coffee. First she selected the beans—aged Sumatra today—ground them, put them into a press pot where the correct amount of hot water sat, waiting, straw into gold, and then she pressed slowly down with the heel of her hand, watching the elixir steadily darken, twilight into blackest night.

For a while she sat at the zinc-topped table in the center of the room, staring out the window as dusk crept through the grounds and shadows rose like temples among the trees. She emptied her mind of all that had gone before and simply breathed in prana.

When the coffee was ready she poured it into a cup that had been preheated and took her first sip, then another, and another. She set the cup into its saucer and with the complex taste of the Sumatran soil in her mouth her mind turned to sisters. She had three, though two were dead. Two of them she had never met. Though they came from the same mother, they had been born at different times in different places: America and Russia.

But, as always, her thoughts turned to her twin, Ana. Once they had been close. As children they played together, finished each other's sentences, thought alike. But at some point all that changed—or rather Ana changed. She became distant, then uncommunicative as her mind turned toward religious extremism, when that became her entire world.

For a time, Lucinda had wanted nothing to do with her, but gradually, after she contrived to meet Sam Wells, after she worked her magic on him, after he was hooked and she understood the true enormity of what being his wife might entail if only she could harness all the horses and get them moving in the same direction—the right direction—she decided a rapprochement was the correct way forward. Of course, she gave Ana all the money she wanted to build up First Flag, her fanatic cadre of Omega. She did this not out of the goodness of her heart or for family, she did it out of cold calculation. Her money fueled Ana's fanaticism, allowed her to take on more and more risk. Inevitably First Flag became more visible, which was Lucinda's aim. She used Ana and First Flag as a cat's paw, to keep attention away from her, what she was building here in America—the main event. And it worked spectacularly. Ana was relentlessly pursued, finally shot to death in her castle, her entire cadre killed in an explosion that tore her hideaway apart.

She took more coffee, feeling the darkness entering her like shadows moving in the corners of a room. She closed her eyes, the better to savor the confluence of flavors.

Now, out of the four sisters, only two remained—herself and Evan Ryder, whom she had never met and trusted she never would. She had been following Evan's career path as best she could. So much of it was classified and even her best hackers couldn't penetrate the cyber-vaults in which her exploits were hidden. But she knew enough. Her sister was dangerous—deadly dangerous, which is why she meant to keep her as far away from Omega as humanly possible. Especially after the fiasco of last spring. Foolishly, she had tried to get rid of Ryder. She had vastly underestimated her older sister's prowess. Worse, the failed attempt on her life had confirmed to Ryder the existence of an American cadre of Omega, the last thing Lucinda had wanted. Now she was obliged to live with the specter of being stalked by her.

On the other hand, for the past nine months she had used her contacts to hold the far-right ragtags' feet to the fire. They, riddled with FBI informants, had risen up again and again, another smokescreen she had manipulated into being, behind which Omega's real work was being accomplished, week after week.

With the last sip she opened her eyes. Darkness had overrun the estate, ribboned by the probing security lights. She hated those lights, even knowing they were essential. She was someone who preferred darkness, shadows, the night, especially after the full moon had been obliterated and the velvet came down. Thick and hard. What was stifling to some, frightening to others, was for her a release. The darkness meant freedom of a sort she could not obtain during daylight hours when phone calls, Zoom meetings, people coming and going took up every moment.

She was weary, but not because of the long day, the revival, or keeping a tight rein on her forces across the United States. After all, she had a phalanx of assistants, low-level functionaries, and computer experts to handle all the coordinating and heavily encrypted communications within the far-flung member councils. No, the heaviness she felt at the end of each day was due to something else altogether.

I need a cigarette, she thought, rising. She crossed to the door that led out to the vegetable garden, lying pale and fallow now in the security light. Her back to the mansion's wall, she opened a new pack and removed a cigarette. She'd been trying—and so far failing—to cut down, but nicotine was the only drug that calmed her.

It was times like these, she thought, when she missed Ana the most. It wasn't that she regretted using her twin—after all, Ana had made her own bed in Crazyville, all Lucinda did was give her enough rope to hang herself. None of this meant that Ana's loss hadn't left a hole inside her, a deep gulf that could never now be crossed. She was forever marooned on her side of the shore, the vast unknown darkness of Ana's world wiped off the face of the earth. It was curious, she thought now, how Ana's insanity had in some way defined herself, as if only by contrasting herself against madness could she assure herself of her own sanity.

The silence of winter was near absolute. A rare bird call or insect chirrup. No leaves rustling in the wind that rushed through the bare branches, merely the sound of the wind itself, like that of a giant sucking his teeth.

She extracted her lighter, was about to flip it open, when a shadow leaned over, presented a flame for her. She inhaled, straightened up and blew a cloud of smoke above their heads. Ambrose's familiar scent had identified him even before he moved into the light. For a time they smoked in companionable silence. Ambrose was Wells's only son, named by his mother after her favorite writer, Ambrose Bierce. Ambrose, who had, rather lazily she supposed, chosen to stick close to his father. His motives were of no import to her; she had set her sights on him from the moment they met. Early on, she discovered that Ambrose was the keeper of secrets. Not only did he know where all the bodies were buried in his father's life, he had excavated a secret about each of the men in his father's inner circle and so was able to manipulate them whenever he wished. Which, she supposed, was why he was in charge of keeping the family's vast business interests secure.

Between Lucinda and the First Son there sparked an incontestable sexual tension that drew them both like trembling moths to a flame. Around each other their bones grew soft, their hearts hammered, a thin sheen of dew gilded their skin. Not that anyone else, especially the Old Man, for that is what they called him in private, was any the wiser. They were both far too canny to give themselves away. In public, so to speak, they were all business, a relationship the Old Man understood and admired.

But they were connected by another, even deeper, emotion: their antipathy toward the Old Man. They were both venal, in their way, recognized that trait in each other and admired it. Ambrose had good cause for his antipathy. In the early stages of the marriage the Old Man had treated Ambrose's mother poorly. As the oldest, Ambrose had been witness to his mother's tears, her cleverly hidden bruises. He'd also been old enough to disbelieve her stories of falls or running into doors. He knew abuse when confronted with it online and so knew it when he saw it in real life. He had also winkled out the Old Man's loathsome predilection, the cause of his mother's eventual suicide. Everyone else believed the official line put out by the Old Man's publicity machine that she was drugged up, mentally unstable, and out of control. Alice had seen to that. Alice, his willing accomplice; she did everything he asked of her.

A nightbird was singing, alone, the last of his kind to have stayed in his summer habitat. Lucinda thought the sound as sad as a train's whistle in the small hours of the morning, a sound she knew well from her sleepless nights in Slovenia, reflecting on her homelessness.

"I've been meaning to ask you," Ambrose said now, "how it feels to be a goddess."

She laughed softly. "Shall I lie?"

"We know each other too well. To me you can say anything you want."

"Hm." Her eyes closed halfway, as if viewing a scene only she could see. The more she lied the more uncomfortably numb she became, to everyone and everything around her, but it was unclear whether or not she was aware of it. "It feels like sex." Her eyes opened wide, looking directly at him. "Sometimes I actually orgasm from the adulation."

"Those people are so stupid," Ambrose said with a contempt for what he called *civilians* endemic to the Wells family.

"Not so much stupid as ignorant," she contradicted. "And not even only that, actually. We have so successfully painted a picture of a world they desperately want to live in they are sold on its existence."

Smoke drifted from Ambrose's flared nostrils. "But you're not. That was one of your best performances."

"A masterclass in the huckster's old adage, 'There's a sucker born every minute.'"

They watched a crow lift off from a treetop, pass in shadow across the moon.

"So, tell me in more detail," she said at length, "what have we discovered from our trial balloon?"

For a brief moment while he gathered his thoughts Ambrose regarded the end of his cigarette, glowing like a firefly. He was slim and tall, with rather aggressive features, more like his late mother's than the Old Man's. His salt-and-pepper hair was thick and he wore it long, brushed back from his freshly shaved face.

"You were correct. There is a leak in the European network. The file we created found its way into the hands of an American field agent in Vienna, one Arne Armistad," he told her. "SVR agents were hot on his heels. He managed to take two of them out before he was shot to death by a third—a female, no less, posing as his girlfriend."

Lucinda grunted. "What kind of a field agent was this Armistad to have repeated intimate relations in enemy territory."

Ambrose let that go, knowing it wasn't a question; the answer was obvious. "So now the Russians have it."

"Amusing." Lucinda dropped the butt of her cigarette, waited for Ambrose to light the new one between her lips. "So the nonsense we put in there will keep the FSB cypher directorate busy for some time." She shot him a look. "How long will it be, do you suppose, before they start to pull their hair out?"

He chuckled.

She went on. "A leak. Tell me. Have you found the source?"

"Not yet. Our people are still working on the best angle."

She made a dismissive gesture. "Forget that. We don't have time for angles. Send our best operative directly to the beginning of the pipeline. Work forward from there."

Ambrose nodded. "Consider it done." He hesitated a beat before adding, "There's a screwball aspect to the agent Armistad."

Lucinda frowned, let out a cloud of smoke. "Do enlighten me," she said rather vaguely. She had wrapped her arms around herself to stave off the cold, but she was not yet ready to return inside. She continued to smoke ferociously despite knowing she'd be obliged to shower and change clothes; no point in her getting Sam riled up. Not that she gave a fig for Sam, he was simply a means to an end. What she failed to understand was that the persona she had created for herself when she met Wells had sunk so deeply into her she had no real sense of who she was. She despised America and all it stood for and yet here she was living the life of a billionairess without it giving her one ounce of pleasure. These days only one thing gave her pleasure and even that was superficial and fleeting.

Ambrose grunted. "The American field agent did not belong to the CIA or any other clandestine tentacle of the federal government."

"What?" Lucinda's attention abruptly laser focused. "Who the hell was running him then?"

"He was an employee of Parachute."

"Parachute?" Lucinda frowned. "The quantum computing behemoth?"

"The very one."

Lucinda rubbed her chin. "I'd heard their corporate espionage unit is first rate."

"It is," Ambrose affirmed. "Marsden Tribe has developed a critical thinking AI. This is entirely new terrain. It requires new levels of protection. Apparently, Tribe has hired someone to run his own top-notch espionage network, bypassing completely the governmental clandestine spheres."

A wave of apprehension passed through Lucinda's body, as if viscerally sensing a harbinger of trouble. "What the hell is Parachute doing getting involved in our pipeline?" she managed to get out.

"Don't know for certain as of yet. Hellaciously difficult, believe me. Parachute is a tough nut to crack, even for us. Far more resource-taxing than getting to the CIA or the Pentagon. Their quantum computing is proprietary. We're like an amateur runner trying to catch up to a professional marathoner."

Lucinda nodded abstractly. She disliked hearing about the company's inadequacies, especially ones she could not solve by allocating more money to them. "An educated guess will do for now," she said tightly.

"The scope and power of Tribe's espionage network tells me he doesn't trust his own government's ability to beat back the Russian and Chinese cyber-incursions," Ambrose said. "And he's right. The US government agencies' protections are so woefully inadequate they fail to meet even basic cyber-security standards." Ambrose shook his head. "Worse, he doesn't trust America's clandestine agencies that reward case officers for the number of foreign agents they recruit not how successful their networks are. Not surprisingly, those rushed foreign agents are either being killed or compromised and turned."

"Well, he's right about all of that." She shook her head. "But that doesn't explain why or how they've become involved with us."

Ambrose pursed his lips. Sometimes, even for him, it was an arduous task trying to take the temperature of her mercurial moods. Bless him, he understood that some days it was a fool's errand even to try. "The one thing we do know for a fact is that five months ago Parachute hired Benjamin Butler and Evan Ryder."

At the mention of her sister's name, Lucinda froze, her mind whirling at the implications. She stared out at the tips of the black trees at the far edge of the lawn, swaying in the wind. Their soughing seemed to speak to her. Evan Ryder was bad news, she knew that much. Lucinda's twin, Ana, did not survive her encounter with Evan. Now she had her answer. No wonder Parachute was interested in Omega. For nearly two years her sister had been obsessed with destroying Omega—first in Bavaria then last spring in the Carpathians where she got to Ana. All at once, her gaze snapped back to Ambrose. "I want your people on Ryder."

"Butler, too, I imagine."

"Yes, of course. He's proved himself to be another irritant."

Ambrose nodded. "In and of itself keeping tabs on anyone inside Parachute is like trying to grab an eel with your bare hands. Butler is difficult enough now that he's under Parachute's aegis, but Evan is on another level altogether."

"I'm not proposing you have someone follow her at all; that will surely end in our agent being killed," she said thoughtfully. "So . . ."

Ambrose took his time, smoking languidly while his gaze turned inward. "So," he said at length, "I'll send the agent to the contact who originally wrote the file, as we've already agreed to do. And let them wait for Ryder to come to them."

"And Butler?"

"As I said, easier than Ryder. I'll take care of him." Ambrose bit off each word as if it had a bitter taste. "Don't you worry."

A broad grin broke out across Lucinda's face. "And that's why you're the First Son."

He laughed. "And all this time I thought it was for something else."

She arched an eyebrow, inhaled smoke sharply, let it out with a hiss. "To the victor the spoils."

Ambrose lit another cigarette, placed it between her lips as he took out the butt of the one she had almost smoked down, got one last drag out of it before grinding it under his heel.

"Mm. Have you been upstairs yet?"

"You know how worked up Sam gets after his sermons on the mount." Her mouth quirked. "Besides, Alice manages that part of his life."

"Not just that part of his life. That malicious bitch watches over him as if he was ten years old."

Lucinda made a face. "To answer your question Alice hasn't yet texted me that the guest has left."

A ghost of a smile wreathed his lips. "And I suppose 'guest' is as good a name as any."

Lucinda rolled her eyes. "What is this one?"

Ambrose sighed. "Does it matter what he is?"

Her nostrils flared, leaking smoke.

Ambrose shrugged. "You married him." When she made no reply, smoking, silent, he added in a different tone of voice, "Did you know he was closeted when you married him?"

She took several deep drags on her cigarette before replying. "To answer your question, yes . . . and no."

"Meaning?"

Her head was wreathed in smoke. "Since I came on board, Sam's business interests have multiplied like rabbits. I daresay we own more offshore shell companies than anyone. They're well-named. Vast sums of monies are transferred from one to another in a dizzying acceleration. To the authorities around the world the sums are lost in our own private shell game." She tossed her head. "Bottom line, it doesn't matter."

At Ambrose's expression her eyes narrowed, the muscles at her jaw hinges standing out, white as bone. "Don't you dare judge me."

He immediately looked abashed. "That was not my intention."

"Really?" Her eyes flashed. "Then just what *is* your intention?"

He flicked the cigarette out from between her lips, replaced it with his mouth. At once their tongues entwined. He pressed himself against her, but she twisted away.

"Not here," she said thickly, leading him away. "You know better than that."

15

NUREMBERG, GERMANY

The late morning sunlight in Nuremberg was off kilter—bright as spring but curiously carrying no warmth at all. Evan had felt a distinct discomfort the moment she exited the train station. After sleeping through an entire day in the perfumed quiet of Camina's, unable to pull herself awake until the following evening, she had gathered herself, appreciating how much she had needed that uninterrupted rest, and taken a night train to Nuremberg.

Now as she walked down a quintessentially quaint Bavarian street lined with colorful half-timbered houses, storefronts, and Gothic churches made of the local red sandstone, she shivered inside her leather jacket. Glancing up, the sun seemed strange, as if it were cut out of white paper, flat as a disc. It was disconcerting, made her feel as though she was moving through the pages of an Old World children's book. Her sense of unease only increased the farther into the city she went. She recalled Camina Wagner's warning, *"Plenty of ghosts inhabit those streets at night, just not the children's storybook kind. It's no joke, but you'll probably find out for yourself. The past is particularly strong there, close to the surface, spread across the city; it was never truly laid to rest."*

Now that she was here, inside the medieval walls that surrounded the old city, nearing the Hauptmarkt, Evan had a clearer idea of what Camina meant. The city, the second largest in Bavaria, held great significance for Hitler and the Nazis in general. The city was once the stronghold of the Holy Roman Empire. In fact, the Hauptmarkt was built by Holy Roman Emperor Charles IV, himself. It was no secret that Hitler worshiped the HRE and aspired to create an empire as powerful and vast. Nuremberg was also of import to the Nazi Party. Due to its position in the center of Germany the city was the site of huge Nazi Party conventions—the notorious Nuremberg rallies.

As she had promised, she called Camina.

"I'm here," she said.

"Now it begins."

"Isn't that a bit melodramatic, Camina?"

"One would hope so, but you know as well as I do that in our business hope is not to be relied on." There was a momentarily silence. "Peace be with you, *habibti*."

"And with you. Always."

■   ■   ■

Horst Wessel, the man Camina had sent Evan to, had his shop in a traditional Bavarian house—what was often mistakenly called a chalet. It was a *bauernhaus*, a kind of farmhouse. Herr Wessel's cobbler workshop was on street level. It seemed that his living quarters were upstairs.

Evan entered the shop to the tinkling of tiny brass bells. Immediately she inhaled the scents of leather, wax, polish, and glue. To either side of her were shelves of black-lacquered wood displaying the styles of shoes you could have fitted and made to order. The low ceiling was striated with thick hand-hewn beams, black with age. There were several customers, a couple perusing the samples and a young woman being helped by an even younger salesperson in a much-scarred leather apron. The space had an Old World charm that felt cozy and warm in the manner of a family room with a stone hearth in which a fire blazed merrily.

Herr Wessel sat behind a waist-high cabinet facing the door. He looked up from his cluttered workbench, lifted his metal-rimmed spectacles onto his wide forehead, and rose from his stool. "How may I help you, good Fraulein?"

Evan smiled, crossed the shop, and handed Herr Wessel the slip of paper Camina had given her.

He slid the spectacles back onto the bridge of his nose to read the note. He was a barrel-chested man in his early sixties with a corona of hair around the edges of his otherwise bald pate. He had clear blue eyes, a Roman nose, and a square jaw. The age lines in his cheeks looked more like crevices, cracks in a parched land. Evan imagined him as a younger version with thick curling blond hair, a muscular build, and a calculating stare. He might have been formidable then. There was still a touch of that about him.

"Ah, yes," he said in a deep rumbling voice. "You have been expected, Fraulein." He moved an outsized beaten copper ashtray nearer to him, fired a gunmetal lighter, held the flame to a corner of the slip of paper and watched it carefully as it curled and blackened. After dropping it, he used a corner of the lighter to grind the remains into powder.

A careful and exacting person, Evan thought, automatically cataloging him in her memory, as she did with everyone she met. And yet there was something deeply disturbing about him, a sense that behind his eyes lurked pain as indelible as it was old, and if not fear then certainly apprehension.

"Herr Wessel, may I ask—"

"You must be hungry, Fraulein."

Understanding that he didn't want to talk here, she nodded. "Starving actually. I can't recall the last time I ate."

A smile cracked apart the deep lines of his face. "Then by all means we must take a meal." Setting aside his leather smock, he grabbed his tweed coat and came out from behind the cabinet. After a word to his assistant, he ushered her out onto the bustling street.

The restaurant he chose was Ecco Una Cucina, neither Bavarian nor American. So, then, Italian—a kind of a compromise, Evan thought as Herr Wessel asked for a window table. As it was only the beginning of the lunch service, that proved to be no problem. The restaurant was only a quarter full as opposed to the street, which was fairly packed. Hardly surprising as they were barely a block from the center of the Hauptmarkt. Shoppers, holiday makers, a flute of children laughing and pushing each other, the center of Nuremberg looked just like any European city. On the surface, that is. Once Evan looked more closely at the faces of the passersby, she saw a shadow around them and was once again reminded of the restless ghosts of victims of past atrocities, who had not been buried deep enough or long enough to have flown to happier planes of existence.

They were handed menus, ordered, and a bottle of red wine appeared on their table, was uncorked. They each drank half a glass.

"You know why I've come," Evan said as she set down her glass.

"Indeed." Herr Wessel refilled his glass. "Omega is a modern-day incarnation of Gnosticism. As does Omega the name Gnosticism comes from the Greek language. *Gnosis* means 'knowledge.' On the surface the basic tenet of Gnosticism is just this: salvation is transformational. Like its Judeo-Christian forbear, it is of course entirely faith based. It arose in the late first century after Christ, as these things are calculated. But in an irreparable break with both older religions what the Gnostics fervently believe is that salvation can only be attained through the discovery and dissemination of secret, inner knowledge. A central piece of that secret knowledge is that the death and suffering of Jesus were things that only *appeared* to happen. A modern-day analogue would be, oh, I don't know, science. To the Gnostics—and to Omega in particular—scientific facts are not facts at all; there is inner, secret knowledge only they have that rejects science. This numinous knowledge proves that, like Jesus's suffering on the cross, science only appears to exist. It's a screen, a false narrative. When Gnostics look behind that screen, they see the Truth."

Herr Wessel paused as their shared appetizer was set between them, along with a basket of fresh-baked bread. They spent some time eating, while, outside, the crowds, thickening, seemed to rush back and forth with a singular determination like waves anticipating an oncoming storm.

"So, about the Gnostics—or more to the point—Omega," Evan said, wiping her lips. "Where do they get this secret, esoteric knowledge they see as the Truth? From God?"

"No, not at all." Herr Wessel shook his head, called for more wine. "There have been, down through the ages, Gnostic demiurges—humans who are purported to possess the internal pathway to salvation, who know the Truth. But here we come to the widest divergence of Gnosticism. To them the Holy Spirit is female."

And for one brief, frightening instant there rose in Evan's mind the visage of her last remaining sister, Lucinda Wells.

And just as quickly it vanished, a trick of smoke and mirrors, as Herr Wessel raised a finger. "And this is essential to their core beliefs because in one of their heretical Gospels, Mary could not have been impregnated by the female divine being. There is no progeny possible from a lesbian interaction."

"There is no progeny possible from an immaculate conception either," Evan pointed out.

Herr Wessel gave her a skeptical look. "My dear, you are looking for logic in religion?" He shook his head.

"True enough," she said. "But what exactly is the Gnostic Truth?"

"If I tell you that the Gnostic Truth is the exact reverse of what is said you will say, 'But Herr Wessel, this I do not understand.' Well, most do not."

Evan once again felt the anxiety—or possibly fear—emanating from him and was disquieted. Something in the pit of her stomach began to stir and she felt her gorge rise. Something was coming, she could feel it. What—?

"A living example of their Truth must suffice: *'Do not be ignorant of me/*

For I am the first and the last/I am the honored one and the scorned one/I am the whore and the holy one/I am the wife and the virgin/I am the mother and the daughter.'"

He poured them both more wine. Evan didn't even want to look at it. Her eyes kept straying to the street beyond the window glass, the faces of those passing, strained, hard, distressed. Or was she only seeing a reflection of her own mounting agitation?

"I just quoted several lines from a core Gnostic work, 'The Thunder, Perfect Mind.' No one knows who wrote it, only that the poem is ancient. To understand fully, you need to hear more, Fraulein." And he returned to quoting the poem: *"'I am the staff of his power in his youth/and he is the rod of my old age/And whatever he wills happens to me/I am the silence that is incomprehensible/and the idea whose remembrance is frequent/I am the voice whose sound is manifold/and the word whose appearance is multiple/I am the utterance of my name.'"*

Evan felt lightheaded, all the colors around her seemed bleached of saturation, becoming pastels, as if she were seeing a scene from another time, another place. "The sayings of the first demiurge?" she said without conscious volition.

"Quite possibly." Herr Wessel nodded. "You see, I was right to tell you these things. I think you're beginning to understand. The most fascinating part of Gnosticism, what marks it as different from other major religions, is that it is also a philosophy. As I said, at its core it is transformational. You enter into it, accept it, and are transformed into Other."

"So blind devotion."

"Precisely."

Evan's lightheadedness abruptly escalated. She was terribly dizzied. She felt herself falling through her chair, through the floor of the restaurant, through the earth beneath, into the dark fastness of water. And now she was back in the flooded tunnel beneath the Cemetery of the Forgotten, being pushed under by Pasha Shutkov, lungs on fire, drowning . . .

. . . She gasped and Herr Wessel was by her side, one arm around her shoulders. "My dear," he said, "what is happening to you? Your hands are as cold as ice." His face was close to hers, the fissures on his skin deepening with the extent of his concern. "Are you ill? Shall I call a doctor? Take you to . . ."

That was when the glass in the window grew a spiderweb of cracks in the instant before it blew inward.

PART THREE

LOCUSTS

16

"When I was growing up my greatest wish was to fly," Ben said. "Now my desires are more prosaic."

An Binh, the physical therapist Evan's father, Dr. Reveshvili, had recommended, bent over Ben, who was lying facedown on a massage table, naked but for a Speedo, while An Binh needled him.

This was only their third day of sessions, but An Binh had already performed hours of treatments on Ben's injured body. Today's acupuncture was a surprise, as was An Binh herself. She was an athletic-looking woman with a meticulously sculpted face that was at once lined and radiant, which confused Ben, chiefly because it seemed to him that each line in her face belonged there, was meant as some sort of message. He had the strange feeling that her entire history was presented in her face, and yet he could read not one line of it; its language was entirely unknown to him. He had never before encountered a woman so small who was so powerful. Her power, much contained, came from within, he knew that much, and this, among other things about her, intrigued him. She could be anywhere from thirty to fifty as far as he could tell. But then as he grew older it seemed more and more difficult to judge other people's ages, possibly because age had little to do with the extreme experiences and pressures of the people with whom he dealt. And anyway what did age matter? She had a winning smile and hands that his body responded to the moment she touched him. She employed chiropractic, acupuncture, osteopathy, and traditional Chinese medicine on him. But it was clear to him from the start that she also was a master of a number of non-traditional methods, unknown in the West. The moment she first laid hands on him, her fingertips ran not to the place where he had been shot, but to, as she said, "points in your nervous system that nourish your impairment." When the first two-hour session was finished, she said, "You will walk, Mr. Butler." And then she left the gym in Isobel's basement without another word. She never said when he would walk or how she would effect such a miracle that flummoxed the Western surgeons who had exhaustively examined him.

She didn't say "Hello" or "Goodbye" when she entered or exited the gym. It was not, he quickly realized, that she was rude or even curt; she was simply all business.

But now, surprising him, as she added needles to his back, she said, "Tell me about growing up."

"Why do you want to know? I'm simply curious."

"Of course. You are a curious being by design." She took a breath. "Well, my knowing is part of your treatment." Her smile was crooked, like a young child's. "What comes before influences us in the present. For the weak and unlucky it comes to define them."

Since nothing she said or for that matter didn't say surprised him overmuch, he told her. "My story is not so terrible. It's hardly unique."

"Mm." An Binh added another needle. He felt a tiny prick then a flow of warmth running along an invisible stream inside his body. "Your story is unique to you, Mr. Butler. It is what led you to being here now under my ministrations, so it will inform and shape your treatment. Speaking thus is often an unlocking mechanism for the body." She took up each wrist in turn, measured his pulses. "Ah," she murmured to herself under her breath. Then, "Please continue."

"My mother was a Polish Jew. Her father—my maternal grandfather—was a merchant, and a clever one at that. At an early age he married his teenage sweetheart and while she was in her first trimester moved them to Beirut, Lebanon."

"To learn from the best," An Binh said, taking out one needle, applying another in an entirely different spot. Immediately, he felt something shift inside him.

"Exactly. So my mother was born in Beirut, as was I. She married an American lawyer, a WASP from Main Line Philadelphia."

"An unhappy marriage," An Binh said in her non-judgmental manner.

"Not in the beginning." Ben considered. "But, eventually, yes. They were, how shall I put it—incompatible."

"Is that the word you wished to use?" When he made no reply, she went on as if nothing untoward had happened. But she adjusted the needles again; she was decoding him. "What did their incompatibility mean for you?"

"I never wanted to be home with the two of them. But it was difficult being out in the city on my own."

"Why was that?" Having left five needles in him to marinate his nervous system in his own body's healing energy, his qi, An Binh placed a pinch of moxa on the small of his back. When she lit it he felt the heat immediately, and the incense-like fragrance of the curl of smoke lifting from a dried Asian plant not unlike mugwort, boosting the flow of his qi.

"I was tainted three times. I was a Jew, I was an American, and I was pale of face. I stuck out like a sore thumb, a pariah, baited, harassed, beaten, sometimes. There were days I wished I could be the Lebanese equivalent of Clark Kent, so I could fit in."

"And fly at night."

"Like Superman. In Beirut I felt like I was from Krypton, an outsider, a stranger in a strange land. I longed for a secret identity, where I could pass my tormentors in the street and they wouldn't give me a second look."

"I think, Mr. Butler, there is more to your past—much more."

He made no reply; she continued her work. "I too am a stranger in a strange land," she said at length, "here in your nation's capital."

"You don't want to be here?"

"Here is where the money is. I am deeply spiritual, as you see, but I am not about begging in the street with a wooden bowl, I want to live in the modern world with all its modern conveniences because, paradoxically, those things give me the space to find peace." She paused. "But, of course, there is a price. Here is where I am scorned and derided by every MD, every DO who couldn't get into a first-rate medical school. Here is where I ply my trade through word of mouth only. A pariah even in my own country who has chosen the shadows. Living like you in the margins of Western society." She looked down at him. "You have your longed-for secret identity at last, Mr. Butler. But I wonder if you are happy."

There had been a risk in hiring An Binh. To work on Ben, to hopefully heal him, she required information about Ben that was hidden from outsiders. But Isobel put the Parachute quantum computers to work. The result: they knew every day of the woman's life from her birth to a Chinese mother and a Vietnamese father, until the day they agreed to hire her. She described in detail her slow and extensive travels throughout Asia—to Nepal and Tibet, throughout Indonesia and Sumatra, gathering syncretic medical knowledge. She had never been approached by any Chinese or North Vietnamese agent; in fact just the opposite, she said. Both hierarchies avoided her; she was a half-breed, in their eyes a noncitizen.

In sum, she was precisely how she presented herself. As part of their agreement she was living here in Isobel's villa for the duration of the treatment. Isobel made sure she was well-compensated for her time. Still, observing security protocols they were careful not to speak of anything sensitive in her presence. In any event, An Binh was under the impression they were involved with counteracting would-be corporate espionage.

Ben felt an ill-defined sense of foreboding. "What do my pulses tell you?"

At that moment, Isobel stepped into the gym. "How is the treatment going?"

"For today, not quite finished." An Binh began to take out the needles one by one.

"Any news?" Ben said, turning his head.

"Please keep your head still, Mr. Butler," An Binh said without a trace of admonition. He did as she asked.

"Unfortunately, yes." Isobel gestured for An Binh to leave them. Then she stepped closer to Ben, lowered her voice. "That e-file we went to so much trouble to obtain is a dummy."

"A dummy? Are you sure?"

"The computer has sifted through ten million possibilities. It has confirmed there is no message. It's a dead end."

"So, what? It was a ruse?"

"A charm, as we say in Israel, but to what end?"

"Two possibilities come to mind. Either a diversion to keep our eye off the ball, or to flush out a traitor in their pipeline." They both knew that possible traitor would be a Russian mole, since the SVR knew about the e-file even before Evan did.

"Possibly both," Isobel mused.

"And our sales rep"—he meant Evan—"is right in the middle of it."

Isobel crossed her arms over her chest, a sure sign that she was agitated. "I'd very much like to inform our rep."

"They're out of call range."

"I'm afraid so."

"Still, that's best."

"Agreed." Isobel nodded, called An Binh back in.

The therapist helped Ben roll over onto his back and then into a sitting position on the massage table, legs dangling over the side. She then pushed a bar suspended from the ceiling toward him. He reached out with both hands, grasped it. An Binh pulled on a rope and the bar started to rise, Ben with it. She kept at it until he was standing up, his weight supported by his arms and the bar so he was in effect weightless. And yet he stood without any tremors in his legs. An Binh had been working his leg muscles hard twice a day.

"One hand," An Binh said now.

"You sure?" Ben asked.

An Binh's eyes were upon him, calm as a lake at sunrise. "It is your own body that must answer."

He nodded, yet still hesitated. Isobel could see that he was sweating. From the moxa or from anxiety she could not tell. Possibly it was both.

"Body, not mind," An Binh reminded him. "Do not think."

All of a sudden, he let go of the bar with his left hand. Immediately his knees sank.

"Breathe into your qi," An Binh said softly. "Remember to breathe into your lower belly."

He did, and his knees straightened. He was standing, only semi-suspended.

He took one step, then another before he had to grip the bar with both hands.

"Well, would you look at that." Isobel whistled. "It's a bird. It's a plane . . ."

They all laughed, even Ben. Especially Ben, exhausted and happy.

17

A hail of glass, a sleet of glitter, a hard rain, the explosion of plate glass shards battered the table and its occupants full force, blasting the plates, glasses, and cutlery, splattering food onto ceiling, walls, and floor, rocking the table itself.

As for Evan and Herr Wessel, they were lifted out of their seats. Bits of glass clattered against Wessel's back, but his clothes saved him from serious damage. Evan's forearm, up protecting her face, took the brunt of the force, so that for a moment it looked like a porcupine's leg, until she shook the shards off. None of them had penetrated her leather jacket.

Outside, there was singing, which seemed incongruous to her, even absurd, until, recovering from the explosion's aftermath, the words began to filter through the screams and shouts of everyone around her.

Gradually, she realized it wasn't singing so much as mass chanting: *"Behold, then, her utterances and all the writings that have been completed. Give heed, then, listeners, and you also, angels/And those who have been sent/And you spirits who have arisen from the dead/For we are the ones who alone exist/We who follow her, and her demiurge/And we will suffer no one to judge us/You will find us here/And we will live and will not die again."*

She saw the rock then, lying on the floor, perfectly innocent until someone hurled it through the window. Turning, she lifted her head slowly, tentatively, to see a mob of masked men and women, marching, arms linked in solidarity, taking up the entire width of the road. It was they who had smashed the windows of the restaurant, as they were doing now to the windows of other storefronts as they twined like an enormous serpent, restless, relentless, unbroken.

The voices came again, harsh, green with youth, crusty with absolute conviction, lifted as one, which seemed nearly impossible. *"We are hated everywhere and have found love in the places hidden from you/We are Life and what you have called Death/We are the New Law and what you have called Lawlessness/We are the ones you pursue, the ones you seek to restrain."*

The masks, she saw now, were black, with a white cross bisected by a golden O, and her heart doubled its beat until it became like a stone in her chest. She recognized the symbol of Omega.

"We are the ones whom you scorn," the mob continued to chant in their destruction of all that surrounded them. *"You brand us unlearned, but it is from us you will learn."*

She pulled Herr Wessel toward her. His eyes were glazed with terror and in a flash of insight she realized the anxiety she had felt coming off him was in anticipation of this demonstration.

The massed chanting was louder now, ringing through the streets like medieval church bells summoning soldiers at the advance of the newly sighted enemy. *"She is the knowledge/She finds those who seek after her/She commands those who ask of her and the power in her knowledge/The power of the angels, who have been sent at her word/The power of her demiurges in their seasons by her counsel/And of the spirits of every man who exists with her and of women who dwell within her/She is the one who is honored, and who is praised by the disciples/It is she who is despised scornfully by the ignorant, fearful others."*

Everyone in the restaurant was crouched behind tables, or curled on the floor, afraid to move, terrified to try to escape the violence. Escape where? Into the arms of the Omega mob? The answer came with another rock thrown through the window, this one larger, hurled farther than the first. An incendiary fireball of screams and shouts erupted as every customer left in the restaurant made for the door in a mad scrum, pushing, shoving, cursing as they all tried to squeeze through the door at once.

Among them, Herr Wessel who, despite what cuts and scrapes had been inflicted on him, nevertheless attempted to impart one last piece of intel to her. As if he had tuned in to her wavelength, his cracked lips opened and he whispered so softly she was obliged to put her head next to his. "You must . . . this was preordained . . ."

"Preordained?" She wondered if she had misheard him, but his head bobbed up and down.

"I brought you here. I did . . . You know . . ."

Evan shook her head. "What?" she said, but he seemed not to hear her or to have the strength to answer.

The clamor outside, the terror and the dread inside were reaching a fever pitch.

"You must find Schrodinger," he stammered. "Heinrich Schrodinger. He is out there . . . somewhere . . . he's the German demiurge. He—"

"Heed us! Join us! For in our ignorance we possess the hidden knowledge of the universal spirit/You who have told lies about us, heed the truth about us now/For we are strength and we are fear/We are war and we have come."

"I have it on good authority that the origin of the e-file you seek is with someone within Schrodinger's group." Herr Wessel's face blanched bone-white, veins like ropes spasmed in his temples, and he was no longer able to control himself. Like a panicked squirrel running directly into the tires of an oncoming car, he bolted through a narrow gap in the doorway directly into the mass of the Omega demonstrators.

Though Evan hurled herself after him, he vanished into the marching, angrily shouting crowd like a swimmer going under for the last time. The energy they exuded was like a dark force, blotting out the sky. She hit the wall of demonstrators at full tilt, slipping sideways at the last instant. In this way she snaked through the outmost line, but immediately thereafter was elbowed about her head and shoulders by the next line, turned upon like she was a street urchin caught trying to pick the pocket of an innocent tourist.

She struck out, sending two men off-balance, arms flying, stumbling into those in front and behind them. Then someone slammed his hand into the side of her head and she gasped. Stars sparked and her vision clouded at its periphery. She struggled for breath and would have gone under like Herr Wessel before her had she not grabbed another demonstrator's shoulders, fingers digging into the cloth of his jacket. He tried to fight her off, but she kneed him in the groin, slipped off his mask as he bent double, pulled it on over the lower half of her face. She could smell the rankness of his exhalations, beer and wurst combining to turn her stomach. She pressed ahead. Someone pressed a tire iron into her hand. At first, she tried to press it back to him, but then she realized that was not the way to Heinrich Schrodinger. At the same time, she understood that this path she was about to embark on would be a particularly nasty one, so she steeled herself before swinging the tire iron into a shoe shop's window. A cheer went up from those around her, the press of the demonstrators along with their massed chant sweeping her into the heart of the human storm like a rushing tide.

There were more shops to maim and she did her part, sick at heart, but aware that this was the surest route to Schrodinger. Two young men to her left wrenched a trash can off the pavement, used it as a battering ram to splinter a jewelry shop's door. To her right a trio of young women lit torches, tossed them nonchalantly through shattered windows, laughing and chanting all at once. As the violence ratcheted up the formations became ragged, then unidentifiable. The demonstration became a melee. It was inevitable, Evan thought, as she joined in the rampage. The demonstrators had become terrorists. That too was inevitable, she thought, as she was sucked into the mob's center.

Here, as in the eye of a hurricane, there maintained an eerie calm, space between the handful of people in the vortex. This group was almost evenly split between women and men. More of a surprise was that they were almost all young—in their early or mid-twenties. These unruly upstarts were emblematic of the new generation of Germans who hadn't seen, or if they had believed, photos and newsreels of the Holocaust. There was the knife-edged barbarism masquerading as fascism, bent on ethnic and religious cleansing. A bright new world for a new Germany. Forgotten were the chains of the past, the horror, the guilt, the pledge "Never Again." For these young women and men it was "Yes, Again. And This Time We Will Triumph."

She was still contemplating the terrifying repercussions of this Nuremberg branch of Omega being composed of so many young people when she was shoved to her left.

A young man, blond, blue-eyed, Nordic of mien or, if you prefer, Aryan, large and intimidating as only fascists can be, invaded her personal space, glaring at her. Evan wondered whether there was a school of fascism somewhere that turned out these cookie-cutter bullies.

"Hey, you," he said in a voice larded with hateful menace, "I don't recognize you."

"How can you tell with my mask on?" *Keep it aggressive*, Evan told herself. *Keep ratcheting the nasty.*

"Who are you?" Blondie barked.

"Yes, who?" This from another young man. His light eyes crinkled at their corners—a grin or a grimace? It was difficult to tell. A tattooed snake coiled on his right temple. "Perhaps she's a Verfassungsschutz plant, eh?" He was referring to Germany's internal state security service, which the prime minister had put in charge of surveilling the country's right-wing extremists.

"She wouldn't be the first," Blondie said, sticking his face so close to Evan's she could smell him, sweat, aggressive pheromones, a deep bitterness.

"But she could be the last." Leaning in, Snake gripped her biceps, about to jerk her off her feet. "Look at her face. Someone's been at her good. Maybe she's a lousy lay."

Evan buried her fist in the indentation below his shoulder, then swept his hand away. "Off," she said tightly. Behind him the three young women she had noticed before had turned their heads toward the altercation, flowers lifting their petals sunward. The mob in general seemed to have reached the end of the territory they wished to terrorize; they had come to a halt, faced outward, knives and handguns at the ready to intercept any interference. But at this point the street was clear of bystanders. All the tourists and visitors had long ago fled. Shop doors were locked and, where possible, shuttered. The takeover was complete and an unnatural chill, fed by dread and panic, had invaded the street. It felt like the end of the world.

"'Off,' she says." Snake turned to Blondie. His laugh was like the growl of a wolf. "'Off.'" As if he couldn't believe a woman would speak that way to him. His head swiveled back to her. "Is that an order, Fraulein? Hm?" He reached out, ran the back of his hand down her cheek. At the last instant, his forefinger lifted and hooked the top of her mask, started to pull it down.

She reared back even as she slapped him hard across the face. She assumed Blondie would intervene but he did nothing, watching her, arms folded across his chest. The three young women had crept closer, worming their way through the mob. Far off a siren started up.

"Speaking of the Verfassungsschutz," one of the young women said.

The sirens—the sound had suddenly multiplied, like reflections in a mirror—increased in volume. The authorities were on the move, coming their way.

"This is no time to hang around," the young woman said. She had ice-blond hair, dark eyes, a face like a fox.

"We've made our point, yes?" Blondie was clearly addressing Snake. "Let's get lost. We'll reassemble back at—"

"What about this one?" Snake's eyes were centered on Evan.

"What about her?" Blondie snapped. "Let her crawl back to whatever hole she crawled out of."

"The Verfassungsschutz," Snake said, venom in his voice.

Blondie shrugged. "She's gotten into your head, Rolfie boy."

Rolf drew out a handgun. "I'm gonna make sure she's out and stays out, permanently."

Blondie, who had turned his head toward the direction in which the sirens were fast approaching, whipped around. "Not now, you idiot. Bloodletting is the last thing we need."

"And what if she is Verfassungsschutz?" This from the fox-faced woman. "Starting an all-out war is not what today is all about."

Rolf gritted his teeth. "It is now."

"Anyone can pop someone," Blondie said. "You think that makes you a big man? Put the fucking gun away."

When Rolf made no move to do so, the fox-faced woman said, "You hate her so much, why don't you teach her a lesson the right way? Fight her bare-knuckle."

Blondie slapped Rolf on the shoulder. "More fun in hurting her than killing her, eh, Rolf?"

The sirens wailed. The Verfassungsschutz was closing in. The mob was dispersing quickly, silently slipping into shadowed side streets and back alleys.

"That I'd want to see," Blondie said with a smirk, but whether it was for her or Rolf Evan couldn't tell.

"But not here," Fox-face said.

Rolf shrugged. "So take her with. It will be fun beating the living shit out of her."

18

MOSCOW

Minister Kusnetsov saw Alyosha leaning against Kata and pointed. "You!" he barked. "Get the fuck out of here! Now!"

But Kata put a hand on Alyosha's arm. "Stay right where you are," she said. "This is where you belong."

That was last night. Kata had been in this windowless cell now for sixteen hours. It was made of rebar reinforced concrete, a foot thick. It, like all the cells, was soundproofed. As the saying went, *In the Lubyanka no one can hear you scream.* As the cells were unpainted there was always a haze of concrete dust that, settling in the first hour of her incarceration, clung to her like a second skin. Intermittently, she coughed. A stainless-steel toilet was affixed to one wall, a bunk to the opposite wall, on which she was now perched. A blanket as thin as the mattress provided scant relief from the damp chill. In the center straddling a large drain, ominously stained, a metal chair, similarly stained, was bolted to the floor. The glaring overhead light, screened off by a metal grid, went off at odd intervals, staying off just long enough for her to fall asleep, only to be jerked awake when it came on again. She was deep within the dreaded innards of the Lubyanka, where she and Alyosha had been taken. She had not seen nor spoken to Alyosha. Despite her assurances of protection, for all she knew Alyosha could be dead—or worse. And anyway, she couldn't even protect herself, let alone another person.

The center of her face throbbed as if it had grown its own heart. It had been bandaged upon her arrival, the clotted blood cleaned off. She touched her cheeks. Swollen and no doubt discolored. *That fucker, Borya,* she thought. *At least I gave better than I got.* And then she sighed. *I saved Alyosha from him only to get her into this.* She felt disgusted with herself. *Better to get that out now. I'll need all my faculties when Kusnetsov arrives.* Sooner or later, she was sure he would.

One other thought was uppermost in her mind: Lyudmila would be so disappointed in her. She had an attachment to Lyudmila that went beyond friendship. She had reached out and saved Kata when she was at her most vulnerable within the FSB structure. But Kata knew very well there was nothing even Lyudmila could do for her now. In the Lubyanka, she was beyond anyone's help.

She closed her eyes, as if that gesture would make her invisible to the constant surveillance of the CCTV camera set up near the ceiling, but it did no good. She knew very well there were three things that happened to prisoners unfortunate enough to wind up here. All of them began with torture of the most excruciating kind. Then: a lifetime here, which was short; a lifetime in a Siberian labor camp, which was shorter; and death. There were no other possibilities she'd ever heard of, not even in the tall tales bandied about within the FSB known collectively as Legends of the Lubyanka.

Her eyes sprang open at the sound of the door opening. Someone stood in the doorway but with the glare of the light it was only a shadow. The screech of metal against concrete invaded the cell as the figure, dragging a chair with him, entered. She could see now that it was Minister Kusnetsov. The door swung shut behind him with an echoing clang.

He positioned the chair so it was facing the one already there, sat in it, then gestured to her to take a seat in the bolted-down chair. She rose, stepped over to the empty chair, stood behind it, fingers clutching the back. Her knuckles were white with tension.

Kusnetsov looked up at her in her blood-stained dress. He had divested her of both her emerald ring and the necklace of emeralds and shark's teeth before they'd left the dacha. The ring was the symbol of her power and status within his sphere.

"Sit." His voice was soft, neutral. When she made no move, he said, "Kata, we will not have our talk until you are seated."

She moved backward, never taking her eyes off him. When she felt the sharp edge of the cot against the backs of her knees, she sat down.

Kusnetsov smiled and shook his head. "In the chair, Kata." He gestured. "I won't ask again."

When she did not rise, he clucked his tongue against the roof of his mouth, made to rise. "If I leave here now I won't be back." His eyes glittered. "Neither will anyone else."

She believed him. She had no choice. When she was seated opposite him, he said, "I have news of your friend."

"Is Alyosha alive or dead?" Her voice sounded thin and creaky, as if it needed to be oiled.

Kusnetsov drew a bottle of water out of his pocket, handed it to her.

She hesitated briefly, then thought, *What's the point?* Opening it, she drank half of it in one go. "Alyosha?" she said, her voice stronger.

Now it was his turn to hesitate, and she knew she deserved it. Her gaze, however, did not falter. She still had the power—pathetic though it was—to deny him that satisfaction.

He seemed to have crawled inside her head, reading her intentions because his smile returned. With a start she realized there was something distinctly reptilian about it, and she felt sickened.

"Your friend is alive," he said, deliberately not using her name. "In fact she's in the cell next to this one."

"Is she well?"

"We need to talk about other matters."

He paused as if daring her to exert her will in a fruitless situation that could only humiliate her further. The moment he revealed himself she felt a surge of rage she found almost intolerable, as if an army of fire ants were crawling over her skin. In the moments following, another part of her took a step back, understanding this was a test—not from him but from herself. She had never been adept at self-discipline; she was always slipping her leash, which is what constantly infuriated the minister. She knew that if she was ever going to get out of here, let alone be reinstated, she had to tread very carefully. She had to show him that she would toe the line, that she would not cross it again, that she would not even come near it.

In this frame of mind, she said, "Let us speak of them then."

"You attacked and severely injured a high-ranking official of the FSB."

"I retaliated after he attacked me." She pointed to her heavily bandaged nose and surrounding it the deep purple bruises marring the flesh around both her eyes.

"You were intruding on—"

"His beatdown and imminent rape of a subordinate."

"She's not in his directorate."

Her face flushed as she felt a spurt of outrage trying to clog her throat. *Take a step back*, she warned herself. "That's your answer," she said in slow measured tones.

He shook his head again. "Face facts, Kata, no one cares about your friend." He shrugged. "Whether or not she gets raped is of no consequence to any of us in power."

"Have you no humanity in you?" she said in the same measured tone.

"I am who I am, Kata. We are all leopards in this jungle."

For some reason she struggled to comprehend, these words sent a chill through her, and her mind flashed on Alyosha.

"And as for you," Kusnetsov said. "You will have to pay for the crime you committed. Borya Igorevich is dead. Blood poisoning. Your aim was true. The spike heel you jammed into him punctured his femoral artery. By the time he hit the hospital there was nothing to be done.

"So," he added briskly. "A capital crime. Death."

She felt the crushing weight of fate come down on her. Is this really where her life had led her, into a trap where even gnawing her leg off wouldn't free her?

But in the darkness enshrouding her there remained a sliver of hope. She had one card to play, the one she had been holding in reserve. The problem was it was a down card—she would not know how high it was until she revealed it and saw his response.

Endeavoring to set herself on this single-minded course, she forged ahead. "Did you see Borya Igorevich before he was carted out?"

Anger flared behind the minister's eyes. "You don't get to call him Borya Igorevich," he said stiffly. "He is neither your friend nor your equal. If you mean Director Arsenyev—"

"Just answer the question, Minister." Now was not the time to address him informally as she had previously.

His teeth clacked together and he shook his head. "What a fucking piece of work you are. I put it down to your American upbringing. No sense of propriety or politesse."

She laughed harshly. "Politesse in the FSB. Come on, Minister. Cut the bullshit. You and I both know we find politesse an inconvenience. I too am what I am. You can't expect me to change my spots, and you cannot force me to do it." He started to refute her but she gave him no chance. "Since you can't or won't answer my question I'll just carry on. Borya Arsenyev, director of Department 73, is a member of Omega."

Kusnetsov opened his mouth, closed it again just as quickly. He fairly goggled at her. "Slava Baev was so wrong about you. Not only are you a dangerous criminal, you're also deranged.

"I've had enough of you to last me several lifetimes." He stood up.

Kata gave no sign that his words meant anything to her. She had turned to stone; she had set her mind to it. Nothing he said against her now would affect her in any way, shape, or form. She stared at him, unblinking, immobile. Implacably, she went on. "If you had taken a look at the director—a close look—you would have seen his tattoo."

"I did see it, as it happened. But I was more concerned with Borya Igorevich's state of health."

"Then you missed what I didn't." She took a breath. "Sit down, Minister. Please."

Kusnetsov hung back. He looked at her as if he had opened a box only to find inside an uncoiling hooded cobra. "You can't expect me—"

"Leave then." She forced herself to shrug, to keep her voice nonchalant. To show any weakness now would be a fatal mistake, her instincts were quite clear on the matter. On the other hand, she needed to maintain the right degree of respect or she would lose him—and her life. Alyosha's too, she had no doubt. "But no gambler worth his salt leaves with cards still on the table. Bets unfinished."

He gave a small bark, reminding her of a dog at the end of its leash. Then he too shrugged. The moment he sat down she knew she had him. But after all, what she said next was for his benefit as well as hers and Alyosha's.

"You told me you believe Pasha Shutkov was betrayed. You insinuated that the leak came from inside FSB." She cocked her head. "You remember that?"

The minister suddenly looked bored. "Vividly."

"As it turns out you were right; I was wrong."

Kusnetsov peered at her with narrowed eyes. "Continue."

She took a breath. "Alyosha's lover was Pasha Shutkov."

"How is that pertinent to this conversation?"

Pointedly she ignored his nonchalant response. "It happens that Director Arsenyev was hounding Pasha to get the same Omega tattoo," she said. "I was about to ask her if she knew of any other members of Department 73 who had the tattoo."

"Pity we can't ask the director." But Kusnetsov's tone had changed, no matter how subtly.

"I very much doubt you'd have dragged anything out of him."

"Don't be naïve," the minister scoffed. "I'd bring him down here."

"It wouldn't matter," Kata said calmly, authoritatively. "Omega is a faith-based organization. They are, to a person, unshakable in their beliefs. That's what makes them so dangerous."

At this, he leaned forward. She knew he was interested in what else she had to tell him.

"So as it turns out, your dear Borya Igorevich was not only director of Department 73, a division of SVR so highly classified that almost no one knows where it trains its agents, he was also a traitor to the Russian Federation. Department 73 works outside the normal constrictions of the FSB, its mission so vital that it's virtually autonomous." Her eyes grew bright in proportion to how deeply his were looking inward as he digested the implication of what she was saying.

"Is it any wonder that Pasha Shutkov was compromised? That an enemy of the Federation knew he would be in Vienna?"

For some time, Kusnetsov did not move, sat still, staring at her. Time seemed to telescope, as if a whole day was passing before Kata's eyes. This strange temporal sensation dissolved the moment he stood up. He stepped to the door, taking his chair with him, and glanced up at one of the CCTV cameras. At once the door opened.

"It will be taken care of, believe me," he said. "Within the day we will uncover the ones with the Omega tattoos and bring them here."

"Under articulated interrogation, I imagine."

He shot her a hard stare. "You imagine correctly."

She shook her head. "A waste of time, Minister. First because these men are trained for immunity to torture. Second because, as I said, Omega is faith-based. They'll give you nothing."

"In that event, they will be shot dead."

"Leaving, what, the remaining men who may or may not be Omega recruits or potential Omega recruits to continue on."

Kusnetsov gripped the back of the chair he'd brought into the cell. "The answer is to wipe them all out. Remake Department 73 from the ground up."

"The problem with that," she said, "is that we now have proof of Omega's infiltration of the FSB." She cocked her head. "Whom would you trust to head the new Department 73?"

He barked a laugh. "Please don't tell me you're angling for the job."

"I already have a job."

His face darkened. "You have nothing," he answered her savagely.

She neither cringed nor hesitated. She saw her path clearly now. "You didn't offer me the head of Zaslon for nothing, Minister. I can be of use to you now. I'm the only one you can trust absolutely to root out Omega."

"You killed Borya Igorevich. You will pay for that crime." His voice, dark as midnight, echoed through the room with a terrifying finality.

19

"You're Heinrich Schrodinger, I take it," Evan said as her blindfold was removed. They had taken her mask and they'd pulled theirs down as well, revealing their full faces.

Blondie gave her a big grin, turned to Fox-face, waving the blindfold like a flag of victory. "Listen to her, Ghislane. Now she invokes Schrodinger's name."

So was he Schrodinger or not? Would Schrodinger be part of the riot or would he only have masterminded it?

Ghislane's eyes narrowed as she gestured to one of the women she was with, a petite blonde with sharp cheekbones and chin. "Elke, pat her down. Make sure she isn't wearing a wire or a GPS tracker."

Elke looked vulnerable which meant, Evan thought, she must be the opposite—she wouldn't have lasted ten minutes with this bunch if she wasn't. Elke stepped forward to comply. Her hands when they reached out were strong, efficient, assured. Evan was aware of her strength and force of will. Many would not until it was too late. Her eyes did not leave Evan's, looking for a flinch or the inner withdrawal caused by fear. She found nothing of the sort. Evan made no move to stop her; there was no need. She was clean. She wanted them to know it. She wanted them reassured. She had grabbed this opportunity that fate in the name of Herr Wessel had gifted her and run into it with her eyes wide open. She knew the risks she was taking with these people. They glared at her with a black hatred that might have withered anyone else; Evan merely skated past it like a water spider skimming the surface of a toxic lake.

"She's good," Elke said, stepping away after she'd done her work.

"Keep an eye on her," Ghislane said.

Blondie's face darkened. "That should be my job."

"You," Elke said with a curl to her lip, "probably want to jump her." She observed Evan with a critical eye. "I guarantee this one wouldn't let you. Like as not she'd hurt you first."

Blondie growled at her.

"That's enough," Ghislane barked. Then, to Evan, "Hey, you. You got a name?"

"Evan."

Ghislane lit a cigarette. She gave her an enigmatic look, blew smoke in her face. Evan didn't blink and Ghislane noticed that. She noticed everything. "Whether Evan is your real name or not you're going to be sorry you ever stepped into this hornet's nest."

Late in the afternoon the light fell at winter's bidding. So near the solstice, the longest night of the year, the turning of the tide, the day was weak, wounded by the distant sun. An icy wind followed, rushing through the stunted field, making it whisper, giving a false sense of summer's insects. But there was nothing there, no life at all.

They were somewhere in the countryside, how far from Nuremberg she couldn't say, but judging by the length of the ride not too far from the outskirts. Far enough, anyway, that the police sirens were no longer an issue. As they were leaving there had seemed to be more and more sirens blaring and they'd had to make several detours in the green florist's van they had shoved her into. The Verfassungsschutz were clearly out in force, no doubt due to a flurry of urgent calls by terrified shopkeepers.

Evan did a further assessment. Pumped up with anger, bitterness, and malice, this cadre's hair-trigger reactions were no surprise. But as with all terrorists their animus was inverted. Turning it outward was an unconscious survival instinct, preventing them from being plowed under by their own self-hatred. That knowledge was a psychological weapon she could use. Ghislane, clearly the dominant female of the group, was someone she thought she could deal with. She above all the males would be inclined to talk before delivering a pounding.

But first she needed to get past Rolf.

No time for more thought as Blondie reapplied her blindfold. She was bundled back into the van and off they went. She judged they drove for about twenty minutes, but of course it was impossible to say in what direction. She was sure they had not re-entered the city, however, for there was hardly any traffic noise.

At length, the van decelerated, rolled to a stop. She was hauled out, sent stumbling along a deeply pitted gravel path that hadn't been tended in some time. She was halted abruptly, roughly. A metal door screeched open on hinges badly in need of WD-40. Pushed from behind, she felt the man-made solidity of concrete beneath her feet, the surface perfectly level. The scents of human sweat, pot smoke, spilled beer, the sour reek of cheap wine. She heard the echoing of their footfalls, their voices, and knew they were in someplace large, abandoned. But, considering the remnants of scents, hardly forgotten. Repurposed, perhaps, by itinerant druggies collecting locals for all-night raves.

As he had before, Blondie turned darkness into light. He removed her blindfold and Evan blinked, eyes adjusting to the gloom. They were standing on a narrow walkway that overlooked a vast rectangular space with rounded ends that had once been a swimming pool. On either side of the erstwhile pool were lines of what looked like lockers or, anyway, doors to other parts of the building, the same as those at her back. Above her soared a domed ceiling held aloft by thick masculine arches interspersed with large windows.

"*Volksbad,*" Ghislane said. "This public bath was abandoned two decades ago. We use it now." She inhaled deeply. "At night we charge admission to those eager to get totally fucked up."

"It's quite the scene." Blondie grinned. "Maybe you'll get to see it."

"The hell she will," Rolf said, and there was laughter all around. "She'll be lucky if she ends up blind as a bat."

There were six of them: Blondie, Rolf, and Uwe, and the three females—Ghislane, Elke, and Romy. Together, they took her through one of the doors, down a flight of stairs that stank of urine and vomit.

"Your headquarters needs a good cleaning."

"Yeah?" Rolf said. "After I'm done with you, you can go over it on hands and knees with your tongue."

It wasn't that fear was unknown to her. She had in fact been living with fear all her adult life. It was that she had been trained to consider fear a companion, to walk side by side with it, rather than having it in her face. Fear caused you to make the wrong decisions, to hesitate when acting instantly without thought was the only thing that would save you.

And so she entered the arena of the drained pool with the others. In the center they stopped. Blondie gave her one last shove.

"Those who are about to harm you salute you," he said in an ironic tone. "Isn't that right, Rolf?"

A lopsided grin from Rolf, who had a mouth like the blade of a chainsaw. He handed over his pistol when Blondie held out his hand. Then they all left, climbing back up out of the pool, turning to watch.

She and Rolf, all that was left.

She lifted her head and her gaze settled heavily on Ghislane. "Bread and circuses," she said with a quirk at one side of her mouth.

And that was the moment Rolf chose to attack. He rushed at her like a maddened bull, and like a matador she stepped aside in a perfect matador's *molinete*. She stuck her foot out to trip Rolf up but she was overly confident. Reaching down as he hurtled forward he grabbed her ankle, yanked her off her feet. Down she went to the ringing applause and cheers from the avid spectators.

Rolf loomed over her, punched her in the stomach. All the air went out of her. She saw lights flashing behind her eyes and a certain darkness at the periphery of her vision. She knew she was in a vulnerable position, especially with a male of Rolf's size and weight. She had to get out from under.

She slapped him hard across the cheek then spat in his face. His rage rose over the top until all he could think of was what she had done to him. Spread-legged he bent over her, hauled her to her feet by grabbing her sweater and the shirt beneath it. He ripped them both down the center. He was hellbent on humiliating her before he pulped her face and body, stripping her naked in front of his compatriots.

This was precisely what she was aiming for when she spat, playing on his weakness as a male. She had embarrassed him in public—now she would have to pay dearly. She could see all this in his eyes as he glared and grinned, reaching for her bra.

Enter when pulled—the lesson emblazoned in her mind. Instead of resisting Rolf as he expected she stepped forward and to her right. This brought her against him, nullifying his own superior force. Baffled, he stumbled backward, and she tore away from his grip, turning her back to him in the same movement. Her right arm lashed out, the back of it smashing into his exposed throat.

She watched, gimlet-eyed, as he fell to one knee, wheezing, clutching his throat as if to contain his pain. But again she underestimated him; she was too close. He drove his left fist up into her sternum. She bit her lip, almost crying out, but her training superseded her shock and pain. Grabbing the wrist of his extended arm she swiveled to her left, pulling him with her, using his momentum so that his legs battered her extended knee. Doubling over he went down with a heavy thud.

Silence from the blood and circus onlookers.

Rolf wiped his saliva-slick lips with the back of his hand, spat out a tooth in a pink cloud. When he rose there was a knife in his right fist, the blade long and narrow—a switchblade. He'd had his fill of bare-knuckle fighting. Clearly the rules of this gladiatorial match were fluid as long as he controlled the tide.

He came at her, warily this time, circling, feinting and withdrawing, trying to draw her out, figure out her strategy. He was a street brawler, born and bred to it, she could see it in his eyes, the way he held himself, the bulging of his muscles. He was used to winning fights by brute strength, overwhelming his opponent with the vicious force of his attack. Here he was on different ground and now he knew it. From here on in he would be far more dangerous.

Her stomach and chest felt like they would at any moment collapse. She knew she had to breathe through the pain, force her muscles that instinctively were contracting around the impact sites to relax, to give way, otherwise her strength would be greatly diminished. Red meat for him to feast on.

He kept circling. She stood her ground. When the enemy was in constant motion, being confronted by utter stillness unnerved them. And so it was with Rolf. He could not decode her strategy, and so, impatient, he abandoned his, came at her with a feral growl. His face was thunderous, filled with homicidal intent. Still, she did not move. Now he expected her to move toward him and was prepared for that, she could see it in his eyes, the atavistic cleverness of the animal. Instinct. But his instinct was of the street mob, the cut-and-slash variety, which made him unprepared for the unexpected.

He closed in, knife held before him, the point slightly elevated the better to facilitate the plunge through her ribs, into her heart. The classic killing strike. Neat, clean, quick. But only perhaps.

At the last instant, when the tip of the blade was millimeters from the flesh he had laid bare, she twisted sideways, the blade slicing through her leather jacket rather than the space between her ribs. As he pulled it out, she slammed her forehead into his nose. The bridge collapsed and with a satisfying squirt blood gushed down into his mouth, dripping off his chin. He lost control of the knife and she kicked it skittering across the concrete floor of the pool.

A raging bull now, he gripped her throat, cutting off her airflow. He drove her backward into the wall, used the heel of his hand to crush her windpipe. His free hand mashed against her breast, mauling it painfully.

But she'd had enough. Using the stiffened ends of her fingers she broke through the soft flesh under his chin then, whipping him around, smacked the back of his head against the wall of the pool. The strength drained out of him and she stepped away as he collapsed. She didn't know whether he was breathing but she didn't care. He had hurt her, maddened her. He had taken up all of her concentration but now he was nothing to her. Nothing at all.

The taste of iron was in her mouth. Blood? His? Hers? What did it matter; she was standing, he was not. She gave out a rasping cough. Her throat felt ragged, raw as a freshly butchered slab of beef. Her chest was on fire, her stomach ready to rebel. She leaned an arm against the wall to steady herself.

Head bent, she rested her forehead against her upflung forearm. They could not see the tears streaming down her face, but Rolf could have felt them if he was still alive. He wasn't, though. She hadn't set out to kill him, hadn't meant to, but he had forced her hand. She was sick at the exhilaration she felt coursing through her. The rebound effect of clearing her mind of all thought, all emotion, during the confrontation. All the frustration and helplessness she had felt as a young adult trying to make her way in the clandestine services—always dismissed, undervalued, the side-eye contemptuous looks when with a smirk she was sent off to the file room with the other women who didn't know better. But she knew better. She was born knowing better, and this determination served her well as she slogged her way through the byzantine morass of the clandestine services.

Somehow she had talked her way into the field agent training academy, but upon her graduation no one wanted to take her on as a partner even though she posted top of her unit.

Until Ben. Ben had been willing. She knew she was lucky then, knew it even more now. Without Ben's help she likely would have returned to the prison of the file room. He read her dossier, recognized her abilities, looked past the fact she was female, and took her on. He soon saw that he was right. She was smart, more than physically capable, and she was clever. So much so that for the first ten days in the field he called her Little Fox. Until she told him to cut it out. To his credit he did. He never underestimated her. Ever. He trusted her completely.

Rolf embodied all the smirking males who had consigned her to a bit part, who had constantly hit on her even as they derided her, disbelieved her skills. And this disappointed her. She had strived to keep all emotion out of the fight, but in the end, she failed. It had been different with Pasha

Shutkov. She had been fighting for her life with a professional equal. Rolf had no chance against her. Not really. Something dark and ugly had reared up from deep inside her, lashing its tail, snapping its jaws. Now Rolf was dead and she felt no remorse.

So what? she asked herself. She breathed and breathed again, slowly, deeply, down to the base of her belly. No shallow breaths to the top of her lungs for her. Her tears dried on her cheeks and she wiped the tracks away so no trace of them was left.

She lifted her head. If these people wanted more from her she would do it. What? Take on Blondie now? So be it. She found she didn't care. Either she was in or she was dead, those were the two paths that she had forced upon herself when she decided to try and embed herself in this cadre. Herr Wessel knew what she wanted, knew where she should go next. And now, for better or for worse, here she was, as triumphant as she had ever been, as vulnerable as she had ever been.

This was her life, a hair's breadth from someone who was bent on killing her. But how else would she know she was alive? This was what she was born for, what she needed to go on. To achieve.

Somewhere above her she heard the click of a gun slide. A bullet was being chambered, a bullet meant for her.

Well, then.

"No." Ghislane's unmistakable voice.

She looked up, saw Uwe with a pistol pointed at her. As she watched, Ghislane stepped to Uwe's side, placed her hand atop the weapon. Slowly, inexorably, she pushed it down until it was pointed to the floor of the walkway.

"Bring her up, Dieter," Ghislane said to Blondie.

So Dieter wasn't Heinrich Schrodinger. And why should he be? He showed no characteristics of leadership. Just another foot soldier in Schrodinger's cadre.

She waved Dieter off. "Don't bother." She crossed to the ladder. "I know the way up."

20

"So where is Heinrich Schrodinger?" Evan asked.

"Right here in front of you," Dieter said.

"Yeah, no." She shook her head. "I don't think so."

Ghislane grunted. "Give it up, Dieter."

Elke bared her teeth at him. "Like I said. She's too clever for you."

"What would you know about it?" Dieter shot back.

As Elke advanced on him Ghislane held her back. "You don't want to do that," she said to Dieter, her words clipped, sharp as shark's teeth.

So, Evan thought. *Fissures in the ranks.* She wondered whether they were along gender lines or whether there was something else eating away at the group.

The four of them were in a large room off the pool area. It was windowless, two tiers of wood benches along three walls. The door had a diamond-shaped glass panel at eye height. A steam room, then. The rest of the group—Romy and Uwe—were still in the pool, cleaning up the mess so as not to scare the pair of DJs coming to set up the electronics for tonight's rave.

"So," Evan prompted.

Ghislane gestured for her to take a seat. "You must be exhausted after your exertions."

Evan smiled through the pain racking her with every beat of her heart. Her vision pulsed with it. "Not so much."

Elke's eyes seemed to spark. "I got tired just watching you."

"Dieter's still watching me," Evan said, zipping her jacket all the way up. He'd seen her down in the pool with her sweater and shirt split down the center revealing flesh and bra.

"Dieter's a pig," Elke said.

"Just a guy," he responded.

Elke shrugged. "Same thing. You see everything through the lens of the male gaze."

"And you call yourself a Nazi," he sneered.

Elke had had enough of him for the moment. She climbed up to sit on one of the second-tier benches so she could face Evan, who was still standing, eye to eye. Evan had to give her props for that. She was acutely aware that none of the remaining five had evinced any outward sorrow at their compatriot's demise. It was as if he were a weapon, once emptied discarded in the woods. Were they sociopaths? Was she?

"Schrodinger," Evan said doggedly, to shake the last question out of her head.

"Why are you so interested in Heinrich?" Dieter slouched on a lower bench, elbows on the upper tier. "Who the hell are you anyway?"

"And what were you doing at our little demonstration?" Ghislane added, eyes narrowed. Unlike Dieter, she was hunched forward, elbows on knees, chin resting on her fists.

Good questions both. But Evan had had ample time to come up with answers. "I'm American, from Washington, DC," she said. "I was sent by Lucinda Wells to—"

"Omega?" Ghislane laughed.

Elke sat upright, elbows lowered. "We don't hold no truck with stinking American Omega," she added with no little heat.

"You're wearing the Omega masks," Evan pointed out.

"Sure we are," Dieter nodded. "But what does it mean?"

"It means," Elke answered his rhetorical question for Evan's benefit, "that any photos taken, any of us caught, it's Omega takes the blame, not us."

Evan had to admit she hadn't been expecting this twist. "If you're not Omega, who does Heinrich Schrodinger represent?"

Dieter rose, began to prowl restlessly around the room. "There is no Heinrich Schrodinger."

"There is and there isn't," Ghislane corrected him. "Strictly speaking."

"Oh, come on." Dieter tossed his head.

Which made Ghislane smile. She turned to Evan. "Clever girl like you must have heard of Schrödinger's cat."

"I'll bet Dieter hasn't," Elke interjected. When no one said a word, she went on. "Tell us, Dieter. Tell us about Schrödinger's cat."

"What's the big deal?" Dieter shrugged. "The cat was the guy's pet." He sneered. "What, was this cat a Nazi too, is that it?"

Elke laughed. Ghislane made a sour face.

It was left to Evan to answer. "It's a thought experiment in quantum physics, proposed by the Nobel-winning scientist Erwin Schrödinger. Say you place a cat in a box along with a toxic random subatomic event that may or may not occur. Schrödinger argued that without visual confirmation the cat should be considered as simultaneously dead and alive."

"See?" Elke crowed. "I told you she was a clever one."

Ghislane climbed down, seated herself on the lower bench. She patted the space beside her, a clear invitation.

The muscles of Evan's legs were starting to involuntarily tremor so she took the proffered opportunity.

When she was seated, Ghislane continued. "In a way Heinrich Schrodinger is our own Schrödinger's cat."

Dieter threw up his arms. "For the love of God, Ghislane, he doesn't exist!"

Elke bared her teeth at Dieter again. "Oh, but he does."

"Elke's right." Ghislane turned to Evan. "He lives in the minds of others. As a prime example, you came here looking for him, so in that sense Schrodinger exists."

Evan saw the light at last. "But otherwise not."

Ghislane nodded. "Correct."

"Alternatively," Elke added, "you could say she is Heinrich Schrodinger."

"This is your cadre," Evan said to Ghislane.

"Not that I wasn't forced to fight for it. Almost all the males were against it. Scandalized, one might even say."

Dieter stopped his prowling, stood in front of Ghislane. "I was not *scandalized.*"

She ignored him. "That was why I was so impressed by how you took Rolf apart."

"It was his choice," Evan told her.

Elke snorted. "Rolf was an idiot."

"He was damn good at breaking heads," Dieter insisted.

Elke laughed into his face. "Until he came up against this one."

Dieter's eyes glittered, a snarl on his lips, as he glared at Evan, stepped toward her.

Ghislane shot Dieter a warning look and he thrust fisted hands into his pockets, turned away.

"True, Elke." Slapping her thighs, Ghislane rose. "I don't know about you, Evan, but the events of today have conspired to work up a mighty thirst."

"That suits me," Evan told her. "I have many questions."

"As have I," Ghislane responded. "But honestly this place is just too depressing to stay in one minute longer. *Komm mit, meine freunde.*"

With that, they left.

They exited the *volksbad* via the pool area. No sign of Rolf was left down there, not even a smear of blood. But there were people milling around—they passed through too quickly for Evan to reach an exact count—but because it was too early even for the DJs' arrival, Evan was certain these people were "Heinrich Schrodinger's" cadre. They watched her with vicious eyes and scornful expressions.

The crowd didn't look all that big, but when Evan pointed that out, Ghislane grinned. "It'd be a mistake to judge by this crew. I have hidden resources."

Then she signaled to Dieter to stay. "Do what you can to calm them down," she said. "The riot set them off on an adrenaline high."

Dieter shook his head, and with a sideways glance at Evan, said, "I'm going with you."

"You think she needs a guard dog?" Elke laughed. "Idiot." She tossed her head. "Do as she says."

"What's with the two of you, anyway?" He leered. "In bed with each other when the lights go out?"

"You see?" Elke said to Evan. "The male gaze. Two women can't be friends unless they're lesbians."

"Damn straight," Dieter retorted.

"Shut up, you Neanderthal." Ghislane pointed at him. "Do the job assigned you."

■ ■ ■

"It's not good but it's local."

They entered the Bayern Sports Bar ten or so miles from the *volksbad.* Immediately they were enveloped in a pall of smoke, smelling strongly of spent tobacco, sour beer, and idleness. The gray fug hung motionless in the air, a second ceiling, as if it hadn't moved in decades.

While Ghislane and Evan sat at a small round table wedged into the corner of the darkened room, Elke remained up front at the copper-topped bar above which three flat-screen TVs were showing various football matches from the European Champions League. The usual white noise of bars the world over was periodically drowned out by the triumphant shouts and angry yells from drunken fans. Elke gave their order, then joined them, sitting on the outer corner of the half-moon banquette.

Elke had ordered them draught beers, which came in enormous ceramic steins with metal tops. Also, plates of wurst and sauerkraut, a loaf of coarse black bread and a platter of rosti potatoes as large as a hubcap.

Finding she was famished, Evan loaded a plate, began to eat with great gusto, washing down mouthfuls of food with the good strong beer.

"Unlike Dieter we welcome your presence here, Evan," Elke said.

Ghislane nodded. "It signifies to me that my band of outriders has come into prominence, that we are making waves in this deluded world." She laughed, baring small, uneven vulpine teeth. "I'm sure Lucinda Wells would be jealous."

Evan swallowed. "Do you oppose her aims?"

Elke looked to Ghislane.

"Aims? I don't know about that." Ghislane sucked down more beer, ordered another round for them though Evan's stein was still almost full. "But I do know that I don't give a shit what happens in America and neither, I am convinced, does Lucinda Wells."

At this pronouncement Evan set down her knife and fork, wiped her lips. The conversation had just become interesting. "Tell me."

Ghislane shrugged. "Why should this surprise you? Unlike her husband, Lucinda Wells isn't a true believer. She's a cynic. In my opinion she married the old man for a power grab. She's using him the way he uses the masses of the great white unwashed."

"She's certainly got a way with words," Evan acknowledged.

Ghislane grunted. "Like all great con artists." She grabbed the stein as it was set in front of her, took a long draught. "You listen to her, that queen bitch. Close your eyes, and you're almost in love with her. It's no wonder Wells married her." She cocked her head. "I wonder what his children make of her. Stepmothers are always bad news, always wicked in their own ways."

"Received wisdom is that Lucinda and Wells meshed over their political and religious beliefs."

Elke grinned. "Don't you believe it for a minute."

"It's the story she had their flacks put out," Ghislane explained.

"She's as masterful a spin doctor as my beloved Goebbels once was," Elke said.

Ghislane, one eye looking out for Evan's reaction, shrugged. "It would scarcely surprise me to find Lucinda had studied his playbook."

"First lesson," Elke interjected, her forefinger raised, "whatever you do, whatever lie you're spinning you accuse your enemies of those same actions, those same lies. Nothing reflects back on you, only on your enemies." Her voice grew more emphatic, her words more fluid as she warmed to the subject that was clearly dear to her heart. "It's the ultimate Big Lie. And the beauty part is it never gets old, you can use the strategy over and over, ad infinitum without your constituency being the wiser. In fact, the more you repeat your lies, the deeper they sink into the poor suckers' consciousness, the more potent they become."

"You sound like a historian," Evan said, "not a student of religion."

"In Gnosticism," Elke said, "they go hand in hand."

They were silent for a moment as the crowd noise ebbed and flowed with the action on the TV screens. Evan was about to ask Ghislane about the chant her people shouted as they marched when Ghislane said, "You know, Evan, you present me with a conundrum."

Evan was disciplined enough not to reply. Ghislane cocked her head, as if listening for something beyond that incredible surf of the football fans. The vicious catcalling from the punters at the front necessitated them putting their heads close to each other in order to hear.

"On the one hand I'm not sure you're an emissary from Lucinda Wells," Ghislane said at length. "On the other I don't think you're part of the German Federal Police." She finished off her beer, wiped her upper lip with her forefinger, was about to call for a third when she noticed her companion hadn't even finished her first.

She reached for Evan's second stein. "Mind?"

"Help yourself."

Ghislane stared at her, took a long draught, set the stein down with a bang. "So."

Elke was eating slowly and deliberately. "The question remains . . . who are you."

"You're right; I'm not an emissary from Lucinda." Evan had, of course, thought this through. Nevertheless, she was flying by the seat of her pants, and still deliberately without backup. She had to bury herself in the lies she was about to weave into whole-cloth, the only way to gain a foothold in this group. "The truth is Lucinda doesn't know I exist. I'm an Omega foot soldier, and while I'm a staunch believer, I'm also a keen observer. And I've witnessed too many changes in Omega since Lucinda became Wells's wife."

Ghislane's eyes narrowed. "Dazzle us with an example."

"Okay." Evan nodded. "For one, Wells's business dealings have multiplied tenfold since she arrived on the scene."

Ghislane shrugged. "Their business is of no interest to us."

"Well, it should be." Evan leaned farther forward, lowered her voice even more, obliging Ghislane to lean closer as well. "None of those businesses are traceable. They all lead back to shell companies in the Bahamas, Grand Cayman, and, most especially, Malta."

"Home to the most corrupt government on earth."

Evan nodded. "Not an easy title to get."

They all laughed.

Elke shook her head. "So you're here for what exactly." She chewed, swallowed the food almost whole.

Evan nodded. "I worry that Lucinda's leading Omega astray, that her aims aren't *our* aims."

At this, Ghislane paused in her eating, put her knife and fork down. "So. What is it you want, really?"

Evan took a breath, pressed on toward the climax of this "romance" she was spinning. "There are only two kinds of people in our world. Ideologues and profiteers. It seems clear now that the three of us are one and Lucinda Wells is the other."

Ghislane sat back. "Everyone wants something, Evan. What do you want from us?"

"Help," Evan said at once. "Heinrich Schrodinger owns such a fine rep I thought he could provide some way for me to stop Lucinda before she destroys the American Omega."

Elke's eyes narrowed. "But now you've found that Schrodinger doesn't really exist."

"He exists in Ghislane." This was a crucial moment. Flattery was tricky, especially in situations like these. You needed to be completely sincere, to make sure you didn't lay it on too thick. "It's you I'd like to get to know and talk with."

Ghislane drank some more. She seemed to have an inexhaustible thirst for beer. Her eyes narrowed as she continued to evaluate Evan. "What I like about you, Evan, what I see and neither Rolf nor Dieter do not, did not, is you're a keeper of secrets. How do I know that? You have the eyes of a 6D chess player."

Evan's lips gave a twitch. "Meaning?"

"I have it. I'm a 6D chess player. So, I have no doubt, does Samuel

Wainwright Wells. Well, he must, right? I mean, he's the center of the American Omega movement, no matter what that queen bitch thinks." Ghislane shook her head. "Lucinda is something else altogether. She's a boomslang in human form."

Evan knew something about boomslangs, the deadliest snakes in Africa. Its fangs were in the rear of its mouth. Once it bit a victim it began to chew on its flesh until it succumbed to its toxins. Seemed an apt description of Lucinda Wells, Evan thought.

Ghislane continued. "Any time there's a challenge to our point of view there's always a deeper dimension we will arrive at to dispute it, a new interpretation that keeps our faith alive. If someone—say yourself, for instance—comes up against a wall of what some insist on calling reality, that exposes a weakness in your faith. That's when you need to look deeper to find the truth because the so-called reality most people are living in is a delusion—it's completely and utterly false. I, my followers—and Wells's, too—are in a spiritual war, and we've been called into action."

Evan slapped a rapt expression on her face; since she was intrigued it wasn't difficult. "I agree completely."

Elke leaned toward her. "You see, Evan, our eyes have been opened. We see the truth all around us."

"It's hidden in plain sight."

"Precisely." Elke finished off her beer. "Gnosticism tells us that what we call 'truth' is fungible. What others see as facts are lies meant to delude fools even more."

Ghislane nodded. "People like Wells have claimed over and over that those demons, those who try to push their lies on the world, are real, their powers are real, the darkness they drag along behind them is real— they walk the streets and avenues of every city on earth."

"Prime examples," Elke continued, "Hillary Clinton and George Soros who encourage and feed the cause of evil."

"Do you want me to believe that your protests aren't for Germany for Germans?" Evan said. "Kick out all the immigrants?"

Elke sat back. "Listen to her, Gizzy." She leaned forward suddenly, elbows on the damp table. "As Ghislane just said, like the evangelicals in America, we're in a spiritual war. In that kind of war no prisoners can be taken; they're too dangerous." Her finger drew a circle in spilled beer. "Say you live in a house, say that house is invaded by raccoons. You try to kill them, don't you, because raccoons are destructive and inevitably some of them are rabid. But they're clever these raccoons and some of them evade you, stay alive. Those are the ones you trap. And they must be killed, Evan, because if you let them go even miles and miles from your house they will return."

Ghislane was nodding, giving Elke her head.

"In short, we're on the front lines, fighting for a better world." Elke laughed then, a raucous sound not unlike a crow. "Is this why you came here, Evan? Is this what you wanted to know?"

21

Kata was undeterred. She could scent the change in the air, subtle as it was. "I also killed the original Kata Romanovna," she said.

"Stop." Kusnetsov waved away her argument. "Borya was one of my FSB directors."

"He was a traitor. He attacked Alyosha Ivanovna and then me. Kata Romanovna was worth ten of that prick Arsenyev."

The minister rolled his eyes. "What you're asking is impossible."

"And when you asked me for the impossible—that I rid you of Dima Nikolaevich, my former boss, because he was also a traitor—what did I do? I obliged you. I fed him to your favorite sharks. Or had that incident slipped your mind?"

He stared at her, spitefully silent.

"Who knows how much damage Arsenyev has already done to *your* FSB?" she went on. "Who knows what secrets he's been spilling about our operations? Who knows how many of our networks have been compromised?" She shook her head. "Now that Arsenyev is dead I'm the only one who can find out."

The minister made a dismissive sound. It turned his face ugly, feral. "And how would you do that? You've already said that interrogation won't work. Neither will killing them to make an example of them."

Her eyes were lit like lamps. "There is a way."

He smirked. "I'm sure you'll tell me."

"Not here I won't."

His face darkened. "I don't need you. I don't need any woman."

"I'm not any woman," Kata said. "That's your problem. You need me and you know it."

"Bitch," he spat.

She nodded. "Thank you."

She watched his face turn even darker. Then he turned away from

her, kicked the chair through the doorway, and followed it out. The door
clanged shut behind him, the echo rolling around the cell like thunder.

Eight hours she waited. He made her wait eight hours, thinking that
in the darkness—for the light never came on—suspended in time, she
would wonder and fear for her fate. But he was wrong. For the first time
since she had been incarcerated Kata breathed freely, feeling a great
weight lifted off her chest. She spent those eight hours in meditation,
which, due to her impulsiveness, her inner rage, was more difficult for
her than for others. This made her descent into the meditative space all
the more rewarding. Not that she was aware of that until afterward when
the door opened, for she had emptied her mind of all needs, all want, all
anxiety, all cares, all anger. All thought. In the brilliance of nothingness
she floated, free at last.

The door opened, spilling a lozenge of light into her cell and she surfaced, smiling inwardly at what she had accomplished.

There was no guard. Kusnetsov, standing in the corridor light a few
steps from the doorway, gazed into her cell, but said not a word. Kata
rose. She kept her eyes on the minister. She was very calm.

He did not move until she stepped out into the corridor. His nose
wrinkled as she came close. "You stink," he said.

She stared back. "Let me sniff your armpits."

Without another word he went to the cell to her left where a guard
stood waiting. Kata followed him. Kusnetsov nodded to the guard who
unlocked the door, swung it wide open.

Kata pushed past both men. Alyosha came to meet her. She stumbled,
Kata caught her, held her tight. Her eyes were glazed, pale as a gull's underside. Her lips, half-parted, were dry and peeling. Clearly she hadn't
been treated well.

"I'm so sorry," she whispered in Alyosha's ear. "I promised to take
care of you."

Alyosha rested her head against Kata's shoulder. She seemed exhausted. Kata looked over her shoulder to see Kusnetsov staring at her.
Their glares met midway between them like protons slamming together
at high speed, creating something different, something new.

He seemed to want to say something but could not bring himself to
do so. To cover the fact that he had little choice he shook out a cigarette,
lit it, and drew the tar and nicotine into his lungs. To punish her for her
victory he forced her to wait in silence, smoking slowly, staring over their

heads, until what was left of the cigarette was too small to draw on. Letting the butt go, he flicked it into Alyosha's cell. A petty gesture that in the past would have made Kata smile. Not now, possibly not ever again.

He turned on his heel. "Well," he spat over his shoulder. "What are you two waiting for?"

■   ■   ■

Hours later, in Kusnetsov's sprawling apartment in the so-called Golden Mile, the area of Khamovniki between the Boulevard and Garden Rings, Kata, showered, wearing clothes reluctantly provided by the minister's sour wife, occupied an oversized chair upholstered in tobacco leather. Ovals of buttery light from a variety of table and standing lamps illuminated the gemstone colors of the Tabriz carpets, gave the living room a warm and welcoming glow.

Alyosha, sufficiently rehydrated, was upstairs in a guest bedroom, tucked in bed, too depleted even to eat.

Kata held a plate on her lap, filled with quarters of cold squab, mounds of red cabbage, and mashed and buttered parsnips. On the round table to the right of her chair was a large cut-glass tumbler of vintage port, the deepest ruby color she had ever seen.

Across from her, one knee crossed over the other, Kusnetsov reclined on a sofa covered in a French floral print. He held a similar tumbler, but of iced vodka, from which he sipped from time to time as they spoke in soft, almost velvety tones. If one had witnessed the scene in the dankness of the Lubyanka earlier it would have been near impossible to credit the change that had come over both of them.

"So," Kusnetsov began.

She lifted one leg, flexing her foot. "To tell you the truth these Converse sneakers are more comfortable than the Louboutins, even though they're a little big."

"Small feet." He gestured with his vodka. "Tell me your solution to the Omega problem."

Kata put aside her plate. "As I said, trying to weed out the traitors in Department 73, even if you execute them all, will prove fruitless. Omega is like a hydra. You cut off a head or two here and there, others take their place. Who is to say that the infiltration is limited to Department 73? It stands to reason the rot has spread outside it.

"No." She shook her head. "In this case we must find the source, the person who has been recruiting FSB personnel."

"You think it's a single individual?"

"That's the way Omega works. The origin of persuasion lies in a single voice. More than that and in the best case the message gets diluted. In the worst case, it gets muddled."

The minister finished off his vodka, set the glass aside. He changed position, hunched forward, fingers laced. "Tell me how you will implement this plan."

"I can't," she said. "I have no position inside FSB."

He waved away her words. "Don't play coy, Kata. You wouldn't be here now if you weren't still working for me. God only knows where your friend would be."

"As it happens Alyosha Ivanovna is part of my plan," Kata said. "She's the key to it, really."

"How so?"

"She works for FSB SIGINT."

Kusnetsov grunted. "Never heard of her."

Kata smiled. "Precisely. Neither has anyone but her direct superior, and I daresay he wouldn't recognize her if he bumped into her in a hallway or elevator. But she has access to the FSB file servers."

"Not the ones that matter."

"You will grant her access to those, Darko Vladimirovich."

His nostrils flared, as if he had scented something unexpected. "And if I do—which I will add is a big if."

"There has to be a choke point," Kata said smoothly. "A place where the infiltration into the FSB happens. We start with the late Director Arsenyev's dossier—all of it. From there we proceed to the dossiers of the other members of Department 73 who are aligned with Omega. Alyosha can give me a list of Pasha's buddies who'd also been inked. I'll start there, analyze those findings." She took a sip of her port, the sweet liquor warming her stomach. She watched his expression over the rim of her glass.

Kusnetsov shook his head. "What you propose will not be possible for the head of Zaslon."

For a moment Kata froze, then she put a smile on her face. That it was dry and brittle as a leaf in November was for her alone to know.

Kusnetsov rose, took her plate and sat back down. There was still a good amount of food left on it, and he used her knife and fork to excise a triangle of squab, chewed it thoughtfully. "While you were enjoying your last hours of incarceration I had time to consider your position. It was a mistake to give you a directorship. I came to realize that you were being wasted as a manager. You bridled being behind a desk, no matter how many orders you dispersed. Your skill set is built for the field, so into the field you must go.

"Therefore"—he lifted the fork—"since you have made an acceptable case for yourself and Alyosha Ivanovna I have decided to create a directorate for the two of you, plus in the future a small personally vetted cadre, if needed. Of course your friend will stay where she is. To anyone who would care to look, nothing has changed so far as her work status is concerned. From tomorrow on, she will have blanket access to *all* the FSB server files."

He said this as if it was his idea. *Never mind*, thought Kata. *He's giving me what I need*.

"Does this new directorate have a designation?"

"Only internally—and by that I mean you, me, and Alyosha Ivanovna. The designation is Directorate O."

"Are we reading in Director General Baev?" She was speaking of the head of the SVR.

"I will deal with Slava." A smile played across Kata's face, mirrored now by the minister's expression. "Welcome home, Kata Romanovna."

He crossed to where she sat, pressed her deadly emerald ring into her palm. At almost the same time he swooped down, kissed her hard on the lips. The moment his lips opened against hers, she pushed him back. She slithered out of the chair, out of his would-be embrace.

"You are drunk, Minister."

He shook his head. "Not a bit of it. I feel like celebrating this new phase of our relationship."

He stepped closer, and closer still. Again she pushed him back. "You disrespect your wife, Minister. She is upstairs warm and all unsuspecting in your bed. It is past time you joined her."

"So you won't indulge me."

She tried to judge his frame of mind, failed. No matter. "That kind of relationship will imperil the important work in which both of us are involved."

"Bitch," he said, this time meaning it in a different way, because he knew she was right.

She acknowledged that when she answered him. "You are very welcome, Minister."

■   ■   ■

Never again will I risk calling him Darko Vladimirovich, she resolved as she undressed in the darkened bedroom. She looked at the bed, and all at once was shattered by how alone she was. A stranger making her uncertain way in a strange land with Lyudmila her only friend, the only person she could rely on. But Lyudmila was far away, hidden where no one—not even Kata—could find her. In fact, Kata thought now, due to Lyudmila's obsessive security concerns Kata had no way of contacting her. She was obliged to wait for Lyudmila to initiate contact.

Half-dressed, Kata sat on the bed, looked around a room where nothing was familiar, where there was nothing of hers—not even her clothes—except the emerald ring, which she had slid on her finger and now worked around and around, almost unconsciously.

What troubled her most was that she was used to being alone, and yet now, at this moment, she felt the chill of her solitary life creep through her like a bout of malaria. She rubbed the heels of her hands into her eyes. *What's the matter with me?* she asked herself.

But self-pity wasn't her thing. She snapped out of her black mood, finished undressing. Padding into the bathroom she washed her face without looking at herself in the mirror. She needed no confirmation of how haggard and thin she looked. Back in the bedroom, streetlights filtered through the blinds, striping the floor and bed. She stared at the bed. How cold and unwelcoming it looked. Nevertheless she turned back the covers, crawled in, laid her head on the pillow, and stared at the ceiling.

A soft knocking roused her from a restless twilight sleep. She turned her head, watched the knob on the bedroom door move. A pillar of light entered the room. Someone had turned on the lights in the hallway. She tensed, her mind and muscles prepared to defend herself.

But it wasn't Kusnetsov; it was Alyosha. For a moment, she just stood in the doorway, unmoving. Kata was astonished by how fast her heart was beating. Then Alyosha closed the door behind her and crossed the space between them, lifted the covers, slid into bed beside Kata. It was only then that she realized Alyosha was naked.

Alyosha turned her back to Kata, sighed. Alyosha's body felt colder than the night. Kata was about to wrap her arm around the other woman when she pulled back. In the light coming through the blinds, her gaze moved over Alyosha's shoulders, taking in the hard ridges—the welts deep enough to have dried into scars. Lifting the blanket slightly, down and down her gaze drifted. Reaching out, her fingertips light as feathers, she traced the scars as if she were a blind woman reading a horror story in braille. Her breath caught in her throat. Was there any part of Alyosha's back that wasn't disfigured by scars? Most were old, but she could tell by feel that others were newer, perhaps only a week or so old.

Sickened to her soul, Kata placed herself ever so gently against Alyosha, spooning her. Her right arm enclosed the other woman, holding her so Kata could feel both rhythms—heart and breath.

Tears welled over her eyes, scalding her cheeks, leaving tracks down her cheeks and falling onto the place between Alyosha's shoulder blades. She kissed that spot as gently as the flutter of a butterfly's wing. It seemed to her now that her life was thin and bone-dry. Only now was it clear to her how much her younger self had wanted to love Evan, how much she had craved Evan's love in return. Instead, she had gotten this life. Nobody's fault but her own, that was undeniably true, but it wasn't until this moment, holding another human being whom she cared for, that she understood life's wider connections.

Tracing Alyosha's scars had been an intimacy she had never imagined. Knowing the terror and agony Alyosha had been put through by men—most probably even Pasha, whom she claimed to have loved—she would never again look back on her own past with the rage of a blackened heart. In the face of this woman's woes, her own suddenly faded like an old photo, folded and creased so many times its image had passed into the murk of time.

She closed her eyes. But wished-for unconsciousness came only when she gave herself over to the gentle sighing breaths of the woman she held, and just before it did she whispered in Alyosha's ear, "I will take care of you. No one will hurt you ever again. This I swear on my own life."

Rocking on their joined breath's eternal tide she at last fell into a deep and dreamless sleep.

22

Night, and a time for listening. Lucinda Wells sat at a café table in the vast matrimonial bedroom of the Wells estate. One knee crossed over the other, she regarded the inverted images on the enormous flat-screen TV mounted on the opposite wall in the full-length mirror affixed to the closet door to the right of the bed. The TV was in place of the fireplace and magnificent scrollwork mantel the Old Man had demolished to accommodate his "eye on the world," as he referred to the TV. In point of fact it was unsurprisingly tuned to Titan News, which for some time now was cutting back and forth between the Omega-instigated riots in Miami, Portland, Minneapolis, Chicago, Detroit, Philadelphia. The worst—or best, depending on your point of view—was currently in Los Angeles, where an entire black family had been shot to death by a white cop in training. Ambrose had been in touch with myriad precinct captains within Omega's fold to make sure the spate of non-white killings continued. In Miami it was two Hispanic brothers, in Portland it was three Chinese men—purportedly dope smugglers, but actually paperclip importers. In Minneapolis it was a bunch of Sikhs who worked for a national delivery service. It was a snap for police in that city to identify someone with outstanding warrants, who'd recently been denied his meds, and manipulate him into admitting to the multiple shootings, then kill himself. Now, according to the interview being shown, the FBI had been forced to step in. According to the scroll along the bottom of the screen, the gist of the interview with Jon Tennyson, one of the high-ranking agents in charge, was that the home-grown terrorist threat level in the states being enflamed by the riots had become the FBI's highest priority. For a moment, Lucinda let her assessing gaze rest on the FBI agent. He looked like he'd been a linebacker in college, maybe ex-military. In any event, a heavyweight. His face was lined and jowly, heavy as his body. Though he might once have been good-looking, she judged, he was a decade past that now. He had the lantern jaw of Dick Tracy or some other cartoon character. She didn't take him seriously.

Diversions to the left, diversions to the right, she thought smugly, *and you, Mr. Tennyson, stuck in the middle.*

Everything, in other words, was going to plan. Better, even, since the news channels were also broadcasting images of the violent riots in Germany—Berlin, Hamburg, Nuremberg. Neo-Nazis. Led by their own radical ideologue named Schrodinger. But so what? Their insurrections only added to the chaos that would usher in the Old Man's new world order.

As for the Old Man himself, he sat under the covers on the near side of the vast California king bed. His back was against a padded leather headboard Lucinda despised. It and the wanton destruction of the mantel were but two of many cuts of a thousand knives she suffered to keep herself at the center of Wells's business interests while she worked clandestinely on the transfer of power from him to herself.

Lucinda was dressed in a silk negligee imported directly from Paris, which showed off her long shapely legs to great effect. She sipped black coffee and with a dessert fork delicately picked at a freshly made Štruklji—a kind of buckwheat strudel filled with poppy seeds, walnuts, and honey. It was a dessert she'd become fond of when she lived in Slovenia, after she had run away from her parents, the Reveshvilis, and her sister Ana.

"The secret to amassing dedicated followers," he said now, "is giving them precisely what they want. These dedicated followers of mine—the disenfranchised, the frightened living through difficult times, the ones who feel the ground crumbling under them, whatever rights they had slipping inexorably away from them—want to be saved. They want to be reassured that no matter how bad life is for them it's going to get better. They need a guarantee, you see, and what better way to do that than to show them a direct path to God.

"Religion is the mother to whom they all come to suckle, ingesting the milk of the righteous." A smile overspread his face. It was, Lucinda thought with an inward shudder, the smile of the lunatic, the asylum habitue.

"So soon," he said now. "Three days until the longest night, until our magnificently coordinated chaos. The government will crack, it will topple, the old guard busy with the devil's work swept away."

He paused then as if going over his words to test whether there was a better way to express himself. Evidently deciding there wasn't, he looked up at her from the sheaf of papers he had been poring over, his stare demanding her approval.

She sent off her best smile to him as if it were a kiss blown from her open palm. She could stomach him being a bigot and a militant extremist. And as for his firm belief in an archaic patriarchal society, she'd had plenty of experience dealing with that during her years in Slovenia. But his unceasing rigidity in all matters public and private was wearying to say the least. Daily she fought against his diktats eroding her sense of her own individuality. One reason why she fucked Ambrose as often as possible. Sex with him and the balm to her secret malice was her only safety valve.

She hated the Old Man with the icy antipathy a python has for a rat. She examined him in the same way, especially when he was asleep, face shrouded in charcoal shadow. A stripe of lamplight illuminated one ear, pink, fleshy, vulnerable. She liked to imagine wielding a long hatpin, inserting it into the whorl of his ear canal all the way to the drum and then, leaning in with all her weight, driving it slowly, slowly into his brain as he opened his eyes to his waking nightmare.

But now he was wide awake. "The milk of the righteous." As she reached to refill her cup her negligee, which had been carelessly tied, fell open, revealing the lustrous alabaster of her breasts. "I like that."

"Mm."

Samuel Wells returned to his reading as if he had been regarding a blank wall. *Well, why not?* she thought. She was the wrong sex. An adder could not have looked at him with more malevolence. But engrossed as he was in the day's updates he was mindfully unobservant. And yet, she thought, he exuded a manic energy, a rapaciousness, when he seemed at rest.

"Progress," he said, almost to himself. His forefinger traced the words he was reading. "Real progress."

These paper updates were Ambrose's doing. With the exponential proliferation of hacking, malware, and worst of all, ransomware, data breaches even into the highest reaches of governments were becoming commonplace. As Ambrose rightfully never tired of preaching, *No one can hack a piece of paper.*

She continued to sip her coffee, staring at a spot on the headboard just over his left shoulder, her gaze for the moment turned inward. Her thoughts drifted back to the young man she had left behind in Ljubljana,

Slovenia's capital. He was an artist, painted in oils, beautiful portraits that penetrated to the heart and soul of his subjects. She loved him—the first and only time she felt the flutter in her heart and not simply in her loins. But what was she to do? He was a genius of a kind most people did not understand or felt inclined to support. From his portraits he made just enough to live on, little more. But he loved her as much as she loved him, of this she had no doubt. He was honest, kind, empathetic. She walked away. She had to. She had come to think of him as a fish on a line being reeled in without him any the wiser. And besides, Samuel Wainwright Wells had come to the city to broker a deal for the dominant petrochemical concern in the area. She set her sights on him, alone among his retinue of men, went home, spent the entire night researching him online. Then she spent the next morning calculating the best way to grab his attention.

What was he now to her, that Slovenian artist? She could scarcely recall his name, his face not at all. But his cock, oh yes. His member was graven in her mind. But that was another time, another place. She'd been younger then, different. But perhaps, she thought now, only younger. From the moment she slipped out from between Rebecca Reveshvili's thighs she was who she was. The stamp of her life already imprinted itself upon her like stigmata.

Only one person from her time in Slovenia stayed alive in her memory. She never knew the old woman's name. She had eyes like cabochon opals. As compensation her hearing was better than a dog's. She recognized Lucinda's footsteps from a hundred yards away and always her deeply lined face broke out into a smile. Every day, rain, shine, or snow she sat on her bamboo stool outside St. Nicholas's Cathedral, bent over her offering of flowers—the freshest flowers Lucinda had ever seen; she could smell them even now. She called Lucinda *čudovita ptica. Beautiful bird*. Lucinda brought her food every day, rain, shine, or snow. She thought of her as *miška, little mouse*. Each day Miška gave her the single best flower of her wares as payment for the food. Lucinda never asked her where she lived, never even thought about it until this moment, when it was years too late.

Oh, Miška, was anyone there to bury you, to mourn your passing? she asked herself. *Are your flowers still the freshest in heaven as they were in Ljubljana or have they withered and died?*

Now her husband, Samuel Wainwright Wells, raised his head from the scrutiny of his reports, lifted his eyes to the high vaulted ceiling. She knew what was coming and closed her eyes to slits.

"Hear me, you hearers/and learn of my words, you who know me/I am the hearing that is attainable to everything/I am the speech that cannot be grasped/I am the name of the sound and the sound of the name/I am the sign of the letter and the designation of the division. And I am the light living in shadow/hark unto me, you hearers of my voice/To you I bestow the great power/To absorb my word and to act on it."

More drivel from that damn ancient Gnostic poem. She wished it had never been unearthed, never been translated from the Egyptian Coptic. The Old Man was obsessed with it, insisted that she use parts of it for Omega's daily prayers.

She watched him through her slitted eyes, his head thrown back like a seer in a mystic trance. Bits of spittle gathered at the corners of his mouth as he continued. *"Give heed then, you hearers/And you also, the angels and those who have been sent/And you spirits who have arisen from the dead/For I am the one who alone exists/And I have no one who will judge me/For many are the pleasant forms which exist in numerous sins/And incontinences as well as disgraceful passions and fleeting pleasures/Which men—"* Of course men, Lucinda thought bitterly. *"—embrace until they become sober/And go up to their resting place/And they will find me there/And they will live/And they will not die again."*

And listening to this crap once again furthered her conviction that the poem was a complete fake. It was purported to be written by the feminine divine power, the intermediary between the Divine and so-called mankind. But the proof of its invalidity, that it was in fact written by a man or a group of men bent on gathering to them religious power to rival that of the Christian and the Jew, was that line near the end that the Old Man uttered in complete ignorance. *Which men embrace until they become sober/And go up to their resting place/And they will find me there/And they will live/And they will not die again.* Not men and women, not all humanity, not—and she would in this case even accept this misnomer—all mankind. No, *men.* Just *men.*

No, the entire Gnostic thing on which Omega was based disgusted her. It was for the weak of mind, the lost, the wandering, the terrified. But in a rising sea of fear and change the far-right sectarian religion was only the mirage of a life raft. Everyone frantically climbing aboard would sink like a stone and drown in a sea of faith built on lies.

As the Old Man continued to intone random bits of the poem she slowly parted her legs so that the silk slithered off her knees, then her thighs, revealing her intimate nakedness. He took no notice, of course, but of a sudden his gaze came down from the heavens to alight on her face. And as it did so he began to speak to her of The Hidden Book of John, how Christ came to John after his crucifixion and resurrection and told him these secrets: the moving Spirit of Wisdom Sophia bore a son without her male counterpart, how this son grew in darkness, how he created the world of humankind that was neither of Sophia's Light nor of his Darkness. It was instead a Dim world with elements of each. Seeing the bitter fruits of her transgression Sophia repented, and so was allowed to enter the Dim world of humankind in an effort to impart her Light into those who would listen to her words. Those who rejected her words were doomed to wander the Dim world in darkness, ignorant of the hidden Truth, oblivious to their true nature. And when they died were damned to hell.

"You are Sophia," Samuel Wainwright Wells said to Lucinda now. "I recognized the Light in you the moment I saw you. I was determined to take you, to have you by my side forever and always."

God forbid, Lucinda thought just as her cell buzzed. A text from Ambrose. She read it without lifting it from the table, intermittently flicked her eyes up to engage the Old Man's so he would suspect nothing.

Agent in place. Preparing for arrival of target.

Engaging her husband's gaze, Lucinda allowed herself an inner smile. The sure end of her relentlessly inquisitive sister, Evan Ryder, was now not long in coming. She sat back, finished off the last of her Štruklji, savoring its familiar sweetness with satisfaction.

It was then that the Old Man threw off the bedcovers, pushed up the legs of his pajama bottoms.

"Time," he said, wriggling his toes.

An iron vise gripped Lucinda's heart, squeezing it so that she had difficulty breathing. Still she rose, stepped over to the bed, knelt on it. She had no choice. This was a nightly ritual she could neither alter nor postpone.

Bending from the waist, her face hovered over his right foot. Then, eyes closed as if that might save her the humiliation, she took his big toe in her mouth and began to suck.

23

NUREMBERG

One of the screens had changed. It was now playing a tape of the Rolling Stones concert in Havana. The raucous rock clashed with the roars of the football fans. Jagger looked not unlike a football star slithering around center stage but his wide-mouthed salacious grin was all his own. A fist-fight broke out, quickly snuffed by one of the bartenders, burly, bearded, and inked, perfect for occasions like this one. In due course order was restored.

Not that it mattered to Evan. In fact it seemed to her that an atmosphere of animosity suited the moment perfectly.

"Now I'm wondering whether you will join us," Ghislane said thoughtfully.

"I have an even better idea," Evan said. Now that Ghislane had given her an opening it was the right moment to force the issue. "I could be your emissary in the States. You say you're not Omega, and don't care about what happens in America. But you should. You'd have many supporters there, connections, funding. Omega could help you without even knowing it! I'm ambitious and I'm smart. I can leapfrog my way up the Omega ladder. But in order for that to happen you'll have to help me get rid of Lucinda."

"I like that idea." Elke smiled. "I like it quite a bit."

Ghislane was silent, her eyes turned inward. At length, she said, "It might be possible."

"I'm thinking it could be."

Elke laughed. "No wonder you've got the teeth of a lion and the heart of a tiger." She led the way past the seething bar and out the door. "Where'd you grow up?"

"Near the Gierather Wald, outside Köln. My parents run a psychiatric clinic there." This much was, of course, true. "For years that gorgeous forest was my playground."

They had left the bar behind, were out on the sidewalk. It was already

dark, evenings and nights came early this time of year. It had begun to
rain, but as they stood talking the rain hardened into vicious sleet, pock-
ing the sidewalk, making a hissing noise like a snake.

Ghislane squinted through the weather. "I'll have to consult others
about your offer."

Evan was elated, though she wondered who those "others" were. Far
too risky to ask. "I was hoping you'd say that."

Elke eyed Evan. "We're stronger with you than without you, no
doubt."

Ghislane told Elke they'd talk it over in the morning, her tone making
it clear it was time for Elke to leave them. Nevertheless, Elke hesitated.
"Go on, Elke," Ghislane said with a short laugh. "It's growing late. I'm
sure Evan is exhausted. I can see it in her eyes."

"Oh, sure, but overwound too." Elke grinned. "I'm heading back to
the *volksbad*. I want to work off some steam and I was hoping Evan would
come along. I've discovered that dancing and tension cannot coexist."

"Another time," Evan said, and without thinking, "Will Dieter still
be there?"

"Who knows with him?" Elke made a face. "He makes it look like
he's out to protect Ghislane, but if something happened to her he'd be
the happiest person on earth. He'd step into the vacuum and take over."

"She's right," Ghislane said. "He's sure he can do a better job, the idiot." She shook her head. "Plus which he hates you now for what you
did to Rolf. They grew up together. He wouldn't want you to see that he
cared, Mr. Tough Guy, but they were close."

After Elke said her goodbyes, Evan turned to Ghislane. "Will Dieter
prove a problem?"

Ghislane shrugged. "Everyone proves a problem sometime."

Evan looked around. The weather had swept almost all the pedestri-
ans off the streets. The few who remained were either half-running to
avoid the sleet or huddled in doorways, staring up at the low roiling sky
in search of a break in the clouds signaling the storm was waning. A car
horned blared somewhere down the street. Tires shushed, grinding the
sleet into slush. A gust of wind scoured their faces.

"You must be freezing," Ghislane said, her voice scarcely switching
gears, "what with your ruined shirt and sweater." She gestured. "Best
come home with me and you can choose one of my outfits."

■   ■   ■

Ghislane lived in a neat white rowhouse with a red roof and a tiny fountain on its minuscule front lawn. The house was in Dutzendteich, more or less midway between the neighborhood lake and the Nazi Rally Grounds.

Ghislane unlocked the door and stepped aside for Evan to enter. Evan had been expecting a none-too-clean hippie crash pad Ghislane would be sharing with three or four other females in her group. But this house was the polar opposite. In the entryway a slender marble sculpture rose from a black wood base. Streetlight filtered through the front door's frosted glass top illuminated the twisted form of an elongated dancer. Several steps farther on an alabaster bust of what might be a Roman emperor looked disdainfully down at her from its niche in the wall.

The living room was furnished with sofas and armchairs of leather, pale wood, and fabrics of geometric designs. The brightly painted walls served as backdrop to more sculptures and abstract paintings. This residence clearly belonged to a person of means.

"My mother bought it for me when I turned eighteen," Ghislane said, dropping her sopping coat on the floor. "My mother picked out the furniture and the colors." She ran her hand through her glistening hair, squeezing out most of the water. She paused, staring at Evan. "Take off your jacket, for God's sake." She gestured at the back of a chair. "Make yourself at home."

Ducking away, she returned with two fluffy bath towels, threw one to Evan, began to wipe her hair and face with the other. Then she tilted her head. "Let's get you some new clothes."

As they passed down the hall, more small sculptures gazed back at them indifferently from small niches. "Everything in here my mother gave me," Ghislane said as she forged ahead. She glanced over her shoulder at Evan. "My mother said to me, 'Gizzy, I have given you everything you could ever want: a proper education, a luxe abode, a wardrobe the envy of all my friends, a social circle of young men and women from the highest rung of the social ladder.' 'No, Mother,' I said. 'These are the things *you* want. You never thought to ask me what *I* want.' And she brushes aside my words. 'Oh, darling,' she says, 'I know this is just a phase. I do. But, really, hasn't this little rebellion of yours gone on long enough?'"

Ghislane led her into the bedroom, deeply shadowed by the weak light drifting through the windows that overlooked the street. "This is what happens when money overruns you—you become numb. The extravagant things you have amassed in order to prove your worth to your social cohort blind you to the people closest to you."

In this she was not wrong, Evan thought, having come to much the same conclusion. This was a smart, clever woman she was dealing with. A dialectic intellectual, almost, in her way, a philosopher. She realized it would be fatal to underestimate her.

Ghislane turned on all the lamps and the bedroom leapt into existence. It was expansive, with a queen-size bed, a dark walnut wardrobe that looked like an antique, and a low Danish Modern dresser. The two pieces should have clashed but for some reason they harmonized instead. The room was large enough to also hold a delicate escritoire and a modern mesh task chair. The door to a bathroom broke up the wall opposite the windows.

Crossing to the wardrobe that served in lieu of a closet Ghislane swung the doors wide and gestured with her open hand. "The choice is yours, Evan. Come have a look and then take your pick. They're all silks and cashmere."

Evan turned around. "As you said, designer fashions too."

Ghislane gave her a lopsided smile. "I haven't worn a thing from there."

"Where are your clothes?"

"Right here." Ghislane went to the dresser, opened drawers. There Evan saw T-shirts, men's long-sleeve shirts, jeans, wool sweaters. Nothing fancy, nothing expensive.

"This is more like it." Evan gestured. "May I?"

"What's mine is yours."

Evan paused for a moment. Having run her fingertips across the array of expensive fashions in the wardrobe, and now looking at the clothing in the dresser, she was struck by how often since she had left DC she had been dressed in other people's clothes—first Karl's, then Camina's, and now Ghislane's. She found it curious that she kept putting on and taking off and putting on again other people's clothes with consummate ease as if the *her* inside had diminished to the size of a pea, that there was no longer anything of her original self on which to hang them.

She leaned over the open dresser drawers and the air was suddenly perfumed by the scents of myrrh and frankincense. Instantly she was transported back to western Iran, where years ago she and Ben had crossed the border in the dead of a moonless night to extract an imam who wanted asylum. In Iran she had looked up at the blinding pinpoints of stars and could not help but think of the Magi who brought presents to the baby Jesus. They were Zoroastrian and they had traveled all the way to Bethlehem from their home in western Iran. But only if you believed in such things. The exotic scents that swirled around her were, however, real enough.

Reanimating herself she plucked out a denim shirt and a slate-gray cable-knit. Keeping her back to Ghislane, she shrugged off her leather jacket, stripped off her useless sweater and shirt, donned the ones she had picked out. They fit well enough. Both felt snug and warm against her skin.

Outside, night had come down like a hammer, with the wooly dark of winter. The sleet had turned to snow; the streets were all but deserted. The bedroom glowed like old gold, lusterless, dense, collecting on the bedspread, the floor, the other surfaces like the contents of a treasure chest.

"So I was right." Ghislane's arms were crossed over her chest. "You never really wanted to join us."

"I told you I wanted information."

"Did we provide enough for you?" Ghislane's voice held a keen sardonic edge.

"I'd say I learned quite a bit." Evan picked up her jacket and slid into it.

"You're not going, are you?"

Evan shrugged. "I can't very well stay here."

Ghislane stood arms akimbo. "Why not?"

Evan laughed. "That's an odd question. We don't know each other."

"Maybe we've only scratched the surface."

"*A* surface," Evan corrected.

"How cynical you are. But, honestly, Evan, you have proposed a partnership of sorts between us, how will we know if it can work if we don't come to know each other? If you leave now."

The streetlight outside the bedroom had gone out. The near absolute darkness outside felt cocooning, comforting in its way as it cut her off from all life beyond this room, this rowhouse. Evan appeared to hesitate. She didn't want to seem suspiciously over-eager to remain. But she had been hoping for the invitation. She needed to know if she had been talking to the real Ghislane, and if this young woman could actually help her find what she came to Nuremberg to find. If what Ghislane had shown of herself was a façade she knew she'd be able to crack it. Besides, why go out into this wet, chill night? Staying made more sense than leaving, and she didn't think there was any danger forthcoming here.

Ghislane grinned in her vulpine way. "We can roast chestnuts in the fireplace and tell each other ghost stories. We can drink hot chocolate and be little girls again."

"Sounds cozy," Evan said with a dry edge. "But you are right. We need to know one another."

Ghislane stuffed her hands in the pockets of her black jeans. "You don't believe me then."

"I have no reason to."

"Okay, fair enough." Ghislane nodded. "You want to know about me?" She unbuttoned and removed her long-sleeve shirt. Underneath she was wearing a singlet. Both arms were revealed all the way up to the shoulders. She had two sleeves of ink, the tattoos beautiful, intricate, colored—the fanciful style Evan had seen in photos of Japanese yakuza—a dragon dancing amid stylized clouds ran up her right arm, a roaring tiger clawed its way along her left arm.

Evan peered at the sleeves, taking in every detail. "Gorgeous. Must have cost you a fortune."

"Dead right. I sold a number of sculptures my mother had placed in here. God knows I had no use for them."

Evan laughed. "You're joking."

"When it comes to money," Ghislane said, "I never joke."

Evan took a breath, shrugged out of her jacket and Ghislane's sweater, set them on the bedspread.

"Those beers have finally caught up with me." Ghislane inclined her head toward the bathroom door. "Make yourself comfortable. I'll be back in no time."

Alone in the room, Evan's natural instincts took over. She silently and quickly went through drawers, checked behind the million-dollar wardrobe, the bedside table. The top drawer revealed nothing she wouldn't expect: brush, mirror, a paperback book, vibrator and lube, tissues, and so on. She was about to close the drawer when her eye was drawn to the paperback, a thick one. Intrigued, she moved it so the light fell on its cover. *The Cusanus Game* by Wolfgang Jeschke in the original German. She had read the novel in English and loved it. It imagined a future of worldwide madness brought on by the massive migrations of Muslims out of the Middle East and North Africa due to their native lands becoming too hot and dry to be inhabitable. She could see why it would appeal to Ghislane. She was about to put it back when she saw the corner of a silver frame.

Carefully she pulled it out. She was staring at the image of a young Ghislane making a teenager's goofy face. Beside her was a tall, elegant man. He held a cigarette in one hand, his other arm around Ghislane's waist. He was handsome in the classic Aryan manner—light hair, light eyes, a wide forehead, the nose and mouth of a Norse demigod. He seemed completely at ease smiling aristocratically into the camera. Her father perhaps? Oddly, there was something vaguely familiar about him, but for the life of her she couldn't bring it to mind.

Hearing the *click-clack-click* of Ghislane's boot heels she quickly put the photo back under the book, slid the drawer in, sat down on the bed.

"You okay?" her host said as she returned to the bedroom.

Evan nodded with a genuine weariness. She didn't for a moment trust anything this woman told her. On the other hand she could not fathom what game she was playing, hard-ass one minute, warm and fuzzy the next. She suspected that neither was the real Ghislane, but then who was she? Possibly she was intrigued by Evan or wanted something from her. Certainly, she was intrigued by Ghislane. "I guess I'm more tired than I realized."

"We'll kick your fatigue to the curb. I've got just the ticket. C'mon." Ghislane led the way into the kitchen, flipped on the lights. It was a big, bright, cheerful space. Butter-yellow walls, butcher block island, stainless-steel sink, refrigerator, and stovetop. "All mod cons," she said, spreading her arms to encompass the entirety. "All the money spent makes me want to throw up."

"Why live here then?" Evan asked.

"Because contrary to local lore I'm human."

Ghislane might have been making a sardonic joke, and yet equally she may have given an honest answer. Humans were complex—they often hated and loved something—or someone for that matter—at the same time.

Ghislane filled a kettle with water, set it on the stovetop. While the water was heating she fetched down two oversize cups and a square bottle with a label Evan could not read. Ghislane then made tea, but as it turned out the tea was only an excuse to drink. The cups were filled mostly with a clear, slightly viscous liquid.

"Slivovitz," Ghislane said as they took their cups into the living room, sat in cozy upholstered chairs. Unlike most women, she did not fold her legs up under her. But then Evan didn't either; the position made it impossible to spring up quickly in case of emergency.

Ghislane pushed hair off her forehead. "I'll tell you about my parents if you like. Rich, indolent, living off the sweat of their workers."

"All right," Evan said. It didn't matter to her what Ghislane wanted to say, she simply needed to take Ghislane's temperature, to feel solid ground beneath her feet because she was walking so close to the cliff edge. "Anyway, I never expected hot chocolate."

Ghislane guffawed. "Too right." Her eyes were half-lidded, her inked animals glowing in the lamplight.

She took a long pull from her cup. Evan tried to do the same, but she was unused to slivovitz and even diluted by the tea the potent plum brandy made her eyes water and set her throat on fire.

"You want to know about me? Okay, here it is. My father was an angry man," Ghislane began. "He was angry until the day he died. What caused his deep-seated anger? No one knows, not even my mother. *Especially* my mother." Another pull from her cup. "He took his anger out on her. Until I was old enough, then he started in on me."

Ghislane switched from the liquid mixture to hashish. When Evan declined she merely shrugged, continued to hold the aromatic, musky smoke deep in her lungs, releasing it after the longest time with a hiss like a steam engine.

"He craved a boy, you see; his manhood demanded it. Instead, she gave him me, so I suppose it could be said that he was angry at her womb. But, really, his anger preceded my mother's unspeakable failure. But I know nothing of his early life. He wouldn't even tell us where he was born. He must have had family: a mother and father, at the very least, but his lips remained sealed about them, about possible siblings. His past is a mystery, a closed book to which only he had the key."

"If he wanted a boy so badly why didn't he divorce her and try with another woman?" Evan asked.

Ghislane bared her teeth. "Simple. All the money belongs to my mother. The company, the factories, the investments. Everything."

She held more smoke, her voice coming thin as if through a bad cell connection. "Her family is very powerful, very influential, vindictive as hell. He couldn't—or wouldn't—meddle with that." She laughed bitterly. "Maybe in the end that's what killed him."

Evan noted that Ghislane said *"her* family" not *"my* family."

After taking up the hash pipe Ghislane had lost interest in the plum brandy. Meanwhile, that same liquor was lighting up Evan's esophagus.

When it hit her stomach and its acid she wondered whether it would set off some kind of gastric bomb.

"Of course they don't like me at all. I'm what d'you call it? Excommunicated." She shrugged. "Like it makes any difference to me."

"And your mother?"

Ghislane restocked her pipe, lit up, drawing the smoke in more slowly, more thoughtfully. "Well, shit, she's of no use to anyone—but her family dotes on her; she's the youngest of the three sisters." Her eyes looked glassy through the smoke haze wreathing her head. She waved her arm around. "This is her passion, or maybe her obsession. All these *things*— and what do they add up to, hm?" She drew on her pipe. "Then again every so often I sell one thing or another to fund the group."

A short silence descended and Evan had the curious sensation if she didn't break it open it would smother them both.

"You asked me before if I'd gotten enough information," Evan said.

"Mm hm."

Ghislane's eyes were slits behind the smokey haze. Was she awake or drifting off to sleep?

"You don't sound like you and Elke did before. You sounded like religious zealots."

"Ah." Ghislane shifted slightly. "That's for our rank-and-file, who are believers. That's how Elke and I roped them in. They're like sheep, those ones. They'll believe anything as long as it's religion-based. Like the Wellses, those creepy American white supremacists. I know quite a bit about them, you know. America is in thrall to the Deep State. And who controls the Deep State? Jews and libs, supposedly, but you and I know it's Wells and reactionaries like him."

Ghislane's breath soughed out like the wind in the willows. "Here in the fatherland the neo-Nazis are convinced that these deeply offensive influxes of Muslims will destroy Germany from the inside out." She sat up as if suddenly pricked by a bed of thorns. Her eyes were alight, shining in the buttery lamplight. "Who could have thought of such a diabolical scheme, hm? Our neo-Nazis ask themselves: Who is evil enough to use these immigrants as pawns? Who holds a grudge against us? Who keeps rummaging through our past? Who refuses to let our own dead rest in peace? 'I'll tell you who,' they say over and over. 'The Jews.'" Ghislane shook her head. "And then the lie, told over and over, becomes their truth. 'The goddamned fucking Jews,' they say."

24

NUREMBERG

A clock ticked off the seconds somewhere far away inside the townhouse. Odd that Evan hadn't heard it before. The metronomic beat fought its way through atmosphere turned as frigid as a meat locker. Evan was dizzied again and for a moment or two the river water had taken her under again, clasping her to its depths. She gave a tiny gasp as if awakening from a nightmare.

Evan stood up, paced slowly around the room. She was desperate to look at anything except Ghislane's face. The woman had genuinely startled her and for that she was as angry with herself as she was with Ghislane.

"You all right?"

Evan flinched at the sound of Ghislane's voice.

"My God, you're not a Jewess, are you?"

"I'm not," Evan said in a rather strangled voice. And then, stronger, "Not a single drop of Jewish blood in my ancestry." What else was she going to say? Ghislane seemed to have excluded herself from the bigoted beliefs in that little speech, but Evan was no closer to knowing the truth about her, or about the Omega e-file. In order to stay in place she needed to carefully string Ghislane along the line of neo-Nazi thinking. To do that she knew she was required to espouse a repugnant ideology.

"Huh," Ghislane was saying now, "well, that's a relief. I was worried I'd offended you."

"Why would you say that?"

"Well, you're American, and I know how Americans—"

"Certain Americans," Evan corrected her. "And then I'm Omega so . . . In any event, there have always been fascists in America. Notorious fascists like Virgil Effinger, Seward Collins, Charles Lindbergh, the Ku Klux Klan—the list goes on. The Brits, too. You've only to look at the history of the Royals. That family's half-German, anyway."

Had nothing changed since the rise of Adolf Hitler? Evan asked herself.

Did the false promise he held out of a white Aryan world still glitter like gold? It was still so irresistible to so many because change was always terrifying to people. In the 1930s it was the fall into abject poverty after World War I, now it was the constant influx of immigrants fleeing their own abject poverty, Hispanics and Muslims both. Then as now the outsider was the enemy that needed to be eradicated so the country could be cleansed. This insidious form of fascism was like a brood of cicadas, lying dormant for years only to emerge as a whole new brood, more virulent than the last.

"Nevertheless," Ghislane said, "I feel as if I've made you uncomfortable."

"I'm uncomfortable here in Germany." A lie; her parents lived in Germany. "In Nuremberg." True enough. "I'm unnerved by what has happened since I arrived here." Lies are so much more believable when they're strewn with the truth.

"I can't say I blame you. I regret the Roman Forum thing back at the *volksbad*."

Evan shrugged. "What's done is done." As if being thrown into the drained pool with Rolf to kill or be killed was of no import. "I was just wondering . . ." She turned to look at Ghislane. "About your father."

"He died a lifetime ago. Fell down a flight of stairs one night when I was thirteen. Probably drunk."

"I'm so sorry." Evan was trying to square the image of Ghislane's father she'd seen in the photo with what Ghislane had just said. That man did not have the appearance of a drunkard. But then again how much could you really tell from a single photograph?

"Don't be. I didn't shed a tear, believe me." Ghislane jerked her shoulders as if wanting to rid herself of a memory—her memory of him. "He treated my mother badly and me even worse."

"What exactly—?"

Ghislane's eyes flashed. "Like I said, a lifetime ago." Meaning she didn't want to talk about it. Fair enough. She put the pipe aside. Apparently even she had had enough hash for the time being. She cleared her throat. "I didn't really mean to provoke you, but I needed to know . . . because . . . well, this is a concern of a number of my people, most notably Dieter."

Dieter again, Evan thought. Something would have to be done about him if she was to get anywhere with Ghislane. Horst Wessel had been convinced the message to American Omega had emanated from inside this group. The longer she spent with Ghislane the more she suspected that Wessel was right. Evan turned her full attention to what Ghislane was saying.

"We found out someone in the group had a Jewish mother." Ghislane sat with her arms crossed. Despite how much hash she had smoked she appeared less relaxed now. "Can you imagine? How could she possibly be trusted?"

"And now she's . . ."

"Gone," Ghislane said with a ripple of her upper lip. "Gone and forgotten."

Evan was about to ask her what that meant when Ghislane rose with surprising alacrity. "It's time I showed you. . . ." Her voice petered out as she disappeared into the kitchen. She returned moments later with a carving knife. She held it as if she were about to stab Evan to death, but there was no sense of violence behind her eyes. No dullness either. Rather a clear sense of purpose.

She stood in front of Evan, knife held in her right hand. Slowly she opened her left hand, revealing the pale palm. Her gaze never left Evan's face as she drew the knife blade across her palm. Blood welled, rich and thick. Then she curled her fingers over the cut. Her left hand was a fist. She had not flinched or made a sound. Not even a flicker of her eyelids.

"It's not that I don't feel pain," was all she said.

It sounded like a partial sentence, the following words abruptly cut off. But Evan knew better. Ghislane was demonstrating something about herself, something elemental, primal. *It's not that I don't feel pain,* she was saying. *It's that I've felt pain so often I don't care about it anymore.* She means she's damaged, and it's the damaged who are cold-blooded, the damaged who are the most dangerous. She thought about the girl whose mother was Jewish. *Gone and forgotten,* Ghislane had said. In other words, dead. And immediately her mind went to her sister, irredeemably damaged. Cold-blooded? Dangerous? Was Bobbi, then, better off dead? *Better dead than to turn out like Ghislane,* Evan thought, and was instantly ashamed.

The knife lay on the table behind Ghislane. The thin ribbon of blood running along the edge of the blade turned the knife murderous. It was no longer for chopping vegetables although it might still serve for carving meat.

Ghislane opened a drawer in the same table, removed a strip of white cloth which she wound around her palm. She tied it off with her right

hand and her teeth, and Evan wondered whether this was a ritual often performed, or whether it was a ritual altogether. Either way, the act
of self-inflicted wounds said something profound, something terrible
about Ghislane's fractured psyche.

"Do you feel better when you hurt yourself?" she asked.

Ghislane gave her a quizzical look. "Doesn't everyone?"

"No," Evan said. "Not everyone."

"You?"

"I don't draw blood."

"Of course." Ghislane gestured toward Evan's wound, her bruises.
"You can't tell me you don't feel good when you win a fight."

"It doesn't work like that for me," Evan told her. "I hurt myself in
other ways."

Ghislane's eyes opened wide, questioning, avid, like a pelagic bird.
"Tell me."

Having put one foot into the darkness, Evan hesitated. Ever since
Ghislane revealed her group's rabid anti-Semitism, and likely her own,
the way forward had become more perilous than she had bargained for.
On the other hand, there was no backing out now; the only way forward
was to enter the darkness fully. That meant opening herself up to Ghislane because her sense of the other woman was that as a consummate
liar herself she was a bloodhound for lies. She could sniff them out. Even
when she wasn't sure she smelled a lie she knew something was off.
Evan knew that if she lied now the game was up and she might as well
walk away without discovering who created the Omega file that got Armistad killed. Having come all this way, having almost died more than
once she could not allow that to happen.

"My sister." She looked Ghislane straight in the eye and did not blink.
"I was not good to her. I looked down on her, played tricks on her, sometimes hurtful tricks. Once, when we were children, I left her alone over-
night in a cave near where we lived." It all came out in a rush, as if she
were vomiting up a poison that had lain festering deep inside her. "And
as adults, I didn't approve of her lifestyle; I didn't understand her, didn't
take the time. I didn't love her enough."

"That's all?" Ghislane sneered.

"Do you have siblings?" Evan asked her.

"I don't."

Did she or didn't she? Ghislane thought and acted like an only child.
"Then you can't know. I didn't understand until it was too late that Bobbi

was a piece of my own heart. There's a hole there now that can't be repaired. No one can take her place."

"Where is she?"

"Dead. So is her husband." Evan's mind flashed back to finding Paul Fisher hastily buried in the Fisher backyard. Suddenly the room felt claustrophobic, as if the walls were closing in on her. She went past Ghislane to stare out the window. The snow had ceased, and this changed the aspect of the night completely. As she looked the full moon emerged from behind swiftly racing clouds, carpeting the sidewalks in a luminescent blue. Shadows reared up suddenly, taking on ominous shapes, then receded after a car's sluggish passing. The snow looked thick, boggy, as if it might suck you down like quicksand. She didn't like the look of it and it made her feel even more cut off, as if she were in the desolate Berber desert.

"I never knew who I was," Ghislane said from behind her, voice soft as velvet, slow, as if she were measuring each syllable, tasting it on the tip of her tongue. "I never felt comfortable in my own skin. Does that make sense?"

"Of course it does." Again Evan found herself thinking of Bobbi. Is that how her sister had felt, right from the beginning? Is that why she took the FSB's offer, thinking she'd leave everything behind, start afresh?

Evan was about to ask her to elaborate when there came a knock on the door. Ghislane crossed the room to the entryway, pulled open the door. Two sets of footsteps, one heavier than the other. She turned from the window to see Dieter standing in the living room, a venomous look on his face.

"I knew you'd be here." He bit off each word as if they were forkfuls of schnitzel.

"Why is he here?" Evan asked.

"Get out, Dieter," Ghislane snapped.

"Fuck you."

"You see how it is." Ghislane sighed. "'In this world there is no justice, only mourning for what was lost, piece by bloody piece as we move through it.'"

Evan looked hard at Ghislane and with an internal shiver wondered whether she was already a corpse. Nihilism had been fathered by Nietzsche. But you couldn't trust Nietzsche, let alone admire a man who wrote, "*Woman was God's second mistake*." So screw him and nihilism to the outhouse wall.

Dieter, untroubled by such existential concerns, had drawn a pistol from behind his back.

"You killed Rolf. I don't know who you are. For all I know you're another Jewess."

"She isn't, Dieter," Ghislane said calmly.

"What, because she told you?" He scoffed. "Please. They all lie, these Jews. Lying's in their filthy blood. It's one of the sicknesses they carry." He gestured wildly. "And you—you called for that Roman circus. It was you who started the boulder rolling down the hill that killed Rolf."

"Rolf had his chance," Ghislane said with utter calmness. "Rolf wasn't up to the task I set him. He failed. No one's fault but his own, Dieter."

A shadow behind Dieter's eyes told Evan he'd reached the end of his rope. No words would dissuade him from what he'd come here to do.

Ghislane's eyes opened wide. She saw it too. "Dieter, don't."

Dieter growled deep in his throat, aimed the pistol, and fired.

25

NUREMBERG

Ambrose Wells had made an excellent choice. Christian Bardo was one of those mercenaries other mercs aspired to be. Broad of shoulder, narrow of waist, with tree trunks for thighs and chest muscles like armor. As for his face, his features were unremarkable. Neither handsome nor ugly, his was a face no one remembered. Except those he trained with, who felt a certain fear every time they were picked to fight against him.

He came by his athleticism naturally. His parents were born in Hamburg. At the ages of nineteen and eighteen, respectively, they immigrated to the States and shortened their name from Bardenhaupt.

Bardo's father had been a professional soccer player until his retirement when his knees gave out. He got his killer instincts from his mother, an ex-MMA fighter with a short but storied career in the ring, afterward in the tabloids and on Instagram. Completely uninhibited, she liked showing off her body as if she were a pole dancer. She even had a lucrative FansOnly account. They never spoke about their life in Germany and he never asked.

It was not a surprise to either of them that he was restless. After time in Greece, Italy, Spain, and the Balearic Islands he wound up in the fatherland. In a bar in Berlin, he was recruited by a band of Israeli and American mercenaries who had either been schooled by the Israeli Defense Force or had once been members of the U.S. military's Delta Force. They were not in the business of stealth; they were poppers, merc argot for quick in-and-out missions. In other words, wet work. Easily bored, they were in no way stakeout artists, though not surprisingly the females in the band possessed a significantly less impatient mindset.

It was just a short hop from Berlin to Nuremberg. It spoke well of Bardo that he had a natural aversion to Nuremberg—possibly picked up from his bandmates, though paradoxically being headquartered in Berlin for business reasons apparently caused the Israelis no ethical problem. Because of its constantly morphing political unrest and the alarming rise of neo-Nazism, Berlin was a natural epicenter for the work for which they were handsomely paid. Elements within the government and the federal police were occasional clients. Smart as Bardo was, his attention was so finely focused it never occurred to him that the work he and his group were engaged in was not so very different than that of the *Einsatzgruppen*, the Nazi death squads within the SS.

Though he had been sent a complete packet on his target and where she would end up, for him the night was still young. He had plenty of time to get to where he needed to be. He'd been in Nuremburg for three days now, more than enough time for him to scope out the best bars and dance clubs. In Berlin, where the nightlife was second to none, save surprisingly the Beirut waterfront, he'd become something of a club aficionado. Nothing prepared Bardo for his missions as an hour or three drinking, hanging out at the fringes of dance floors, observing the young scantily clad women, bare arms raised, butts twerking, mouths half-open in a kind of ecstasy the club DJs laid on them.

His club crawl naturally led him to the outskirts of the city where incessant rumor had it an illicit drug- and sex-fueled rave ran full-throttle all night long. On the way, his stomach growling, he drove past a crowded popular-looking pub, and pulled into a parking space up the block. As he was about to get out of the car he saw Evan Ryder with two other women on the sidewalk near the pub's entrance. He closed the door, started the car, but by the time he pulled out and managed to make a U-turn, he'd lost Ryder and one of the other women in the swirl of weather and young people milling outside the pub, laughing and smoking.

He kept his eye on the third girl, instead, as she was alone and heading in his direction. Blond, petite, with a pixie's face. *Center of my wheelhouse,* he thought. *Lucky me.* She picked up a waiting taxi, part of a lineup waiting for fares.

He made another U-turn and followed.

■   ■   ■

The *volksbad* turned out to be nirvana for him. It contained in its age-stained innards everything Bardo could want, as well as opportunities he had never dreamed of finding.

The place was vast, the EDM music ricocheting across the thickly beamed expanse, filling it with ten million molecules in frenzied motion. The DJs were good, the participants even better. He soon discovered that the crowd was made up mostly of transients—kids taking temporary time out from their backpacking around Europe. He crossed to the makeshift bar, got himself a drink in a plastic cup. He took a sip, couldn't identify it as anything in particular, settled for holding the cup. Vari-colored strobe lights lit up the space, making it look larger than it probably would be come morning.

Where was she, his pixie? His eyes roamed the vast space, the writhing crowd, then he himself did slow circuits of the room. Time passed, hours slipped away, and all he felt like doing now was drink some more and pick up any hot girl and pin her to the bathroom stall wall.

The current DJ, clearly into Martin Garrix, segued from "Pressure" to a lit remix of "Drown." At that moment, Bardo clapped eyes on his target. In her thick-soled boots, fatigues, and a camo singlet she was dancing with a cluster of maybe drug-buddies or drunken strangers. With this sort, his experience was that it scarcely mattered. Getting lost in the BPM while high was the sole objective. He understood these people. After all, he'd once been one of them. Now that he was older he'd morphed into a predator at their fringes, awaiting his opportunity. He began to move in a twisting clockwise direction, approaching her in a slow and oblique fashion.

It wasn't that he didn't like girls, but, really, when you came right down to it, what were they good for beyond what he was about to do with the blond pixie? Otherwise, they just got in the way, even, he wasn't ashamed to admit to himself, the female members of his band. Why should he be ashamed of anything? He'd more than earned the right to do as he pleased. He wasn't above the law—he was beyond the law.

He waited, still circling, then made his move. The thicket of bouncing bodies exuded sweat, alcohol, and pheromones. Cutting through all that fragrant flesh, he came up close on the blond pixie's right. The guy across from her got a shower from Bardo's tipped cup. Before he even had a chance to shout, Bardo had taken hold of the blond pixie's hand, dragging her toward the opposite side of the dance floor.

After only three or four strides she recovered her bearings, wrenched her hand from his and hissed at him. Instead of going after her, as she might have expected, he gave her an exaggerated shrug and started off in the direction in which he'd been dragging her.

Silently, he counted slowly toward ten. He'd reached nine when he felt her come up beside him.

"What the hell was that all about?" Pixie had to shout in order to be heard.

He shrugged again, began again to walk away but this time she kept step with him. At the edge of the dance floor he turned to her. "You are a nosy little thing, aren't you?"

He caught her arm as it came around to slap him. With his fingers encircling her wrist he drew her to him, not hard, but not softly either. He judged, correctly as it turned out, that she wouldn't like either extreme. He wanted her intrigued, not pissed off. And now that her blood was up he didn't want to give her what she wanted too soon.

He stared into her eyes, measuring how far gone she was by the dilation of her pupils. *Not quite yet*, he thought. Now was the time to smile.

"Stefan," he said into her face.

The confusion behind her eyes remained, yet she responded. "Elke."

"Well, Elke, don't let me keep you off the dance floor."

"I'm bored with the dance floor," she said, already wrecked and with a blurry eye toward nighttime adventure.

"I'm new here," he said into her ear.

"I'm fucking not."

"Take me wherever you want to go, then."

One of the first rules of seduction was to make the girl think she was in control.

Her elfin face expanded into a conspiratorial grin and she took his hand. "This way."

■ ■ ■

The night was icy, cleared now of the foul weather. After the overheated interior, the wind instantly dried the sweat on her face, in her armpits and the hollow of her spine. Elke zipped her jacket up to her throat. His back was hunched against the cold. It took only a minute for their noses and ears to redden. The sky was clear and on the side away from the city, black and star-studded. He pointed, picked out Sirius, the Dog Star, right away. "It's my good-luck star, the one my mother said I was born under."

He told her it was the closest star to Earth, besides the sun of course. *As if I'm a child*, she thought. She laughed, a rough animal sound. He held her closer and she snuggled in. He smiled but she noticed it was not at her. Who was that smile meant for? she wondered. She had glimpsed his interest the moment he saw her, arms above her head, body shaking, eyes half-closed in near-ecstasy.

She led him due north. After 1,500 yards a small building appeared out of the darkness.

"It's an old hunter's cabin," Elke said. "It's abandoned. No one's used it in ages." She chuckled. "Well, not for hunting, anyway."

The door was unlocked. It groaned on rusted hinges as she pushed it open. It reeked of earth and damp. An animal smell overlaid everything. Animals in rut. She saw him grin in the gloaming. *I know his type,* she thought. The night air had cleared her head somewhat.

Elke went straight across the room. She'd been here often. Striking a match, she lit some old newspaper that lay crumpled beneath a neatly stacked square of branches. It took three matches to get the damp newspaper going but at last a flicker of red light rose up, then another and another, joining together. The fire flared high, licking at the blackened firebrick. She wanted heat now—a lot of it. It was colder inside than out but she did not shiver. Her indifference to the cold started deep where her bones lay white and hard, iced over.

He came over to where she crouched, feeding the fire in small increments, and put his arms around her. He took off her jacket, having already doffed his coat. He pressed against her back. His hands came up to cup her breasts and he heard her say, "Hrm." Like an animal that had found its burrow. Her hair smelled of smoke and sweat and lemon oil. He buried his nose in it, inhaling deeply. She took out her cell phone, fired up a radio app, and music began to fill the room. Drawing her up he led her to a place just a little way from the crackling fire, where the heat had begun to warm the wall like the inside of an oven.

He took her in his arms and they danced to some Achim Hox electro house—"I Need You So." She broke away and for a time they danced a foot apart, her arms raised, eyes closed. While he watched her with gimlet eyes.

They came together, rubbing up against each other. He pushed down her fatigues and she helped him, making sure her underpants came down as well. He licked her ear, the velvet skin behind it. "Hrm," she said again, somewhere between a murmur and a groan.

Then he slammed her face with his fist.

Scheisse! Her knees gave out and he caught her as she fell into his arms, against his chest. *What the hell?*

With one hand he unfastened his trousers. They pooled around his ankles. He had already outgrown his underwear. Pushing them down he entered her. She cried out and put her arms on his roped shoulders. But he was going too fast, sawing in and out of her with a violence she needed to stop.

"What are you—?"

"Shh," he said. "Shh."

But she would not be quiet, not for him, not for any man. She was strong, and she swiveled powerfully enough that he slipped out. She grabbed his member and hurt him. At the same time the flash of a knife blade jabbed toward him. He knocked it to one side, squeezed her wrist so tightly anyone else would have been forced to drop the weapon. She kept her grip on it, ignoring the pain in her wrist, and was able to slash through his skin into the viscera.

Now they were at war.

Enraged, he delivered a kidney punch. She dropped the knife then, subsided so completely he had to hold her up. He turned her away from him. He stared down at her buttocks and grew even harder. He pushed and pushed and pushed. So enraptured was he that he did not feel her fingers gripping the base of his member until, clamped into a fist, they twisted him, then letting go, they slapped his scrotum so hard he gasped, saw stars.

As he took an involuntary step back he slipped out again. Whirling, Elke drove a bare knee into his testicles, doubling him over. Locking her fingers together, she slammed her knuckles down on the back of his neck. Driven to his knees, he tried to grab her, arms lashing out blindly, but she danced away, evaded them easily.

She shoved the heels of her hands against his shoulders and began pushing his upper body into the fire. Bent backward, his knees snapped and cracked and popped in protest. She saw him stunned, paralyzed by a woman who was not afraid, who had the will and the strength to fight him off.

She felt a surge of triumph as she continued to hold the initiative even though the heat from the fire was now scorching her eyes, drying her lips. She drove him back, her heart so black, a fireball, all her humiliations turned to rage as if by an alchemist's draught. Vicious tongues of flame licked toward the back of his shirt.

He bit his lip but uttered no sound at all. Again he reached out and again she evaded him.

She kicked out to send him into the flames but, using the strength of his abs, he was able to lever his upper body up and capture her foot between his hands. He twisted violently. She cried out, hit the floor hard, jamming her shoulder, her temple smacking against the floorboards. She was out of it for a brief moment while he crawled away from the fireplace furnace. He turned on his back like a turtle, rubbing against the floor in an effort to smother any clinging sparks, but Elke, already sufficiently recovered from her fall, reached across him, plucked out the top piece of flaming wood and dropped it onto him.

He yelled and threw it away from him, whipped onto his side, began scrambling to his feet, stumbled.

Elke saw her chance, grabbed her shed clothes and cell phone and sped across the room. But he was already regaining his feet and he rose with the piece of burning wood she had dropped on him in his hand. Ignoring the scorching of his palms and fingers, he hurled it at her retreating back. The flames caught her as she was about to open the door. The fire climbed onto her sweater like a tiger digging its claws into her flesh.

She arched her back, turned the doorknob. If she could only open the door the cold night air would snuff out the flames. But now Bardo had also retrieved the knife. He rushed at her, blade held in front of him in the hand-to-hand killing position.

She yanked the door open, felt the blessed relief of the cold wind on her face, her shoulders, her back where the skin was curling, blackening, flaking off. The night was icy, crystalline. She pulled blessed air into her lungs.

Then the knife—her own knife—slipped between her ribs. The world seemed so far away, the laughter, the music from the *volksbad* a distance of miles instead of yards. Lights blazed, remote as the constellations. Branches of illumination cast onto the newly fallen snow like party streamers. She was at that party but that seemed in another lifetime. Another world, rhythmic, drug-addled, familiar and now lost to her. Pain shot through her as if she were a tree hewn in two. A hand grasped her shoulder, threw her backward onto the floor. The hilt of the knife protruded from her side. She was gasping as if she were on the moon without a spacesuit, thrown into a black vacuum. Dimly she heard him say, "I saw you outside the pub with Evan Ryder. She went off with your friend. Tell me where she is right now."

She turned her head, shot him a venomous look.

He kicked her. She bit her lip to kill the groan forming in the back of her throat. She was glad at least for her silence.

"First you, then her." His face was red in the firelight.

Fuck you, she mouthed, and he cursed, kicked her again. The air had turned frigid with the slowing of her heartbeat. Even the blood running out of her felt cold. The initial shock of his second kick was an onrushing train, and when she regained consciousness he was gone.

Alone. The dying fire crackled in the hearth behind her without warmth; fire crackled through her body like lightning strikes. With agonizing slowness she lifted her cell phone. Her hand trembled so badly she dropped it, picked it up, dropped it again. For a time she could do nothing but stare at the phone as it went in and out of focus. Once, she found she couldn't remember what it was.

She dipped her hand into her own blood and her mind snapped back to reality. But so did her pain—she'd never felt such pain in her life, had never even imagined such a thing.

Tried again to use her phone, but between its blood-spattered slickness and her trembling she could not get a grip on it. She moaned piteously, had no idea where that awful animal cry had come from. There was a rattling in her chest every time she tried to take a breath. She coughed. Blood drooled out of the corners of her mouth.

She stared at the phone, concentrating all her remaining energy on it. Finally she left it in place near her mouth, pressed a nerveless fingertip against a key. When Ghislane answered she began to speak in a thready voice stitched with insupportable pain.

26

Kata was in her office doing absolutely nothing, staring absently out the window at the cluster of new, twisting skyrises in one section of Moscow's skyline. They had been built in an attempt to drag the ponderous city into the twenty-first century. They were as far from onion domes as it was architecturally possible to get. You might even think you were in Dubai or London, for that matter. What was wrong with these people? Who were they trying to impress? Anyone with an ounce of sense in their head knew that modernist Moscow was only millimeters thin, beneath it the real Moscow resided, with its dusty streets, its crumbling tenements, its hulking blown-out factories rife with the clotted oil and grease of the early twentieth century.

Her gaze as well as her scattered thoughts were turned outward in a mostly successful attempt to ignore the insistent summonses from the man who used to be her immediate boss, Comrade Director Stanislav Budimirovich Baev, the head of SVR. In the next moment, the brief text came through on the encrypted phone Kusnetsov had given her. Alyosha had the second one—the minister possessed the third, and that was it.

Level-XIII now, read the text from Alyosha.

Breathing a sigh of relief, Kata swiveled her chair around, rose and left the office, striding down the hallway where only soft, hesitant murmurings disturbed the deathly silence. Dust motes spun in the air at her passing, whirling like dust devils in the weak December sunlight dribbling in through the windows.

She took the elevator down to the lobby, crossed it diagonally, pushed open a nondescript metal door with the legend DVORNIK in Cyrillic—JANITOR—and stepped through into a dimly lit corridor that smelled powerfully of disinfectant. At the end of this stood an elevator door. To the left was a panel with a piece of glass polished like a marble embedded in it. She placed her left eye directly in front of the marble. There was a satisfying click, a hiss, and the elevator door opened.

Arriving at level-XIII, which was their code for where SIGINT was housed, she found herself hurrying faster and faster toward Alyosha as if running toward a lover. But was it to Alyosha she was propelled or what Alyosha had unearthed in the archives?

But why, she asked herself now, couldn't it be both? She had never before entertained such a thought, it never entered her mind that she would. There was a glare at the corners of her eyes, entirely internal, that she could not parse. It was as though gleaming mysteries from deep inside her had begun to rise from the moment she and Alyosha bonded over iced vodka and the punishment meted out to Borya Arsenyev.

A fingerprint scanner allowed her entry into SIGINT itself. The space smelled like a nineteenth-century coal chute, which it indeed once might have been. Everyone was hunched over their terminals inside malodorous bays thick with electronics, sweat, moldering food, and quiet desperation. No one was allowed out for a meal or even a coffee break. Reeking toilets were available through a pair of doors on the far side of the windowless room. Indeed, once you clocked in for your ten-hour shift you were forbidden to leave for any reason whatsoever, except by stretcher. Those instances were not as uncommon as might be assumed. And, of course, SIGINT itself was active right around the clock. Spying on your enemies—and your so-called allies—never slept.

Alyosha had related this depressing information in the hours when there was no one else to hear save for Kata herself. Kata electronically swept her townhouse morning and evening without fail; she did not trust anyone from the FSB to do it for her. Still, there was a paranoia that ran through all of the big cities, Moscow and St. Petersburg especially, that could not be entirely erased. Not that Kata minded. Paranoia was like a razor blade held close; it honed her edge even when she was in repose.

She saw Alyosha standing in the center of the vast room, her face questing like a hawk scenting a great horned owl. But this particular hawk was a friend, Kata thought, who would not hurt her, and who she had pledged to keep safe from harm.

"What have you found?" Kata said quietly as they stepped inside Alyosha's cubicle. It was larger than the others, dominated by three monitors set in a shallow curve like the old Cinerama screens or the newest gaming monitors.

Alyosha's sly smile curved her lips like those of the Mona Lisa who, Kata was certain, knew secrets that even da Vinci—the genius who painted her—and afterward all who looked at her image did not. Alyosha placed a slender forefinger across her luscious lips, keeping Kata silent. Paranoia again and always.

"I can't take anything out of here," she whispered. "Especially the deep intel Minister Kusnetsov gave me clearance to search through." She pointed. "But here, look at these."

Kata scanned the pages Alyosha had extracted from the dossiers she had pulled from the FSB servers. Six pages, six names, including Borya Arsenyev's.

"We're looking for a choke point," Alyosha continued. "Isn't that the phrase you used?"

Kata nodded. "The place where Department 73 was being infiltrated by Omega either directly or indirectly."

"I think it's indirect." Alyosha's forefinger ran down each page. "A couple of names keep popping up. I'll see where it leads."

She was about to go on when Kata heard her name being called. She looked up, heard her name again, stepped out of Alyosha's cubicle. Baev, her former boss, saw her, signaled with his head. When she hesitated, he said, "Now," loud enough to stiffen the backs of the workers nearest him.

Without even a glance over her shoulder at Alyosha, Kata picked her way along the narrow aisles between the open bays.

"Outside, turn left, three blocks, cross the street. Ahead you'll see a green kiosk, buy a packet of chestnuts. Wait for me on the far side of the kiosk." Before she could respond Baev hurriedly walked away, but not before she saw the storm clouds darkening his face.

■　■　■

Kata put her back against the kiosk, which was warm from the burner heating the chestnuts. She held her wax paper cone in one hand, staring at nothing in particular. She did not have a good feeling about this abrupt rdv. Baev was out of bounds, of this she was sure. Just as she was sure Kusnetsov had no idea of the meeting, hence Baev's insistence on a spot outside the office.

The snow had stopped some time ago but the day was overcast and very dark above the violent light pollution of the city, a dome in which airliners thundered at will but migrating birds got lost.

The head of the SVR arrived soon enough, fastidiously knocking icy slush off the bottoms of his shoes. His fingers plucked a warm chestnut from her packet. He wore a heavy wool coat with wide astrakhan collar and lapels. The style was vaguely military. His eyes searched her face as if it were a map of the edge of the world.

"Did I ever tell you the story of my grandfather?" Clearly he did not want an answer so Kata didn't give him one. "He was a high-level Bolshevik in the 1917 revolution. After the Tsar and his regime were deposed and killed he attended the meetings of the Bolshevik hierarchy. In the first two the question was raised concerning democratic elections, which had been a promise the Bolsheviks made to the peasants. The questioner was peremptorily told there wouldn't be any elections. In the second meeting he brought it up again. This time no one bothered to answer."

"I imagine that man was your grandfather."

"No," Baev said with a sly smile. "It was Stalin." He popped the chestnut meat into his mouth, chewed reflectively. "My grandfather knew precisely what was going on—that the Bolsheviks never had the intention of mounting democratic elections or democratic anything, for that matter. Stalin did not; he had no idea at that time what the Bolsheviks were all about."

"But he learned quickly enough," Kata said.

"From my grandfather." Baev reached for another chestnut, rolled it around between his fingers. "He learned all my grandfather had to teach him and then he had him killed. Did it himself, in fact. Over dinner, no less. Ran him through with an old Cossack saber he'd 'liberated' from a White Russian during the Revolution. Then, by all accounts, he sat back down and ate two portions of honey cake—his and my grandfather's."

Kata gave him a cynical look. "I'm sure if I look hard enough I'll find a moral there somewhere."

"Just what the hell do you think you're doing, Kata?" Baev's voice was thick, clogged with bitter emotion.

Now she said what she'd held back before. "I don't work for you anymore."

Baev's eyes narrowed. "Of course. You're now one of Darko Vladimirovich's bitches." He meant Kusnetsov.

"If you say so," she said mildly. If his aim was to rile her up he would be disappointed.

"I do say so. Friends become enemies in the blink of an eye." He leaned toward her. "Just what the fuck are you doing for him?"

Without taking her eyes off him, she plucked out a chestnut, began to nibble on it. "Mm. These are good."

At this impertinence, his eyebrows lifted. "I wonder if our dear minister knows he's got a scorpion in his shoe."

"I doubt it." She made a show of chewing contentedly, while in reality she was on edge. Placed between Baev and Kusnetsov was like being caught in a vise squeezing slowly shut.

"But one of these days he will."

"You're sure of that?"

"As sure as you and I are standing here now," Baev said. "You're unreliable, Kata. I don't mean in the usual way. If you were you'd be useless to us. No, in the usual sense you are the polar opposite of unreliable."

Kata spat out a sliver of shell. "Speak plainly."

"You are unknowable, possibly even to yourself," Baev said. "I used the wrong example before. Scorpions are utterly reliable. You know precisely what they're going to do and when they're going to do it. No, you're a tiger. Tigers are altogether unpredictable. Are you going to be charged or ignored? Are you going to be eaten slowly or all at once? Who knows?"

"Someone must."

Baev shook his head. "Yes, but they're all dead."

Kata took a moment to gather her thoughts. "Okay, you are your grandfather and Kusnetsov is Stalin. When he has no more use for you—"

"Or when I gather too much power."

She acknowledged his addition. "When either of those two things happen—"

"It will be off with my head. And just like with Dima you'll be the one who volunteers to do it." Dima Tokmakov had been the former head of Zaslon.

Kata's lips twisted at the allusion to the Queen of Hearts in *Alice in Wonderland*. "So what am I doing here? Are you attempting to enlist me to save you?" She shook her head. "Not a chance."

He appeared to ignore her remark. "Rumor has it that Borya Igorevich Arsenyev, the director you killed, was a member of Omega."

Kata did not even blink. "I can neither confirm nor deny—"

"For the love of St. Stephen, come off it." He waggled a finger in her face. "Listen, I had a deal going with someone inside American Omega—intel for money. Everything was nice and simple."

"Nothing is nice or simple, Comrade Director. You of all people should know that."

Again, he ignored her interruption. "And yet only now do I find out that Omega has infiltrated Department 73."

"Maybe inside FSB itself," Kata said evenly. "That's what I'm doing."

Baev grunted. "The thing is I don't trust Kusnetsov."

"Why should you?" Kata replied. "I don't."

"So . . ." Baev took a breath, let it go. "What are we going to do about it?"

Her brows knit together. "What do you mean *we*, Comrade Director?"

"Stop calling me by my title," he said waspishly. "The way you say it makes me sound like trash."

"Stanislav Budimirovich." She cocked her head. "Is that better?"

He made an exasperated sound as if he were blowing into a tuba. "The one thing I know about you is that your hatred for Omega is unsullied by the currents swirling around you."

"You're doing business with Omega, you shit."

"Now I prefer Comrade Director." He laughed, but she did not join in. "My job is to collect intel from whatever source may be available. That's what *I* was doing. But not now, not anymore. Not after knowing they want to have their strudel and eat it too."

An icy wind had started up, knifing along the street. The wax paper cone and its contents went flying in a wicked gust, the chestnuts tumbling off the curb, sinking into the slush of the street, ground to paste by the passing vehicles.

"Ah, well," Baev said. "Nothing lasts forever."

"Some things have a life span of a mayfly." She turned her attention from the lost chestnuts back to Baev. "Who in particular were you dealing with inside American Omega?"

"I have a name," Baev replied, "but it's probably operational nomenclature. I don't even know whether it's a man or a woman."

"The name, Comrade General."

"Will you assist me? I like my head just where it is."

She sucked in the icy air, held it in her lungs as if it were weed smoke. Was she considering or procrastinating? The name might very well prove useful to her purpose.

"I'll do what I can," she said at last.

Baev snorted like a horse after a long run. He nodded. "My contact's name is Schrodinger."

27

It was Ghislane launching herself like a missile who took Dieter's bullet. It passed through the meat of her left upper arm. Ducking down, Evan grabbed a small bronze sculpture of the Roman Caesar Caligula doubtless worth thousands and hurled it. It struck Dieter square in the face, his nose vanishing beneath it in a welter of blood and cracked cartilage.

Ghislane was able to wrench the gun out of his hands before he knocked her aside. Blood gushing down the front of his shirt, the lapels of his jacket, he snapped open a butterfly knife. Its slim wicked blade flashed in the lamplight, a dazzling bolt running its length. Ghislane took his attack. Rather than retreating she stood her ground, grabbed his wrist, pulled it toward her, over her canted hip. The rest of his body followed, over and down like a waterfall sluicing over a shelf of rock.

As soon as he was down Evan was there, jamming a knee into his solar plexus. He coughed blood, the white of his eyes were crimson, but the pupils were dead set on her. His mouth opened, lips pulled back from teeth in a predator's rictus.

He waited and when her weight was fully on top of his, he scissored his legs, toppling her. Grabbing up the bloody ruined bust of Caligula, he brought it down hard. Only Evan turned her head at the very last instant and prevented it from cracking her skull. As it was, it slammed into her ear, making her head ring. Dieter delivered a vicious kidney punch that caused her legs to draw up in agony.

He rose, hauling her up with him, and pushed her against the wall of the entryway. His own blood was drying over his face like a war mask. Half-dazed, her body racked with pain, Evan nevertheless drew him toward her as if he were a lover on whose lips she was about to plant a kiss. Instead she bit clear through his lip, tearing off a piece of it, spitting it into his face. He had no time to respond before she slammed her forehead into what was left of the bridge of his nose. With a roar of pain, he reared back, where Ghislane was waiting with his gun in her hand. She placed the muzzle against the side of his head and squeezed the trigger.

28

Kata arrived home long past normal working hours. As she stepped across the threshold all the lamps blazed as if there were a party going on. She was scarcely surprised; Alyosha had told her that she was afraid of the dark. She was like a child who was sure monsters lurked under her bed or in her closet. Unlike a child Alyosha's monsters were her abusers, Pasha Shutkov and Borya Arsenyev. That they were both dead mattered not at all. The barrage of pain Alyosha had been subjected to was never to be forgotten. A form of recovery was the best that could be hoped for.

Alyosha was sitting up against a cloud of pillows in Kata's bed when Kata entered. She was halfway through *Anna Karenina*. Now she looked up, her large eyes clouded with Anna's world, as if she had been dreaming while reading.

"I waited for you longer than I wanted," she sighed.

"Isn't that the essence of life?" Kata shrugged out of her coat, toed off her boots.

Alyosha's expression snapped alert, considering this as a true existential question. Kata let her think about it while she padded into the bathroom to perform her ablutions.

"I suppose you're right," Alyosha said when Kata returned. "I'd never thought of it in that way."

Yet another reason Kata liked this girl so much; Alyosha was a thinker, had so much potential that until now had been entirely wasted in the kingdom of men. "I've been meaning to ask you. Alyosha is the diminutive for Alexei, a man's name."

Alyosha looked away for a moment, staring like a cat at the play of lamplight across the near wall. "It was a joke," she said at length. "Though he never said it I think my father had been expecting a son. He always said I was as strong as any boy."

Kata laughed in the way reserved only for Alyosha.

"He was very good to me, took me everywhere with him." Then she turned back, her eyes directly on Kata. "You're so late."

"I'm sorry. I had lots to do when I left you. For one thing, Baev kept me longer than I wanted."

Alyosha grimaced. "Is he also a beast?"

"I think that's a prerequisite for advancement in the FSB." Kata undressed, shedding shirt and pants, and Alyosha averted her gaze, a pink flush rising up her neck into her cheeks. Kata was well aware of the girl's change in demeanor since the night of their first encounter in the dacha where Alyosha, emboldened by Kata's coming to her rescue, had joined in the attack on Borya. But the change had come not after the attack, but after Kata told her of Pasha Shutkov's death. Alyosha said she had well and truly loved Pasha even as he well and truly whipped her night after night. Rage, helplessness, and a tenderness that continued to unmoor her warred for ascendancy inside her.

Kata drew on the silk sleepwear—shorts and an oversize short-sleeve shirt—that she folded and laid out on the bed each morning.

Returning her gaze to Kata again, Alyosha gave a little shiver. She had said that she was always cold at night, even colder deeper into the night, and that she hardly slept. Though they were about to share the same bed for a second night, Kata had a strong feeling that it would be like the night before, just sleeping—for Alyosha *had* slept with Kata's warmth beside her—and in the morning awaking with Alyosha's body pressed against her back, Alyosha's elbow on her hip, her forearm wrapped around her waist.

"What did he want?" the girl asked now in a small voice. Lamplight burnished her face, highlighting her forehead and cheekbones, the shadowed hollows underneath further accentuating how thin she was. And yet, while there was virtually no fat beneath her skin there was plenty of strength both physical and mental. She had survived so much. Her topaz eyes were limpid as tide pools, slowly revealing their inner depths the closer you got to them. Kata felt the quickness of her pulse, the exaggerated trip-hammer of her heart in her chest and her throat. A line of sweat crawled insolently down her spine. Her thighs felt heavy.

"Tell me about your breakthrough first." Kata sat down on the edge of the bed. She had to restrain herself from reaching out, pulling the girl to her, encircling her with her arms, pressing her lips against the side of her neck, feeling the rhythm of her pulse. Alyosha was like a fawn, easily frightened by anything she perceived as a physical assault. In this intimate setting even laying a hand on her shoulder might set her off.

Alyosha's face fell. Kata knew she hated disappointing her new friend and savior. She wished she wouldn't feel that way. "Ah, well. I hit a dead end. I was so excited that I'd found the choke point, but when I dug deeper the converging lines vanished."

"Forget about that. It's okay," Kata said reassuringly. "To answer your question, Baev has become terrified of Kusnetsov, and for good reason. He's been trafficking with Omega."

"Not a smart move."

"No. But Baev is desperate to stay one step ahead of Kusnetsov."

"Intel for money?" Alyosha intuited.

Kata frowned. "But that's just it. American Omega doesn't need money. It has more of it through the Wellses and their cohort than they'll ever need."

Alyosha shook her head. "Then I don't understand."

"Neither do I." Kata got under the covers. "Baev said his contact's name is Schrodinger."

Alyosha's eyes lit up. "Oh, wow." She set aside her book. "Kata, I think we might have found our choke point. The name Schrodinger appeared in Borya's dossier."

"In what capacity?"

"No idea. A slip of paper with that name scribbled on it was in Borya's file, a bit of ephemera a completist clerk stuffed in there without questioning who Schrodinger was or why the name was written on the paper."

"Written by Arsenyev?"

Alyosha shook her head. "No. I know his writing. It's not Pasha's either."

"I wish I could see it," Kata said. "It would be a big help."

Alyosha sat up, her legs crossed yoga style under the covers. Shyly, she handed over a rumpled slip of yellow lined paper that had obviously been ripped off a writing pad.

Kata took it. "Alyosha, this was a very dangerous thing to do."

"I thought it was important," Alyosha said. "This is what we do now, no?"

"It is." Kata smiled. "You're a wonder."

Alyosha shrugged. "As far as SIGINT is concerned, no one will miss it because I'm betting no one knows it was ever there."

Kata nodded. "Nevertheless I don't want you making any more changes inside SIGINT."

Alyosha folded her hands in her lap. "I promise. But I was exceedingly careful."

"No doubt, no doubt." Kata took a long look at the note. "Baev gave me the phone number he was using to contact this Schrodinger."

"And did you try it?"

Kata sighed. "The second reason I was late. After ditching Baev I went to see a friend of mine."

A cloud passed across Alyosha's face. "Why didn't you come back to SIGINT? I could have—"

"As it turns out you couldn't have because my friend couldn't and this is all he does, all day, all night, every week. He's the best hacker I know. He's never failed me before. This time he did. Secondly your request would have been on a security record somewhere and I don't want you questioned." Without thinking, she put her hand out toward the girl, but almost immediately drew it back. "Excluding you, I don't trust anyone in SIGINT. In fact, after my talk with Baev I don't trust anyone inside the entire FSB."

"Does that include Minister Kusnetsov?"

"Him most of all." Kata waved a hand. "In any case, the number Baev was calling is a zombie—no records, nothing. It doesn't exist. Though my friend said it likely linked to another number and another and another and so on, bouncing all over the globe."

"So that's a dead end."

"We have a confirmation of the name Schrodinger."

"So it seems likely Comrade General Baev wasn't getting his intel from someone in American Omega, after all."

"Oh, but I think he was." Kata reached over for her brush, was about to run it through her hair.

"Let me do that."

Alyosha took it out of her hand. Fingers brushed against fingers with an unmistakable electric charge. Kata could swear she felt the excited atoms swarming from her to Alyosha and back again. She gazed at Alyosha but the moment their gazes intersected the girl's eyes slid away. Still she brushed and stroked Kata's hair with infinite tenderness.

"Go on," Alyosha said softly, her voice hoarse with barely suppressed emotion.

"Baev has dealt with *dezinformatsiya* long enough to know it when he sees it," Kata said, picking up her train of thought with some difficulty. She cleared her throat of the novel sensation lodged there. "It appears likely that this Schrodinger is itself a cutout, someone who has a connection inside the American Omega."

"So Schrodinger is an operational name."

Kata nodded, and Alyosha's palm brushed against her temple. "So now what?"

"So. Now I go to the only source we have: *Devyatyy Krug*, Department 73's training site."

Alyosha set aside the brush, ran her hand over Kata's hair as if giving it a final polish. "I know the place. You must take me with you."

"That's just what I won't do," Kata said. When Alyosha started she made a gesture to calm her down. "We now know the local choke point is somewhere inside *Devyatyy Krug*. I have to go alone; you've been seen there with Pasha Shutkov. Your presence is sure to stir up gossip among the men, which is what we don't need." She cocked her head. "Oh, don't look like that. We're a team now, Alyosha. Isn't this what you want?"

"What I don't want is to be stuck in front of a computer screen in SIGINT the rest of my life."

Kata put her hand over Alyosha's. A tiny spark of heat went through her and another barrier inside her began to melt. "Have patience. For this mission I need you here in SIGINT to back me up." At that moment it was impossible to think that when provoked Alyosha was capable of terrible violence. She liked that. She liked it very much. Kata smiled in a way she never had before. Possibly it was a child's smile and this both dizzied and elated her. Her adoptive parents never held her. The Russians chose carefully and wisely. The couple had been trying to conceive without success. They took Evan in and fell in love with her, but with Bobbi they were different. Perhaps they didn't intend to be. But Evan came first, Evan was their golden child. The suspicion that they hadn't wanted to take her was never far from her thoughts. Yes, she had cried when they died, but not because she loved them. The abruptness of their deaths was a shock. But the truth was she felt nothing for them. She cried because they had left her all alone and she was terrified that Evan would leave her as well.

"Afterward," Kata said, after clearing her throat of memories, "there will be time to move up."

"Out into the field," Alyosha said. "With you."

"If you wish it."

"I do." Alyosha nodded. "More than anything."

Kata, so unused to compassion, bent her head as if in prayer. "It is done."

Alyosha blinked, like an owl at night, searching. "All right," she said at length. "I'll back you up when you go to *Devyatyy Krug*. I'll be patient. But in return I want you to do something for me."

Kata tipped her head forward. "What exactly?" But she knew; she'd known from the moment the two of them had sat side by side on the carpet of the dacha's upstairs bedroom drinking and talking softly while Borya Igorevich Arsenyev lay six feet away, Kata's broken-off heel in his leg. She just hadn't expected this moment to arrive so soon, and yet she knew she would willingly acquiesce to Alyosha's quid pro quo, which was actually nothing of the sort because this was no business transaction and she could no longer deny that she burned for it as brightly as Alyosha did.

Alyosha's eyes were luminous, as big as moons. Lamplight fired her hair, picked out her cheekbones, the tip of her nose, her half-parted lips. She slid closer and, leaning in, whispered, "I want you to touch me . . . here and here. And here."

"Yes." Kata's heart, that treacherous cinder, had burst into flame. Her throat was tight, ached in a way it never had before. And she repeated in a rush of heated breath, "Yes."

29

They had a doctor on board. Of course they did. Ghislane's wound was not serious in that the bullet had gone through the meat of her arm without hitting a bone. As for Dieter, Ghislane had made a call. "He'll be gone by the time we get back," she had said as Evan helped her into the shotgun seat of her car. "The place will be neat and shiny."

Which made it clear to Evan that this wasn't the first time a dead body had to be spirited out of Ghislane's townhouse. She had thanked Ghislane for taking the bullet meant for her. Ghislane seemed not to have heard her, she was too busy glowering at Dr. Brady as he clucked over her wound. Apparently he disapproved of flying bullets.

It was while Dr. Brady was finishing the last of her stitches that Ghislane got the call from Elke. She listened to the first couple of words, pushed the doctor away. She tried to ask questions but Elke had stopped talking, although the connection remained open. Ghislane, blanched white as snow on a tree branch, used one of her GPS apps to locate precisely where Elke was.

To Evan she said, "We've got to go," as she slid off the operating table. "Where to?"

At the same time Dr. Brady tried to hold her back. "You're not going anywhere, Ghislane. I haven't bandaged you up."

Ghislane slapped his hand away. "I'll live, Brady. Don't you worry about that."

"But there's the risk of infection," he protested. "You must—"

Ghislane held out her hand. With a sigh Dr. Brady opened one of his drawers, spilled out a dozen capsules. "Two a day for—"

She was at the door when he pushed a glass of water at her. "Two, Ghislane. Now. This is no joke."

"It's for your own good," Evan said.

Ghislane glared at them both. "You're taking his side now?" Nevertheless she took two of the antibiotic capsules, swallowed them without aid of the water. At the same time he slapped a pair of self-adhering gauze pads over her wound.

"Happy now?" she snapped.

"Not in the least," Dr. Brady said, clearly unhappy. "Let me give you an injection for the pain so—"

The rest of his sentence was cut off by the door to his surgery slamming behind them. Ghislane sprinted down the hallway to the front door, Evan at her heels.

"Take it easy," Evan called to her. "You'll bust a stitch."

Without a word Ghislane wrenched open the door using her good arm. The frosted witching hour air swirled thickly around them, taking their breath away.

"What's happening? Where are we going?"

Ghislane said nothing as they scrambled into her car, a battered VW that nevertheless sounded like an Indy racer when she stepped on the gas. The initial acceleration punched Evan back into her seat. Then simply, "Elke's been assaulted."

Ghislane drove maniacally fast, doubly dangerous because of the icy roads. She didn't seem to care but it was Evan's first time in the car with Ghislane driving and her heart was in her throat.

"It's bad—I think terribly bad," Ghislane said as she screeched around a corner, the rear of the car fishtailing. "The poor thing could hardly speak. She may be dying. She may be dead already. I don't know."

"Who assaulted her?"

"She didn't say or if she did it was too garbled to make out, and anyway he wouldn't have given her his real name. They met at tonight's rave at the *volksbad*, from what I could gather. Elke wasn't making a lot of sense. Come to that, she wasn't breathing all that well either."

Up ahead the light was changing from green to red. She not only ignored it but accelerated through the intersection, leaving bursts of angry truck horns behind her. It was after two in the morning; there were scarcely any cars on the road.

"But—now listen to this—whoever assaulted her, one thing she made clear, Evan: she claims he told her he's after you." She shot Evan a quick look. "Can you credit that?"

Unfortunately, Evan could.

Ghislane grunted as she fishtailed around another corner. One thing Evan had to say for her, she was an excellent driver even in bad weather.

"Okay, you're pissed. I get it. But sooner or later Dieter was going to try to take you down for what you did to Rolf," Ghislane said at length. "They didn't always see eye to eye but through it all they had each other's back."

"Pity," Evan said, "but I'm tired of repeating that Rolf gave me no choice."

Ghislane sighed. "Neither did Dieter. That's the kind of people they were. But their bullyboy strength was what made them good soldiers."

"Lovely group you had here," Evan said tartly.

"Never mind my group." Ghislane risked another glance; it was brief but weighted with incipient fury. "Is Elke right? Is her assaulter after you?"

"I'm afraid it's quite likely."

"*Scheisse.*" Ghislane huffed. "Because of you I have two of my people dead, and one gravely wounded, at the least."

"You've also put down an insurrection."

"Bitch."

Evan nodded, accepting the epithet. "I'm sorry about Elke. Truly I am."

"Fuck your sorries, Fraulein. And fuck yourself. If Elke dies, her blood is on your hands."

"She won't be the first," Evan muttered under her breath.

"What was that?" Now Ghislane was staring at her. "What did you say?"

"Nothing." Evan turned her head, stared out the window as the darkness sped by and saw only shadows, moving and changing as if alive.

■   ■   ■

"She's up there." Ghislane pointed. "There inside the old hunter's cabin."

The souped-up VW swerved past the seething entrance to the *volksbad* and its milling throng, haloed in a cloud of cigarette and pot smoke, off the curved driveway. They jounced onto the dead grass, covered over now with a blanket of fresh snow. Ghislane was out almost before she slammed the gearshift into park. The VW jerked to a stop, its metalwork groaning in complaint.

Evan followed her as she wrenched open the cabin door, the high *skreee* of its rusted hinges sounding as loud as Gabriel's horn. Evan had earlier scrabbled in the car's glove compartment, and now thrust the flashlight she'd found there into Ghislane's hand. It threw off a wider and more powerful beam than either of their cell phones' flashlight apps.

And there she was, Elke, staring at infinity with glassy eyes open wide. Surrounded by a lake of blood, her mouth half-open, her forefinger still on the smeared keys of her cell phone.

"*Gott im Himmel!*" Ghislane raced toward her friend, the beam of the flashlight swinging back and forth so that Elke moved from light to shadow and back again in time with Ghislane's churning legs and arms.

Evan came up behind her as Ghislane crouched over her fallen comrade.

"Elke," she called. "Elke! It's me, Ghislane. Wake up! Damn it, wake up!"

Lowering herself beside Ghislane, Evan put two fingers against the side of Elke's neck. She had seen enough dead people to know there would be no pulse. The air around Elke was rank not only with her own blood but with the stink of a surfeit of alcohol and drugs.

"Ghislane," she said as gently as she could. "She's gone."

"No!" Tears rolled down Ghislane's cheeks. The flashlight fell from her fingers. "Jesus no."

"Elke's gone," Evan reiterated.

Those two words must have finally gotten through Ghislane's shock and disbelief. She whirled on Evan, slapped her across the face. "*Hündin!*" She screamed. "*Fotze! Blöde fotze!*"

Nails turned to claws, she lunged for Evan's eyes. Thwarted, she went for her cheeks, connected with one nail before Evan batted her aside. She sat back on her heels, weeping openly now. "Look what you've done. Look what you've done to my girl."

Her eyes narrowed, even overflowing with her rage. "I told you what would happen to you if Elke died," she cried. She wasn't even in control of her voice, which was shrill as a buzz saw wrecking metal.

"You said her blood would be on my hands." In contrast, Evan's voice was low, perfectly calm. "And it is. I accept that. If not for me—"

"If not for you she'd be alive!"

Considering the debilitated shape Elke was in while she was still alive Evan did not think that was altogether true. Tonight for whatever reason Elke was ripe for a predator. It was a pity, an outright disaster, and as Evan had just told Ghislane she wouldn't shy away from her part in the girl's murder. But—

Ghislane growled deep in her throat. "I told you I'd kill you."

"I assumed you were speaking metaphorically."

Ghislane rushed her, her hands curled into fists. "You don't know what she meant to me."

"But I do." In the same moment, she drew Ghislane to her, hugging her close.

"What . . . what're you doing?" Ghislane moaned. Her fists beat a tattoo against Evan's shoulders. Then feeling Evan's hand in her hair, her head came down onto Evan's shoulder. "Oh, God, oh, God. Elke, where are you now?"

"Beyond the pain you and I are both feeling," Evan said into her ear.

Ghislane hissed, began to struggle again but Evan maintained her firm hold on her and her embrace would not be denied. The dying fire crackled, wind battered the old boards, insinuated itself through cracks in the brickwork. A fistful of shouts, a car's engine backfiring, drunken laughter indistinguishable to the two women inside the hunter's cabin from sobbing.

It took some time for Ghislane to understand that Evan's embrace was not hostile, that she wasn't being imprisoned. She was being consoled. The tension collapsed within her, all at once, as if she were a marionette whose strings had been cut. Her head lolled against Evan's shoulder and she took quick gasping breaths.

"Slow down," Evan whispered. "Slow down, that's all you need to do."

After another interval during which a renewed sleet started to crackle and pop against the cabin's roof and walls like buckshot, Ghislane sighed.

"She's dead." Her voice strained, thin as tissue. "Elke's dead."

"Yes," Evan said because she knew Ghislane needed to hear that affirmation.

Ghislane sighed again, deeper this time, air hissing out of her. "She was not like me." Her voice was small but steady now. "She was born into poverty. Her family had nothing, scraped at the very earth, clawed for money, often stole it. Sometimes beaten for it. Other times thrown in jail. They never lived; they were too busy surviving."

"That's something, isn't it?"

Ghislane took a moment, after which she said, "Yes. I suppose it is. But not something to be proud of."

"Oh, I don't know. Surviving instead of dying . . . I'd say that's a pretty big victory."

Ghislane gave a tiny laugh almost immediately submerged into a sob. She cried again until she was dried out.

"She made it perfectly clear to me how much she despised the Nazis, the neo-Nazi movement."

"Then why was she with you?"

"For one thing, she was my best friend. For another, she was my history guide." Ghislane sighed. "She studied them, the Nazis, and Goebbels's propaganda tricks that she saw being used by not only the neo-Nazi movement here in Germany but in the fascistic authoritarianism infecting your own country. She found some of the films Leni Riefenstahl made at his request as Nazi propaganda. God knows where or how much she had to pay for them. There's a black market for Nazi relics. The more she studied the more convinced she became of the danger of the Fourth Reich being resurrected and spreading out from here. 'We are the epicenter,' she would tell me over and over. 'We have to stop the movement now before it becomes too strong and overwhelms us.' At this she would grow intensely agitated. I think at some point she began a love affair with drugs, either to dull her anxiety or to forget about the sinkhole opening up under Germany. It's likely both."

"So neither of you are what you seem?" The subtle disconnect Evan had noticed between Ghislane and the neo-Nazi's loathing for Jews was beginning to make sense now.

Ghislane exhaled a long-held breath. "We do our job well, don't we? That's partly how we recruited the group. But for us it's a front."

"I don't understand."

"I've told you all I can. Maybe too—"

"Finish what you started, Ghislane."

Ghislane closed her eyes for a moment. "The situation's not as simple as that." She shifted a bit but seemed reluctant to have Evan let go of her. It seemed she had found a kind of stasis that kept her from exploding, whirling in all directions. It may be that Evan was preventing her from losing her mind.

"History. That isn't my thing. I'm only interested in the eternal now— what's tangible, whatever I can see in front of me. But then I don't know." She shook her head. "It was Elke who made me see what a baby I am— doing all this to derail the family's status. I thought that if I humiliated them thoroughly enough I'd shake them out of their ivory cocoon." Her hands turned into fists, white knuckles slowly emerging like the Wolverine's adamantine claws. "I despise them so—their money, their power, their insulated world. Above all their smugness. All they think about is money and what it can buy them. If that's happiness I'd rather be dead."

She was silent for some time after that. She seemed to be listening—to the decaying sound of the last of the smoldering wood caving in, the sleet, the soughing of the wind. Then she turned her head, saw Elke again in her lake of blood and gave a sharp intake of breath, as if reliving the moment they came upon her like this.

"I liked her right away." She was caught up again in her memories. "She was such a street-smart person. She had gone through things I've never dreamed of. It made her tougher, you know. But also angrier. I felt her anger; I felt our kinship through it. I picked her out of the gutter, literally, where she'd been lying for a night and a day. She was a reclamation project. To help her, I thought. To get her back on her feet. But I see now that saving her was entirely selfish. The real reason I did it was to make me feel better about myself, believe that I was worth something."

"You gained a friend," Evan said.

Ghislane ducked her head. "She owed everything to me and she never stopped repaying me. Even though it sometimes went against her convictions she did everything I told her to do, all the dirty work a girl like me wouldn't—couldn't lower myself to do." Ghislane pulled away enough to look Evan in the eye. "And you know what? I did nothing to stop her. I liked it, reveled in the adulation. I mean, who wouldn't?" Then her face fell. "No, no, there'd be plenty who wouldn't." She gestured with her chin. "You, for instance."

Evan almost lost it then, thinking of Bobbi who so longed to be her sidekick but never knew how to tell her big sister. *Not that it would have mattered*, Evan thought now. *I was so successful at pushing her away.* All at once her inner voice echoed Ghislane's lament. *Where are you now, Bobbi?*

Ghislane at last broke away, began to crawl on hands and knees. She stopped once to press her hand against her wound, which was throbbing terribly. Then she continued crawling from where their fight had thrown them back to Elke's side.

"And now her death"—she whispered—"no, no, her life with me, what I ordered her to do, over and over—I see now that I'm no better than my parents. I was born an elite and, *fick mich*, I'm still an elite. I hire other people—the indigent who have no other choice—to do what, if I were a real revolutionary instead of pretending to be one, I would do myself."

Head down, staring fixedly at Elke as if her gaze could pierce through the flesh and blood to find her essence. "She was the real revolutionary. She clashed with many of the group, but she sparked debates among us. Even though she rubbed some of them the wrong way she kept them on their toes, she kept them thinking."

"Did that include you?"

Ghislane stopped abruptly, as if she had caught herself in a truth she didn't mean to reveal. "I don't know you at all."

"You know me as well as I know you."

Ghislane rose, shaky but seeming determined. "I need to get out of here, go home." And as she felt Evan come up beside her, she turned to look at her and said, "I feel like sleeping for a week." She stared down at Elke's half-shadowed face one more time. "I don't want to leave her, but I must. This—her murder—changes everything."

Evan badly wanted to ask Ghislane what she meant, to go deeper into what she'd been talking about—her parents, her motives, her self-reckoning—but some instinct, honed in the field, warned her to keep silent, to keep her interest at bay. Suspicion, she had learned, was like a genie—once out of the bottle it was impossible to put back in. Nevertheless, she was beginning to suspect that beneath all the bluster and speechifying Ghislane was a decent human being—lost, perhaps, but decent.

She revealed none of this, understanding this was a critical moment for Ghislane, perhaps even a turning point in her outlook. Instead she said softly, "We need to take care of Elke."

Ghislane nodded. "I'll stop somewhere, call my people from a public phone. They'll come fetch her."

"That's the best we can do for her? No funeral or—"

Ghislane's eyes blazed for a moment before dulling out, depthless, half-dead. "We need to bury her as quickly as we can. My people have to be discreet, come here, in and out as quicky as possible. People use this place regularly but we can't afford to take the time to clean up. This is the world we live in, Evan."

With visible effort she turned and went through the door. Evan picked up the flashlight and swept it and her gaze around the room for anything they might have missed, but there was nothing. Even the fire had died.

Ghislane called her name from just outside the door. "You coming?"

The sleet had stopped, at least for the time being, but the sky was still low, choked with clouds corrugated as a tin roof. Evan caught up with Ghislane, a sudden thought overtaking her as they crunched along. The sleet had turned to an icy skin over the snow.

Ghislane reached the VW, opened the door, then turned back. "It's too late to do anything for Elke, you know. Too late to make amends."

"I can find who murdered her," Evan said.

"The only way is to . . . he wants to find you. You're the target. Elke was just a stop along the way."

"Just a stop," Evan echoed. "She deserved so much more than that, didn't she?"

"Yes, she did."

"I agree. So then. I think I'll stay here a bit longer."

Ghislane gave her a stern look. "I think you're wasting your time."

"I want another look inside the *volksbad*. Maybe someone saw him."

Ghislane inclined her head. "Okay. Will I see you again or are you done with us, done with me?"

There was nothing to say to that, so Evan turned and threaded her way toward the endless throng polluting the air outside the *volksbad*. But her eye was on the VW, and the moment she saw it going down the driveway, she climbed into the back of the first taxi in the wait line.

"Follow that VW," she instructed the driver. She'd always wanted to say that.

30

Ensconced in his den, one of the rooms in the mansion Lucinda was forbidden to enter, Samuel Wainwright Wells, notepad on his lap, sipped his Pappy Van Winkle bourbon from a cut-glass lowball glass.

He was currently engaged in conversation with Alice Stanwick, his nurse and personal secretary. She had begun schooling him when he was ten years old and she was fourteen going on twenty-five, a rare and precocious genius. She had been handpicked for him by his father, Louis, a towering man, brilliant, volatile, ruthless, with a massive ego that would hit you like a stone wall if you crossed him in even a minor way. Such was his power in those halcyon golden days that he had been known to reduce his rivals to near bankruptcy or suicide. Starting when she was seventeen, when Alice wasn't schooling young Samuel she was in bed with Louis.

She had left the fold soon after Louis died. She was thirty-four, and she spent the next decade earning her RN, then traveling throughout the Far East—Japan, Indonesia, China, Tibet, Sumatra, finally Nepal— studying with the great healers and shamans, learning their trade, and then returning home, to Samuel, with their secrets. No matter how far she went, she never lost touch with Samuel. They exchanged long letters, phone calls as often as possible. She made sure the connection between them would never be broken. Wherever she was in the world, she remained his first teacher, his most trusted adviser.

Now, she was still as rare and precious a light in Samuel's life as she had been when he was a young boy. She had pale clear eyes, a patrician's nose, and rouged cheeks. She had not shed a tear at Louis's funeral or interment. But within a week she had donated all the expensive clothing Louis had bought for her to Goodwill and bought a new wardrobe of plain practical outfits in black, white, and camel. Ever since, her dress remained always nondescript. It occurred to Samuel that consciously or unconsciously she had chosen the colors of death. Mourners in the West wore black. Mourners in the East wore white. Camel was the color of the desert, a forbidding place, trackless, bereft of life.

She was the only person he trusted absolutely, the one he knew would never lie to him. Everyone else around him did; he took that as a matter of course. It came with the territory when you were so very wealthy. His father had taught him that, along with the admonition, "Never allow anyone to call you rich, son. That word is for people of a lower class. What we possess is wealth." Samuel Wainwright Wells never forgot a single word his father said.

They were seated in a pair of persimmon wingback chairs with a marble and wrought-iron café table between them. To their right was an oriel window guarded by green watered-silk curtains pulled back with swags. Across the room a large wall-mounted flat-screen TV played soundlessly. For a couple of minutes they watched the images. The TV was programmed to auto-change to a different newscast every two minutes.

"Look at them," Alice said conversationally. She wore her still-thick hair unfashionably long. It was the color of silver and shone like metal. She was knitting him a sweater. In her later years she had taken up knitting as a way to keep her fingers nimble, protecting their arthritic joints from stiffening up too badly. "They're like the flying monkeys from *The Wizard of Oz*," she said, referring to the coast-to-coast rioters, whose disturbances were, according to plan, ratcheting up. Mass shootings, looting, drummed-up protests devolved into full-scale riots, burning big-box stores, retail storefronts, overturned vehicles. "Soon the entire country will be on fire," she said.

"Can't be soon enough," the Old Man grunted. His face twisted, the seams down his cheeks seemed to crater, but perhaps that was only a trick of the light. "Now," he said without looking at her.

Alice was at once on her feet. "The periods between—"

"I don't want to hear that," he thundered, and bit his lower lip. "None of my business."

She unlocked a cabinet, drew out a tray with four Styrofoam beds meant for syringes. Only one remained. She drew it out, went through the familiar ritual: alcohol on cotton ball, clean his upper right arm, uncap the one-time-use syringe, inject him. He made a face, like a child forced to drink cod liver oil. "It burns. Oh, how it burns."

"You know that means it's fresh and working." Alice turned away, disposed of the used syringe so no one would find it. "You've used . . ." She halted, thought better of the rebuke. "That was the last dose."

He glared at her as if his eyes were a weapon. "Order an immediate delivery. Do I have to tell you everything?" The serum gave him an unpleasant, almost feral edge while it was being absorbed by his body. But she knew this, she had been trained well, and his sharp words flowed over her like water over a rock.

Alice, back in her chair, called in the order on her cell. "I don't care if it costs more. And increase the standing order from one tray to two." She listened. "Do I care what it costs?" She disconnected, uninterested in a reply.

She glanced up at the riots flitting across the TV screen. She knew she needed to change the subject; he became low if he dwelled on his medication. "The people. These sheep. With their blood up they're an unthinking mass."

"When I was in college," Samuel Wainwright Wells drawled, "I observed an experiment. Rats responding to electrical stimuli. Get them to do this, get them to do that, as you wished." He gestured at the screen. "Same thing."

"Well, not quite." Alice contemplated the ceiling, her mind turning over, turning, always grinding facts to dust, like grist in a mill. "Today there are so many forces at work in our favor, destabilization chief among them. When people feel threatened as whites do now they turn to like-minded people. Religion, faith empower them in a world that threatens to marginalize them. You promise them strength, Sammy. You promise to protect them from the encroaching tide of people of color, radical libs who want to take away whatever's left of their lives."

Needles clicking, stitches lining up like good soldiers at attention. "You provide hope and, just as important, an outlet for their rage. You provide targets they can blame for the country's upheaval. You give them everything they need to express themselves, to reassure themselves they still matter. The result: a sense of belonging is more important than facts. Because facts contradict this sense of belonging, which is all they have.

"In short," she concluded, "you have given them a magnifying glass which turns sunlight into heat, a way to burn their enemies alive."

"What a victory, Alice! No one in this country has ever accomplished what I have! No one had the vision. No one had the nerve."

"Or the wherewithal," Alice interjected drily.

Samuel grunted, either in admission or in contempt. "By recruiting the radical right to my cause while demonizing the radical left I have effectively split this country right down the middle. That message is playing out

overseas in Germany, France, Italy, Turkey, but it will be all the more potent once Titan-Firstar begins televising internationally tomorrow. Just
in time for our nationwide American insurrection where we begin to
take back our country from the left-wing socialists." Samuel's expression
was smug. "The contracts are all signed, sealed, and delivered. Dylan
sent me e-copies." Dylan Soames was the corporation's chief lawyer sta-
tioned in London. "He's done a stellar negotiating job. Got better terms
than we had initially discussed."

"Soames will go far," Alice acknowledged. "He takes orders well."

The rioting kept Alice's interest for only the length of two channel
cycles, then her attention moved on. She watched Samuel's gaze riveted
to the screen of his notepad. *No time like the present*, she decided.

"Unlike Ambrose," she said conversationally.

Samuel stopped his obsessive scanning.

She lifted an immaculate eyebrow. "What are they up to now?"

Samuel looked down at his notepad. Pressed a key. "Still outside
smoking, like they do every night as soon as I retire up here with you."

"I find it amusing," Alice said, "that they still have no idea."

"Especially since Ambrose is head of security."

Alice clicked her tongue against the roof of her mouth. "They're making those CCTV cameras as small as a snake's tongue." She shook her
head. "What a world. Time keeps racing ahead, Sammy."

He nodded. "The less years we have left, the faster time goes." His
gaze never strayed from the notepad screen. "You know the saying, Alice,
days pass slowly, years pass quickly."

"Too right." She started a new row. "Still smoking, are they?"

"No," he said, his eyes riveted to the screen. "They're done. They're
moving."

Alice clicked her tongue again. "It's sad, really. Human beings are so
predictable."

"Not us, Alice."

She chuckled. "No. Not us." She put her knitting aside. "Shall I order
a late dinner?"

"Why not?"

She reached for the internal phone. "The usual, then? Bone-in rib eye,
rare, fries, extra crispy, apple pie."

"Hold the à la mode," he said distractedly. He was watching Lucinda
with a strange avidity Alice would rather not be witness to. His wife had
just come within view of the wide-angle lens. She and Ambrose were

holding hands, like teenagers. There was a rapt expression on his wife's face, eyes hooded, lips half-parted, he'd never seen before. He ought to be jealous; he might have been years ago, but his tastes had changed. He now found women repellent, especially older women trying to recapture something from their youth that was so ephemeral that even back then it was impossible to define.

As if reading his thoughts, Alice said, "You're not in need of punishing yourself, Sammy."

His finger stabbed out, changing the scene again from one camera to another.

"Wealth washes away all sins," she continued.

His eyes flicked up for just a second. "Now you sound like my father."

"Yes," she said, with an enigmatic smile. "Isn't that marvelous?" She had taken up her knitting again, but the needles remained still. She looked up at him. "Well?"

"They're going at it like demented ferrets."

"Yes, well, we're all animals in the end, aren't we?"

He sighed, turned off the screen; he'd seen enough. "It's the betrayal, Alice." He pressed his thumbs against his closed eyelids.

"We knew what she was when she was romancing you."

"A nonbeliever." When Alice did not deign to confirm such an obvious remark, he continued, nettled. "Of course I saw what she was, which is why I married her."

"A bolt out of the blue, she was." Alice dropped her gaze, resumed knitting.

"I needed a female who could embody what our scriptures reveal as the left hand of the Holy Spirit, the one who whispers into the ear of the demiurge. And I tell you this, Alice, she's perfect for the role. It was as if she were sent to me—to *me*, the demiurge, in order to put the final cement in the merging of American Gnosticism and American evangelicalism."

Alice frowned. Had she dropped a stitch? Not possible, surely. "She's a con artist, albeit an exceptionally skilled one."

He nodded knowingly. "And like all skilled con artists she's got charisma to spare. And she radiates sexuality like an atomic furnace. Every man who sees her, hears her speak, is lucky enough to feel her hand against his is immediately entranced. These big boys will follow her into the gates of hell."

He put aside his notepad. He did not want to look at it again tonight. "She's also made the company a ton of money."

"It will be her money in time, as well as Ambrose's," Alice said sourly. "I have a new will." He grinned. "I have cut them out."

She peered at him over her reading glasses. "They'll fight it tooth and nail."

"They'll be given a settlement and they'll take it." He tapped his fingernail against the notepad's screen. "Have you forgotten about this?"

It was rare to hear Alice laugh; she was not born to laughter. Or pleasure, for that matter.

"Well, she *is* an immigrant, after all. And a nonbeliever to boot," Alice said with no little asperity. "She deserves nothing but scraps. *They* deserve nothing but scraps." And under her breath she muttered in a litany, almost like a prayer, "Thank the divine power that watches over us you didn't have a child with her."

Clearing her throat she raised her voice to a normal conversational level. "But now we must circle back to the question of betrayal, Sammy. The constant abominable fornication between your wife and your son."

"Yes, down through history the con artist is a louche character, one with loose morals or none at all. A liar, a thief, outcast from the divine power's sight. Only hell and damnation await them."

"So the Slovenian. But Ambrose . . . ?" She allowed the unfinished question to hang in the air between them before continuing. "She offered him the apple. It was between her legs and he gobbled it wholesale. She has taken him into darkness."

He closed his eyes for a moment, then shook his head as if trying to rid himself of black thoughts. "Is it his lust for her or hatred of me that caused this to happen?"

"The age-old question." The knitting needles clacked softly together like the progress of insects across a headboard. "Why can't it be both?"

31

"Someone to see you," Isobel said.

A wary edge to her voice caused Ben to look up from his notepad. He was enveloped by an upholstered armchair set by a window in Isobel's library, which, with its Steinway baby grand was as much music room as library. When she was agitated Isobel came here to play a piece by Debussy or Erik Satie. It was her place of sanctuary from the quantum-speed world she otherwise lived in. The room was ringed by mahogany shelves stocked with books from all over the world in many different languages, modern and ancient. Sapphire-blue curtains flanked the two windows. The streetlights had come on many hours ago. Darkness fell early and swiftly with the winter solstice only days away.

"He doesn't have an appointment." Isobel's smile was off, by a lot. "But then he doesn't need one."

Instantly Ben was on high alert. "DOD?" He thought of his old boss General Aristides.

Isobel shook her head. "FBI."

"Wait, don't tell me. Is his name Tennyson? Jon Tennyson?"

Isobel's eyebrows lifted. "As a matter of fact it is."

"Send him up." Ben turned off his notepad, on which he had been replying to the latest text from Zoe. "And let his shadow up as well."

"He's alone." She frowned. "You sure about this?"

"Yeah, I am," Ben said. And just in case. "I may not like him but he's a straight shooter, Izzy."

She nodded. "I'd like to take you at your word, but you know how feds raise my hackles." She left to fetch Jon Tennyson from the foyer down-stairs where two of her men were—as she would put it—entertaining him.

Ben was not a little surprised that the FBI agent would want to see him. It had been May, seven months ago, that he'd last seen Tennyson and his partner, Jason Leyland. He and Evan had come across them at the late Paul Fisher's house. Fisher had been married to Evan's sister Bobbi. He wondered what could have brought the FBI agent here. Ben had had a previous life with his own black shop within DOD, but that had been abruptly terminated by the outgoing president. Just as he had no wish to go back, he resented anything from that time intruding on the new life he and Evan had made for themselves here at Parachute. He was well rid of being in the government's clutches and was not inclined to do them any favors. And yet he felt an obligation to see Tennyson, to hear what was on his mind. Too sentimental by half, he thought.

When Isobel returned, Tennyson in tow, she said, "An Binh doesn't want you staying up too late." It was an unnecessary reminder, but perhaps, Ben thought, it was directed at Tennyson, a way of cueing the agent that his time with Ben was limited.

Tennyson looked pretty much unchanged as he stepped across the threshold and came toward Ben.

"Jesus, Butler," he said, "this place is more secure than the Pentagon."

When Ben made no reply, he took a different tack. Clearing his throat, he said, "This visit is a surprise for both of us."

"I'm not about to make it any easier for you." Putting aside his notepad Ben took up a cane and stood, took several slow but firm steps toward the FBI agent.

Tennyson's eyes opened wide, but he said nothing, instead sticking out his hand. Ben looked into Tennyson's eyes for a moment, then shook the hand.

A rueful smile quirked one side of Tennyson's mouth. "Yes, well, I was a bit harsh with you and Ms. Ryder during our initial meetings."

"Not as harsh as your partner."

"Leyland, yeah."

"Where is he, by the way?"

"I sent him back for training."

"What? To not be such a prick?"

Tennyson grinned.

"Does that mean you're a bigger prick than he is now?"

Tennyson snorted. "In a manner of speaking." He unbuttoned his coat. Shrugged it off. "Say, d'you mind if we sit?"

There was a sofa nearby and Tennyson walked as slowly as Ben over to it. When they were both seated Ben said, "From your initial reaction I know you heard about—" He gestured at his legs.

"Well, I'd heard you'd been shot overseas. Congratulations, by the way, in getting rid of that extremist network."

There was a sharpened note to his voice that alerted Ben to a deeper meaning, possibly a hint to why he was here. Never mind. For the moment, they were getting reacquainted, which considering their previous adversarial positions was necessary for both of them.

"Then I assume you heard that I was crippled."

Tennyson looked a bit alarmed at Ben's directness. Clearly he was not a man used to candor. "I . . . well, yes." He brightened. "But obviously that was incorrect."

"Out of date, more like." Ben waved a hand in dismissal. "Congratulations on your promotion. How high have they elevated you?"

"Section chief of the FBI Joint Counterterrorism Task Force. I liaise with the CIA now."

"Poor you," Ben said and they both laughed, and just like that the ice was broken. If forgiveness wasn't in the air at least a détente was.

Tennyson sat forward on the sofa, elbows on knees, hands clasped together under his chin. "The truth is . . ." He cleared his throat again. "The truth is I, we—I—need your help. Yours and Ms. Ryder's."

The Ben of a few weeks ago would no doubt have said something sharp and brittle, spoiling for a fight. But this was now. Here was a new Ben, reborn. "Go on, but I'm sorry to tell you that Evan is currently overseas and completely unreachable."

Tennyson frowned. "That's regrettable. We could use her unique method of tackling problems."

That caused a smile to break out across Ben's face. "Ah, so you've seen the light."

"Hindsight has its uses," Tennyson said, "for those willing to reevaluate."

"Indeed." Ben was thinking of his own recent reevaluations. But he also wondered whether he was guilty of judging Tennyson too quickly. He put his hands together. "So. How can we help?"

"We?"

"I'm part of a huge corporation, Tennyson. When you get me, you get Parachute. Well, part of it anyway."

"Okay, I accept that." Tennyson gave an anxious look around. He seemed to want to be anywhere but where he presently was. "Look, I—"

Ben held up his hand. "I think it's time we invited Isobel into this conversation."

The FBI agent looked even more nervous. "Is that really necessary?"

"Really, it is," Ben said with such force all Tennyson could do was nod in acquiescence.

Ben pressed a key on his cell. They waited in silence, staring at each other, two boxers unsure whether to rush each other or retire to their corners.

When Isobel stepped into the room it was with An Binh at her side. Ben let out a breath he hadn't been aware he'd been holding. Whatever détente he'd come to with Tennyson seemed ill-fitting and rickety as a shack about to be hit with a wrecking ball.

Isobel smiled her warmest smile, stood with her hands clasped in front of her. She did not introduce An Binh but Ben had the distinct impression that oversight was by design. He would not have been surprised to learn that it was at An Binh's own request. It seemed to him that at this stage of her life she preferred being anonymous.

"How can I help?"

"It seems," Ben said, "the FBI is in enough difficulty to require our assistance."

At this Tennyson winced, but, gathering himself, said, "There's a specific reason. Last spring when Evan Ryder returned from the Far East she was abducted as she left the airport."

"Yes," Isobel said. "Old news."

"Yes, I know." Tennyson nodded. "However, there's a thread left dangling. Ms. Ryder herself believed she was abducted at the behest of Samuel Wainwright Wells."

"True enough," Ben said. "But there were no direct links."

"Maybe there is something. I think we can agree that Ms. Ryder was being forced to drive to somewhere within a certain radius of the airport." Tennyson spread his hands wide. "Mr. Butler, did she describe to you the events that took place while she was being abducted?"

"Yes," Ben said. "Of course."

A beam of light seemed to snap on behind Tennyson's eyes. "That being the case . . . This has really been nagging at me. I have to fly out to Los Angeles tomorrow—these riots." He shook his head as if in bewildered amazement. "I wonder if you'd be willing to take a quick drive with me now, guide me as far as that aborted journey went. I've read the report over and over but there are details that are still not clear. You were there; maybe you'll remember something from that day, maybe being there again will jog your memory. Perhaps from that we can determine if your theory about Wells is correct."

"It is correct, Tennyson. Jesus, Evan and I have spent two years building the case against him."

"Really?" Tennyson cocked his head. "Care to share?"

"It's right here, Mr. Tennyson," Isobel said, and right on cue she handed the FBI agent a thick file.

He took it graciously. "Well," he said, digging out his reading glasses. He sat back, set the dossier on his lap and, opening it, began to read through it with the alacrity of a speed reader, tracing the lines of type with the tip of his forefinger.

Ben and Isobel looked at each other, silently communicating. She tapped her watch and he nodded. An Binh was waiting to help him to his bedroom for the night. Nevertheless, he held up a hand, indicating they should wait.

At length, Tennyson looked up, closed the file, and stowed his reading glasses back in his breast pocket. "Okay," he said, "color me convinced. But nothing in here is a smoking gun. It's all circumstantial."

Isobel had had just about enough of this interloper. She didn't know him from a hole in the wall. Moreover it was clear to her that after their past history Ben didn't much like him. "Get out," she said, in no uncertain terms.

"As you wish. Parachute isn't my territory."

"You bet," she flared. "And it never will be."

Obediently, Tennyson rose. Without looking at Ben he said, "Obviously, I've come to the wrong place." As he came abreast of her he said, "Mind if I keep this file?"

"Be my guest," she said. "That's a copy."

An Binh chose this moment to speak. "Please stay a moment." She turned to Ben. "What Mr. Tennyson has asked of you—this must be a personal decision, not a corporate one."

As Ben leaned on his cane and struggled to stand up, Isobel glared at An Binh. Both of them contrived to ignore her. He'd become good at that, especially when two or three times a day she'd ask him if he'd heard from Evan. He hadn't. She was worried; he wasn't. But then she didn't know Evan like he did. He was confident in Evan's uncanny abilities in the field. When she had something to report she'd contact them, not a moment before.

Tennyson turned around and in his eyes Ben could see that he was reluctant to leave. The naked look made him realize it wasn't that he didn't want to leave here defeated. He really did need Ben's help.

"Tennyson, you understand . . ." He took a slow but firm step, then another and another. "I'm still damaged goods."

"Nonsense," the FBI agent said. "All you need to do is sit in my comfy SUV and tell me where to go, what to look for. Besides, you look as healthy as a race horse."

Ben looked at him as if he had just surfaced from a deep sea dive, a fish clamped between his jaws. He almost laughed. This was a different Tennyson than the one he and Evan had butted heads with last year. He took another step. Pain flared in his left hip and he stumbled, almost fell. Isobel moved to help him, but Tennyson's hand on her arm halted her. She shot him a vicious look but nevertheless stayed where she was, allowed Ben to right himself on his own.

"My hooves aren't yet sufficiently shod," Ben said with a self-deprecating laugh.

"But they will be," Tennyson said with an uncharacteristic grin. He gestured. "The truth is I can't go any further on the case against Wells without your expertise. That file I just read proves it. An hour and a half of your time. No more. That's all I'm asking for."

Isobel gave him her best dark look. "I say stay here, Ben. It's too soon. Granted, An Binh has already done you a world of good, but you've really just begun."

"I get it." He shook his head, gave An Binh a quick look. Her face was as usual impassive, but he suspected he knew her heart now just as she knew his. "*This must be a personal decision,*" she had said. She was right.

"This could be the break Evan and I have been searching for," he said. "I can't pass this up. I want to go with him, Isobel." He shrugged. "But I work for Parachute, for you. Are you ordering me to stay?"

"I'll do no such thing." Isobel crossed her arms under her breasts. "That's not how you and I ever operated. It's not how we operate now."

He nodded. "Then I'm going."

"Of course you are." She said it not as an accusation. She turned and without another word left the room.

An Binh stayed a moment more, long enough to give him a look. He knew. She smiled with her eyes.

■   ■   ■

"We really pissed her off," Tennyson said when they were both in his Chevy Tahoe and he had stowed the file under his seat. The Tahoe had been repainted a matte black—just like Evan's car—to keep it anonymous. FBI agents didn't normally drive matte colored cars, hot-rodders in tees and motorcycle jackets did.

"Nah," Ben said. He zipped the window down, reveling in the wind on his face. Even the chill of Washington winter felt good. He felt refreshed, more himself, and he knew why. He was on the hunt again, not cooped up inside Isobel's electronic-lined birdcage. "She wasn't angry, just resigned."

"Good woman then."

"Good *person*," Ben said. "Better than most men I've encountered. Far better."

Tennyson maneuvered the Tahoe nimbly through the dregs of late night traffic. The violet glow of the metropolitan area that sprawled across the Potomac into Virginia spread through the dark. "High praise from you, Butler."

"At this point," Ben said, eyes half closed against the wind, "you might as well call me Ben."

"Jon," Tennyson said.

They were crossing over into Virginia, on their way to Herndon, the area near Dulles Airport where Evan had parked her car, and from where she'd been abducted.

"Leyland is waiting for us at the airport. We'll pick him up, then drive to the lot in Herndon where Ms. Ryder's car was parked," Tennyson said.

Ben turned to look at him. "You were pretty sure of yourself, then."

Tennyson barked a laugh. "Not really. When it comes to you and your partner, Ben, I'm never sure of anything."

"So if I'd said no you would have left him hanging out on his own?"

"Leyland's a big boy. He knows how to take care of himself."

Thirty minutes later, they pulled up to the curb where Jason Leyland stood hunched over against the cold, hands thrust deep into the pockets of his overcoat.

He gave one look at Ben sitting shotgun, nodded perfunctorily and got into the backseat.

"Took you long enough," he growled. "Fucking cold out there."

Tennyson glanced at him in the rearview mirror as they took off. "What'd I tell you, dipshit. Play nice."

They quickly left the concentration of Dulles's lights behind, and for some time after that Ben was occupied with giving Tennyson directions, first to the Herndon parking lot, then on to the crash site, Ben recalling with crystal clarity the route Evan's abductor had ordered her to follow before she had taken charge, almost killing herself in the process. Streetlights steadfastly rose like ranks of sentinels, whipping by them, their shadows blackening the interior of the Tahoe in metronomic precision.

A rude sound from the backseat caused Tennyson to shoot Leyland another look but Leyland just wrapped his arms around himself and grumbled.

"What's that?" Tennyson said.

"Nothing, boss." Leyland put his head back, spitefully pretended to go to sleep.

"Bear right at that fork," Ben instructed, "then a right at the first signal."

Moments later, Ben said, "The crash Evan caused was just along here."

"Wild-goose chase," Leyland brayed. "Nothing but a waste of time."

"It appears," Ben said, "your remedial tutorial didn't do your personality any good, Leyland. Once a prick, always a prick, I guess."

Tennyson grunted. "You can lead a mule to water, but you—"

Glass shattered, the Tahoe bucked and jerked, and there was a ringing in Ben's ears. Something heavy banged against the back of his seat, along with a warm spatter of Jason Leyland's blood and brain matter.

Ben had just enough time to think, *My God, I'm following in Evan's footsteps* before Tennyson lost control of the Tahoe. The SUV swerved in ever widening S-turns before hitting something in the road. The vehicle lifted violently on two wheels before tumbling over onto its roof. Airbags deployed, slamming against him in a white cloud, and he lost consciousness.

■   ■   ■

When he next opened his eyes, he and Tennyson were suspended by their seat restraints upside down. The airbags had deflated into sad squashed marshmallows. It was painful to turn his neck but he did so anyway, looked into Tennyson's face.

"Tennyson," he said in a shock-thickened voice.

The FBI agent's eyes were open and staring at him. "Ben. You have blood running out of your nose." As if they were having a beer at a local tavern.

Ben automatically wiped the blood off with the back of his hand. He winced. Everything hurt.

"Ben. What the hell happened?"

Ben had to wade through the fog of his memory, laden as it was by pain and trauma. *I'm in shock,* he thought, even as he said, "Leyland was shot. In the head. Through the rear window."

Tennyson's eyes had the bewildered look of a bird after it strikes a windowpane. "But how did we—" He gestured.

"Fallen branch across the road. Big. Hard to see in the dark, swerving like that. You were trying to control the car. I saw it too late to warn you."

"Shit. That wasn't supposed to happen."

Ben's brow crinkled. He was concentrating on the feeling in his legs and feet. Both there, he thought with enormous relief. "Did you see anything in the rearview mirror?" he asked.

"I saw Leyland being an asshole."

"No. I mean headlights?"

"I don't . . . Huh . . ." Then he vomited. "Ugh." His eyes, when he looked back at Ben, were red-rimmed, bleak. "I don't remember headlights. I should have—"

"Forget it," Ben said. "Let's concentrate on getting out of here. Especially because it stinks."

"Ha," Tennyson said just as there was a knocking on his side window. Ben started. Tennyson slid down the window. "How about you get us the fuck out of here," he said to the unknown figure standing by the car. He unlocked all the doors and immediately his was pulled open. What looked like oversized hedge clippers began to cut their way through the restraints.

"Jon . . ."

"Hold on, Ben. No one's forgetting about you."

Ben was thanking his lucky stars Tennyson had backup in place. Smart guy—smarter than he'd given him credit for.

He concentrated now on leveling his breathing, taking it slow and easy. He'd be out of this cage any moment. Tennyson was being handled gently out from behind the wheel.

Ben heard him say, "Take care of my friend."

Someone outside the Tahoe pulled Ben's door open. He stuck his head in. Ben tried to turn his head but was hit with a massive stab of pain. He subsided. There was nothing else to do. Leyland dead. A mission spiked before it got started.

He saw the thick blade of a hunting knife flash momentarily across his limited vision field. Then he was being cut from his harness, the blade sawing industriously through the webbing.

"Thanks," he murmured.

Hands lifted him out, returned him to a right-side-up position. He collapsed into someone else's arms. The world around him was speeding in a circle, around and around until he no longer knew which way was up, which way was down.

Icy hands took hold of his face like a vise, forcing him to look into a familiar face. Tennyson.

"Hey there, Benny boy." Tennyson's voice held a hitherto unheard roughness; it was heavy from a life of inciting fear, inflicting pain. "Surprised? I'll just bet you are." He grinned. "Well, life is full of 'em, surprises, some of 'em real nasty." His fingers dug into Ben's cheeks. "I'm just sorry I couldn't get you *and* Ryder. What a coup that would have been, right? But you're not so bad a catch."

Dizzied and still in shock Ben watched as the men who came for him and Tennyson doused the inside of the Tahoe with gasoline, stepped back and threw a lit match through the open window. They all took a couple of steps back as orange flames and black smoke engulfed the SUV. Then, with a great *whoosh!* of heated air that stung his cheeks, seared his throat, the Tahoe exploded. Its electronic guts and the man still inside fried to sticky blackness.

"A fitting end to that prick Leyland." Tennyson's grin was as scythelike as a new moon. The rest of his face was glowing, painted red by the inferno. "You've been expected, you see. For over a year, in fact." A laugh like metal on concrete. "Ben, my friend, welcome to your own private level of hell."

32

NUREMBERG

Evan in the taxi, a rattletrap vehicle with a hole half as large as her foot in its floorboards. For a while she watched the blur of slushy tarmac and cinder road until she realized the sight was mesmerizing her. It was like watching a whirlpool rushing at her. She looked up, on the edge of the backseat, peering through the filthy window. If there was any incipient dawn light in the sky, it was smothered by the thickness of the moist heavy cloud cover.

"How about putting your wipers on?" she said.

The driver laughed. "You're about five years too late, Fraulein."

"You can keep that VW in sight?"

"No sweat," he said. "You caught the right driver. Relax."

Relax was about the last thing Evan could do. They jangled and shivered along, all the while keeping the VW's taillights in view, tiny eyes glowing in the murk.

Evan couldn't help thinking of Elke, feeling the burden of Ghislane's rageful accusations. Who was this person she had picked up at the *volksbad* and taken back to the hunter's cabin? Why had she done it? How wrecked was she, and whose fault was that? Evan had declined her invitation to accompany her, so she had been alone. Poor Elke. *If only I'd gone with her, as she asked, she'd still be alive*, she thought. But she was not in a business that allowed what-ifs. If you let yourself go down that rabbit hole you'd end up putting a gun in your mouth. Evan reached into her pocket, let her hand brush against the eyeliner container, the gift Camina had given her just before they parted.

Peace be upon you, sister, she thought.

In truth, Evan couldn't understand how Elke had been so careless, stuffing security into the back of her mind. Again her mind kept returning to the interior of the cabin. Everything neat and tidy, the fire burned down but not altogether out—and there in the middle Elke lay in a pool of her own blood. Evan had noticed defensive wounds, scraps of blackened fabric. Elke must have put up quite a fight, but her murderer had been too much for her. Putting all the pieces together she concluded that whatever his identity he was a top echelon professional.

She considered a moment, her mind in overdrive. The first and simplest explanation was that he was a professional merc. It tracked. Someone had hired this particular merc to run her down and kill her. Presently she could only think of one group this train of thought led back to: Omega. She recalled in vivid detail how she had been abducted in her own car from a parking lot near Dulles airport last year, how in retrospect she had suspected that they were headed to the Wells estate out in Herndon, Virginia, but had no proof that this was so. The incident that had almost killed her was another in a long line of circumstantial evidence she and Ben had amassed but which no law officer let alone a court of law would find actionable.

She blinked out of her private thoughts as the taxi slowed. She leaned forward. "What's happening?"

"Your friend up ahead has stopped driving like a maniac."

"Can you follow with your headlights off?" Evan said with some urgency in her voice. "There isn't much traffic here and I don't want the driver to get suspicious."

"I should be taking a video of this," the taxi driver said as he turned his lights off. "None of my friends will believe it."

"They won't hear about it either." Evan leaned forward, dropped a 100 euro bill onto the seat beside the driver.

"Not a word." He was hunched forward, concentrating on following Ghislane. The route Ghislane was taking was familiar to Evan—it was leading back to her house. But twenty minutes later, the VW slid right past Ghislane's townhouse and kept going. Darkness engulfed them.

"What's up ahead?" Evan asked.

"The old Nazi Party Rally Grounds." The driver pointed at a spot through the windshield. "You see there that huge building, that's the Documentation Center. Looks like something out of a Murnau Expressionist film like *Nosferatu*, doesn't it?" He snorted. "A monument to the so-called Thousand-Year Reich."

"Plenty of ghosts inhabit those streets at night," Camina had cautioned. *"Just not the children's storybook kind."*

Evan leaned farther forward so she could see through the windshield. The VW was slowing. To one side of the center was another building, smaller, shadowed, and just beyond lay the lake, still as glass, as if painted onto the night. Like most things in Nuremberg, the Silver Lake had an odd and unsettling history. The crown jewel of the rally grounds was to be the world's largest stadium. Albert Speer, the Nazi's chief architect, drew inspiration for the monumental structure from the Panathenaic Stadium in Athens. He boasted to the Führer that it would seat an astounding four hundred thousand spectators. Excavation began in 1937 but with the war effort straining Germany's resources it was never built. After the war, with the northern half of the pit filled up with seeping groundwater, a lake was allowed to form. Some said, and she was sure Camina would be one of them, that the water was inevitably mixed with the blood of the multitudes who had been killed.

As was her wont Evan kept checking the immediate vicinity for any sign of human activity. The last remnants of snow lay across the open space, long mounds seeming like corpses wrapped in shrouds waiting long decades to be properly remembered and interred in the icy ground.

"It's no joke, but you'll probably find out for yourself. The past is particularly strong there, close to the surface, spread across the city; it was never truly laid to rest."

They had lost the VW in the deep shadows thrown across the vast staging area, now a parking lot. The driver drove the taxi toward a stepped grandstand, a building in the style of an ancient Greek temple. "Here is the Zeppelin Tribunal," the driver said in the slick intonation of a tour guide. "You see the three tiers just to the right—that's where Hitler stood up on the so-called Pergamon altar the architect, Albert Speer, designed for him from the original Greek structure in Turkey. Hitler stood up there like the Greek god Zeus, looking down on and addressing a quarter of a million German soldiers and civilians."

Evan, in no mood for a history lesson, got out of the car. She looked around for the VW, for Ghislane herself, wondering where she had got to, where she had been going. She needed to find this out. She headed away from the taxi, but the driver caught her by her sleeve.

"Hey," he said. "Hey, you forgot your change."

"Keep it," she said. "You earned it."

"I can't do that." He leaned out of the taxi window. "Listen. Hey, listen to me. I know this area like the back of my hand. I think I might know where your friend is headed."

That got Evan's attention. She turned back, stuck her head into the open window.

"Where d'you think she's going?"

Two things happened almost simultaneously. She saw the dark spots of blood on the front of the driver's ripped shirt and she thought of Elke's firelit corpse in a pool of blood. Elke's blood? But he already had a grip on her head and he slammed it down on the bottom sill of the window so hard Evan's eyes rolled up and she collapsed into the snow.

PART FOUR

BOOMSLANG

33

Devyatyy Krug—like its namesake, the ninth level of hell—was a bleak place at the best of times; even in summer it was hot, humid, and pestilential with black flies that bit like demons. Now, in the dead of winter with the longest night just over a day away, it was intolerable. The wind swept down out of the Siberian taiga, icy, bitter, hinting of the vast coniferous northern forests and its apex predators, gray wolf packs. Its harsh knife-like edge beat the treetops, scoured the clear-cut open space surrounding high wooden walls, likely stolen from the forest itself.

Kata hated it the moment the FSB chopper dumped her out just outside the impregnable perimeter of the Department 73 training facility. As the chopper headed in she had felt a suffocating atmosphere mindless of the steel frame protecting her as if she had plunged five fathoms down into a murky sea. Up above in the real world dawn had broken, but here surrounded by the seemingly endless green-black pine forest a twilight gloom prevailed, gray, dense as a lowland fog.

She was expected. The door swung open with a squeal like pigs being slaughtered, and as she crossed the threshold *Devyatyy Krug* swallowed her whole.

The interior was its own thing, a small industrious town, sooty and fly-specked, gamey with the business of killing human beings. Row upon row of corrugated steel huts gave the place the unfortunate aspect of a gulag, but perhaps, Kata thought, the effect was deliberate. Men were sent here to become ruthless weapons, hardened, immune to any and all extreme circumstances. Behind a bewildering labyrinth of mock streets lined with mock houses, bare fields covered now with snow trampled to icy slush and firing ranges for all manner of small-arms weaponry.

She was met just inside the front door, on the edge of what looked to be a parade ground but here must serve an altogether different purpose. She noted the single wooden pole, dark stains on the ground swept clear of all snow, slush, and shards of ice.

The acting commandant reared up before her, a grizzled tank of a man, ex-GRU, who had been lured away from the Russian army by promises of money and promotion. He had received both, of course, but in keeping with making a pact with the devil, the unspoken details made all the difference. For his recompence he was duly sent into the depths of the wilderness to supervise the ten thousand methods of terminating the enemy. What did it matter, Kata thought, if you were as rich as Croesus, elevated to minister, even, if you were consigned to the ninth level of hell?

This then was Thoth Abramovich Novikov who stood before her with a face formed into what she intuited to be a perpetual scowl. After all what did he have to be happy about? More death? More blood? Kata, unintimidated by neither his size nor his expression, scrutinized him. He looked like the kind of man who would easily anticipate a human sacrifice, if only to relieve the monotony of simulated killing repeated ad infinitum by his recruits.

Novikov grunted by way of greeting. "Where is Borya Igorevich? He is overdue. When is he returning?"

Clearly they didn't get the latest news up here in the wilderness. Possibly they got no news at all; news was a distraction not to be tolerated during training.

"Arsenyev is dead," Kata stated in the same matter-of-fact tone she used for ordering coffee.

"Dead?" Novikov's monumental eyebrows lifted like a pair of Kamov helicopters taking off. "How dead?"

"He was molesting a friend of mine." Kata stared at Novikov, daring him to make a move. "I drove the heel of my shoe into his femoral artery. Blood poisoning."

Novikov's eyebrows rose even higher, ridging his wind-beaten forehead. "You?"

"Shall I make a believer out of you, Thoth Abramovich?"

He started, then scowled at her use of the informal address. "I know you are the minister's creature. How may I be of assistance?"

That was better, Kata thought. "Minister Kusnetsov wishes me to inventory your personnel."

"My personnel?" Novikov's eyebrows had yet to descend to their normal position. "In what way?"

"My objective is no concern of yours." Kata knew how to deal with these officious lunkheads. "I am to be assigned an office that is both comfortable and most importantly private. Immediately."

His eyebrows at last descended. "As you wish."

"And you will provide me with a complete list of your personnel." Alyosha had in fact provided her with dossiers on everyone in the compound. She had memorized them on the flight from Moscow. "Within thirty minutes I will begin interviewing them one by one in alphabetical order of their last name. Clear?"

"Absolutely." Novikov's hand swept out. "This way if you please."

As they began walking toward the largest of the corrugated-metal huts, she added, "I shall require a carafe of freshly brewed coffee along with a meal that is hot and edible."

He answered in the affirmative but took the opportunity as he pointed out the "corporal punishment stake" in the center of the open space to clandestinely ogle her large square-cut emerald ring.

■　　■　　■

"We might as well start with you, *Gospodin* Novikov," Kata said as soon as she was settled behind the cheap metal desk in the room the acting commandant offered her. She had moved the desk so the window was behind her when she sat at it. She raised the blinds all the way up so that the sullen light would spill over her back and into the face of whoever was sitting in the green metal chair facing her. When she raised her left hand the emerald shot bolts of light through each of its facets, projecting geometric shapes on the walls.

A carafe of coffee had been brought, along with something that, though hot, appeared completely unpalatable. She ignored it, poured herself a cup of coffee and took a sip. It nearly tore out the lining of her throat. It was all she could do not to cough and sputter, but Novikov was scrutinizing her every expression, surely ready to make a cutting remark when she spit out the liquid. When she did not he subsided in disappointment.

"Right," Kata said briskly. She scanned the three sheets of computer printout that had been brought with the coffee and whatever the hell that was squatting on a plate. She pushed the plate to the farthest corner of the desk and then flicked it over the edge. She observed Novikov as before he had studied her, but she could see no change in his expression as the plate crashed to the floor, its contents spattering one leg of the desk.

"When I said edible, Acting Commandant, I meant edible." She gave him the mildest look. "I can only hope you run your recruit's training better than you run your kitchen."

"No one complains," he said.

"I'll bet they don't."

She removed a sheaf of papers from the titanium case she had carried all the way from Moscow. She gestured. "Let's begin, Acting Commandant." It was not a request. She looked up. He didn't move.

"Have a seat," she said conversationally.

"I prefer to stand."

Her eyes narrowed for a moment. "That won't work, I'm afraid. I'm going to need a writing sample from you."

"What?"

She sighed. "Shall we not make this more difficult than it has to be?" She glanced at her watch. "I would prefer not to spend the night here. And I can tell you quite candidly you don't want that either."

She extracted a pad and a pen, shoved them over to his side of the desk. He sat but did not hide his displeasure. Hunched over to keep the light out of his eyes he looked like a warthog. However there was nothing cartoonish about his brute force or his position here at *Devyatyy Krug*.

"Please write your full name," Kata said, shifting her papers back and forth. She did not look at him; she was staring fixedly at the scribbled note Alyosha had discovered in Borya Arsenyev's dossier and had smuggled out of SIGINT. "Now write down this number." She recited the cell number Baev had told her was his contact for Schrodinger. "Lastly," she continued, "write the word *Schrodinger*." She spelled it for him.

When he was finished she ripped off the top sheet and compared what Novikov had written to the note from Arsenyev's dossier. Not a match. Not even close.

She looked up. "That will be all, Acting Commandant." As he rose, she consulted the computer printout of the personnel she had been given. "Please have Aslanov come see me."

Ten minutes later the requested recruit knocked and entered the room. By then she had drained half the carafe of coffee and used the facilities to empty her bladder.

"Please sit."

She watched Aslanov as he took the chair, squinting against the light. He was a fair-haired young man, slim but from what she could see all muscle. His eyes were like stones; he looked at her but clearly saw nothing of interest.

"How long have you been here, Aslanov?" she asked in a completely disinterested voice.

"Eight months."

"Did you know Pasha Rodionovich Shutkov?"

"Everyone here knows Pasha Rodionovich," Aslanov said. "Everyone wants to be like him."

"Do you want to be like him, Aslanov?"

"Most assuredly."

"Shutkov is dead."

For just an instant a slight spark illuminated Aslanov's eyes. "That's not possible."

She watched his face. "Why do you say that?"

"He's the best of us."

"He's as dead as the corporal punishment stake outside."

She spun the pad and pen at him, asked him to write the word "Schrodinger." He stared at her for a moment, then shrugged and wrote it. Even upside down she could see he hadn't scribbled the note. She sent him away.

"Next," she called through the partially opened door. And ten minutes later, "Next," again.

"Donlov," she said as the mountain of muscle subsided into the chair across from her, "tell me, have you ever received punishment out there?" She hooked a thumb over her shoulder at the window and the parade ground beyond.

When he made no reply, she said, "Donlov, this isn't a test of your loyalty to Department 73. No need to keep secrets from me." She gestured. "In any case, it was an inquiry, not an order."

He nodded. "Once. My first week here. Once was enough."

"What was done to you? An old-fashioned flogging?"

He laughed. "Sure. That's what it was." He held up his left hand. The pinkie was a stub. "Commandant Arsenyev has an array of garden shears."

Jesus, Kata thought. *Just like the Japanese yakuza.* "Now Novikov has the shears."

"I don't know," Donlov said. "I hope to God I never find out."

She administered the writing test, to no avail.

Three hours later, she had gone through the entire list save one without finding who had written Schrodinger's name. The last was the cook, who refused to be taken away from the tools of his trade with which he was assembling dinner. If it was anything like what Kata had been served earlier in the day there was no reason for him to even be in the kitchen.

She could have ordered Novikov to bring him to her but apart from the short visits to relieve her bladder she had been sitting for too long. She needed a break. Throwing her pad and pen into her briefcase, she snapped it shut, went out of the drab office she had been assigned. It didn't take her long to find the kitchen—she had only to follow the vile odors lofted on the wind that shrieked through the gaps in the wooden stockade fence.

Cooks should be fatter than a Wagyu steer, shouldn't they? But possibly this one was smart enough not to eat his own cooking. He was thin as a nail, tall as a basketball player. He didn't turn his head as Kata peered at him through the clouds of steam rising from a trio of enormous cauldrons. It was from these the noxious odor was emanating, as if he were boiling dozens of sweat-soaked socks.

His name was Egorov, whey-faced, pale of hair and beady of eye. He wore a stained singlet and baggy khaki pants tucked into combat boots. When Kata was close enough he turned. Sweat was pouring off him like water from a fountain.

"What?" he snapped. "I'm busy."

"I can see," she said. "Is there any particular reason why you're being a prick?"

Egorov bared his teeth. "Flattery will get you everywhere." He rolled shoulders thick with wiry hair. "Plus, what the hell is a woman doing in here?" Kata almost gagged at the thought of what was inadvertently falling into those cauldrons.

"I need a writing sample from you."

"Get lost, sister."

She grabbed the ladle out of his hand, slammed the bowl of it against the side of his head.

"Ow! What the—?"

She dragged him away from the stovetop to one of the stainless-steel chopping stations. "Egorov, were you born this way or did this damn place turn you sour?"

"Huh." The cook shook himself free of her. "You have no idea what it's like here. Sometimes I think I'd rather be in a gulag. At least then I'd know who I am. Here they strip you of all identity. You become a cog in Department 73. They beat every bit of individuality out of you, tell you the pain makes you stronger, but, shit, I'm here to tell you all it does is breed doubt and dread."

Kata was unsettled by Egorov's insight. Served her right for judging him by his appearance and crustiness. It was becoming clear to her why Department 73 was ripe for Omega infiltration. People who were lost, who were physically or psychologically abused, were prime candidates for a quasi-religious organization whose clear aim was to overturn the entrenched order. Which meant that someone smart, clever, and psychologically astute had correctly targeted Department 73 as a soft spot in the FSB infrastructure. The mysterious Schrodinger? Or was that merely a nom de guerre?

She opened her case, took out what she needed, set the pad and pen in front of him. She told him what she wanted him to write.

He looked up at her then, his eyes filled with a curious light. "Schrodinger. Huh."

She frowned. "What does that mean? Do you know the name?"

Now he hesitated.

"Too late to backtrack, Egorov."

"Yeah, well, okay." He shrugged. "Sure I heard the name before."

"Write it for me."

He nodded, complying. No match. Her heart sank. She thought she was onto something with him. Then she looked at him with narrowed eyes. "So how did you hear about Schrodinger?"

"Shutkov," he said at once. "Pasha Rodionovich told me about him."

Kata shook her head. "In what context?"

Egorov drew up his singlet and there it was: the O and the cross, just as it appeared on Arsenyev's chest.

"Omega," she said. "So Schrodinger is the Omega contact outside Russia?"

"So far as I know."

"What else do you know about Schrodinger?"

Egorov shook his head. "Nothing. Honest."

She took out the scribbled note to show him. "Someone here wrote this note. Who?"

Egorov's simian shoulders rose and fell. "How should I know?" He squinted then, took the note, held it up to the light. "Something odd about this handwriting."

Kata's heart rate ascended precipitously. "You've seen it before?"

"No." He pursed his lips. "Yeah. Maybe."

She took it back from him, scrutinized it again as she had done so many times before. *"Something odd about this handwriting."* What? What could it be? Her mind backtracked over the day's events from the moment she stepped into the copter until right this moment. There was something there, something niggling at the corner of her consciousness.

"Something odd . . ."

And then she had it. Like being zapped by a bolt of lightning.

■ ■ ■

Thoth Abramovich Novikov was in his office, his cell phone pressed against one cheek, when Kata strode in.

He glanced up, his body tensing behind the heavy wooden desk, polished dark as ebony. "You never heard of knocking?"

"There's a time and place for everything," she said.

"Is that right?" He said something inaudible into the phone, cut the connection. He sighed, opened the center drawer, tossed his cell inside. "Have you finished interrogating my people?"

"Yes," Kata said. "And no."

Novikov's eyebrows once again took off, rising up into his domed forehead. "What kind of answer is that?"

"The correct answer."

He made a disgusted sound. "I've had enough of your games, *devchachiy*."

"Girlie?" Rage ripped through her. "You're calling me girlie?"

"There's a time and place for everything," he said, mocking her.

She took out the scribbled note.

His upper lip curled. "I already saw that. I already wrote the name out for you."

"With your right hand." Kata bent forward, placing the note squarely in front of him. "I know you're ambidextrous, *pizdobol*." *Fucking liar.* "Now write the name with your left hand."

"You want me to use my left hand?"

"That's right, asshole." She spread out the note, flattening the creases. "Do it now."

Novikov reached into the center drawer, which he hadn't bothered closing, and before she could make a move drove the curved blades of a garden shear through her left hand, pinning it to his desk.

"How's this then, princess?" He grinned like a pumpkin moon at Halloween. "Happy now?"

34

FAIRFAX COUNTY, VIRGINIA

The only thing Ben knew for sure was that he was alive. Everything else was a blur, from where precisely he was to how he had come here. The shooting of Jason Leyland, the crash, the burning and subsequent explosion of Tennyson's Tahoe with Leyland in it—all of these most recent waypoints were blurs, a confusion of time and space that try as he might Ben could not arrange in the proper order, let alone make sense of.

Presently he became aware that his mouth was dry. Licking his lips he tasted salt and copper—snot and blood. A thunderous bell kept ringing in his ears, a warning for an oncoming earthquake. The rhythm was familiar. Eventually he realized he was hearing the beating of his heart striking inside his rib cage. Fire in his blood as waves of pain threatened his consciousness. What didn't hurt he couldn't feel. He was in a kind of limbo—half-alive, half-dead. He was nowhere and everywhere at once: time and space had collided, melded. He was baffled, set adrift. Lost in the darkness surrounding him.

There came a time when he heard a door unlock, open, close. The clatter of low-heeled shoes. A woman. A female interrogator? What would that be like?

"Dear Ben." Yes, a female voice, young, with a slight Eastern European accent. Full throated even when speaking softly, as if the woman behind the voice was used to projecting into a microphone or upon a stage. "It's said that all good things come to those who wait, and I've been waiting for this moment for many months."

He heard the scrape of a chair being moved, probably facing him. Which brought up the vexing question of not only where he was but his actual physical condition. He had no feeling in any of his extremities. Was he in restraints, was he hanging by his wrists? For that matter, where was the floor? Years ago, during his field training, he'd been locked into a sensory deprivation chamber. Floating in water at body temperature, without even the thinnest fingernail of light to orient him he had found each of his senses switching off one by one: five lights in a slick corridor, the lights extinguished one by one until he'd felt like a mummy encased in a sarcophagus. Pleasant it wasn't. He'd lasted a little over twenty-four hours, which was something of a record at the time.

This was how he felt—or more accurately didn't feel now.

"Patience is a virtue we both possess," he said. He needed to regain some form of control and his only way was through his voice. Snark cut through even the heaviest of silences.

"I'm gratified to hear you say that, Ben." The voice was smooth as well as cultured but it was deliberately devoid of a regional accent. Just as he couldn't place himself locally he couldn't place this woman's country of origin. More darkness.

"My name is Lucinda," she said. "Welcome."

Lucinda? Lucinda *Wells*? "Where am I?" Ben asked, but he knew. The place he and Evan had been trying to get into for more than two years.

"Precisely where you need to be," Lucinda said.

"Is that a Zen koan?"

A spotlight snapped on, illuminating, oddly, Lucinda Wells, not him. She was even more beautiful in person than seen through a camera lens. There was a magnetic quality about her that even the best cameraman or director could not fully capture. An allure possessed only by the female sirens of old Hollywood—Elizabeth Taylor, Greta Garbo, Marilyn Monroe, Catherine Deneuve. She fairly took his breath away, and of course then he understood why the spotlight was on her, not him. Compared to her he was insignificant, a bug she was about to wipe off the sole of her shoe.

"'Nothing Goes Away,'" Lucinda said. "That is a koan. I was simply stating a fact." She wore black form-fitting leggings, an oyster-gray silk shirt open at the neck, ankle boots with wicked sharp toes. "I'm just disappointed Evan isn't here with us today."

A bit of light spilled onto the floor and, looking down, he realized he was in a chair, wrists and ankles bound to the metal arms and legs with thick plastic zip ties. "And why is that?"

"She would embody another koan, Ben, namely, 'More of the Same Can Be a Whole New Thing.'"

The scrape of chair legs. She was moving closer to him. He felt the heat coming off her like something radioactive. A waft of Dior's J'adore invaded his nostrils—ylang-ylang, Damascus rose, French and Indian jasmine. He'd met a woman in a Tangier bar many years before who'd been wearing it. They'd had drinks. Intoxicated by the heady floral perfume as much as from the alcohol, he'd taken her to his hotel room and feverishly stripped off her clothes. Afterward, twisted sheets damp and musky, she'd almost killed him with a tiny .22 she had secreted under the pillow. She'd thought he was dozing after the long and satisfying bout of lovemaking. He'd only been waiting, patient as a hooded cobra.

Funny how scent could bring back memories so powerfully.

"Well, it's no wonder," he said now. "Everyone likes Evan better than me." He was desperately trying to keep his head together, to be witty while he gathered his wits about him like armor. "I've always told her that if we broke up I'd have no friends left."

Lucinda laughed. "I prefer my men have a sense of humor, Ben. I am so gratified that you do."

Along with the faint accent, she also had a precision to her English that made it clear she had learned it by working very hard at it. "Anything to oblige."

There was a short silence after which her tone changed completely, bristling with steel filings. "Do you have any idea why you're here, Ben?"

"In our line of business, Mrs. Wells, guessing is a fool's game."

A sardonic smile curved her perfect lips. "And you're anything but a fool, Ben, isn't that right?"

It was a comment not a question so he kept quiet. Clearly she'd worked the answer out on her own.

"So." She put her hands together in her lap like a schoolgirl. Oddly, the prim gesture only ramped up the intensity of her allure. "How is my dear sister? More importantly, *where* is she?"

"Of course you want to know," Ben said. "Evan is your last remaining sister."

Lucinda's eyes narrowed. "The one who murdered my twin."

"No. Actually that was me. I was protecting Evan. Ana was about to throttle her to death."

Lucinda scoffed. "I don't believe you. You're protecting her again."

"She tried to stop me. She wanted to speak with Ana, but you know Ana, she wasn't having any of that. She was crazy, but you know that better than anyone. Evan didn't care. Ana was her sister, one like you she never knew existed. She had already lost one sister; she didn't want to lose another."

"That is quite a tale you tell."

Ben shrugged. "You're like everyone else, Mrs. Wells. You'll believe whatever you want. Whatever fits your worldview."

He'd hit a nerve. He could see it in her face where a small muscle in her right cheek began to spasm.

"You are the one who is in denial, you are the one who is delusional." She had the habit of people for whom English is a second language of not contracting the words she wanted emphasized. Evangelists had that habit too. "You and your criminal partner. You think you know everything. You are sure you have it all figured out, what is shadow and what is light, what is good, what is evil."

He'd gotten her blood up. In her heightened state she slipped off the chair she'd been sitting on, stood in front of him, legs slightly apart, fists on hips.

"You are not afraid, Ben. I'm wondering why that is?"

"I suppose it's because I've been here before, Mrs. Wells. Not in this room, of course, not sitting in front of you. But in other rooms like this one, with other people just like you. It's never ended well for them."

"What an arrogant bastard you are."

Ben shook his head, tried not to wince at the pain the motion caused him. "You don't get it. I've already died and come back."

Lucinda lifted an eyebrow. "That makes you immortal?"

Ben barked a laugh. "What it's done for me, Mrs. Wells, is this: I no longer fear death." He shrugged. "So have your people—maybe it'll be Tennyson, your turncoat FBI agent, won't that be ironic?—beat a tattoo on me."

"No one's doing anything to you, Ben," Lucinda sniffed.

"About Tennyson." What Ben had to say was more important than whatever lies she chose to disgorge. "In my experience turncoats are the least reliable people. The most difficult step—the first betrayal—has already been taken. It's an important threshold. To do it again is nothing at all."

She watched him for long moments and he wished he knew what was going through her mind. He was not going to make the mistake of underestimating her. She was clever enough to hook Wells, expand his business empire, and, who knows, maybe behind the scenes even run Omega as well.

"Mm, well, my experience has proved there's a platinum lining to everything, this situation being no exception." She took a step closer. "There is an excellent reason why I'm not going to touch a hair on your head, Ben. At least not yet anyway."

Her smile was as entrancing as the light of a full moon, as ominous as the blade of a scimitar. "Now that you're here, now that I have you, you're of great importance. Capturing you has altered my plans and, as I said, I believe it's for the better. I will be able to look her in the face before I kill her."

"Who are you kidding? You don't even know where she is."

She put her face close to his and it was like inhaling her most intimate parts. "You're the bait, Ben. You don't know where Evan is, but I do."

His eyes opened wide. He couldn't help it. Even if there was a grain of truth to what she said . . .

"What do you think she'll do when she finds out where you are, hm?" Lucinda's smile widened. "She'll be coming here to save you. That's her MO. That's her weakness. She cares. She will move heaven and earth to free you."

"How d'you know where she is?"

"I sent someone to the end of the line that she's following."

"You?" His stomach dropped as if he were in a plummeting elevator. "You had that encrypted e-file created and sent to yourself?"

She laughed. "Don't look so surprised. There was nothing of interest in it, Ben. We had a leak somewhere in Europe. I needed to flush it out."

Ben cursed under his breath and cursed again. They had sent Evan into a bear trap. Still . . .

"She'll mow down whoever you sent."

"Well, now, that is a distinct possibility, one that I would look forward to now that I have you under control."

"It won't make a difference." He knew he was being mulish, but what else could he say? The fact was he was terrified for Evan, more than he had ever been in their long and difficult history.

She lifted her chin. "Ah, now I see it. You love her."

"What?"

Her smile held an even sharper edge. "Yes, you do."

Ben struggled to ignore her. She was just needling him.

Her upper lip curled, which made her seem slutty. At that moment he lost all respect for her. She was like any other hustler who had found a rich mark, living in the moment. Hers was a severely constrained life, but he didn't pity her; he hated her too much for that. There were many reasons for that hate but the main one was how much he could see the resemblance to Evan. He hadn't had enough time with her twin Ana to consider it, but here it was staring him in the face. It was only *in extremis* that you discovered your deepest truth. He loved Evan. He had loved her from the indelible electric moment they had first met. For the sake of their work he had buried his love deep, even going so far as to deny it to himself. Only once had they given in to physical temptation, but if that night had brought his love out of the vault to which he'd consigned it, he never spoke of it. And in any event what was the point? Supposing he confessed his love to Evan and she responded in kind. What would be the result? They'd start living together and he knew with a rock-solid certainty that that would lead to a kind of death. His work—and hers— would be forever compromised. He would spend his time worrying about her and she him even more than they already did. He would be a dead man walking.

He smiled through the pain of this truth. "Evan will get to you too."

Lucinda clicked her tongue against the roof of her mouth. "There I have to disagree with you, Ben. You see, I've studied your methods. Your methods are Evan's methods. But neither of you know me at all. You don't know what I'm capable of. You don't know my method. You don't know the Omega Rules. And that, my friend, makes all the difference in the world."

At that moment, he felt a presence behind him, but it was already too late.

35

Christian Bardo dragged Evan from where he had assaulted her beside the taxi. He hauled her into the deep shadows of the Zeppelin Tribune. Unlike the other structures in the area this one was constructed of limestone, much softer than the concrete used elsewhere. As a result much of the façade had crumbled away. Still, the main part was still standing.

An essential part of the Nazi propaganda was the deeply-held myth that the Third Reich was the natural successors to the Holy Roman Empire, whose seat was right here in Nuremberg. Possibly some of them— Hitler surely—believed it. But the truth was more practical in nature. They built these monuments to the Thousand-Year Reich here because Nuremberg was a central location with superb rail service.

Bardo, hand grasping the collar of Evan's jacket, paused to take in his surroundings, to immerse himself in the history of the place, triumphant not for a thousand years but barely a decade. *The hubris of great men*, he thought, *is the same for madmen and megalomaniacs.*

A moment later, a whip-poor-will's call snapped him back to the present. He stared down at his prey and decided to have some fun with her before he stripped the flesh off her. Bardo took her to the door that led into the Golden Hall. It was locked, of course, as the building was inaccessible to the public, there being inside numerous decorative swastikas, now illegal in Germany. Bardo had little difficulty unlocking the titanic door, and they slipped quickly through into the hall itself. Its ceiling, high above them, was patterned with solid gold. Along the right-hand side of the hall were niches, presumably for statues of fallen Nazi heroes. Presumably, because no one really knew the true nature of this building. Nevertheless, it held the particular aura of a church, the holy religion of Naziism. This was heightened by a gigantic footed stone firebowl. This and its twin outside were lit during the almost liturgical night sessions held on the field just in front of the Tribune building.

What would the proud Nazis think of this place now, he asked himself.

Would they be ashamed of themselves? But, no, the Nazis didn't feel shame. Remorse, either. *Not unlike me,* he thought.

She was getting heavy now, so he pulled her up onto his shoulder in a fireman's lift, headed down the hallway, through a doorway on the right and down a flight of limestone stairs imprinted with gold swastikas. He turned on the flashlight app on his phone. Down here, the floor was smeared with the detritus of history. He could almost hear the echoes of the long-dead two hundred fifty thousand shouting their synchronized responses. Proud young men, loyal to their Führer rather than to their country. The old Germany was dead to them. Long live the Third Reich!

Poor deluded fools, Bardo thought as he paused to peer into a room. It was much like the others he had passed. It was as good as any to begin his wet work. As he slid Evan down off his shoulder two items fell to the stone floor from the pockets of her jacket: a cell phone which he kicked away and an eyeliner pencil case which he ignored. Women and their vanities, he thought with contempt. How they even lived their lives was a complete mystery, one he had no interest in penetrating. With that last thought, he laughed. Real echoes bounced off the bare architecture of the room as he set Evan down, back against a wall. Dust and cobwebs fluttered up, settling on her outstretched legs.

Crouching down he divested her of her leather jacket, set it aside. He stripped off her upper layers until she was naked from the waist up. He sat back on his hamstrings, drinking her in. Elke was a skeleton, wiry and feral, compared to this one, he thought.

There was little malice in him at this point, only the kind of curiosity a surgeon had in what was opened up before him. Her skin seemed pale and was stippled now, roughened up by the icy interior.

He studied her hands first—the fingers, then the backs, last her palms. Her knuckles and pads were armored with callus. Moving up her arms he could feel the tension of her musculature. She must be very strong, he thought. Stronger than the females in his group who always seemed to be preening themselves in front of each other, oiling their biceps, smacking their hard abs and flexing like weight lifters. In this they were so much like their male counterparts they disgusted him. They had no business acting like men.

This one, he suspected, would be different. He was almost sorry he had caught her by surprise, that he'd knocked her out before they had a chance to engage fully. But that had been his plan all along. An un- necessarily underlined paragraph in his orders had warned him about her, not to take her lightly just because she was a woman. The warning had pissed him off, not to mention the way it was written as if to a child who lagged behind the rest of the class. As if Ambrose Wells was making it clear that Christian wasn't professional enough to handle her otherwise.

He clamped her cheeks between fingers and thumb as a way of proving to Ambrose Wells and to himself that she was completely under his control. This pleased him immensely up until the instant her eyes snapped open.

■   ■   ■

Evan had regained consciousness at the moment he began to study her hands. She awakened not from a prince's kiss but from a professional assassin's touch. It was all she could do not to throw up. The tiny hairs on her arms rose as well as her gorge, an atavistic response as if she were a porcupine reacting to danger.

But when she felt him at her face and her eyes flew open, for just a fraction of a second it wasn't Christian Bardo's eyes she was looking into. Rather, it was Elke's stony, unseeing eyes in her strong beautiful face. And beyond Elke's eyes, the infinity she saw just before she died, as defined by a line from William Butler Yeats, *The blood-dimmed tide is loosed, and everywhere, the ceremony of innocence is drowned.*

She smiled, a baring of the teeth, just before she slammed her forehead into Bardo's at precisely the angle and exactly the spot she had been taught to stun an assailant: a vee, slightly indented, the most vulnerable spot on the forehead.

Bardo's eyes bulged, then briefly crossed, his grip on Evan's head relinquished. She shoved him back, but he had already recovered, grabbed for her, the edge of her hand fell onto his wrist like an anvil, and she was free. She kicked him on the point of the chin, stooped to pick up her cell and eyeliner case but stopped halfway. The muzzle of a Sig P365, a small eight-shot handgun that packed a wallop, was aimed at her.

Luckily, he was still reeling from the blows Evan had dealt him when he fired his first shot. It spit off the wall behind her, but so close a sliver of marble lashed her cheek. She was just able to snatch up her phone, the eyeliner case was out of her reach, and then was off and running as he righted himself, tried to aim at her moving figure. A squeezed-off second shot just missed due to her zigzagging movements and the dimness of the illumination.

Into the icy darkness of the interior she ran. Moments later her peripheral vision registered a piercing beam of light probing the hallway behind her. Elke's killer had a Sig and a flashlight. What did she have to protect herself?

She had her wits.

The hallway kept turning to her right as it ran around the inside periphery of the building. At one point she thought she heard whispered voices and turned on the phone's flashlight app. Nothing. She switched it off almost immediately and moved faster in case he had pinpointed the flash of light. The whispers could have come from the ghosts of the Holocaust Camina had warned her about or they could be the echoes of her pursuer's boots. In any event, it was clear that not only this building but the entire complex was haunted by history that refused to be swept away, forgotten, denied. It was here. It was real. It would remain.

"Why bother running, Evan? You know I'll find you wherever you are." His shouted voice was picked up by the walls, ricocheting around her, taunting her. Buried in those echoes were the shouts of Hitler, Bormann. Goebbels, still potent, still terrifying all these decades later.

She picked up her pace though she didn't want to run too fast lest she miss a place to hide. But every doorway she passed opened into a room identical to the one in which he had dragged her. No windows, no egresses. Nothing that could help her. Time seemed to dilate and then contract. Minutes passed when she was sure she had lost him, then in the blink of an eye she heard his voice closer than ever.

"When I find you I'm going to do to you what I did to your friend Elke."

She gritted her teeth and kept on.

"What a juicy bit of meat she was. I can still taste her. Yum!"

He was baiting her, hoping his goading would make her turn back and in her rage run right into the bullets he was planning to pump into her chest.

Her spatial intuition told her she was about halfway around the building, and still there had been no side corridors, no turnings, just this one corridor off which doorways to nowhere sprang at her like old dogs.

"I can see you now," he called. "Your bottom bobbing as you run. The view is so fine maybe I'll let this go on a bit longer."

His taunting almost did its job. She nearly missed the door. It was half-open and her first thought was that it led to a room just like the others, but unlike the others there was a glimmer of light coming through this door.

Skidding to a stop, she slid through the partial opening, then wrenched the door shut behind her. There was no inner lock, bad luck for her, but as she switched on her flashlight app she could see ahead of her another partly opened door beyond which was a narrow stairwell. It went down, an open ironwork spiral like a nautilus. A whiff of sewage accompanied humidity as high as summer. Without another thought she descended as fast as she was able, sometimes skipping two or three treads at a time while holding onto the tubular handrail. She was perhaps two-thirds down when the tread she landed on after skipping the intermediate two shattered in a shower of reddish metallic particles. It had rusted through.

She tried to pull her foot out but that only led to metal shards digging into the flesh above her ankle. She heard him, a wolf's primal howl as he scented his prey. He was almost at the top of the stairs. His shadow, three times his size, slanted across the doorway. Desperately, she looked around, saw a jigsaw of pipes, wheels, levers and, below them, a series of furnaces and other machinery she could not identify. Shining her light down she could just make out the sheen of black water. Part of the subfloor had given way to the seepage of groundwater that had been a problem here since the 1930s. Ironically, the filling of the lake had only exacerbated the problem. The water looked to be about six feet below the concrete subfloor. It moved in a sluggish, hypnotic tide, the stench it gave off was more than putrefaction, it was the miasma of a charnel house, as if corpses had been indiscriminately thrown into it. Evan gagged. Again she was drowning in the river water under the cemetery in Vienna. The breath rushed out of her, a hand on the top of her head pushing her down, down into the black murk. Her lungs burned.

"There you are!"

His triumphant cry from the top of the staircase jolted her, making her shoulders twitch. The light made him seem ten feet tall, angular, out of proportion. He banged the barrel of the Sig against the handrail, sending a shock through her hand, up her arm. Sweat beaded up, rolled down her forehead, the back of her neck. Her underarms were a swamp.

Forget him, she thought. *Free yourself first.*

Shoving her phone into the deep pocket of the black jeans she had donned at Camina's, she crouched down and pried at the rusted ends of the grid that held her fast. She heard him coming down the staircase. With each step he banged the Sig against the handrail.

"Here I come," he was fairly laughing at her. "Prepare yourself, bitch."

Her nails cracked as she bent up the ends of the grid. Sweat ran down into her eyes, stinging them, blurring her vision. But now she turned her foot. Bent up more of the ends, dug her fingers through, untied her boot laces. The hammer-blows of metal against metal sent tremors all down the staircase. Scraping the back of her hand, she managed to push off her boot. She lifted her heel, gingerly raised it through the jagged rent. Lines of blood oozed up along the top of her foot as she guided it through the widened hole.

He sent a bullet whistling just over her head. If they had been captains on the high seas that would have been a shot across her bows. Now her foot was finally free, she could continue down. But was that the right course? He'd expect that and if she'd learned anything during her time in the field it was when outgunned do the unexpected.

Instead of continuing her descent, she leaped over the handrail, grabbed onto the thickest of the vertical pipes, swung herself around so that the pipe was between her body and Elke's killer. As soon as she was in place she loosened the grip of her knees, then her hands and down she went.

The friction had reached burning level when she hit bottom. Knees bent, she allowed her legs to act as buffers so the jolt was minimized. But now what? She stood three paces away from where the groundwater had eaten away at the concrete, creating a drop-off into the underground pool. The stench from the water made her eyes tear.

Her pursuer, already more than halfway down the stairs, bypassed the rusted tread. Swinging his body out, he jumped down the remaining distance. He was on her back while she was only half-turned. She blocked him as he tried to swipe her temple with the Sig's square black butt, but that left her off-balance and vulnerable. He stuck out his leg, hooked it against hers, brought her down heavily against the concrete floor.

His right hand lifted, came down, the butt of the Sig striking her just beneath her shoulder bone. Lashing out with the edge of her hand, she connected with the inside of his wrist, the nerves sparking up along his arm with such force that he dropped the handgun. Evan kicked out, sending the Sig spinning out over the edge of the floor, down into the water with a heavy splash.

With a war cry, her attacker jammed his forearm against her windpipe, bore down. She wriggled her body back and forth trying to squirm away from him. She succeeded but now her head was out over the drop-off. The violent movement of her shoulders caused the friable concrete to crumble beneath her until a third of her body was suspended off the floor's edge.

Her attacker took the opportunity this afforded him to push her farther and farther off the edge of the floor. Without looking she knew the black water loomed below her, who knew how many feet deep? She could feel the current drawing her, sucking the air from her lungs. How many decomposed bodies would she get tangled in, a soft net holding her down, making her sink to the bottom where strange creatures swam and crawled.

She reached up to scratch at his face. Her nails raked down his cheek before he managed to immobilize her arm, pinning it to her side. He lashed out with his flashlight, opening a gash just above her left eyebrow. Blood rolled down, settling into the valley of her eye socket.

The crumbling concrete dug painfully into her naked back. She could feel herself beginning to bleed. Sensing the end was near, he reared up over her, grinning like a death's-head. Evan, on the verge of blacking out, had to keep her mind from the thought of the water below her, but she kept flashing back to her hand-to-hand with Shutkov and her lungs letting out an unanswered scream for air.

He tossed away the flashlight and used his fist, reveling in the contact of flesh on flesh, bone on bone, getting off on the immediacy of it, the passionate domination. His violence was sexual; it fueled more violence. Her vision came in flashes now, interspersed with blackout. She saw his fist coming toward her. Blackout. And again. Another blackout. She saw his exposed wrist, a line of scars. How many? Blackout. Fist. Blackout.

Is this how he had killed Elke? The thought of Elke, left to die like a cur in the street, sent an electric bolt through her. All the years of suppressed rage inside her from how she had been mistreated, her opinions ignored, the ugly insinuations that her rise through the DOD was strictly due to her fucking Ben, or kneeling in front of General Aristides, Ben's former Pentagon rabbi. All the seemingly small humiliations she had suffered in silence in order to advance her career, in order to prove she was a team player—the field instructor taking her behind the obstacle course, promising her top grades if she just . . . The flat of his hand on her head, pushing her down, down, the sergeant who had cornered her in a bar, the lieutenant who had called her into his office, locking the door behind her before exposing himself and, worst of all, the moment after the big black SUV rolled up beside her as she walked to work, the door opening and General Aristides beckoning her in, now flew out of her like a clutch of furies. So strong was the explosion she could actually see them, claws out, fangs bared, red eyes fixed on their prey.

Her rage, her furies, told her what to do. She relaxed her entire body. Immediately she saw his reaction—the surprise as his eyes widened. She arched her back, her free hand cupping one bare breast.

"Look," she whispered. "Look how hard you've made my nipples." She offered them to him, saw the confusion on his face, his anger pivoting swiftly to lust because for him anger and lust occupied the same place in his brain. She put her hand behind his head, pushing it down as others had pushed her head down. He let go of her other arm and her fingers found the place between his legs, he was already hard. Good, the furies chorused. Excellent.

Their deft fingers guided hers in opening his pants, drawing him out. He was panting now. She could smell his sour breath on her cheek and neck. His mouth dipped first to her blood on her face—the blood he had caused—lapped it up. His bloody lips fastened onto her nipple, nuzzling.

But when she squeezed his balls so hard tears came to his eyes he reared up, his eyes veined with red. She struck him on the point of his chin. He gasped. She spat in his face. He gasped again, tried to breathe, but nothing inside him seemed to be working. She hit him in the throat, shoved him to the side and he toppled over.

She was on him in an instant. She thought of all the times she fought to get away from the pawing of men, their animal instinct that ran so deep the moment—this moment—was all that existed for them, the future, the consequences were lost in the blizzarding need for sex and power. Because their lives had taught them that it was easy to feel powerful when you were with a woman whose career was in your hands.

She screamed with the power of her furies. She slammed her fists against his jaw muscles and when his mouth flew open, she jammed her fist in as far as she could and kept it there while his eyes widened, the whites glistening like eggs fried in butter, his nostrils flaring. His arms flailed, the muscles spasming, but she had the leverage, controlling them with her knees.

He began to cough and spit. His head swung from side to side until she slammed the heel of her free hand into his horsehead just above his eyes. Using all her strength, she bore down with her fist. He gagged and kept on gagging.

"Helpless," she whispered. "Now you know how it feels, how Elke felt."

She was torturing him. Dimly a part of her brain acknowledged that, but the image of Elke, the taste of her own blood would not allow her to finish him off. Not yet.

"You're a bad bet, you know that? You're an accident waiting to happen. You live off fear, the fear of your victims. You get off on it. Pulling a trigger, sinking in the knife, they're the same as an orgasm for you. No difference whatsoever."

She ground her fist even deeper inside him. "That's how it was with Elke, wasn't it? You loved every minute of it. The more violent it got the harder you became." She laughed. "Like now. You're hard as a rock."

She took a breath, let it out slowly as if she had just taken a drag on a joint. Space-time had condensed for her, bubbles in her brain popping like exploding stars.

"It disgusts me that you're enjoying this." Her smile was a reservoir of assaults and agonies, humiliations and self-hatred. "This will soften you up."

She drove her elbow down into his sternum. Its crack echoed like a rifle shot. And then again higher up. The fracturing of ribs a fusillade from a firing squad.

36

Blood leaking from the back of Kata's hand drew Novikov's gaze like a carrion bird to an open carcass. He licked his lips.

"I may not be up to date on today's news," he said, "but I know about Kata Romanovna Hemakova, don't I?" He nodded. "Yes, I do. You're something of a legend, *devchachiy*." Novikov's sausage-like forefinger hovered over Kata's emerald. "I know what this is and it's not for decoration." The fingertip pressed down on the center facet. "It's your weapon, *devchachiy*. An extremely effective weapon if even half the stories about you are true. But now, sadly for you, I have rendered it impotent."

His grin was back, so close she could smell his sour breath. "Now it will be me asking you the questions. I have established my power over you and unless you want to—"

A mid-sentence silence. The acting commandant's mouth dropped open as Kata gripped the handle of the garden shears with her right hand. Staring him right in the face with the gaze of a medusa she pulled the shears out of the desktop, through the flesh of her hand, freeing it without wincing, without even making a sound. She ignored the blood oozing from the wound, pooling on the desk, black on black.

"What . . . how can you . . . what are you?" Novikov's eyes were opened so wide she could see the whites all around.

"For you, Thoth Abramovich, I am Eris, goddess of discord, war, and murder." Leaning forward, she thrust the bloody tips of the shears against the hollow of his throat. "Bring out your vodka."

"What?" He was still in shock.

"You heard me." Jabbing the tips through his skin so he yelped.

His gaze shifted, possibly because he could no longer bear her scrutiny. "You're bleeding," he said without an ounce of irony.

"That's the least of it," she said.

"I don't understand."

In that moment she realized how stupid he was, how stupid every man she knew was. *I don't understand.* They look at you and never see beyond the need to mount you. *I don't understand.* How could they possibly?

"Vodka, prick," she commanded.

He tried to move away but the shears followed him so he stopped, remained perfectly still while opening the door to the half-size refrigerator next to the right-hand side of his desk. Out came the bottle of vodka. It was half-full.

"Now pour it over my left hand," Kata said.

As if in a dream he did as she ordered. The alcohol was white hot as it entered her wound but she gave not the slightest inkling that she felt any pain whatsoever.

"So, now we get down to it," she said. "Who is Schrodinger?"

"Man, woman, I don't know," Novikov said. "Schrodinger is the person I text with."

She snapped the fingers of her right hand. "Let me see your phone."

"You won't find the texts in there. They told me to use an app called Kein Platz."

"No Space."

He nodded. "The app erases texts ten seconds after they're sent. There's no way to retrieve them, nor do I know the incoming number. Kein Platz blocks that."

She snapped her fingers again and, sighing, he brought forth his cell from the middle drawer.

"Pull up the app," she said. "What was your last exchange with Schrodinger?"

"I would be remiss if I didn't point out that you're still bleeding."

"All over your beautiful desk, yes."

He reached for the inter-compound phone. "I should order the doctor to come—"

"Yes, you'd like that." She cut the telephone line with the shears. "By all means call him with a coded message. He will burst in shooting, I imagine."

Novikov subsided back, his eyes hooded. *I should play poker with him,* Kata thought. *He can't hide anything. I'd take him for everything he's worth.*

"Then at least let me get my first aid kit." He gestured with his head. "It's in the cabinet over there against the wall."

"Sure," Kata said. "Let's put your service to the test."

She stepped back, allowed him to scuttle across the office. He swung open the door to the cabinet, pulled out a white metal box with a green cross painted across its top. His anxiety made him overanxious. He made the mistake of opening the box there and then instead of bringing it back to his desk, so when his hand curled around the Janz pistol Kata was already there.

"You are a very bad boy, Thoth Abramovich." Lifting his pinkie finger, she snipped it off at the base. Novikov yelped and jumped backward. He held his maimed hand with the other, squeezing it tight while Kata lifted the pistol off its bed of wrapped sterile gauze.

"Your service was found wanting. You need to be punished." Kata wagged the barrel of the Janz at him and he took up the first aid kit and, as he should have to begin with, brought it over to the desk, along with his severed finger. "Now," she held up her wounded hand, "sterilize and wrap."

"What about me?" Novikov fairly whined.

"We'll get to you when you're finished with me."

He did a better than decent job with her hand. The bleeding had almost stopped which was more than one could say for the stub of his finger.

"If we put that on ice," he said, indicating his severed finger, "there's a chance it could be reattached."

Kata laughed as she began to wrap his wound. "No chance in hell."

He began to sputter. "But you could—"

"And you could tell me about Schrodinger," she said with a finality that caused him to shudder.

She flicked his pinkie so it spun around on the desktop. He shrieked, then nodded. "Okay, all right." He shuddered again. "I need to sit down."

She kicked a chair over and he sat, sighing heavily. "Okay, well, I'm Schrodinger's conduit, I admit that." His meaty shoulders lifted, fell. "Why not? I have nothing more to lose. I'm the true believer."

"Show me," Kata ordered.

His hand shook as he fumbled the buttons of his dress shirt open. She pulled the front apart, revealing the cross and the entwined O, the sigil of Omega.

"What about your boss, Arsenyev? He had the tattoo as well."

"He went along with it, but he wasn't a true believer," the acting commandant said morosely. "He thought it was some kind of joke, a hobby for the recruits." He glanced up at her. "It gets unbearable here, especially in winter."

"And what was your last communication with Schrodinger?"

"My whole hand," he cried, "it's killing me."

"Answer the question."

Almost in tears from pain, Novikov blurted out, "He texted that something is happening on December twenty-first."

"What?"

"I don't know, I swear." He moaned. "Please!" He raised his hand. Kata just stared at him. "Okay, okay. Schrodinger also said—be ready . . ."

"For what?" Kata asked.

"I don't know," he yelled. "I swear. I assumed he was going to let me know when the time was right."

Kata could believe that. It was strict security protocol. "That's it?"

"Yes. I swear it. That's all I know."

She believed him. His eyes were now swimming with incipient tears. She finished up bandaging his hand. "Go to the refrigerator and get ice."

With a grateful glance in her direction he scurried to the half-refrigerator, scooped out two handfuls of ice, dumped them in a glass bowl sitting on the windowsill and placed it on the desk. He looked at her like a cowed badger.

"Go ahead," she nodded.

He picked up his finger and, gagging, dropped it into the nest of ice he had made.

Kata graced him an almost gentle smile. "Now call muster by the central pole."

"Then I can have my finger back?"

"Absolutely." She nodded. "You and your finger will be reunited in plenty of time."

With a sigh of relief Novikov rushed to do as she ordered.

■   ■   ■

An armada of clouds obscured the sun, turning the afternoon sky the color of bleached bones. The thirteen men of Department 73 arrayed in ranks in front of the post in the center of the open ground looked straight ahead, facing the acting commandant. Kata had buttoned up his shirt. He had his field jacket on. He looked both imposing and important. None of the men had any idea that Kata, standing directly behind him, had the point of the garden shears pressing into the spot that if she jammed it in would puncture a lung.

Novikov, to his credit, had put on his official face with the same diligence a stage actor puts on his makeup. Kata thought he must be thinking of his severed finger floating in its bath of ice.

"Now that everyone is mustered," Novikov shouted, according to the script Kata rehearsed with him, "you will all strip to your waist."

The men, well-trained and obedient, did as they were ordered. There was bewilderment on the faces of some. One or two, she noticed, tried to hide apprehensive looks, tried to keep their eyes focused on Novikov, who wasn't about to give anything away.

Watching over his shoulder, Kata saw first three, then four of the men with the Omega tats, including the cook. "Here we go," she whispered in Novikov's ear. "Do exactly what I told you to do or you'll die gasping for air right where you stand."

Novikov blinked heavily. His breathing became erratic and she only hoped he wouldn't pass out from the pain in his hand.

As she slapped the Janz into his hand, he said, "There has been an infiltration of Department 73. Our former commander allowed it, but he was wrong and I will not." He lifted the Janz, fired off four shots in succession. All the men with the Omega tats staggered backward and collapsed onto the hard-packed winter ground.

Novikov was a crack shot, one bullet each was enough for the kills. But Kata was uninterested in such crisp and quick deaths. The farther she was away from her victim the less she enjoyed the ritual attendant to violent deaths. Here, she felt nothing at all. It was as if these men had never existed.

"Let this be a lesson to you who remain," Novikov said, oblivious to anything but the throbbing pain in his hand, as Kata relieved him of the pistol. "Neither Omega nor any other outside influence will be tolerated within these walls. Those men on the ground were traitors to Department 73, to the FSB, to Mother Russia. Their fate was just and deserved."

He was in formal parade-ground stance, his chin thrust out. Proud little soldier. His false pride made Kata want to slam her fist into his face.

"Dismissed," he shouted, furious.

Sooner than could be imagined the parade ground was deserted. Apart from Kata, Novikov, and the four dead Omega recruits, only the constant wind, dry and piney, remained.

■   ■   ■

Novikov clutched the plastic sack containing his precious iced pinkie as he climbed aboard the helicopter that had brought Kata to *Devyatyy Krug*. The rotors were already whirling, the engine whining up as he sat beside Kata. She handed him a pair of cordless noise-canceling earphones and mic and placed one on her own head.

"All the heavy lifting's been done, Thoth Abramovich," she said through the closed system. "You did well. The pilot called ahead. We'll get you to a specialized clinic in Moscow. You and your finger will be one again."

Novikov nodded, clearly relieved. They were rising rapidly. The copter turned around, lifted even higher, heading back toward Moscow. His forehead wrinkled. "What about Department 73? Will I still run it? Will someone else be in charge?"

"Well, that's entirely up to me," Kata said, without having a clue whether or not that was true. "What do you think?"

"Me?" Novikov shook his head. "If it were up to me I'd never set foot in that hellhole again."

"I can't say I blame you. Have you a family, Thoth Abramovich?"

"An older sister, a niece and two nephews—her children."

"I mean your own family. Wife? Children?"

"I never would have accepted this post if I did. No marriage could survive that."

"You mean to tell me there is no one?"

Novikov gave her a watery smile. "Well, there is a woman. Juliet Danilovna Korokova. She's a captain in the GRU. That's where we met."

"Is she also Omega?" Kata asked.

"What? No, surely not." Novikov looked away, out the open doorway. "The subject never came up."

Kata knew he was lying. His body language gave him away.

"You mean she never saw your tattoo?"

He shrugged. "I got it while I was at *Devyatyy Krug*."

"Yeah, I don't think so."

His head turned so quickly she heard a vertebra crack. "What . . . what d'you mean?"

Kata smiled. "Let's just hope she'll be waiting for you." She leaned over, unsnapped Novikov's safety harness before he had a chance to protest. She hauled him out of his seat and over to the open door.

"Wait! What are you—?"

"Not to worry. I'll give Captain Juliet Danilovna Korokova your best," Kata said as she kicked him out of the helicopter. She caught a glimpse of his horrified face before he was torn from her sight in a sky congested with derelict clouds.

37

NUREMBERG

Evan found her boot stuck between two balusters a couple of treads below where her foot had gone through the rotten tread. She took the opportunity to sit down while she drew on the boot, laced it up. For some time afterward she sat, forearms on drawn-up knees. She felt sick to her soul. The atmosphere of this place was toxic, massed with the ghosts of the dead. She could hear the echoes of Hitler's demagoguery, Goebbels's high cackle, Bormann's goading. They pressed down on her like a bunker on the verge of collapse. She grabbed the sides of her head, scalding tears squeezed out of her by three choked sobs. Then she lifted her head, wiped her cheeks of tears and blood that still leaked from the cut over her eye. She examined the cell phone she had lifted from her victim.

It was locked of course. No fingerprint reader and she knew why. A dead man's fingerprint would open the phone as well as a print from a live one. Logic dictated that to be absolutely secure he would change the code periodically. How in the world would she . . . ? *This is how you learn*, she thought. Closed her eyes. Put herself in his head. What would he think of that was both easy to remember and secure? Amid the blackouts the image of his fist, over and over again. And his wrist with its line of scars. How many? Four? How many? Eight. Eight scars, one fresh. One for each kill, the last for Elke.

She entered the numeric equivalents of the letters: 5–9–7–8–2–0.

Open sesame!

She scrolled through the phone. His name was Christian Bardo. He was indeed one of those mercenaries Camina Wagner had warned her about. His group was based in Berlin, but took on assignments all over the world, though they specialized in German targets.

It was then she came across the packet of intel on her Ambrose Wells had sent Bardo. And after all this time, there it was in black and white: the smoking gun she and Ben had been seeking. A direct link from the

Wells family to assassinations, terrorism, dirty money—for Bardo was being paid from a cutout account in Grand Cayman. With the info on Bardo's cell it only took Evan a few clicks through the dark web to discover that Ambrose Wells was paying Bardo from a shell company that had been on Parachute's list of probable money laundering assets.

That's a bingo! she thought, heart rate hammering. *We have you now.* She sent the data to Ben's and Isobel's cell numbers, then secreted the phone carefully away in the jeans' other pocket. It was worth its weight in Bitcoin.

At length, she stood, climbed the spiral back up to the empty room. Retracing her desperate route around the circular corridor she at length stepped into the room where Elke's killer had first dragged her.

"You'd better put these on." Ghislane held out Evan's bra and the shirt and sweater that had once been hers. "You'll catch your death of cold." She was kind enough not to mention Evan's cuts and bruises.

Numbly, Evan slipped into both layers, shivering as she did so. "Why are you here?"

"I saw the taxi drawn up where there should be no taxi and came to investigate." She turned Evan around to face her. "Did you kill him? Is he dead?"

Evan nodded. "He was posing as a taxi driver."

Ghislane took her into her arms and hugged her tightly. "You did what needed to be done. You've avenged Elke's murder."

Ghislane held her at arm's length, cocked her head. "I would like to ask you why you came here."

"I was following you. I saw you going into the Documentation Center. Again, why are you here?"

Ghislane ignored the question, merely said, "You didn't—you don't—trust me."

Evan grabbed her jacket, slid it on. She casually picked up the eyeliner case from the floor and put it in her jacket pocket. "We don't trust each other."

"We each have our reasons, don't we?"

Evan eyed her. "I doubt that's ever going to change."

"Pity." Ghislane produced a handgun, a compact Beretta 92. Aimed it at Evan's chest.

"Is that really necessary?"

"We don't trust each other, that's been established," Ghislane said. She waved the Beretta. "Come on." As she followed Evan out of the building she added, "You know what happened to the curious cat."

Evan gave a small grimace. "Deader than Schrödinger's lab animal."

■   ■   ■

The Documentation Center brooded about a mile away from the Zeppelin Tribunal, on the other side of the lake, sluggish and tarry-looking, with its horrid underpinnings. The two women were silent during the short journey in Ghislane's VW. The grounds were eerily lit, the shadows extending like elongated fingers, grasping and malevolent. The silence congealed, seemed to suck all the oxygen out of the car's interior. She felt entombed. But the air, cold and breathless when Evan wound down her window, offered little relief. Save for the creaks of the car, the muttering of the muscular engine, an otherworldly stillness reigned. She gasped, felt every ache and pain she had suffered at Bardo's hands. Blood pounded behind her eyes. She struggled against losing consciousness.

The Center reared up before them, oversized, thuggish, casting its own monstrous shadow across the Nazi Rally Grounds. The enormous building resembled the Roman Forum, both in its façade and its round shape. It was the most heavily tourist-trafficked building on the grounds, so Evan was surprised to step into an apartment on the closed-off top floor. The place was comfortably furnished in the style of a London gentlemen's club with sofas and wingback chairs artfully arranged on Tabriz rugs. A white marble fireplace along one wall was topped by a mantel sporting a French ormolu clock, above which hung a stag's head with massive eight-point antlers. The walls were adorned with books on shelves, black-and-white portraits of upright mustachioed men, some in Field Grey Prussian military uniforms, staring determinedly into the camera. Neoclassical cornices from another era ringed the ceiling below which small intarsia tables set with lamps with fringed shades occupied nooks and corners. Morning sunlight danced cheerfully through the windows. Along one wall was a stand containing a line of African violets below a long grow light.

"Wait here." Ghislane put away her handgun, disappeared down a long wood-paneled hallway. Evan stayed where she was. Having come this far she had no intention of leaving. She had the distinct sense that she had come to the last station in her search for the hidden German module of Omega and the source of the cipher. Looking around she couldn't help but be impressed. It took a great deal of wealth and political influence to have created this velvet-lined private sanctuary within a national historical site.

She crossed the room to where the African violets lived. Reaching out she felt the velvet of the purple petals.

"Are you an African violet aficionado?" A male voice, rich, aristocratic, used to commanding others.

Evan turned to see an older version of the man who had his arm around the young Ghislane's waist in the photo she had uncovered in Ghislane's townhouse. If anything he seemed more handsome now with silver streaks above his temples, lines of age and wisdom creasing his face. His eyes were a piercing raptor blue. He wore a Field Grey wool suit cut along the lines of the Imperial German Army uniforms worn by the mustachioed men in the photos on the wall.

She took all this in, her heart pounding with a martial drumbeat in her chest. *End of the line,* she thought, *and here I am.* "I'm more of a March violet aficionado," she replied. March violets were cynical opportunists who joined the Nazi Party only after it was a sure thing, when Hitler officially became dictator in March of 1933.

He frowned. "You don't say."

"I'm a student of history."

"I *am* history."

Was he kidding? Evan asked herself. Or just insane? "You're Ghislane's father."

He made a noise in the back of his throat. "Let's get you fixed up first, shall we?"

Crossing to a sideboard, he fetched a first aid kit. Deftly, he cleaned the cut above her eye, slicked on an antibiotic cream, then used a butterfly bandage. "At least it's stopped bleeding."

She thought it interesting that he didn't ask her how she came by these wounds, and she was grateful for that. She had no desire to go back over her encounter with Christian Bardo.

"There." He put away the kit, turned back to her. "Would you like an ice pack?"

"I'm fine, thanks." Though her entire face throbbed to the beat of her heart she had no desire either to show weakness in front of him.

"As you wish." Still, he brought her a glass of water and four ibuprofen, which she promptly popped and drowned in the water. His smile brought out a dimple in his left cheek. "Schrodinger at your service."

"So there *is* a Schrodinger after all."

"After a fashion," he said with a quirk to his lips. "No one has yet looked in the box."

"And with a sense of humor, too," Evan said. "But surely Schrodinger's not your real name."

"My grandfather served the Kaiser in World War I."

"One of the old line Prussian officers, I take it."

His blue eyes gleamed like marbles. "Precisely so, Fraulein Ryder."

"So you know my name."

"We've known it from the moment you insinuated yourself into my daughter's group."

"And yet you made no move to stop me."

His smile made him even more handsome. He was quite a dazzling specimen—an über-mensch, as Wagner would say. "Ghislane likes you, Fraulein. She likes you very much. She's my only child, so I am in the habit of indulging her."

"Really? That's not the way she tells it. A defiler. She told me. And you're supposed to be dead."

Ghislane appeared then, smirking. "Everything I said was true, only it wasn't about my father. I appropriated Elke's past." She put a hand up to her mouth in exaggerated coyness. "Oops. Was that bad of me?"

"Not at all." Evan gave her the blandest smile she could manufacture. "Just par for the course."

"So," Ghislane's father said, "are you here to save us or to destroy us?"

"That depends entirely on you."

"Mm, no." He shook his head. "Whether you like it or not you have a major role in this."

Evan waved away his words. "Are you or are you not a part of Omega?"

"Well, now that depends. Which part of Omega are we speaking of?"

Disgust flooded Evan. "It's all one and the same."

"But it isn't," the man calling himself Schrodinger corrected. He lifted a finger. "It was Schopenhauer's opinion that 'religion is the masterpiece of the art of animal training, for it trains people as to how they shall think.' That is my opinion as well."

"So what the Wellses espouse—"

"Is utter nonsense," Schrodinger said. "It gathers in the weak-minded, those fools who take the limits of their own field of vision for the limits of the world."

"Schopenhauer again," Evan said.

His eyes lit up. "Ah, I'm beginning to see what sparked her interest."

"Ghislane brought me here at gunpoint."

She didn't understand why a smile crept across his face.

"My daughter would not have shot you."

"And I wouldn't have run away."

"Of course you wouldn't," came a familiar voice. "This is where you are meant to be."

"Wait." Evan's heart skipped a beat. "What?"

And then there she was. Ghislane had stepped aside to accommodate Lyudmila Alexeyevna Shokova. Tall, slender, a runway model's long legs, Lyudmila's ice-blue eyes were shining. Her blond hair was pulled back from her high-cheekboned face in a ponytail. Her eyes drank Evan in in the way a thirsty woman drains a bottle of cold water and asks for more. To Evan, she seemed even more beautiful than ever. She wore black skintight jeans, a midnight-blue men's shirt with French cuffs, a plain gold choker.

"Lyudmila." Her voice was little more than a raspy whisper.

Lyudmila gathered her up in her arms as she scrutinized her. "You've been through the mill. For this I apologize."

"You know I would—"

"Run through fire for me, I know. And I you. This is what the two of us are to each other." She gripped Evan's shoulder, lowered her voice. "But it's important you know that both Pasha Shutkov and Christian Bardo were operatives dangerous to what I am preparing. I could not allow them to continue; nor could I risk involving one of my own field agents in their extermination." Leaning in, she kissed Evan on both cheeks. "But I do apologize the task I gave you was so perilous, but there is no one else I can trust."

Evan smiled. "A few weeks in Sumatra will cure the meat-shredder you put me through." She and Lyudmila had spent an idyllic three weeks on the island last spring. It seemed like a lifetime ago.

"I'm so happy you're here." They hugged before Lyudmila held her at arm's length. "Let me look at you." She shook her head, a smile curling her lips. "Still the consummate soldier."

"Why would I be anything else?" Evan indicated Ghislane's father. "This man . . . Schrodinger or whatever his name really is—"

"Bernhard-Otto von Kleist." He gestured at one of the photos. "My grandfather, General Robert von Kleist."

"*The* Bernhard-Otto von Kleist?"

Von Kleist bowed from the waist, every inch a gentleman from the old school. Now Evan understood why he looked familiar in the photo of him and his daughter. He was a master fixer. Every prominent pol in the EU came to him when they needed help of the sort only he could provide. As such he shunned the spotlight. So much so that there were few photos of him, which is why she didn't recognize him right away.

She turned to Lyudmila. "But this still doesn't explain what you're doing here in his aerie."

"Oh, no." von Kleist spread his hands. "I'm the visitor here, just like you."

Lyudmila took a step toward her. "This is where I live, Evan. This is from where I run my entire network."

"And von Kleist?"

"Darling, much as I hate to admit it, there are times when men are indispensable."

They both laughed then, heartily, deeply, while the von Kleists looked on.

The moment of levity ended as quickly as it began. Evan's expression clouded. "But why didn't you tell me about all this?" She gestured at the apartment, at von Kleist.

"Precisely because of Bernd. Do you really think that if you came here without having gone through what you have you'd be ready to accept him as an ally—as my partner?"

Evan was about to refute her when she closed her mouth. Of course she wouldn't have accepted this man. Of course she would have started to doubt Lyudmila. Of course Lyudmila was right; she always was. Once again Evan had to wonder what Lyudmila's overall scheme could be. She had never been able to discern a pattern, although she knew damn well there was one. Lyudmila never did anything at random. Her life post-FSB, post-Politburo was one vast jigsaw puzzle into which she was placing the pieces one at a time. And only she knew what the puzzle would look like when completed. But one thing was for sure, Bernd von Kleist was a major piece she had put in play.

"I think it's time we all got to know each other better, eh?" von Kleist crossed to a cabinet on which was set a chased silver tray with old-fashioned, highball, and shot glasses. Bending down he slid open a door, pulled out an iced bottle of vodka.

As he poured, he said, "You know, being around Lyudmila as much as I have been I've developed a taste for vodka." He gave a little snort.

"My grandfather is probably rolling over in his grave. Imagine, a German and a Russian allied." He shook his head, laughing.

Ghislane helped him bring over the shot glasses and the bottle. They sat on a loveseat and chairs grouped near the window. After toasting and swigging down the first shot, von Kleist went around and refilled everyone's glass.

"Now would be the time, Ghislane," Evan said, "your group . . ."

"Was created by me and Bernd," Lyudmila said. "It's there to gather information from and about Omega. We got part way, but not as deep as we had hoped."

"We suspect that Ambrose Wells, the son, shared his suspicions of a problem somewhere in Europe with Lucinda," von Kleist continued.

"It seems that he and Lucinda have become rather close." Lyudmila's smile turned contemptuous. "Lucinda sleeps with the son. The Old Man sleeps with well-paid men."

Evan thought about this for several moments, about how rotten everything had become. How even the people who were on the right side were no longer with the angels—if they ever were.

"So you were ordered to create the bogus coded message to send from here to DC."

Ghislane nodded. "They knew we were the best, and they still trusted us. So they used us to find the leak in her system."

"Not yet realizing we were the leak," Lyudmila said. "Which means Ghislane's group has more or less run its course. We don't want any of her group rolled up."

Evan thought of Elke and of Bardo, her murderer, and that led her back to his cell. She drew it out, was just about to show Lyudmila the smoking gun that led back to the Wellses, when the phone vibrated. She looked down at it as if she were holding a scorpion, pressed a key and up popped a text.

There was no text, however, only a photo. Evan gasped. There on the phone's screen was an image of Ben, strapped to a chair. His eyes were closed, his head canted to one side. She saw the dark dot, with trembling fingers zoomed in on a puncture wound. She went rigid.

"Evan?" Lyudmila was up out of her chair. "What is it? What's happened?"

But before Evan could show her, Lyudmila's own cell chimed. She looked at the screen, pressed a couple of keys, looked again.

"Listen." Lyudmila's face darkened as she looked up at Evan. "Text Ben immediately. Less than twenty-four hours from now, sometime on December twenty-first, there is going to be a nationwide event staged by Omega and its followers."

Evan thought about all the protests, the riots, the mass shootings she'd seen on TV the last few days. "The country's already in a state of . . . What kind of an event?"

But even as Lyudmila was shaking her head Evan was texting Isobel on Bardo's phone, asking her to have Parachute staff get on the quantum computers and immediately search for anything they could find about an Omega-led insurrection planned for December twenty-first. A return text hit her like a sledgehammer: Ben had gone off with the FBI agent Jon Tennyson and had not returned.

"I've got to get back to DC," Evan said, rising. Her voice was shaky and her legs felt weak. Everything that had happened to her during the last week came crashing down on her like an avalanche. "But I can't call Ben. I can't . . ."

Stepping forward Ghislane grabbed her, steadying her.

"Let me see," Lyudmila said.

Wordlessly Evan showed her the photo, and they both read the new text that had just come through.

Lyudmila glanced up into Evan's face. "Did you send the intel from this phone to Ben?" When she saw the look on Evan's face, she sighed. "The text makes sense now. Lucinda knows you'll be coming."

Evan looked down at the text again, all her cuts and bruises coming to the fore in a ferocious tsunami of pain.

1st shot horse administered. 2nd in 6 hrs. Omega Rules. You lose Ben. You lose everything.

38

"Thank you for taking me to the airfield," Evan said. Isobel had had a Parachute jet flown over from Berlin. It was now fueled and ready to take her back to DC the moment she arrived.

"It's nothing." Ghislane trod hard on the accelerator and her souped-up VW leapt forward, skimming around vehicles. It was early enough in the afternoon that the traffic hadn't yet built up to its rush hour crescendo. "After all that's happened I wanted a chance to talk with you—alone." She slowed for a light, came to a stop. "It occurred to me that since you appeared we've both been playing roles. We were never ourselves. I regret that."

"So do I," Evan said, meaning it.

"I mean I've been doing that—playing a part—ever since I formed this group with my father and Lyudmila's help. It was a kind of game, you know. And I can't deny I enjoyed it—being important, pleasing my father, knowing I was part of his plans."

The light went green and she took off like the VW was a rocket.

"But now you're not so happy," Evan said.

Ghislane nodded. "When I looked down at Elke's body last night—I don't know, something happened inside me. I crossed a Rubicon that until that moment I didn't know existed. I liked Elke; I really cared for her. I'm going to miss her. I think I'm going to grieve for her more than for anyone I've lost before."

"I'm so sorry."

"I know you are. I know I was angry—and I took it out on you."

"For good reason. It was my—"

"No, listen to me. I came to realize that I was angry at myself. I put her in harm's way. I'll never forgive myself for that."

"But you must," Evan said, "otherwise what's the point of living? You have to go on, Ghislane, but with your eyes wide open. You can't keep doing things because other people want you to—no matter how much you love them. You have to know yourself to know what you want. And it's especially difficult for us women. We're all so busy looking to others—fathers, mentors, other women who we're sure are better than us, more successful than us—for approval." She shook her head. "That's no way to live a life—any life."

Ghislane was quiet for some time while she weaved in and out of traffic. Evan wondered whether she was talking about Ghislane or herself. She didn't know whether she had drawn Ghislane closer or driven her away. As Ghislane had said, they had spent their time together playing specific roles.

"My father wasn't lying," Ghislane said after a time. "I do like you."

"How can you tell? You don't know me."

Ghislane gave her a sly smile. "You can't tell me that bits and pieces of you didn't slip out when we were together in my home."

"Maybe." Evan looked out the window. "Maybe."

They were close to the airfield now and Ghislane slowed, taking the off-ramp to the exit.

"Look at it this way," she said, "we're both good at acting." She laughed. "We should be in the Royal Shakespeare Company."

Wouldn't that be something, Evan thought. But then, "I'd be no good under the lights."

Ghislane laughed. "Yeah, I guess that's where we differ. I love the lights. I'm sorry the gig's ending."

She pulled up adjacent to where the Parachute jet waited, its ultramodern fuselage sleek and somehow ominous. Sunlight spun off its curved silver surface.

She still thinks of what we do as a lark, Evan thought. A game—despite the people who have been killed because of it. She turned to look at Ghislane and knew she'd learn in time.

"Okay, well, that's it." Ghislane turned away, suddenly awkward.

Evan put a hand on her forearm. "Ghislane . . ."

Ghislane turned back, smiling. But her eyes were magnified by incipient tears. "Sorry I pulled the gun on you."

"I believe your father when he said you'd never pull the trigger."

"Yeah," Ghislane laughed. "Anyway, I'm rotten with goodbyes. I don't know how to—"

Evan hugged her tight. "It's okay."

Ghislane pulled back. "Will I see you again?"

"Perhaps." Evan opened the door, the chill rushing in. "Someday."

"Right." Ghislane nodded. And then, all in a rush, "I feel like I'm losing something rare."

Smiling, Evan took her hand briefly, squeezing. "Rare isn't singular."

"Something real."

She looked straight into Ghislane's eyes. "You know I have to go."

"Of course I do," Ghislane said a bit too fiercely.

"Good. So." Evan continued to regard her. "Now that you know what to look for you'll find it again."

Ghislane nodded as Evan slid out of the car. There was something forlorn behind Ghislane's eyes.

Evan ducked back down. "You will, you know," she assured her. "I have faith in you."

Ghislane looked away for a moment as if embarrassed, and Evan turned to go.

"You'll get back in time," Ghislane called through the open window as Evan set out toward the stairs that were a part of the fuselage. "I have faith in you."

■ ■ ■

Evan stood for a moment just inside the doorway of the plane while behind her the stair swung up into the body of the jet. She was even more impressed by the sophistication and comfort of this Parachute aircraft than she'd been by the one that had flown her to Vienna, four days and several lifetimes ago. Wide leather seats that swiveled, work stations with what must be laptop computers, though they didn't look like any laptops Evan had ever seen. Even wider aisles, and in the rear leather sofas on either side of a circular bar within which a young female attendant was busy at an electric blender, mixing someone a drink.

And that someone was the biggest surprise of all. A tall man, rangy and solid looking. He had thick, dark hair, worn long, an oval face with a prominent nose, a wide almost sensual mouth, strong jaw, and the extraordinary violet eyes of Elizabeth Taylor.

"Ryder, come on in," he called in a clear well-modulated tone of voice. "Don't be shy." Then he laughed, big white teeth appearing, shining like little LED lights. "Shy's not the right word—not for you. But I know you must be surprised to see me. I know I would be if I were you." He spread his large, long-fingered hands. "But after all this is my plane."

This then was Marsden Tribe, the hermit genius who broke the enigma of quantum computing and founded Parachute. He was the polar opposite of a pale-faced nerd who hadn't seen the sun in a decade. While she was familiar with his voice from the bit of his TED Talk she'd tuned in to, Evan had only a hazy idea of what he looked like. She'd never much cared; she had more important things to concentrate on.

He waved her over and she sat on a low-backed stool beside him. He wore jeans, a battered leather flight jacket over a midnight-blue shirt. The bartender, who had the look of a PhD slumming as an executive assistant, stopped the blender, poured the contents, thick as a milkshake, into two tall glasses. The liquid was the color of Tribe's eyes. She set one glass in front of Evan, served Tribe the other. A moment later she brought up an ice pack, and with an easy smile slid it across to Evan.

With a nod of appreciation, Evan picked it up, placed it against her throbbing cheek.

She watched Tribe out of the corner of her eye. The man had charisma, no doubt about it. There was an electricity circling him like an aura that made the hairs on her forearms stand. His golden skin. Each line and crease of his face seemed to belong, to have a meaning, a place in his life, as if he had somehow conquered time. Something stirred inside her, uncoiling, stretching. For an instant she had difficulty drawing breath.

The rising roar of the engines penetrated the cabin.

"Strap in," Tribe said briskly.

Looking down Evan saw that the stools were bolted to the deck. A harness was attached to the stool. She did as he said. He was already strapped in. The bartender had somehow disappeared. "Hold tight to your drink."

The brakes came off and they were released down the runway, picking up speed with every foot they traversed. In no time at all Evan felt that floating feeling in the pit of her stomach as the plane roared into the sky. The deck tilted as they rose far more steeply than a commercial aircraft. Her ears popped. They were already going extremely fast.

"Drink," he said.

She did and her ears cleared. Whatever was in the concoction was slightly sweet, slightly tart and completely without alcohol and yet it did give her system a lovely immediate boost.

"You're looking better already," he said. "You came in here looking half-dead."

"Atta way to sling the compliments." But she ran a hand over her face, feeling the bruises, the scars. "I must look a fright."

"Not at all. You look interesting."

To her horror she felt a flush creeping up her throat into her cheeks. She drained the glass quickly. "What's in here anyway?"

"Sugar and spice and everything nice." He winked. "My own recipe. You'll never get it out of me and Joyce is sworn to secrecy."

Joyce popped up again behind the bar seemingly from out of nowhere, a bowl of soup and a double patty hamburger on an oval tray.

"When was the last time you ate?" Tribe said, but Evan was too busy wolfing down her food. It wasn't until she'd smelled the soup that her stomach growled, informing her that she was famished.

When she was finished, she noticed that Joyce held a small mother-of-pearl box in her right hand. She opened it. Evan saw neat rows of joints. Tribe plucked out one and lit up, using a heavy gold lighter. "Want one?" he said through an exhalation.

"Thanks, no."

"Quite right." He inhaled again, held the smoke in. "It's one thing for me to be eight miles high, quite another for you, Ryder." When he grinned he looked like an impetuous teenager. "You should sleep, get some rest while we're in the air."

"I can't. Not when Ben's life is at risk. Not when the country could go up in flames tomorrow."

He regarded her candidly. "So how will not sleeping help Ben or the country?"

"It won't." She bit her lip. "But I—"

"Actually, you're right again. There is something we can do from this aluminum can." He nodded at Joyce, who drew out a bottle. "I understand your weapon of choice is vodka—Russian, high end. Am I right?"

"You are indeed." Through the icy frosting Evan recognized the bottle: Jewel of Russia Ultra Black Label.

"Nice," she said as Joyce poured a generous amount into an old-fashioned glass. Even Lyudmila would be happy to drink this silky, complex liquor, she thought. Silently she toasted her as Marsden blew aromatic smoke up to the ceiling.

Tribe suggested they move to one of the sofas. When they were seated, he flicked ash off the end of the joint into a cut-glass ashtray built into a low table.

"I'll be honest with you, Ryder. This whole espionage adjunct is an experiment. I've been deep into a new innovation for my quantum computers: time and memory crystals." He waved a hand. "I doubt I'd even have gotten into espionage if it weren't for Isobel. What I do, what Parachute sells as a platform is enormously valuable. It has to be safeguarded. This is why I agreed. Also I trust her absolutely. She's the professional's professional. Her contacts are deeper, more wide-ranging than you could imagine. Even better, I've learned that she has a gift of insight. She extrapolates from what's happening today and can see where events will lead three and five years down the road. That's an invaluable trait, one I recognize as precious."

He took another long toke, watched the smoke curling out of his half-open mouth. "Unfortunately, Isobel's macro method of looking at the world and its future contains a drawback. She sometimes misses the importance of the here and now. This is what has happened with the Omega threat. She failed to take it seriously enough in the moment; her gaze was elsewhere, further out—on, if she's right, an appalling threat we will be coming up against next year."

He waved a hand. "However, this oversight, serious as it is, has been mitigated by you and Butler and, I might add, her utter faith in you both. You two have had your sights firmly on the Omega threat and now, thanks to your intel, we know precisely how acute their immediate threat is. Our quantum system has picked up microbursts of conversations within the Omega network—which I might add is far more extensive than even you and Ben know: police chiefs, legislators, military personnel—talk about the Deep State, this is it." He gestured. "The federal government isn't equipped to find these microbursts let alone listen in on them. We know—we know a lot and learning more each second."

He pressed something on the tabletop and it lit up. It was a computer screen. Several more taps with his fingertips and a 3D holographic rendering of a very large house appeared above the screen.

"The Wells mansion," Tribe said. "The schematic includes all the electronic surveillance, HVAC, plumbing, the whole eleven yards." He turned it so that she could look at the mansion from all sides, so that they could figure out the best way in—and out.

"Where did you get this?"

"My quantum computers have been working overtime since Isobel got your text."

"And Ben? Do we know where he is?"

"He was taken to the mansion, that much we do know."

"How?" she said. "How did it happen?"

"You remember those FBI agents from last year."

"Tennyson and Leyland."

Tribe nodded. "Tennyson, it turns out, works for Omega. He lured Ben out. There was an ambush. Leyland was shot to death, Ben abducted, and Tennyson's vehicle torched. It's at the FBI crime lab now but, you know bureaucracy, it's going to take time for them to come to any definitive conclusions."

"Time we don't have."

"Twenty-four hours, or less—we don't know exactly what Omega's got planned for tomorrow, the twenty-first," Tribe told her. "Seven fewer hours by the time we touch down at Dulles."

She was staring fixedly at the mansion. "He's still there? Ben?"

"The place has been under Parachute drone surveillance, so yes, we know he's still there."

A shiver went all the way through her, invading her marrow. "But still. Ben may not make it out alive."

Tribe turned the hologram over so they could see the equipment that lay underneath. "None of us makes it out alive, Ryder. It's just a matter of when."

39

"Welcome back to the U S of A, Mr. Tribe. The District of Columbia welcomes you."

"Thank you, Darryl. Always a relief to be home."

"Ain't that the truth." Darryl, a bruiser with bloodshot eyes and the red-veined nose of an inveterate drinker, gave no more than a cursory glance at the three passports—Tribe's, Joyce's, and Evan's—then handed them back to each in turn.

Tribe rose out of his seat. "How's the fam?"

"Just fine, thank you," Darryl said. "Say, my oldest asked me to tell you he's loving working at Parachute."

"Justin's a fine young man. He's got a great career ahead of him."

"I appreciate that, Mr. Tribe. And so does Justin, that's for sure."

Darryl deplaned shortly after that. Joyce was once again nowhere to be seen. At the top of the steps, Tribe took Evan's hand. "Until next time, Ryder." His smile made her heart flip over in her chest.

But that was all the respite she was going to get. The airtime from Germany to DC was normally around eight and a half hours. Somehow Tribe's jet made it in seven. Since Germany was six hours ahead they'd only lost an hour. They landed at approximately 5 P.M.

Isobel was waiting for her on the tarmac, a purring SUV at the ready just behind her. Evan looked over her shoulder but there was no sign of either Joyce or Tribe.

■　■　■

"The prodigal field agent returns," Isobel said as they settled into the backseat. The SUV immediately took off. A soundproof glass panel slid up, sealing them off from the driver and what looked to Evan like a diminutive figure, maybe only a shadow, but a quick flash of getting into the taxi driven by Christian Bardo drove all thought of it out of her mind. She gave a little shudder.

Isobel turned to her. "Are you all right?"

"Tribe and Joyce took good care of me."

"I should damn well hope so."

Evan's brow furrowed. "Ben?"

"Nothing new. They haven't moved him." Isobel drew out a laptop. "But then they wouldn't, would they?"

"Meaning?"

"He's the lure, Evan. Clearly, it's you Lucinda Wells wants. You caused her twin's death. Ben pulled the trigger but he'd never have gotten close to her if it hadn't been for you."

"Does Tribe know Lucinda is my sister?"

Isobel's eyes were bright and steady. "If you're asking whether I told him, no, I didn't. But Marsden has his own ways of finding things out."

Having spent seven hours with the man Evan had no doubt that he did. Ways she couldn't even imagine. That was the kind of power he wielded.

As if she had read Evan's mind, Isobel said, "But even Marsden's power has its limits. He tried to get the FBI to turn over Tennyson's SUV to our forensics team. Even when he told them they could get results within two hours they turned him down flat."

"Tribe didn't tell me that."

"Well, he wouldn't, would he?"

Evan felt the air go out of the little fantasy she had been building around Marsden Tribe and now she felt foolish. "That's the government for you," she said to cover her embarrassment. "Stubborn to a fault."

"Ah, well, every woman falls under his spell." She laughed. "It only takes a moment or two with him."

She realized that Isobel had been studying her for some time. "Did you?" she said a little too sharply.

"I'm a special case."

"Meaning?"

Isobel lifted an eyebrow. "You really want to hear this?"

"I do."

"Okay. You know someone too well, the thrill is gone."

Evan looked away at the buildings streaking by as they headed toward Alexandria. When she turned back she noticed a black leather briefcase sitting beside Isobel's left calf. Isobel lifted it up, snapped it open, took out a slim laptop of the same design she had seen in Tribe's aircraft. But that wasn't the only thing inside the briefcase.

"Loaded for bear," Isobel said. "That's the correct American phrase, is it not?"

Evan ran her fingertips over the selection of small weaponry held in place by thin leather straps. "It certainly is."

Isobel opened the laptop on which a two-dimensional blueprint of the Wells mansion was displayed.

"So. You're the infiltration expert. Do we go in hard or soft?"

Evan's thoughts snapped to, like a rubber band. She knew what Isobel meant. "I go in soft—silent and swift. Then at some point, when I give you the signal you cut all the utilities and we go in hard."

"Only one thing wrong with your plan," Isobel said. "You're not going in alone. I'll be with you."

"I don't think that's the wisest course of action. I do best when I'm on my own."

When she spoke next Isobel's voice had acquired a steely edge. "Nevertheless, that's the way it's going to be."

"I'll need a reason," Evan said. "A really good one."

"Inside the Wells mansion are two separate targets: Ben and Lucinda. No matter how good you are, Evan—and believe me I have no doubts whatsoever as to the extent of your expertise—you won't be able to get to both."

Evan knew she was right. She didn't like it, but she had to accept the reality of the situation.

"You'll go after Lucinda," Isobel said. "And I'll find Ben and haul him out of there." She hesitated a moment. "You've discussed this with Marsden."

"I did," Evan said. "And I was kind of surprised he was taking such a personal interest in the plan."

"Huh, well, that is easily enough explained. We have neither the personnel nor the government authorization to deal with these expanding riots. And Marsden can't get to first base with the feds to listen to what he has to say—not that he would tell you that."

Evan nodded. She pulled out Bardo's phone—it would show as a number originating in Germany—and punched in a number she had memorized.

"General Aristides, please."

Beside her Isobel gave a start. *What the hell are you doing*? she mouthed.

"I don't care if he's in a meeting. Tell him it's Evan Ryder calling. That's right." She rolled her eyes as Aristides's new phone jockey asked for the spelling. She gave it to him, willing herself to be patient.

"Please hold."

Evan waited for almost five minutes while she imagined the general deciding what to do.

Finally he came on the line. "I was hoping I'd never hear from you again."

"What a lovely greeting."

"What d'you want?" She could practically hear Aristides's molars grinding in frustration. "Have you told Ben what happened?"

"Between us, you mean?"

"You know damn well what I mean," the general bit off.

"I didn't think it was a good idea."

"You're damn straight it wouldn't—"

"But I could, I just might. And everyone else, as well."

He made a sound not unlike a mule ordered to move its ass. "Get on with it then."

She told him everything Tribe would have told him, about Omega, about the Wellses, about the imminent insurrection.

"We're aware of the planned riots, of course, and the local police have been alerted. Other than that, there's been minimal chatter. And believe me we've been monitoring—"

"Either your systems are deficient or Omega's found a way to remain invisible. But I assure you—"

Aristides gave an exasperated sigh. "I've no time for this."

"This is all you have time for, General. Believe me. I'm sending you proof." And she sent him the packets of intel she'd sent Ben and Isobel, also Isobel's overview report of what was being planned for tomorrow, the twenty-first.

"Okay, I'll give this to NSA's SIGINT section and—"

"You don't get it, Aristides. By the time they get to it it'll be too late."

"But . . . but what if it's *dezinformatsiya*? If I muster out all the police, the National Guard . . . Jesus, I'll look like a fool."

"You're already a fool, General. But I'm more than willing to let everyone know your dirty little secret when I tell my story—and believe me, in this day and age everyone will be listening. Social media will blow up. The media will have a field day. You'll be besieged, your superiors will call you on the carpet. They'll draw up a court martial or whatever the hell they do to punish a disgraced Pentagon general."

Silence, drawing itself out like melting taffy, sticky with doubt and fear.

"I won't do it. Go fuck yourself."

"As you wish. I have General Robertson on speed dial." Robertson, a four-star, was Aristides's boss. A man with a Puritan's spirit and an Old Testament glee in inflicting retribution. "So I'll just sign off now and—"

"Send me all the intel you have, dammit—every last freaking scrap of it," Aristides barked in a voice so coarse he might have been gargling with gravel. "And if this blows up, God help you, you'll be in Gitmo before you know what hit you. Clear?"

"Crystal."

She broke the connection, wiped the perspiration off her brow with the back of her hand.

"So?" Isobel's voice was thick with anxiety. Evan had never seen her anxious about anything.

"Call Tribe," Evan told her. "Give him the number I'm about to send you and tell him to start transmitting everything Parachute's quantum computers have unearthed on Omega's plans for tomorrow night."

Isobel nodded. "With pleasure."

■   ■   ■

Ten minutes later they drew up on a side street in Alexandria. Just ahead of them the driver of a medium-size delivery van was lugging two cartons across a small iron-bound wooden loading dock at the back end of an exclusive boutique French laundry and dry cleaners, frequented by the staff of the elite inside the Beltway and in the tony Old Town and Southwest Quadrant areas of Alexandria. But it was late now—too late for any regular deliveries, but not too late to make a special run to the Wellses.

December gloom shrouded the narrow street in indigo. Apart from the two red lights on the loading dock, all was in darkness. Finished, the driver slammed the rear doors of the van, slid a simple vertical bar in place, then went around to climb up into the driver's seat. Evan made a move to leave the SUV but Isobel grasped her biceps.

"Not you," she said softly.

■   ■   ■

An Binh slid out of the shotgun seat of the SUV, ran swiftly and silently to the off-side door of the van, opened it and hoisted herself inside. The engine had started up, the headlights piercing the darkness. An Binh had in her left hand a push dagger with a fat, leaf-shaped blade four inches long. The blade was made of Damascus steel, the same material used in samurai katana or long swords. It was composed of alternating layers of stainless and high-carbon steel—the one for strength, the other for flexibility. It was the perfect material for a blade. This particular one had been forged by hand by An Binh's grandfather who had spent twenty years in Japan studying with a grand master swordsmith. It had great sentimental value to An Binh, therefore she handled it in only the most professional manner as her father had taught her.

By the time the driver turned to look at who had invaded his cab, An Binh's body was neatly folded in the footwell. The tip of the push dagger pricked the material at the juncture of his thighs.

"What is this?" Sweat had broken out along the diver's hairline.

An Binh did not bother answering him. She waited patiently for the double fist sound from the back of the vehicle.

She nodded to herself. "Nothing has changed," she said to the driver in her singsong voice. "Drive."

■　■　■

The moment An Binh swung up into the cab of the van Evan and Isobel, briefcase in hand, were out of the SUV, racing the several yards to the back of the truck. Lifting up the long latch, they swung open the doors and climbed in, closing the doors after them.

Sealed in, they crouched in the darkness as the van began its journey to the Wellses' mansion.

"So who is that riding with us up front?"

"An Binh. The therapist your father recommended for Ben. She's been miraculous, she's helping him regain his ability to walk."

All the breath went out of Evan. She could scarcely get a word out. "Ben is . . . Ben can walk?"

"He can. Slowly at this point and with some help, but yes."

"Dammit, Isobel, why the hell did you bury the lede?"

"It didn't matter at the time."

Evan was aghast. "It didn't—"

"I needed you fully focused on the plan, but thinking about Ben, his progress, whether he was going to fully regain his mobility . . . The time was right now when you saw An Binh."

Evan, flushed with anger, nevertheless knew Isobel was right. She went into prana, breathing slowly and deeply, regaining her equilibrium.

"That doesn't explain why you brought her." There was still an edge to her voice she didn't like. "The less people—"

"It was her idea, actually, and I agreed." Isobel seemed to have ignored Evan's tone. "We have no idea what shape Ben will be in when we come upon him. An Binh will be best at evaluating him and tending on the spot."

"If he's still alive." She saw Isobel's eyes on her. "He did shoot her twin sister, didn't he?"

"Speculation can only lead to false narratives." Isobel switched on an LED flashlight, played the beam around the compartment. Apart from the two containers it was empty. "Let's take a look at what we have, shall we?"

Evan carefully pried open first one container then the other.

Isobel played the beam over the contents. There were bed linens to be sure—Frette Egyptian cotton sheets, each one cleaned, folded, and adorned with a robin's-egg blue satin ribbon. But that wasn't all. In among the sheets Evan discovered small containers in which were nested four sterile syringes loaded with a colorless, cloudy liquid.

"Interesting delivery," she said.

"What the hell is this?" Evan asked. "Some kind of powerful narcotic? Medication for Wells?"

"No," Isobel said. "And yes." With the utmost care she extracted a syringe from its Styrofoam nest, held it up to her beam of light. "As you can see, the laundry is legit; it does fantastic work, it's earned its reputation. However there is another business in the basement of an entirely different nature, as illicit as the laundry is kosher. It's a laboratory and dispensary."

"Drugs," Evan said.

"You would think so." Isobel's nail flicked the syringe, as if striking a warning bell. "But what we have here, Evan, is another of the Old Man's dirty little secrets." She tapped the syringe again. "In here we have something really nasty.

"The Old Man is really an Old Man. He's terrified of growing older, terrified even more of death. He'll do anything, pay any price if he thinks he can stop time, maintain the years he has left ad infinitum."

"Please." Evan made a face. "That's impossible."

"Impossible," Isobel answered her, "*and* insane." She didn't bother to hide her look of disgust. "The serum in here is a distilled concentration of fetal placenta. Wells is convinced being injected with this will keep him from aging any further."

Evan swallowed a sour liquid that had risen from her gut. She was going to ask a question to which she suspected the answer. "Where is this dispensary getting its . . . material?" She couldn't even say the words, couldn't conceive of this actually happening, couldn't believe this could be what was at the end of her long road to the Wellses.

"Aborted fetuses." There. Isobel had said it for her.

"Oh, God." Evan put her fists against her eyes as if to blot out the heinous idea. "Oh, my God."

40

WELLS ESTATE, FAIRFAX COUNTY, VIRGINIA

"Yes," Isobel said. "Quite."

"Only a madman would get caught up in such an abominable notion."

"Oh, he believes it to his very marrow." Isobel put the syringe back in its plastic bed. "Fifty thousand a pop is what they're charging him."

"What does he care?"

"Precisely," Isobel said. "He doesn't care about the cost, he doesn't care about the poor little helpless things he's defiling."

They stopped talking as the van slowed then came to a halt. Isobel opened the briefcase.

"Time to saddle up," Evan said, arming herself.

Isobel shot her a curious look, then shook her head. "Americans," she muttered.

They could hear a muffled conversation—presumably, the driver and the security guard at the rear gate. Mercifully, the back-and-forth was short, the driver clearly was known to the guard.

The van started up again but at a more leisurely pace. Evan and Isobel looked at each other. They were inside the estate. So far so good, but as both of them knew improvisation was often required.

■ ■ ■

From her lotus position on the floorboards, eyes just above the dashboard, An Binh watched the van approach a door in the rear of the estate. It opened vertically, allowing them entrance. The van rolled into what looked to be a cement-walled delivery bay, came to a stop. Lifting herself off the footwell An Binh drove the butt of the push dagger into the side of the driver's head just below his right ear. Immediately and in complete silence he collapsed.

As planned, she banged on the wall separating the driver's cabin from the load area—one, two—pause, three. As she slipped out of the van's cabin she heard the rear doors swing open. She was in a rectangular space clearly used to accommodate incoming supplies, sculptures, and furnishings large and small to meet the fancies of the owners. Apart from the wash of illumination from the rear driveway lamps there was no other light in the space—no windows, nothing on the walls. At the rear was a raised platform similar to the one at the start of the van's journey, allowing larger trucks to offload their cargo directly.

Even as she heard Isobel and Evan Ryder step down onto the concrete apron she saw the door at the far end of the platform open. An elongated shadow flowed into the receiving area—thin, angular, head enlarged, limbs spidery. Then the figure attached to the shadow appeared. Both by nature and by training An Binh was stoic, revealing as little as a stone. This was how she was now.

"Alice Stanwick," she murmured so softly only someone standing right next to her should have heard. But Alice heard. Her head swiveled on her neck. Her eyes seemed to catch fire—a trick of the odd light surely—as recognition dawned on her face.

"Do my eyes deceive me?" She stepped along the cement above An Binh. "Is this the half-breed I left for dead in Nepal?"

"Resurrected," An Binh said in a neutral tone of voice. But she could hear the blood circulating faster through her arteries, the double-beats of her heart expanding and contracting. But within moments she had stilled them all, chilled out her body, calmed her mind, for this was the goal of her heaven-sent invitation to work with Ben Butler inside the otherwise impenetrable Parachute bubble. Butler and Ryder were inextricably linked to Omega. Alice Stanwick worked for Samuel Wainwright Wells, who controlled Omega. This is what patience meant. This was how she had worked her way back to her sworn nemesis.

"You used Wells's money to get whatever you wanted," An Binh said.

"And why not?" Alice scoffed. "It's a way of life for them." A crooked smile creased her face. "I had money, you didn't. You were a child, but you got in my way. You tried to tell people what a fraud I was, that I wasn't a believer in their rituals, their beliefs. You wouldn't stop."

"You weren't. You still aren't."

"But you see that doesn't matter. It didn't matter over there, it matters even less here. There are no accounts of what I did in Asia, either written or verbal. There is an archival silence." She moved farther toward An Binh. "Being Asian—a poor mongrel Asian—you probably don't know the derivation of 'archive.' It's from the ancient Greek *arkheion*, 'the house of the ruler.' And that's what I am to you, An Binh, the ruler—just as every Westerner has ruled over Asia at one time or another."

"Manipulated."

Alice shrugged. "Same thing." She put her forefinger against her lips. "Archival silence."

"I am the antidote to your archive of violence," said An Binh, advancing herself toward the short flight of stairs up to the platform, despite the fact that it made Alice seem taller and herself shorter, exaggerating the differences between them. "I am the demon in your machine." Her smile was ghastly but only to Alice to whom it was directed. "I am the one forever haunting your ruler's house."

"Not for long," Alice said, taking out a small pistol she kept with her from her days and nights in Asia.

An Binh heard the mad slap of boot soles coming from behind her but her thoughts were not on Isobel or Evan, she was solely concentrated on her foe. As of its own accord her left hand swung up. The push dagger was in the air before Alice could squeeze the trigger. The blade struck her precisely where An Binh had aimed it—her lower belly.

Alice gave out an agonized grunt, fell to her knees as her intestines were pierced through and through. An Binh was on the move, up the steps when she signaled to the two women behind her to keep their positions. Her gesture was so emphatic, the action and reaction so swift, so startling that both Isobel and Evan halted in mid-stride.

An Binh was on the platform now, standing over her enemy. She kicked away the handgun. Then as Alice looked up at her she slapped away the woman's hands from the hilt of the push dagger, repossessed it and twisted the blade in a slow widening circle. Alice's eyes nearly bugged out of her head, her mouth dropped open, a string of saliva drooled over her chin onto her shirt.

"Fuck," Alice said, as An Binh withdrew the blade. Alice cupped her hands as her insides began to slide out.

Still bent over, An Binh held her push dagger in front of Alice's face. "You know who made this?"

Alice's eyes were rolling in their sockets. "Who cares?"

"My grandfather made this." An Binh's voice was so quiet it was horrifying. "The man you killed."

"He wouldn't teach me to—"

"Because he knew your heart, and you killed him."

"I offered him a hundred thousand dollars!" Alice's voice turned plaintive. "Who turns down that much money?"

"You know what? He baffled you. He took you inside his own ruler's house, so you killed him?"

"One Asian." When Alice spat her saliva was thick, red with blood. "One lousy fucking Asian. Thousands of them die every minute. One more was nothing to me. Like a clod of dirt on my shoe."

An Binh lifted one foot, set it down slowly. "Like a clod of dirt."

Alice let out a strangled scream as An Binh pressed down harder. Her head shook from side to side as if she could rid herself of the unbearable agony An Binh was inflicting on her.

"Where is Ben Butler?" An Binh said.

"Go . . . go to hell."

An Binh put all her weight down and Alice threw her head back, lips pulled away from her chattering teeth.

"*Nói đi, con chó,*" *Speak, dog,* An Binh said. "Where are you keeping him?"

41

"Fire," Samuel Wainwright Wells said from his bed. "The fire this time."

Ambrose smirked, thinking about how his father was quoting a book of essays on race inequality in America. But why bother? he thought. He had news for his father that was far more unsettling. He turned his attention to the flat-screen TVs. Both of them were filled with the fires in New York City, Los Angeles, Chicago, Detroit, stricken faces of liberals, Blacks, Hispanics.

"The new America is burning." Wells's voice was plummy from long-awaited satisfaction. "We're burning it down. We're returning America back to the people whose ancestors founded this great nation. Tomorrow it all goes up in flames!"

Ambrose stepped closer to the foot of his father's bed. "But then again maybe not."

Wells's eyes narrowed. "What the hell does that mean?"

"There are police actions being readied. The National Guard has been called out and is at this moment being deployed in all our targeted cities. We are going to be shut down before we can even begin."

Wells's empurpled face spun toward his son. "But how is that possible? How could they know?"

"We've been betrayed."

"By whom? You're the head of security! You should know—"

"Alice," he said. It was a reckless thing to say, but tonight he felt reckless. Tonight he felt on the verge of being free from his father's insane tyranny. Free to be with Lucinda all the time, instead of hiding in shadows, picking their precious time together.

"What?" Spittle flew out from between the Old Man's mottled lips. "What rubbish. Alice is a true believer, always has been. Which is more than I can say for you. You never really bought into the core Omega beliefs."

"It's obvious to any objective observer. Alice is the one closest to you. Alice is the one you trust completely."

Wells's face twisted in contempt. "I agree, Ambrose. We do have a traitor in our midst. But it isn't Alice."

"Who then?"

Wells opened his laptop. It had been sleeping like a dragon in its cave, but he pressed a key and it awoke. His fingers danced over the keyboard, bringing up the latest of his videos of the trysts between his son and his wife. He turned the laptop so Ambrose could face his fate.

Ambrose felt a trickle of sweat slide down the indentation of his spine. His face, however, betrayed nothing of the appalling distance he felt between himself and the writhing images on the laptop screen. He heard the animalistic grunts and moans. He heard someone call out Lucinda's name and with a start recognized his own voice. But this couldn't be happening. It couldn't, and yet as the act of love reached its inevitable climax, with Lucinda's "yes, yes, oh, yes, baby!" ringing in his ears, he heard his father say, "We both know who the traitor is, don't we, Ambrose?" Wells was moving about under the covers as if he had been joined by a great serpent stretching its shining coils. "You little shit."

The venom knocked Ambrose out of his semi-daze. His gaze switched from the laptop to his father. Wells's face had erupted in so many twitches and tics he was scarcely recognizable.

"Well, someone had to pin her against the wall, Father." He took another step forward so his knees were pressed against the foot of the bed. "You certainly weren't going to do it. You're too busy sticking it in your visitors."

"What're you complaining about? You're getting paid a king's ransom." Wells's grin was as wide and fixed as a jack-o'-lantern's. "You've had it with me, I can see that far ahead. That's why you betrayed Omega." He sneered. "You're just like your mother, soft as a puddle of mud at your core. The trouble with you is you have no backbone. You never did. I realized that the moment I saw the first video of you and that whore I married. Well, you're welcome to her. You and she have no part in the new will, signed by me, sealed, and delivered to my lawyer. So go your own way—you and the whore of Babylon. You deserve each other."

All of this was too much for Ambrose. The spear of his pent-up hatred, disgust, and greed had at last found its honed point. He leapt at his father, clawed hands outstretched, but the Old Man was quicker than he looked. Grasping the laptop he swung it in a short, shallow arc. The corner slammed into Ambrose just below his left eye, slipping off the bone and into the eye itself.

Ambrose, gasping, recoiled backward, but Wells was scrambling after him. No time to find his personal firearm, a Colt .45 semi-automatic. Ambrose raised one arm to protect himself but his body was at an awkward angle and he tripped over the edge of the bedcovers, went down onto his elbows at the end of the bed. His father reared over him, seeming to have gained in height what he'd lost in years. Younger, stronger, more determined, he brought the edge of the laptop down on the crown of his son's head. Over and over again, grunting harder, louder with each effort.

A crack like thunder but whether it was the plastic shell of the computer or Ambrose's skull he could not until sometime later tell. Ambrose no longer raised his hands; he had no more protection left in him.

There was the stink of the abattoir, rising, engulfing father and son, connected in violence, in shed blood, in death as they never had been in life. There was nothing more to say from either of them. They were beyond words, but then they had always been beyond words, real ones at least. Lies came easily to both of them. But now those hard shells had been breached. Irrevocably shattered.

Ambrose was dead. His father might just as well have been as he lay prostrate over his betrayer, fruit of his loins.

42

A brace of security guards, having responded to Alice's screams, came at them, guns at the ready. Evan and Isobel fired their Tasers and took them down, rendering them mute.

Evan turned to Isobel. "Lights out?"

Isobel nodded. "Now that we know where Ben is being held." She contacted one of the two Parachute drones flying high over the estate, pressed the key designated for activation. There was a second or two latency as the drone linked up with the company's quantum computers. Then everything electronic in the mansion died. Moments later, the mansion's generators were targeted and they too failed.

Within the darkness, Evan said, "Now, if what's left of security have any sense, they'll fall back and wait for us to come to them."

"Don't forget Jon Tennyson is lurking somewhere here."

"I haven't." Evan looked back at where An Binh still hovered over Alice. "What do we do about her?"

"For the moment leave her be. When she's finished—truly finished—she'll find us."

"You do know she set this up. You do know that's why she insisted on coming with us. She knew where this woman was all along."

"When she got her chance she seized it," Isobel said. "You and I would have done the same."

"She had a score to settle."

"Her grandfather. That's a heavy debt to carry for so long, Evan." Isobel tossed her head. "Besides, she's the reason Ben is starting to walk again. She's also here for him. Whatever else was on her agenda is none of our business."

Evan switched on her phone's flashlight app as they proceeded down the hallway and into the mansion proper. Photos lined the walls above oak wainscoting. The floor was polished marble. The ceiling was high, vaulted. She could make out the shapes of upholstered furniture, fine polished tables upon which bronze statues reposed or fresh flowers rose from cut crystal vases.

The mansion was quiet, serene as a windless night or the opening scene of a horror film. She switched off the light.

■ ■ ■

Jon Tennyson stood at his post in the center of the second floor hallway running the length of the mansion. He harbored no remorse for what he had done. His ex-partner was a Neanderthal, better off dead. He despised Ben Butler. Butler saw himself as one of the entitled, a highhanded spook who considered himself superior to the FBI and CIA and above the law. As for Evan Ryder she was all that and more—she was insufferable, felt herself empowered, as some women did these days. Tennyson was of the old school. Women were fine as long as they did not exceed their limits. Ryder was so far beyond the limits she couldn't even conceive of them, let alone see them.

In any event, the dice had been rolled. He was here now, so was Butler and now, too, Ryder. He'd caught a glimpse of her in the CCTV tape from the delivery bay before all the electronics failed. The generators hadn't kicked in, which concerned him the most. Someone had been with Ryder in the bay, but all he'd seen was a moving shadow. Who was with her and was that individual the only one? He didn't know and there was no way of finding out until they came creeping toward him. He grinned into the darkness. Truth be told, he was looking forward to disabusing Ryder of her delusions of power, putting her in her proper place.

Had he heard something? Silently he moved one step to his left, cocked an ear. Nothing. It had taken all his restraint not to kill Butler at the scene of the wrecked SUV, but orders were orders. He felt a certain power working for Ambrose Wells. His orders were carried out instantaneously and without question. He was being paid four times what the FBI handed out to him even with his elevation in rank. His raise had been pitiable, then laughable when Ambrose Wells recruited him. The perks were many, the hours to his liking. Best of all he was above the law.

The sound came again and he froze. It seemed to emanate from the depths of the mansion, where there were so many rooms never used let alone lived in, devoid of life. Yet in his time here he had come to understand they all had their sounds—creaks, groans, ticktocks—as if they required no occupants to validate their existence. A house—this house especially—was a living organism, and by now he knew the various rooms' exhalations as well as he knew his own—

A sharp pain in the small of his back made him cry out, but a hand clamped over his mouth turned his yell into a stifled croak.

■ ■ ■

Evan, the 3D layout of the mansion clear in her mind, had climbed a little used utility staircase, wrought-iron, steep for lack of space. Her nostrils flared; Tennyson's familiar aftershave came to her. Unerringly, she followed the scent through the darkness until she made out a darker figure against the balustrade of the open section of the second floor hallway.

Taking off her boots, she launched herself, silent as a hunting owl, toward the figure. A knee to the small of his back, her hand clamped tightly over his mouth, she bent him backward, heard something snap, a dry twig in the forest that a traveler had stepped on.

She could just make out his agonized face. "This is for Ben," she whispered in his ear.

Then a piano wire was looped around her neck, immediately pulled tight, cutting off her breath. She struggled, but she had been so intent on her target, so caught up with her fury at Tennyson's betrayal, she had temporarily lost contact with her immediate surroundings. Try as she might she couldn't free herself. She was losing consciousness, her hands slipping away from Tennyson, who whirled and, gasping in pain, delivered a punch that sent her deep into a well of tears and regret.

■ ■ ■

She was swimming in the darkness. Shapes floated by her, bumped into her, bloated arms and legs, blue-white skin as luminescent as creatures at the bottom of the ocean. A head appeared out of the darkness, empty eye sockets staring at her, accusatory. She tried to scream, her mouth filled with water and she . . .

Awoke with a start, choking and spluttering. Her throat hurt inside and out. She tried to raise a hand to feel where the pain was coming from only to discover she could not move it. She looked around, bewildered. All her limbs were being tied to an old wooden chair. There was someone beside her, also tied to the same style chair, eyes closed, head lolling on one shoulder. Ben.

In a heartbeat, the moments just before her blackout came rushing back to her. "Ben," she cried. "Ben!"

"He won't answer you," a beguiling female voice said from just be-hind her. "He's too far under."

She started again, looked around the room. It was square, window-less, stifling and bone-chilling cold at the same time. *What is this place?* she asked herself. *A former cold storage unit?* But that question faded into irrelevance once the person with the beguiling voice moved into her field of vision and she got her first face-to-face look at Ana's twin and her last living sister.

"Lucinda." The name popped out of her mouth seemingly without her volition. It came from somewhere deep inside her, from a direction where she'd rather not look.

"So now I have you both—the two people responsible for Ana's murder."

She stood, much as An Binh had stood over Alice, looming like Shiva, the Hindu god of destruction. Like a film star she seemed larger than life, more beautiful, more polished, magnetic, charismatic, enigmatic. Staring up into her eyes Evan saw not Ana, her twin, but Bobbi. She blinked, stared again, but it was true—the woman standing over her might have been a reincarnation of Bobbi. The revelation took Evan's breath away, so that when Lucinda said, "What do you have to say for yourself?" she could not utter a word. She heard the hard, chunked un-dertones of Lucinda's Eastern European background through her pro-nunciation of English, and she switched to German.

"Is Ben alive or dead?"

"Still ticking." Lucinda's smile was like a Madonna's. "For now."

"I wanted to save Ana," Evan said.

"Save her from what?" Lucinda snapped.

"From herself," Evan said. "It was clear she was insane."

Lucinda became instantly furious. "You don't get to—"

"I wanted to talk with her, to understand her," Evan pressed on, "but she wouldn't listen. She was intent on my destruction."

"As you are intent on mine."

"Not you, Lucinda. Omega's. You don't—"

"What are you hens talking about?" Jon Tennyson came around from behind Evan where he'd been tying her up. She could see he was uncom-fortable listening to a language he couldn't understand.

"What did you say?" Lucinda took her eyes off Evan to glare at Tenny-son. She had switched to English. "It's none of your business what Evan and I say to each other."

"I don't work for you." Tennyson's voice was tightly coiled. "I work for Ambrose—"

"Ambrose works for me, moron."

"No, ma'am. Ambrose works for his father."

"And I am his father's wife." Her words thundered in the small space.

Tennyson heaved a theatrical shrug that fooled no one. Evan could see everything he was thinking in his expression. He hadn't expected Lucinda to be part of this. She'd roped him in and now, to crown it all, she was giving him orders. The only thing to do was to stand up to her. He'd cower before no female.

"At least talk like an American," he retorted. "Not like a damn Slovenian immigrant."

"I was speaking German not Slovenian, shit-for-brains." She lifted her chin. "And what of it? Where did your grandparents come from?"

That stopped Tennyson in his tracks. He didn't know? Maybe he'd never bothered to ask his parents; maybe he'd never cared. That wouldn't surprise Evan at all.

Meanwhile, she was working her hands free; Tennyson was as bad a knot-tier as he was a fed. But then what? she asked herself. Her ankles were still bound to the chair legs. If she bent over, they'd see and stop her at once. But if she shifted her weight to the right . . .

The chair overturned and her with it. Her weight acted like a lever increasing the force with which the chair hit the hard cement floor. It shattered and she was more or less free. She pulled a chair leg off her right ankle, slammed it into Tennyson's head. He whirled on her. The blow had opened up a cut just below his hairline. He tricked her with a well-executed feint, slapped the wooden leg out of her grip. But she could see him wince from the pain of the rib she had broken. He pulled his service revolver and she kicked. Her knee caught his hand and the gun went off, the bullet embedding itself in the ceiling. She slashed down on his shoulder with the edge of her hand and, with unerring precision, tore his rotator cuff. He grimaced, the revolver came down, pointing at her, and she drove her fist into his broken rib. He screamed as they grappled for the gun. It went off for the second time and Tennyson's face turned gray. He looked down at the red stain growing, slathering his shirt.

"You unholy bitch." He tried to grab her. She didn't have to move much to elude him. He coughed. A thick gout of blood spewed out. Then his eyes rolled up in his head and he fell away from everything and everyone.

43

Two more security guards went down, bound into the darkness. But there were two more up ahead; Isobel could sense them. She was accustomed to the dark. Long training in the Israeli Defense Force starting when she was in her late teens and then, later, recruited into Mossad, and from there into Kidon, Israel's tip of the spear, the wet work unit, had accustomed her to working in pitch black.

Their scent came to her, these mercenaries. They smelled of metal and burnt rubber. They were like tin machines: young as they were, yet old and out of date. Marsden would have laughed at them, with their antiquated notions of cutting-edge weaponry. They were like Bedouins in the desert to him. To her.

She kept on coming in a semi-crouch, left side forward because a profile was more difficult to hit than a figure approaching head-on. Her gumboots made no sound. Even her breathing was tamped down. When she was close enough to hear their exhalations she came at them with a speed that frightened them. They, too, went down.

Stepping over their bodies, she moved on, climbing steadily, approaching the target with the speed and stealth of a cheetah moving through high grass.

■   ■   ■

Samuel Wainwright Wells called for Alice. Instead he got An Binh. They faced each other in his bedroom. Between them the corpse of Ambrose, erstwhile scion of the Wells family.

Wells's brow furrowed. "Who are you?"

"Money," An Binh said as if she were biting off the head of a serpent.

"What? You want money?" He blinked heavily. He showed no recognition of his dead son, lying at his feet. "Are you here to deliver my medicine?" His upper lip curled, his expression abruptly stormy. "You had better be, otherwise I can't imagine why someone of your kind would be allowed on the upper floors."

An Binh did not blink, did not react in any way. "Your money."

"I already told you," he snapped. Then, sensing something beyond his ken, his eyes narrowed. "Explain yourself, immigrant."

"Your money causes ruination."

He snorted. "A moralist, to boot." His hand cut through the air. "Be gone. You don't belong here."

"You're no longer master of this house." An Binh picked her way across the floor, slowly, ever so slowly. "You're no longer even master of your own life."

Something in what she said seemed to have pierced the semi-trance the Old Man had been in ever since he killed Ambrose in a fit of vicious rage. He was entitled. Alice would understand. Only Alice who knew him best, knew him down to his core. "What d'you mean? Speak clearly."

He was no longer trying to get rid of her. He felt a kind of invisible umbilical between them and grew afraid. A frigid wind had entered the room, penetrating his bones, turning them brittle.

"Years ago Alice, when I was ten—your Alice—came to my grandfather's shop. She tried to bribe him with the money you gave her. He wouldn't take her money so she killed him."

She crept closer, closer and it seemed to him that he was unwilling or unable to stop her advance.

"Then Alice turned on me, pistol-whipped me, so sure of herself and my youthful weakness she left me for dead."

"And yet here you are."

"Alice miscalculated, as she did with many things," An Binh told him. "For instance, that dreadful elixir she's been injecting into you."

"Keeps me strong and fit," he said, his chin raised proudly. "Stopped aging. Stopped time."

An Binh within arm's reach of him shook her head. "Oh, no. Not at all. Alice was a fake, she always was. You have been paying for an abomination that has done you no good."

"That can't be." But he looked down at his hands, saw as if for the first time the raised veins like blue twigs, age spots like blackened craters, the atrophying of his flesh, the desiccation of his nails. He looked up into her face. "I just need more, that's all. Another shot will fix everything."

"Nothing can be fixed for you," An Binh said with such authority he recoiled, sat back on the ricked bedspread. "Not now. Not ever."

All around him on the flat-screen TVs America was burning, but the insurrection was stillborn. Already there were National Guardsmen being deployed, firetrucks clogging the streets, huge planes overflying the burning sections of the cities, dumping mega-gallons of water. Where were his people? Where?

Wide-eyed, he scrabbled for his Colt, couldn't find it. He looked up to see that the Asian woman held it. He was deathly afraid. He had been reduced to being an old man, a frightened child. The terrible irony of time. "Will you kill me now?"

"Why bother?" An Binh let the handgun slip from her hand. Her grandfather had taught her to hate guns, so ugly compared to his exquisite Damascus steel weapons. Her nostrils flared. "Your death is already in this room."

She turned and stepped to the doorway. Ever since she had come to America she had been anticipating her death. She had done what she had come here to do. She had fulfilled her obligation; she was done. But then the image of Ben swam into her consciousness like a fish emerging from around a reef, startling her, and she set off to treat him.

The percussion hit her just after the sound. It drove her to her knees. A .45 caliber bullet to the back, how fitting. She retrieved her breath from where the bullet had driven it. She was back on her feet when she heard the sound. There was a particular noise made when someone stuck their gun in their mouth and blew their brains out—the abrupt *thwack!* of a clean gunshot was replaced by the thick, wet sound as of a defenestrated body smacking onto concrete.

No need to turn back. No need ever to turn back now. She knew full well what was behind her and she was leaving forever. Unsteadily she lurched into the hallway.

One step at a time, she thought. *One step at a time.*

She wasn't tired; she was buoyed by a strange elation that ran through her entire body like an electrical current. She did not yet feel the bullet or the hole it had made, but her progress was marked by bloody footprints.

■   ■   ■

"It doesn't have to be like this." Evan meant it; she'd already lost two of her sisters. Whatever was motivating this one did not, at this moment, concern her. "Blood speaks to blood." She wanted the chance she had missed with Ana, with Bobbi. She wanted time with Lucinda. But there had to be ground rules. "Ben. Bring him around. Let me see he's okay."

"He's not okay." Lucinda laughed. "He's far from okay." She watched, eagle-eyed, as Evan went over to him, took his face in her hands.

Evan lifted his lids, noted with a lurch to her stomach the pinpoint pupils. Where was An Binh? She'd know what to do, wouldn't she?

She looked up at Lucinda. "Help him. Won't you help him?"

Lucinda shook her head. "I have every reason not to."

"You want time with me as much as I want it with you."

Lucinda curled her lip. "Please."

"What is it you want then?" Evan stood between her and Ben, for whom she felt a great and abiding protectiveness. "Revenge, validation, love?"

Lucinda shook her head, for once her vaunted voice failing her.

"Did you love Ana? How could you really? She had moved so far away from you. In her mind you were a distant sun, useful only for pumping money into her insane schemes. Did she even believe in Omega's core values?"

"I don't either," Lucinda shot back. "That's my crazy husband's thing."

"Of course." Evan nodded. "You were only in it for the money. You must've stalked Sam Wells, circling him until it was time to dig your claws into him. Then you wouldn't let go."

"Would you?" Lucinda's eyes opened wide. "Before you say no remember what you said. Blood speaks to blood. Under other circumstances you would be right here where I'm standing, glorying in the wealth spread at your feet."

As she spoke, Lucinda was whipping the piano wire with which she had rendered Evan unconscious. "Come here, Sister. Come here and get your reward. So much blood spilled and for what? Your so-called justice? You, the keeper of morality, you have killed people—how many? How many?—while I have killed no one. Not one person my entire life. Who holds the moral high ground here? You?" She loosed a cutting laugh. Whipping the piano wire now with violent force, she let loose the left-hand handle. It flew out, struck Evan just above her nose. She fell to her knees, her head lolling, her eyes trying to focus.

Dimly, she was aware of Lucinda stalking toward her, Lucinda gathering the loosed handle, forming the loop that would cut through her throat, windpipe. Consciousness rising, she knew she was at last facing her own death. Her arms felt like lead weights. Her mind was trying to

shake itself clear, but Lucinda's strike had been well-placed; it had severed the mind-body connection. Evan saw herself, Lucinda, Tennyson's
bloody body as if from high above. The tableau seemed to have nothing
to do with her, even as Lucinda stepped around behind her, looped the
piano wire around her neck.

She heard a bang. Nothing to do with her. Lucinda's head coming
up, a shout from seemingly far away, another part of the mansion, another room. And it was now or never. With a herculean effort she cleared
her mind, brought her body into alignment with her instincts. Raised
a hand, gripping the piano wire before it could be drawn tight against
her throat. With her other hand, she grabbed for the other broken chair
leg but it was too far away. She strained forward, reached for it, but in
the process her sweating hand slipped from the piano wire and Lucinda
drew it hard against her throat so it bit into her skin, drawing blood. A
commotion close by, too late to help her. The room was dimming. Ben
was slipping away from her as she slid down into black water.

Then suddenly she heard Ghislane's voice in her head. *"Lucinda is
something else altogether. She's a boomslang in human form."* Even now, some
part of Evan's mind was able to recognize the ripening irony of Ghislane's assessment of Lucinda while her conscious mind immediately
knew what she had to do.

She fumbled out the black plastic eyeliner case that Camina Wagner
had gifted her, which contained no eyeliner. Camina had hoped that
Evan would never need to use it, but Lucinda gave her no other choice.
She pressed the bottom. Her consciousness wavered, blackness moving
in and out, turning her weak, slow. She was unaware of Isobel and An
Binh bursting into the room, as she gathered herself for one final act.

Tears overflowed her eyes as the needle emerged like the tongue of an
asp, as she buried it in the inside of Lucinda's thigh, hit the femoral artery
and injected the concentrated boomslang venom Camina had prepared.
More tears, hot as oil, as her heart sank. Once again she had failed. Once
again she could not save a sister. Once again there was only blood, death,
and the darkness into which she pitched, falling, it seemed, forever.

3 DAYS AFTERWARD

Midnight on December twenty-fourth. Kata sat at the upper bar in PP&J, a nightclub, restaurant, strip club on Tverskaya Street, not far from Red Square. Kata was inside the private club, a place where she was well-known and well-liked, principally because she was a *kit*—a whale, in other words a big spender. PP&J was frequented by both the FSB and the GRU. Though there was no love lost between the two intelligence factions the private club was mandated neutral territory, principally because the owner, Vasiliy Ochenko, was the Sovereign's nephew. Rumor had it that the Sovereign himself provided Ochenko with the seed money for the venture and was now reaping 60 percent of the profits. For Kata PP&J was an invaluable source of rumors, secret dealings, clandestine affairs, for which she had an excellent ear, within the two rival organizations.

Mechanically Kata kept drinking shots of iced vodka. The bottle rested beside her, steeped in cubes filling a metal ice bucket. She recognized Juliet Danilovna Korokova, whom Novikov had claimed was his girlfriend, the moment she appeared at the top of the circular stairs. She was big, blond, and busty with the well-formed legs of a runner. Her thick hair was short. She wore neither jewelry nor makeup. She possessed the appropriate no-nonsense attitude of an officer in army intelligence. She had chosen to meet Kata in uniform, and Kata saw by her shoulder insignia that she was a captain in the GRU.

Kata lifted a hand and Korokova came over. They did not shake hands nor did they say hello, but merely nodded to each other as if distant acquaintances passing each other in the street.

Kata signaled the bartender for another shot glass, poured Korokova a drink. The GRU captain looked at the vodka as if it were poison.

"I'm on duty," she said stiffly.

"I understand." Kata took the glass, downed the vodka. "So am I." She put a small oblong box on the bartop. "I have something here for you," she said. "From Thoth Abramovich."

"Ah." Korokova said no more than that, made no move to take posses-
sion of the box. In fact, she barely looked at it. She manufactured a smile.
"I would prefer to proceed in a less . . . public space."

"One of the private rooms?" Kata asked. These were usually reserved
for customers interested in more than a lap dance from the strippers.

Korokova nodded, slipping off the barstool at the same time. She
seemed eager to get the transaction over with. Kata wondered what her
real relationship had been with the late, unlamented Novikov.

They went into one of the empty private rooms. It smelled of incense
and intimate flesh, however it was as clean as a cat's whiskers. Management insisted on complete cleanliness and employed a small army
of older women to keep the club spotless day and night. There was no
shortage of such women in Moscow; they were a hundred rubles a dozen.

The two women sat on facing velvet-covered club chairs. Behind
them was a small circular stage and in the center of that was a brass pole
that rose up to the ceiling. A loveseat against the rear wall and a series of
erotic photos completed the décor.

Between the two women was a low free-form table that belonged to
the 1970s and was inscribed KOROVA MILKBAR across the smoked glass
top. Onto this Kata placed the small box. It sat midway between her and
Korokova. When it was clear Korokova wasn't going to touch it, Kata
leaned over, opened it, took out the contents, wrapped in pink-and-white
striped tissue paper. This lay on the table between them until Kata carefully unwrapped it. Only then did she push it toward Korokova.

"From Novikov with love," she said, sitting back.

Korokova scarcely glanced at it. "What happened to him . . . really?"

"He met a cult that disagreed with him."

"And now you bring me this?"

"It was his dying wish."

Korokova's eyes narrowed. "Does Minister Kusnetsov know about
this?"

Kata didn't even blink. "Minister Kusnetsov sanctioned it."

"I see." Korokova excused herself to use the facilities. As she opened
the door she made way for two men to enter. She closed the door behind
her and the men came at Kata in a classic pincer move.

If Korokova's hostile demeanor hadn't alerted Kata, the woman's
metaled smile certainly had; she manipulated it the way a child guides
fingerpaint. No firearms would be involved, she knew that in advance,
not in PP&J. Still, it was two against one, odds she liked.

She spread her hands, smiling. "Gentlemen, is this what you really want to do?"

"You're coming with us," the one on the left said.

"In here, really?"

"Resistance is futile."

Was this a deliberate reference to *Star Trek* or not? Either way it made her laugh. They didn't like her laughing one bit. They rushed her. Which was her objective.

She buried her cut emerald ring into the eye of the man on the right, slammed the other one's forehead into the wall. Stepping over them she went out of the room where Vasiliy Ochenko was standing, legs spread, arms crossed over his barrel chest.

"Not a good night for them," Kata said, as she passed him by.

Ochenko grunted. "My uncle will take care of this."

"I'd hate to be in their shoes."

Ochenko's laugh followed her all the way to the ladies' room, where she found Korokova in front of the wall of mirrors, staring at herself as if she were a diva.

"A scene fit for a selfie," Kata said.

Korokova started at Kata's voice. Her eyes moved in the mirror to take Kata in.

"So soon." Her gaze returned to studying her reflection.

"When you send voles after a fox . . ." Kata shrugged. ". . . what can you expect?"

Korokova sighed, ran the tip of her pink tongue around her lips, turned to face Kata. "So." Hands on her hips. "What is it you want from me? Surely it wasn't to give back a blackened finger from a man I hardly cared about."

"He cared about you."

"That was his problem," Korokova said. "One of them, anyway."

"The other was Omega." Kata's gaze held Korokova's in an iron grip. "Omega is your problem as well."

At that moment, the door opened. The two women said, "*Vne!*" *Beat it!* at the same time. The woman in the doorway ducked her head, retreating.

The GRU officer turned back to Kata. "Just so you know I'm out of that."

"Explain."

"I came to believe that I was being used the same way I was using Novikov and the others in *Devyatyy Krug.*"

This interested Kata. "On what evidence?"

"Joining Omega was supposed to make the men stronger, more focused, more dedicated because I didn't think the Federation was paying attention to them. It became clear to me quite the opposite was occurring. Omega was breaking their morale, fracturing them and, ultimately, turning them away from their allegiance to the Russian Federation."

Kata considered this for some time. Could it be that the Omega infiltration was based on *dezinformatsiya*?

"Who was your contact?" Kata asked. "Who sold you on Omega?"

"I never met them," Korokova told her.

"But you must have spoken on the phone?"

Korokova nodded. "Code name Pavlichenko."

"So a man."

"I couldn't say for sure. The voice was filtered through a vocoder."

"So it could have been a woman."

Korokova shrugged. "As I said."

Kata was lost in thought. There had been a real-life Pavlichenko, the most decorated Red Army sniper in Soviet history with 309 confirmed kills during World War II. Pavlichenko was nicknamed "Lady Death," her complete name being Lyudmila Mikhailovna Pavlichenko. Using the surname of the most successful female sniper in history as an operational designation was just the kind of bold move Lyudmila would go for. A second Lady of Death—how she would revel in that sobriquet.

Korokova's brow crinkled. "What are you thinking?"

"The two men you sicced on me are toast. Ochenko will see to that."

The GRU officer shrugged. "I'm more concerned with Pavlichenko. Why do I get the feeling you know more about this person than I do?"

That was when Kata realized that her line of questioning had set off alarm bells. She cursed herself for being so lax in her security. Under no circumstances would she allow anyone—especially an officer of the GRU—to start sniffing around Lyudmila. She knew better than anyone how meticulous Lyudmila was about keeping herself hidden from the outside world. Now having inadvertently given Korokova the scent she had to shut her down. Permanently. Of course, she would be implicated in the assault on Kata but one could not count on where that would lead and how long it would take to get there. In the meantime the wheels inside Korokova's head had been set in motion and who knew who she would talk to in the interim. Kata could not risk any delay.

And yet . . .

And yet for the moment she felt no desire to attack Korokova; she'd had her fill of violence, at least for the moment. And in that moment the image of Alyosha rose before her and she longed for her, not for blood-lust. And she thought, *Perhaps it's true: happiness changes you.*

Her gaze refocused on Juliet; the impulse to kill her seemed to her absurd, a complete waste of a life. There was the evidence of her intelligence. No one else had an inkling of Lyudmila's Omega scheme to weaken the FSB. Insight and perception in one person were rare enough, especially within the GRU.

"The future isn't looking too rosy for you," Kata said. "Those two goons are going to sing their heads off about you and what you ordered them to do here in neutral territory."

Korokova's eyes glittered. Her body tensed but she made no move. Kata didn't think she would.

"But there's another path," she said. "Another choice that can lead to a different future."

Kata led the way out. Korokova gave her a quizzical look. "And what would that be?"

"Not here."

They passed through the bar, descended the winding stairs to the front door. The full force of Moscow's December hit them in the face but neither of them felt it.

"We'll talk over iced vodka," Kata said, "and this time there'll be no talk of being on duty."

Korokova's laugh was rough but deeply felt. "What good would it do me?"

■   ■   ■

When she was ten years old Evan loved her eight-year-old sister, Bobbi. They played together, Evan was both patient and parental in the absence of their parents—their father putting in long hours at work, their mother, impatient and short-tempered, sequestered in her private part of the house watching game shows on TV. Evan liked best tucking Bobbi into bed, telling her stories Evan herself made up. Often, when she awoke from night terrors, she would check on her younger sister. Seeing Bobbi's half-shadowed face on the pillow calmed her. She would convince herself that everything was fine and was lulled back to sleep.

But one night when she stuck her head into Bobbi's room, her sister wasn't in bed. Her window was wide open. Heart in her mouth Evan went to the window, looked out. Moonlight flooded the grounds but nowhere could she see her sister. Then a stifled laugh from above made her twist her neck. There, up on the roof, was Bobbi, looking down at her, laughing. Was there spite in her expression, unalloyed joy, both?

Looking back Evan could not say. All she could recall was the overwhelming terror that overcame her at the danger Bobbi had put herself in. From that time forward nothing was ever the same between the sisters.

Evan, lifting lids heavy with drugged sleep and muted pain, remembered that night as if she were still living it, as if limbs shaking, her body frigid with fear, she had just descended into the bedroom with Bobbi in her arms.

"Evan . . . Evan?"

Someone was wiping her eyes and cheeks. Vision clearing, she saw Isobel leaning over her.

"Ben." Her voice like a stalk in winter. "Is Ben all right?"

"He is." Isobel smiled. "He'll be here as soon as he can get out of bed."

"He'll walk over here?"

Isobel nodded. "He will."

Evan sighed, relief flooding through her. To have her Ben back, to see him on his feet was a prayer answered. She looked around at the white walls and ceiling, heard the rhythmic beeping of the medical equipment beside her bed monitoring her vital signs. "Where . . . where am I?"

"At the private hospital on the Parachute campus in Seattle." Isobel pulled up a chair, sat down with her knees against the bed. "Marsden flew us here in his aircraft."

"Ah, then I missed seeing Joyce again."

That got a laugh out of Isobel. "Yes, you've been out for almost three days, healing." She crossed one leg over the other. "Actually, Joyce is here tending to An Binh. In addition to being Marsden's personal assistant she's an RN and a PA."

Evan's mind elided over Joyce's accomplishments for the moment. "What happened to An Binh?"

Isobel's expression hardened. "For reasons unknown she made her way to Wells's bedroom after we left her. Best as we can tell, Wells shot her in the back before eating his Colt .45. She's in a medically induced coma. There's been no consensus as to a prognosis."

Evan absorbed this sobering news slowly, as a teen tries to get her head around calculus. "So Wells is really dead?"

"As a doorpost. As is his son, Ambrose. It looks like Wells killed him."

Evan closed her eyes for a moment. "My God."

"Yes," Isobel said. "Quite the family."

"And Omega?"

"Gone—well, as much as it can be. Its leaders are dead, its lieutenants either held over for trial or being hunted down by the FBI and NSA. Wells's business empire is being investigated for tax evasion and wire fraud. The fires are out, the ruins being cleared. FEMA has been deployed but there's the usual governmental red tape, jurisdictional disputes, where the funding is coming from—so business as usual despite the magnitude of the disaster. What's clear is that billions will have to be spent on renewal and infrastructure, but Marsden has pledged a billion and has induced the other tech billionaires to follow suit."

She huffed. "You'd think this failed insurrection would be a wake-up call, that the country would finally start to come out of its deep stupor, but that doesn't seem to be the case at all. People are more divided than ever." She shook her head. "Some things never change."

"The media?"

"Your friend General Aristides is getting all the kudos. That was quick thinking on your part. When you're feeling yourself again, Marsden wants to thank you in person."

She smoothed her skirt over her thighs. "He's been promoted, by the way, your General Aristides. He's now one of the three top generals in the country alongside Robertson and Lawson."

"Shit doesn't always run downhill," Evan said.

"Hey, he did what you asked."

"Only because I gave him no choice."

A silence built between them, punctuated by the metronomic bleeps of the monitors.

Isobel cleared her throat. "There's one thing you haven't asked about."

Evan's brows drew together. "What's that?"

"Yourself."

"I'm alive, aren't I?"

Isobel laughed again. "Indeed you are." Her forefinger described a shallow arc tracing the line of Evan's throat. "You have a scar there. It will stay with you unless you decide on plastic surgery."

Evan asked for a hand mirror and Isobel gave her one. She stared at her battered face, then moved the mirror so that she could see her throat.

There was the scimitar of the welt, red-black. Ugly now, but never mind. She recalled the bruises Ana had made with her hands a year ago, hidden now beneath the welt. Lucinda, who looked so much like Bobbi.

"Why would I want that?" she said. "It's a gift from my sister."

ACKNOWLEDGMENTS

The fact is I dislike acknowledgments: so many people to thank, so few of them can be named. Those that can are my wife and sterling editor, Victoria; my guiding star at Forge, Linda Quinton. The entire team at Forge/Tor for their unstinting hard work and steadfast dedication to me and to my work. I would also like to acknowledge the fascinating website of the Documentation Center and museums at the Nazi Party Rally Grounds, Nuremberg, Germany, for the facts and virtual tours that added verisimilitude to scenes near the end of the novel.

Thank you all, named and unnamed.

ABOUT THE AUTHOR

ERIC VAN LUSTBADER is the author
of twenty-five international bestsellers,
as well as twelve Jason Bourne novels, including
The Bourne Enigma and *The Bourne Initiative*. His books
have been translated into over twenty languages.
He lives with his wife in New York City
and Long Island.

ericvanlustbader.com